THE SUMMER OF LOST LETTERS

HANNAH REYNOLDS

RAZORBILL

RAZORBILL

An imprint of Penguin Random House LLC, New York

First published in the United States of America by Razorbill,
an imprint of Penguin Random House LLC, 2021
First paperback edition published 2022

Visit us online at penguinrandomhouse.com.

THE LIBRARY OF CONGRESS HAS CATALOGED THE HARDCOVER EDITION AS FOLLOWS:
Names: Reynolds, Hannah, 1988- author.
Title: The summer of lost letters / Hannah Reynolds.
Description: New York : Razorbill, 2021. | Audience: Ages 12+.
Summary: The discovery of a packet of old letters sends seventeen-year-old
Abby Schoenberg to Nantucket to unravel a family mystery about her
grandmother's past, but things get complicated when Abby meets the cute
grandson of a prominent family who wants to stop her from investigating.
Identifiers: LCCN 2021010365 | ISBN 9780593349724 (hardcover)
ISBN 9780593349748 (trade paperback) | ISBN 9780593349731 (ebook)
Subjects: CYAC: Family secrets—Fiction. | Dating (Social
customs)—Fiction. | Genealogy—Fiction. | Wealth—Fiction.
Summer—Fiction. | Jews—United States—Fiction. | Nantucket Island
(Mass.)—Fiction. | Massachusetts—Fiction.
Classification: LCC PZ7.1.R4865 Su 2021 | DDC [Fic]—dc23
LC record available at https://lccn.loc.gov/2021010365

Printed in the United States of America

ISBN 9780593349748

1st Printing

LSCH

Design by Rebecca Aidlin
Text set in Haarlemmer MT Std

To my parents,
who have unshakable belief both in me
and in that I base all parents I write on them.

The former means more than I can say;
the latter—okay, in this case you're not far off.

The New Colossus

BY EMMA LAZARUS

Not like the brazen giant of Greek fame,
With conquering limbs astride from land to land;
Here at our sea-washed, sunset gates shall stand
A mighty woman with a torch, whose flame
Is the imprisoned lightning, and her name
Mother of Exiles. From her beacon-hand
Glows world-wide welcome; her mild eyes command
The air-bridged harbor that twin cities frame.
"Keep, ancient lands, your storied pomp!" cries she
With silent lips. "Give me your tired, your poor,
Your huddled masses yearning to breathe free,
The wretched refuse of your teeming shore.
Send these, the homeless, tempest-tost to me,
I lift my lamp beside the golden door!"

One

April 6, 1958

I am going to try to explain.

I'm not sure I can. I'm not used to explaining things to you, maybe because usually we understand each other so well. I picture us like two roses on the same stem, us against the world, surrounded by thorns ready to prick anyone else who dares to come close.

But I've realized with some things, we will always have a different perspective, because we're standing in different places. You see family so differently than I do, because you come from a luckier, happier world. Sometimes I'm drowning in jealousy, the way you take your family for granted.

I love you. Passionately. Consumingly. Loving you, some days, has been the only thing keeping me going.

But romantic love is only one love, and not the most important. (I can see you shaking your head here, but stop. Even if you disagree, understand I believe this. I prize other kinds of love as highly as being in love.) You are not a knight and I am not your lady in the age of chivalry, and we are not the pinnacle of what matters. I love you and I want you, but what I want and what is right are not always the same. You haven't always had to think about the difference before (you know you haven't), but please do now. I'm making the right choice.

I love you.

But I am not going to change my mind.

Growing up, my mom liked to play a strange version of Would You Rather. It happened when she picked me up from a friend's house—from Niko's, whose mom baked mochi cake, or Haley's, whose mom knit scarves. *Would you rather have Niko's mother,* Mom would ask, *or me? Would you rather have Haley's mom or me?*

Even during the worst fights between us, I knew better than to cross this line. Fights between mothers and daughters transcended almost to an art form: I knew how each thrust and parry would land, and how to aim shots low or high. But even when casting words meant to draw blood, I'd never take this shot. This was the soft spot behind the skull, water to the Wicked Witch, Achilles's unprotected heel. You only struck this spot if you struck to kill.

"You," I always told her, as we walked away from Niko's manicured lawn, or left Haley's porch with its bunting flag in red, white, and blue. "I'd rather have you."

The doorbell rang in the middle of a storm.

The rain pounded against the eaves, nearly drowning the chimes out. Sheets of water streamed across the living room's French doors, distorting the yard and forest into shifting blurs of green and brown. March in New England might officially be springtime, but in reality it was chilly and wet and dark.

I sat curled on the sofa, reading *Rebecca* by Daphne du Maurier. The combination of gothic novel and weather had me on edge, despite the room's bright lights and my steaming mug of peppermint tea. Mom and Dad wouldn't be home for hours; they'd gone to a town hall meeting, which basically counted as a date night in their world. My brother, Dave, was sleeping over at his best friend's house. Mom had worried about leaving me home alone, but I'd shooed her and Dad away; my parents deserved a night out. Besides, I liked having the house to myself.

Most of the time.

The chime sounded again while I stayed frozen on the couch, book clutched in both hands, heart racing. No one had ever accused me of being sensible ("You have a *tad* of an overactive imagination," Dad often said, holding his thumb and forefinger a hair's breadth apart)—but honestly, who wouldn't at least *consider* whether a doorbell during a storm heralded a serial killer?

Best not be a sitting duck for my prospective murderer. I padded through the house toward the front door, positioning my back against the wall as I craned my neck to peer out a window.

A USPS truck lingered in the driveway, headlights cutting through the rain, and a figure dashed toward the cab and leaped inside. The truck backed away and sped into the dark.

Oh. Cool.

Anxiety draining out of me, I opened the inner door to the mudroom, a small, chilly space filled with umbrellas and boots. My toes curled as they hit the cold stone floor. I quickly unlocked the outer door, and wet wind lashed at me. The trees in the front yard bowed back and forth under the gust. A rain-splattered box sat on the stoop. I grabbed it and retreated inside, locking both doors and carrying the box to the living room.

Dr. Karen Cohen, 85 Oak Road, South Hadley, Massachusetts, the address read. Mom. The sender: *Cedarwood House.*

Made sense. O'ma's nursing home had told us they'd be sending over a box of her stuff recently found when cleaning out her closet. I could wait for Mom to come home before opening it. Which a less nosy, more respectful daughter would do.

Or.

Got the box of O'ma's stuff! I texted. Will let you know if it contains secret riches.

I slit the packing tape with a key from the kitchen odds-and-ends drawer. The box flapped open to reveal a cursory note from the nursing home and a brown-paper-wrapped package. Now I hesitated. This had been O'ma's, this twine-tied bundle, something she'd packed away so long ago it had been forgotten. Carefully, I tugged the brittle bow loose, then unfolded the brown paper. At the core lay the treasure: a pile of envelopes, all addressed to Ruth Goldman. O'ma's maiden name.

Bright curiosity cut through me. A hundred things could be inside. We knew so little about O'ma's life, especially from before she met O'pa. Ruth Goldman instead of Ruth Cohen. Who had she been?

I knelt on the living room floor and spread the envelopes in an arc, marveling at the thick parchment and the way the ink bled into the fine weave of the paper. Fifty envelopes at a guess, with a Lower East Side address.

The envelopes didn't have return addresses.

I picked up the first envelope and slid the letter out. Neat, slanted writing filled the page. *My darling Ruth,* it began. *I still can't believe you're gone. I keep looking out the window expecting the car to pull up and you to emerge and say this has all been a mistake. Please come home soon.*

O'pa, I thought, though it didn't sound anything like how my gruff, funny German grandfather had sounded. My eyes slid to the date in the righthand corner: *June 1st, 1952.* O'ma would have been eighteen. A year older than me.

I flipped to the back of the letter for the signature. *Love, E.*

O'pa's name was Max.

I scanned the next letter.

My dear Ruth,

It has been too long since I last saw you. Yesterday I walked through the garden and saw a cardinal on the trellis and thought of the kisses we used to steal. I can't even look up at the widow's walk without remembering the way you used to pace there...

Wow. The most romantic letter I'd ever received had been a text from Matt last year saying *Homecoming: Yes/no?*

No wonder we didn't last.

I sent Mom a picture of the letters along with a flurry of texts:

> **Me:**
> Turns out the box has LOVE LETTERS in it
>
> From some guy named E
>
> Do you think O'ma had a grand love affair before she met O'pa???

Mom must have felt her phone buzz, because she texted back immediately.

> **Mom:**
> What do u mean love letters?

> **Me:**
> Like there's some real purple prose here

They're addressed to MY DARLING RUTH

"It has been too long since I last saw you"

!!!

Mom:
Maybe u shouldn't read them?

Me:
hahahaha

Mom:
Wait for me!!!

Me:
sorry nope

I'll text you the best parts

Mom:
Who r they from

Seriously, Mom had both terrible reading comprehension and terrible punctuation. Why did I need to go to school if adults didn't know how to write?

Me:
I don't know, some guy named E. Gotta read more, have fun adulting

Outside, rain slashed away. Inside, I sank into the letters. E's writing made it clear O'ma had moved to New York City and loved it, though he seemed skeptical anyone could enjoy the city. Different bits jumped out at me:

What we do is none of my mother's business.

A bakery, Ruth? Are you sure?

He wrote about painting the ocean: *I'm happy to report my Monet-esque attempts have become more palatable, though I doubt I'll accurately capture the light on the sea if I paint every day for the rest of my life. Yet never fear; I shall rise to the occasion. The attic no doubt looks forward to being crammed with my poor attempts.*

Mostly, though, he wrote about missing her. He wrote about missing her in the gardens, on the beach, in the gazebo. He seemed wracked with a hundred memories of her. He wrote *Nantucket is not Nantucket without you.*

Nantucket.

The name conjured up a speck of an island off Cape Cod. The Cape: a hooked arm of national seashore and small towns southeast of Boston. But while the Cape and the islands were standard vacation spots for Massachusetts families, O'ma had spent most of her life in New York. When had she ever been to *Nantucket?*

Impatient, I skipped to the last letter (I was the kind of person who sometimes read the last page of a book first; never let it be said I handled curiosity well). It was short and dated almost six years after the first—May 3, 1958:

I'm not mailing the necklace. If you want it, come back to Golden Doors and talk to me.

—E

And dammit, Ruth, don't you dare say this is about anything other than your damn pride.

Surprise swayed through me. What had happened? When had these romantic letters switched to anger?

Served me right for reading out of order. Hoping for more context, I opened the penultimate letter. *Can't we talk about this in person? The operator won't even put me through anymore. You're far too proud, and you don't need to be.*

Man, an operator. What an age.

The one before:

> *Ruth,*
>
> *You're being ridiculous. I'm catching the next ferry to the mainland.*
>
> > *Don't do anything stupid before I get there. I love you.*
>
> > > *Edward*

A shiver skirted across the back of my neck. Lowering the letter, I stared out the French doors. The rain had lessened, no longer obscuring the woods encroaching on the backyard. Tall oaks and pines shot into the sky, their trunks soaked black. Winter had been harsh this year, and even now, mid-March, I had trouble imagining I'd ever feel warm again. I had trouble imagining O'ma as an eighteen-year-old, too. *You're far too proud,* the letter-writer had said. Had O'ma been proud? Elegant, yes. Smart, curious, a little sad, a little difficult. But proud?

Though what did I know? I hadn't even known O'ma had been on Nantucket. I definitely didn't know who this Edward was, or what necklace O'ma wanted back, or why she'd left him in the first place.

Come back to Golden Doors, Edward had said.

I opened my laptop and began to type.

Several hours later, the door swung open and Mom's voice echoed through the house. "Abby?"

"Here!"

She walked into the living room, slinging her coat around the back of a chair. Dad followed. He'd hang her coat up later. "You're still up."

"How was the meeting?"

"Eh, fine. What are you up to?" She dropped down on the couch beside me. Dad kissed the top of my head and left for the kitchen to make tea.

"I think I figured it out." I handed her the letters. "They're signed 'Edward,' and mention a place called Golden Doors, which is the name of a house in Nantucket. The house's current owner is *also* named Edward, and he would have been twenty-two years old in 1952. O'ma would have been eighteen. She could have spent a summer on Nantucket with him."

"On *Nantucket*?" Mom flipped through the letters. "She never mentioned visiting Nantucket."

I gave her an arch look. "Shouldn't you have known about someone who writes 'my darling Ruth'?"

She nudged me with her shoulder. "As though daughters ever ask about their mothers' personal lives."

"Rude. I know about your high school boyfriend and the guy you traveled around Ecuador with after college." I pointed at a company's website open on my laptop. "I was thinking I'd email and see if I could get in touch with him."

She peered at the screen. "They're connected to Barbanel?"

"You've heard of it?"

"It's one of the big accounting firms."

"Yes, the internet told me as much. But what exactly do accounting firms *do*?"

She laughed. "They do financial consulting, audits, taxes."

"So they're not *connected* to Barbanel, they founded it. It's their company. The Edward I was talking about is Edward Barbanel."

Mom's brows shot up. "Really. Well. Explains the house on Nantucket."

"Do you think it's okay if I try to get in touch with him?"

She hesitated. "What for?"

"What do you mean what for? He knew O'ma when she was young. He could know all sorts of things. He could know about her family."

"Abby . . . O'ma was so young when she left Germany. She barely knew anything about her family. Why would anyone else?"

"Because they were in love! And maybe she talked about them when she was younger. Maybe she wrote about her family or her hometown in a letter she sent him."

"I don't want you to get your hopes up about discovering any family history."

"Okay, fine. But even if I don't learn anything—don't you think it's weird she went to Nantucket and never mentioned it? It's weird she was in love with some fancy rich dude and we've never heard about it. And why would some rich guy steal a necklace?"

I knew the general progression of my grandmother's life: She'd left Germany at four years old, traveling first to Paris, then to the States via a steamship. A Jewish family in Upstate New York took her in until she turned eighteen, at which point she moved to the city. She married my grandfather, another German Jew, moved back upstate, raised three children, and retired to West Palm Beach. Was widowed.

Got dementia. Moved to a nursing home. Stopped recognizing her family. Died.

The only time I'd seen Mom cry was when we got the phone call about O'ma.

"What does it matter?" Mom said. "If she'd wanted us to know about this man or Nantucket, she would have told us."

"Bull. You're just mad she *didn't* tell you, so you're pretending you don't care."

Mom looked startled, then pressed a kiss on my temple. "Thank you for your diagnosis, Dr. Schoenberg."

"I'm right, you know. So you don't mind if I try to talk to him?"

"Go for it."

Over the next few days, I dived deep into Edward Barbanel's life. He'd grown Barbanel from a successful local accounting firm, already one hundred years old in the 1950s, to a massive multinational organization, though still privately owned. According to a wedding announcement in the *New York Times,* Edward had married the same year he'd sent his last letters to O'ma, writing *Don't do anything stupid. I love you.* On his eightieth birthday, he handed the running of the company over to his son.

It turned out it was very, very hard to get in touch with the chairman of the board of an exceedingly wealthy company. Emails, phone calls, DMs all went unanswered. However. Wills and ways.

"I talked to Ms. Chowdhury at the library," I told my parents over breakfast, two weeks after the box arrived. "Her sister-in-law knows someone with a family friend whose daughter owns a bookstore on Nantucket. She said she might be able to get me a summer job there."

Mom practically spit out her coffee. *"What?"*

"That was a very long list of people," Dad said. "Did you remember all of them or make some up?"

"Since I can't get in touch with Edward Barbanel, I thought I'd go to him."

"You're not going to Nantucket for the *whole summer*."

Dad sighed. "No one ever listens to me."

"Why not? I need a summer job."

"Not in *Nantucket*." Mom's voice rose several decibels. "Don't you think you're being a little extreme? What about the library? You like working there!"

"Think of what a good college essay this would make. You *know* how competitive scholarships are." I'd need a full ride to afford a private college, and while my grades were decent, a good essay could set me apart. Especially if I showcased how my devotion to studying history was *so* strong, I'd spent my entire summer digging into primary sources about my family. Hopefully that kind of dedication would impress the admissions boards—because honestly, something needed to. Scholarships weren't exactly flying off the shelves for prospective history majors.

"Honey . . ."

Okay, I might not get a scholarship no matter what, but I didn't want to hear it. "Niko and Haley and Brooke aren't home this summer anyway. What's the point of staying?"

Mom's face cleared as though she'd been struck by understanding. "This is about Matt, isn't it? Abby, I know you're upset—"

"Oh my god, Mom, not everything is about some stupid boy." Though admittedly, I *really* didn't want to see Matt, especially after his gracious offer to be "casual" post breaking up with me.

Dad wisely picked up his tea and retreated from the room.

"Are you sure? You read the letters two weeks after you and Matt broke up. You're fixated on them. You can't run away from things, Abby."

My stomach clamped up, squeezing tight around the hurt inside of me. "I don't want to talk about this."

"Abby, honey—" Mom's face melted and she reached for me.

I evaded her touch. "I'm seventeen. I'm funding this and leaving for college next year anyway. I'm not doing anything dangerous."

"I don't understand why you care so much about this!"

"I don't understand why you don't! It's a huge gap in O'ma's life."

"Why don't we compromise and go for a weekend?"

"Mom, I don't want to *be* here this summer!"

She froze. Her voice came out soft and small. "Oh."

Regret rose immediately. We were twined together, Mom and I, our emotions rising and falling based on the other's. "I'm sorry. Just—I want to find out more about O'ma. Don't you? Aren't you a *little* bit curious?"

She shrugged one shoulder, a gesture reminiscent of her mother. "She didn't tell me, so I don't know why I should care."

I wasn't buying her cavalier act. *You're far too proud,* E had written. Maybe O'ma hadn't been the only one.

I'd spent my entire life watching how hurt Mom became whenever O'ma stonewalled her. Their relationship had been strained in a way ours had never been, filled with tense silences and *it doesn't matter* and *how morbid.* Maybe Mom really believed what she'd told me: maybe if O'ma hadn't wanted to tell her, she didn't want to know.

But I didn't believe it. I knew my mother; I'd seen the look in her eyes when we read the letters. O'ma mattered so very, very deeply to Mom. And while she might be too proud to seek out her mother's past, I didn't have to pretend not to care. I could do this for her. Go to Nantucket. Find Edward Barbanel. Find out about O'ma's past.

And at the end of the day, what could my parents protest? A nice summer job at a nice bookstore in a nice town? One of Mom's colleagues even had an aunt on Nantucket with a room to rent (or at least a bed in a room, if I didn't mind sharing). So my parents drove me to Hyannis for the ferry (Dave came, too, but he mostly played video games). Mom asked over and over if I'd packed my toothbrush and my vitamins and my acne cream until I burst out I wasn't an *idiot*, and she looked horribly sad, and I felt like a monster. They stood on the ferry dock and watched me go. Dad wrapped his arm around Mom's shoulder, and she leaned into him. For the first time, they looked small. They waved and waved and I waved back, unsure of what would happen if I turned away before they did, if it would be better or worse to snap the cord.

Two

The high-speed ferry sliced through the Atlantic. I tipped my face up, savoring the heat soaking through my skin, the way the back of my eyelids turned red-gold. Salty wind tangled my hair above my head, then whipped strands into my mouth. A bright, cerulean world surrounded me, all endless ocean and cloudless sky.

A small secret: Mom was right. I did run from things.

Hard to stop, when the act of being in transition made me happier than anything else. I could leave things behind: I had no weights, but no new expectations. The world around me felt charged with potential. I could start again. Anything could happen. Something *would* happen.

Something to distract me from Matt, ideally.

In retrospect, I shouldn't have been blindsided by his decision to break up. "I need to concentrate right now, you know?" he'd said on the last day of February break, when we were out eating burrito bowls. "Harvard's so picky, especially for kids from in state. They want diverse candidates, like from Kansas."

"From Kansas." Two seconds before, we'd been making plans to see the latest blockbuster. Now I watched him shovel rice and beans into his mouth, while my own meal sat like lead in my stomach. He was breaking up with me because of valedictorians from *Kansas*?

"And I need to be doing more interesting stuff, like the start-up internship. I don't have time to date. I like you," the only boy who'd ever seen me topless said. "But, you know."

I'd thought we were going to get married. I barely believed in the institution of marriage, and I'd still thought we'd stand beneath a chuppah. "Sounds like you've made up your mind."

He nodded, then pointed at the chips left in my platter. "You gonna eat those?"

"Go for it." I pushed them over. "Great, well, uh, thanks for letting me know. I'll see you in Psych tomorrow."

He spoke mid-crunch. "You don't have to go. We can talk about it, if you want."

"What would we talk about?" My forehead started sweating. I hadn't even known foreheads *could* sweat. "You made a decision. Good for you, I'm glad you know yourself so well that you know you don't want to date me. Great. I don't want to date someone who doesn't want to date me, so . . . we're not dating anymore. Bye." I awkwardly scooted out of the booth, walking away with as much grace as I could manage.

Perhaps pride *was* a heritable trait.

A horn blew, and people rushed to join me at the rail. A stretch of land had surfaced on the horizon, and soon we could make out a haze of details: tiny gray houses, heaps of green trees, the spikes of steeples. Our ferry curved around a sandy point crowned by a squat lighthouse, then pulled into a painfully picturesque harbor. Dozens of different kinds of boats bobbed on the water, and seals warmed themselves on wooden docks. Above us, gulls cried out, soaring through a blue sky dotted with cotton-like clouds. People geared up to disembark.

Nantucket. Summer home of some of the wealthiest people in America. Home sweet home for the next few months.

The stream of passengers carried me onto the docks, which merged seamlessly with the cobblestone streets of downtown. Leafy trees lined the sidewalks and American flags waved. Clothing boutiques and ice-cream shops stood shoulder to shoulder, and the people strolling through the quaint downtown looked sun-touched and happy.

I clutched my suitcase handle tightly as I rolled it past well-dressed mannequins and nautical bric-a-brac, under hand-lettered signs hanging from horizontal posts. Nantucket seemed like an Epcot version of America, both beautiful and bizarre. I was Alice down the rabbit hole, Lucy through the wardrobe, Dorothy not-in-Kansas-anymore. I'd googled the island, but it still hadn't wholly prepared me.

It had given me the island's general history, though: Originally settled by the Wampanoag, Nantucket had boomed in population in the early 1600s when people on mainland Massachusetts fled disease and invasion, coming to the island for safety. But the British soon followed them, and the majority of the Wampanoag on the island died from disease by the 1760s. Then the Quakers came, then the whaling industry, then the wealthy, who stayed and conquered.

I'd always loved history, but I hadn't realized you could seriously study it until this year. It seemed too easy, like I'd be getting away with something. Like—you could go to school to *read stories* about people from the past? That was *wild*. Literally all I wanted was to go on Wikipedia deep dives about ancient societies and women rulers and the Belle Époque. I'd read everything Stacy Schiff and Erik Larson had ever written. The idea of writing a college essay actually *appealed* to me, if it meant I could write about family history.

If, you know, I found something to write about.

Following the directions on my phone, I turned at a beautiful brick mansion, then walked down progressively smaller streets until

I reached a narrow lane. Gray-shingled houses stood close together on either side of it, surrounded by small lawns and rosebushes. There was an inherent coastal air to these weatherworn homes, with their American flags and signs saying *All You Need Is Love and the Beach* and *Home Is Where the Beach Is.*

I paused at a house with a wooden plaque that read *Arrowwood Cottage.* Tiny white flower buds were carved in the corner. I jumped my suitcase the three steps to the porch, took a deep breath, and pressed the doorbell.

An older woman answered, her silver-streaked gray hair cut in a bob, her purple tunic flowing. Blown-glass baubles dangled from her ears. "Hello."

"Hi. Mrs. Henderson?" I'd met her niece—my mom's coworker—a handful of times when I'd been dragged to college functions. The vague similarity in their features put me more at ease. "I'm Abby Schoenberg."

"Yes, of course. Did you just arrive?"

"Yeah. Yes. I took the ferry from Hyannis. My parents dropped me off." I followed her inside. To the left lay the kitchen, open and airy; to the right a living room, shelves filled with books. A golden retriever jumped up from a rug, barking sharply and hoisting her floppy ears high. She had a coat like browned butter and the long, awkward legs of a dog not yet full-grown.

"That's Ellie Mae," Mrs. Henderson said. "Come on, Ellie, she's a friend."

The golden barked again, then trotted forward and shoved her nose at the front of my shorts. I fell into a defensive crouch and caught her narrow head. She had gentle eyes and tufts of fur behind her ears and knees. "Hi, girl."

She licked my face and panted at me with her terrible dog breath.

Mrs. Henderson laughed. "She's the worst guard dog in the world."

I'd met many of the worst guard dogs in the world and loved them all. "How old is she?"

"Eighteen months. Do you like dogs?"

"Adore them. My grandmother has a beagle." My dad's mom lavished her dog with even more indulgence than she did me and my brother.

"I've always had goldens, but one of my good friends has hounds. You should see her dog point." She smiled fondly, then waved me up. "I'll give you the grand tour."

Ellie Mae trotted faithfully after us as Mrs. Henderson showed me the house. Along with the kitchen and living room, the first floor had a dining room and office. The latter opened into a fenced backyard. On the second floor, she pointed out her own bedroom and her late husband's study. She smiled self-deprecatingly. "Sometimes I think about turning it into another rental, but I haven't had the heart."

To reach the third floor, we climbed a narrow staircase with steps sloping downward in the center. This floor was a single hall, light spilling in from windows on both ends. Mrs. Henderson pushed open a door. "Here we are."

White walls brightened a tiny room with a slanted ceiling. A braided oval rug, blue and white, lay on the pale wooden floor. One of the two twin beds had been neatly made up with white linens and a comforter, while clothes covered the disheveled second. A nightstand with a turquoise lamp stood under the window between the beds.

"This used to be the maid's room, when the house was first built. I've tried to make it a little nicer, though."

"It's great." I rolled my suitcase to the free bed, and looked out the window. I could see Mrs. Henderson's yard, filled with purple flowers and a delicate bird bath, and the neighbors' yards, too, since the cottages were so close together. "Thanks so much."

"The bathroom's across the hall—you and Jane will be the only two using it. The other room up here is for storage." She handed me a key. "Welcome to Nantucket."

After she left, I hung my dresses in the hall closet and lined up my shoes below the bed. I tucked Horse, my childhood companion, under the covers. The site of a ragged stuffed cat on my new roommate's pillow comforted me.

I'd done it. I was here.

Now what?

Muted merriment floated in through the open window. At home, only the unchanging song of crickets filled summer evenings, a more calming noise than this one, which tugged at my chest and made me feel like I should be out there, laughing and shrieking and living.

Okay. I was only feeling weird because I was lonely, which would go away after I started my job in two days. No reason to start wondering if I'd made the right choice. Of course I'd made the right choice. I'd spent the last three months holding on to the idea of Nantucket like it was a lifesaver. You couldn't long for something—*lust* for it—then feel hollow as soon as you achieved it.

Could you?

I felt like I'd abandoned Mom.

I knew I hadn't, technically; she had Dad, who was fairly competent at humaning (not too competent; if I asked him a particularly thorny question while he was walking, he would literally *stop walking* in order to think, and I'd have to go back and retrieve him). And Mom had her temple friends and college bestie and friends from her Children of Survivors group and the parents of *my* friends who she'd befriended. And she had Dave, my brother, I supposed.

Come to think of it, Mom had a *lot* of people. Only sometimes I didn't think she realized it. Sometimes she seemed to think she was all alone.

She wasn't, of course. Even if none of those others had existed, she had *me*.

Except I'd left her.

"Get yourself together," I muttered, sinking down into my new bed. Shoulders back. Deep breaths. I considered calling Mom, but she'd sense my panic. Then she'd panic, and we'd descend in an escalating spiral of panic. So I sent her a cheerful selfie instead and called Niko.

My best friend's face filled my phone, framed by a Stanford dorm room. "Hey! Are you there? How is it?"

"So beachy, you wouldn't believe it, and there are roses everywhere. Wait, are you wearing lipstick? Are those *bangs*?"

"Badass, right?" Niko turned her head so I could admire her high-low cut and the straight shot of bangs across her forehead. "I'm reinventing myself."

"You look amazing."

"I know. I figured no one here knows I've never worn lipstick in my life, so why not. Did you know people put on a lip primer *before* they put on lipstick? What the hell?"

"How's Palo Alto?"

"Everyone bikes everywhere, and no one jaywalks, and they call highways freeways, which is cute. How is bougie island life? Are you wearing cardigans and pearls yet? Is everyone white?"

I made a face. "I'm freaking out. What am I doing? Why am I here?"

"Breathe. You've been there literally two seconds."

"What if I don't make any friends? How did you make friends at coding camp? We haven't met new people since we were six!"

Niko frowned. "Who did we meet at six?"

"It was an arbitrary number."

"Anisha moved to South Hadley when we were twelve, so maybe she's our newest friend."

"Nikoooo."

"Okay." Niko put on her serious face. "Think of this like college practice. You're going to meet people, and you can be whoever you want—you can reinvent yourself, too. Focus on more than your grandma, because you're seventeen, not seventy. Go crazy. Be bold. What's your dad say? Have some chutzpah!"

"My dad is literally the dorkiest person alive."

"I love your dad. Remember how excited he was when you let him chaperone the aquarium trip?"

"Don't remind me."

"He loved the tiny penguins *so much*. I've never seen anything so pure."

I felt better by the time we hung up. So I'd sent myself to an island thirty miles off the coast where I didn't know anyone. But no panicking. I had video calls and deep breathing and towels.

At a little past nine, the door flew open and a girl blew in, a tangle of tiny black braids and flour dusting her shirt. She had double-pierced ears and dark skin and three inches on me. She stopped abruptly. "Hi."

"Hi!" I bolted upright. "You must be Jane."

"Yeah. You're Abigail?"

"Abby."

"Cool. You're working at the Prose Garden, right?" She tore off her T-shirt and pulled on a red top. "Sorry I'm a mess, I just finished my shift."

"Oh? Where?"

"My aunt's bakery." She turned to the mirror and swept two perfect winged lines on her lids. "I've come up the last two summers to help, and also to avoid my brothers and sisters. Thank god Mrs. Henderson has this room for rent. I'm from Rhode Island. You?"

"South Hadley—it's in western Mass—"

"Yeah, nice, I'm thinking about applying to Smith." She straightened. "Okay, sorry to rush in and out, but I have to run."

"Oh." I tried not to wilt. Last thing I wanted was for my roommate to think I was clingy. "Nice to meet you."

She hesitated. A space hung between us, charged with risk and potential. I was an unknown quantity, overeager and possibly too much effort. She had a life and friends and plans and no responsibility toward a stranger.

Yet she offered me a kindness anyway. "You want to come? I'm meeting my friends on the beach. There'll be a bonfire."

Relief and gratitude pooled through me. The anxiety wrapping around me all evening began to unspool. "I'd love to."

The setting sun dyed the sky royal blue as we walked out of town, down North Beach Street and Bathing Beach Road. Sand edged the pavement, cropping up beneath the patchy grass. "So, how'd your aunt end up on Nantucket?" I asked my new roommate. "Did she just decide to open a bakery here?"

Jane laughed. "God, no. We're from here."

"Seriously? That's so cool."

"Yeah, there's a decent Azores and Portuguese population on Nantucket. It's the same latitude, you know, so traders crossed back and forth a lot." She pointed to the globes of blue blossoms I'd already noticed all over the island. "They say the hydrangeas here were actually originally brought from the Azores, which is between Nantucket and Portugal. It's the first land you hit if you sail east."

Eventually the road opened up to the beach parking lot, and we crossed to the sands, the water beyond dark and endless. The moon hung low in the sky, half-full and butter yellow. We kicked off our sandals, and tiny grains of sand scraped at my feet. Jane led us past clusters of people until we reached a bonfire with kids our age gathered around it, drinking from red Solo cups. They wore cable-knit sweaters and striped shirts and Nantucket-red shorts, and their laughter mingled with the scratch of the low-tide against hard sand.

Jane wove her way through the crowd and I followed in her wake. I'd thought teen beach parties only existed in movies, but the scene fit into my heart like a puzzle piece snapping into place. Summer nights were meant for this: toes burrowed in the sand, waves crashing, the scent of salt and seaweed and burning wood. *Be bold.*

"Want a beer?" Jane handed me a plastic cup.

Right. Alcohol. Cool cool. I was a teen and we drank alcohol. Fine, *I* didn't because my friends and I tended toward sleepovers featuring *She's the Man* and homemade brownie sundaes. Also, what if I turned into a weepy drunk who sat in a corner and cried?

But. Screw being the boring girl next door. Screw following rules. Screw Matt—or not, because he'd dumped me.

The problem with your generation, Mom always said, *is you're too rule-abiding.* In her own youth, Mom had made a career of not following rules. I had the insane urge to send her a picture of me, beer

THE SUMMER OF LOST LETTERS   25

in hand, but came to my senses. She'd probably meant for my generation to get better at civil disobedience, not getting drunk at the beach.

Whatever.

I took a gulp of the pale amber liquid and almost spit it out. Wow. Okay. Screw beer, too.

"This is Abby." Jane pulled me toward a trio. She nodded at a short white girl with fashionable glasses and a leather jacket. "Lexi, my old roommate, who abandoned me."

"Don't hate me," Lexi said, an uncomfortable amount of earnestness underlying her wry tone.

"I *suppose* you had a good reason. Is Stella here yet?"

"She gets in tomorrow."

Jane waved her cup at the others in the circle: a Black boy in pale green plaid and khakis, and a South Asian guy. "Evan's from Boston and our token rich kid. Pranav's from London and is an intern at an architecture firm."

Both boys nodded at me.

"Hi." I clutched my Solo cup like a safety blanket. My friends and I shared the same jagged edges, fitting together like broken pottery. What should I do here? Wrap myself in gauze so I didn't cut anyone, or would I then be so blunted I had no shape at all?

I took another sip of beer. It still tasted terrible. Oh well.

Maybe the alcohol chilled me out, though, or maybe Jane's friends were the best, because within five minutes they'd absorbed me into the group, and we were ears deep in an intense debate: If you were leaving Earth and could only take three cheeses on your spaceship, what would they be?

"Mozzarella," Jane said decisively. "You can't make pizza without mozzarella."

"Sharp cheddar," her old roommate, Lexi, said. "And maybe Brie or Camembert. But I also could see a good parmesan being helpful."

"What about American?" Evan said.

Jane stared at him. "Are you kidding me? You can only take three cheeses to eat forever, and you'd include *American*?"

"I like American!"

"It depends what else you're bringing," Pranav said diplomatically. "Also, paneer."

"It's true, Brie might be dumb if you don't have baguettes," Lexi said.

"You definitely can't have baguettes," Evan said. "It's space! Crumbs!"

"Does cream cheese count as a cheese?" I ventured. "Because I don't want to say goodbye to bagels forever."

The group looked at me with consternation, and for a second I was sorry I'd spoken, sure I'd said something horribly embarrassing.

"Oh man," Lexi said after a moment. "I didn't even *consider* cream cheese."

"Good point," Evan said gravely. "And sticky buns have cream cheese frosting."

"If we're going to space, we're not going to have time for *sticky* buns," Jane protested.

"Sticky buns give me joy, Jane," Evan said. "Do you want to deny me joy?"

Slowly, I relaxed, until I was laughing with the rest, laughing and teasing and feeling like a member of the group, and happy, for the first time all day, to be here.

"So you study architecture," I said to Pranav later, once I'd reached the bottom of my Solo cup. "Do you know about the houses on the island?"

Pranav shrugged. Inane to think he was fancy because he had an accent to die for, but I wasn't evolved enough to think otherwise yet. "The important ones."

Lexi rolled her eyes. "You're so pretentious."

I plunged onward. "Have you heard of Golden Doors?"

"Yeah. It's a great example of Federal architecture. Gorgeous. Built in the mid-1800s, before all the rules."

"Rules?"

"Height limits and materials and stuff," Pranav said. "The entire island's a National Historic Landmark District, but Golden Doors was built way before then."

"The Barbanels are one of the super-wealthy island families," Jane told me. "Actual islanders, not like the recent blow-ins. They're also Portuguese! Sort of."

I cocked my head.

"I mean, they're Jewish. But a Portuguese sort of Jewish."

My attention sharpened. I hadn't realized the Barbanels were Jewish; I wouldn't have expected a Jewish family to summer on Nantucket. Though what did I know of the extraordinarily wealthy? They could summer wherever they wanted. As for Portuguese—"Sephardic?"

"What?"

"Oh. It's what you call Jews from Spain or Portugal." Though they'd been kicked out during the Inquisition. My own family was Ashkenazi—descended from Jews who'd settled in France and Germany around the eleventh century.

"Cool." Jane turned a high-wattage smile back on Pranav. "Pranav's right, their house is stunning. They open it up for tours once or twice a year."

Lexi nodded. "I actually have a gig there tomorrow."

I swiveled in her direction. "What kind of gig?"

"Catering. They're having a 'start of summer' party." She shook her head at Evan. "Rich people are weird."

"I plead the fifth."

"Do any of you know them?" I asked the group. "Edward Barbanel and his family?"

Jane gave me an odd look, and I realized the others were, too. I'd come off too intense. "Why so interested?" my new roommate asked.

Evan smirked. "Noah?"

I hesitated. I didn't know these people. They might think it was super weird, me coming to Nantucket to dig into my grandmother's connection with the Barbanels. Also, a large part of me wanted to hold the reason close, like a dragon guarding its hoard. To change the subject by saying, *Who's Noah?*

But how would I find out anything if I didn't talk to people? What kind of historian didn't do interviews? "I think my grandmother visited Golden Doors decades ago. She died recently and we don't know much about her past, so I'm trying to find out more."

"Did she know the Barbanels?" Evan asked.

"I'm not sure. I think—" I hesitated. "I think she knew Edward. They wrote letters."

"What kind of letters?" Jane asked.

Pranav smirked. "Love letters?"

I looked at my feet.

"*No,*" Jane exclaimed happily, and everyone else looked properly interested. "Are you serious?"

"I think so."

"What are you planning to do?"

"I figure I'll check out the house, just to see it—I saw those garden tours online. Maybe talk to Edward Barbanel."

"You should go with Lexi tomorrow," Jane said. "Get the lay of the land."

"I don't want to impose—" I said, hating myself for sounding stiff and timid even as the words left my mouth. "I mean, I *do*, but—"

"You should," Lexi said, her brows slightly raised. "Ms. Wilson is always willing to hire more hands. And honestly, I'm all for shaking up some bougie rich people."

"Thanks," I said. "I won't be trouble or anything."

"You're only invited because I hope you will be," Lexi said, cracking a smile. "We feed on drama."

"Cheers to that," Pranav said, and we all laughed and lifted our plastic cups.

So the next day, I headed to Golden Doors.

Three

Lexi picked me up at five, in a Jeep crammed with other kids from the catering company. I squeezed in the back, wearing black shorts and a white top like the others, and let their music and conversation wash over me as they gossiped casually about people I didn't know.

As the elevation climbed, the houses grew farther apart. Hydrangea bushes, with their globes of tiny flowers, blossomed everywhere, beneath shady trees, over white fences, climbing up trellises. Sea views dipped in and out of sight, the water sparkling like diamonds. I draped my arm out the window and turned my face up to soak in the late-June heat.

We passed rolling green fields, our view of the ocean now almost unbroken, a line of ever-present blue beneath the constant sky. Only giant mansions, with colonnaded porches and drives made of crushed white shells, interfered. Eventually, we turned down an unpaved lane.

And Golden Doors came into sight.

The pictures I'd seen hadn't captured the grandiosity. The house was sprawling and elegant, all gray cedar shingle and peaked roofs and gables and chimneys. Two dozen windows were set on the side facing us alone. A veranda circled the first story, while balconies dotted the second. A widow's walk crowned one branch of the house.

"It's a lot," I said.

"Twenty-five million dollars," the girl next to me said. "Not that they'd ever sell."

Wow. It was nice, but not *that* nice.

"It's not just for the house," a boy added, when he saw my face. "It's also the land."

At first I didn't get it, but then, as we drove around the side of the house to the parking area, I did.

The *land*.

While everyone else bustled about, I stood still. Exquisite lawns and gardens spread behind the house, until the earth dropped away, falling toward the shore and sea itself.

Just as I'd known it would. I knew the gardens E had written of, and the ocean he'd painted. Past the manicured hedges and neatly planted flowers lay a rose garden and a gazebo, and riotous hydrangeas tumbling down dunes to the beach. A shiver cut through me— of recognition, or foreboding. Maybe I'd trespassed too far.

"Come on, Abby," Lexi said. "Let's find Ms. Wilson."

Too late now.

She led me across the lawn, where people raised white tents and strung up fairy lights. Tablecloths billowed in the air before landing on folding tables, where bouquets were then placed at intervals. A clump of workers set up a sound system, and behind them, a woman consulted a clipboard: Lindsey Wilson, who ran the catering company.

We'd spoken on the phone this morning, and she greeted me briskly. "The Barbanel parties are always easy," she said as I scrawled my signature across several forms. "But they're a private family, so don't poke around."

Lexi smirked.

We moved trays of food from the catering trucks to tables and fridges. Trays of sharp Manchego and soft Port Salut; tiers of strawberries and pineapple and cantaloupe; watermelon and feta with sprigs of mint; asparagus and snap pea salad; bowls of olives and of hummus and of baba ghanoush; Brie baked in dough with fig jam.

I caught glimpses of the house, since the party would extend from lawn to living room. Glass light fixtures hung from the high ceilings, and sand-colored curtains framed French doors. The armchairs and sofas were upholstered in cool blues and off-whites to match the low tables. A painting of the beach hung above one fireplace; a gilded mirror above another. Potted plants and fresh cut flowers filled corners. A row of books spanned both mantelpieces.

"There's the current CEO." Lexi nodded at a middle-aged couple standing in the center of the yard, talking to Ms. Wilson. "Harry Barbanel and his wife."

Harry, son of Edward, and Helen Danziger, the wealthy woman he'd married the same year he told my grandmother he loved her. Harry had lots of hair (Dad would be jealous) and dressed in Nantucket reds (known as salmon to the rest of the world). His wife wore a shiny jacket and constant smile. They looked like they belonged in a magazine.

They couldn't have been more different from the adults in my parents' circle, who had an argumentative, unpredictable, hippie vibe. Often, I'd wind up in a debate, and whenever I felt about to win, they'd *pivot* and say, "Have you considered being a rabbi? You'd make a good rabbi, you're good at arguing. You should come to shul more," and suddenly I'd be politely rejecting letting them plan my career trajectory ("But *why* don't you want to be a rabbi?"). Then we wouldn't be talking about me at all, but the new young rabbi at temple who had given such a good sermon on elder orphans, but Joan's neighbor didn't like her because she was too progressive, and also did anyone know if the rabbi had a partner? Susan's daughter might be a lesbian and probably they should get married.

I knew how to deal with my parents' friends. I doubted the same methods would work on the Barbanels.

At seven, guests started arriving in droves. People in white linen pants and monochrome outfits stood in loose circles, stemless wine glasses dangling from their fingers. I circled the crowd with a tray of champagne flutes, unease curling in my stomach. Had O'ma really spent any time here? Had she laughed and tilted her head like these women? Had she stood on this lawn in an hourglass dress, her hair in curls like a character out of *The Marvelous Mrs. Maisel?* The letters had made it sound like she'd spent plenty of time here, but I couldn't imagine it. Maybe she hadn't visited during these parties, or maybe she'd been staff, like me.

O'ma's life had always seemed like a story: dangerous and glamorous, and here was one more unexpected chapter, pages that I hadn't realized had been stuck together. Had she looked as happy as everyone here did? Hard to picture. All her life, she'd seemed a little sad.

Every so often, one of the other caterers would point out a board director or a CEO. Even a senator made an appearance. "Is it always like this?" I asked Lexi when we both dropped off our trays of empty glasses at the same time. "All these famous people."

"Everyone comes to Nantucket in the summer."

Everyone in the one percent, maybe.

By 9:45, the party was in full swing. We'd been told to use the bathroom off the kitchen, but the wait was interminable, so I went searching for another. I wandered deeper into the house, taking in the perfectly placed mirrors on the hallway walls, the tiny tables with fresh flowers. I found another bathroom, filled with thick, lush towels, and seashells, and prints from old newspapers. Good lord, this bathroom was better decorated than my whole room.

On my way back, I peeked down an empty hall and caught sight of framed photos and paintings. I paused.

A quick look couldn't hurt, could it?

I walked down the hall, all my senses on alert, aware I wasn't supposed to be here. In this part of the house, the sounds from the party were softened, muted, like they belonged to another world. What was I even looking for? A photo of O'ma? A framed letter? Ha.

A door to my right swung open.

I jumped back, but the man exiting didn't see me as he strode in the opposite direction. The slowly closing door displayed an office with a giant painting of the ocean. A Monet-esque painting, if you would.

I stuck my foot out to stop the closing door.

And froze. Still as the girl in *Jurassic Park* trying to avoid detection by dinosaurs; still as Medusa's victims after they'd been caught in her sights. Because I didn't *do* this. I didn't break into places. I didn't break rules.

But the painting—

A chime of laughter sounded nearby, and I dove inside and shut the door. I leaned against it, heart in overdrive and hands sweaty. I could get in so much trouble. I needed to leave. But what if I opened the door and someone saw me? And arrested me for trespassing? And threw me in jail (did Nantucket have a jail? Nantucket *had* to have a jail. Who was housed in Nantucket's jail? Tax evaders? Joy-riding teens?). And what if they posted bail but no one paid and my parents were too far away—

I took a deep, calming breath, counting to ten. Okay. Breathing. Important to remember.

I walked over to the framed oil work hanging on the wall behind a massive desk.

I doubt I'll accurately capture the light on the sea if I paint every day for the rest of my life . . .

But this painting had. The artist had used greens and yellows to suggest light penetrating the waters' depths, so the ocean glowed from within. I was used to paintings where the ocean looked foreboding or refreshing; not many made me long to wade into the water.

In the bottom right corner, white script stood out against the blue. Even in scribbled cursive, the two initials were clear—an *E* and a *B*.

My hand rose as if to trace the letters, but years of museum-going stopped me short. Instead, I leaned close, holding my breath as though it might move the waves. I didn't need any more proof. It had been Barbanel. Edward Barbanel had written my grandmother love letters.

I drew back and took in the room. It had all the hallmarks of a well-used study: papers and pens littered the desk; packed bookcases lined the walls. A luxurious carpet covered most of the dark wooden floor, but what I could see gleamed. Beneath the painting, a fireplace was set in the wall, and to the right, a window alcove with heavy velvet curtains looked like the perfect place to curl up and read.

I'd already trespassed—was it kosher to look around a little more, or should I duck out?

Okay, it probably wasn't *one hundred* percent kosher, but surely it was more like marshmallows than bacon.

Hesitantly—as though walking with caution would make my actions any better—I moved to the bookcases, scanning the spines. Nonfiction all: books on business and history and accounting. Fun. Farther down, I noticed flatter spines with handwriting. Binders. I knelt on the ground, tilting my head to see the labels more clearly. *1990–1994. 1994–1996. 1997.*

Albums. Dozens of them.

And these were the most recent ones. A dozen more sat on the shelf below, and my eyes jumped to them, almost faster than my mind. I was afraid to hope, afraid to think they would go back so far—

1947–51.

My breath caught so quickly it felt like my heart had been hooked on a rib. The letters had begun in 1952. 1951 might have been the year O'ma visited Nantucket. Almost reverently, I pulled the album into my lap and opened the green cover.

Not an album—a scrapbook. Small, square sepia-toned photos filled most pages, with the occasional colorful postcard or paper pressed between the plastic. Strangers smiled up at me, women with bouffant hairstyles, men with cigars—

O'ma.

The photo captured her in a moment of laughter. Her perfectly curled hair blew in the wind, and her dark lips were parted. She must have been around my age, skin unlined and eyes wide. I barely recognized her. Wide-legged jeans buttoned high around her ribcage, and a short-waisted, high-collared jacket finished the outfit.

She looked so young.

And so *alive.* In her last years, she'd been small and frail. Who was this vibrant girl who'd been so in love, who'd come to this island and left it and never spoken of it again? I'd known my grandmother; I'd known Ruth Cohen, who'd baked pies and spun stories and complained about air-conditioning, but I didn't know this bold, bright young Goldman girl, who didn't have a husband and a daughter and a granddaughter and a condo in Florida. Who *was* she?

"What are you doing?"

I screamed.

Just a little scream, shrill and quickly silenced. I twisted so quickly I toppled off-balance and sprawled on my back. The ceiling spun as I tried to catch my breath.

A boy my age stood in the doorway, limned by light. He stepped inside and closed the door.

"Oh my god. I'm so sorry. Hi." Scrambling to kneel—why was I such a hot mess?—I shoved the album back onto the shelf and jumped to my feet.

A thunderous frown crossed his face. "Who are you?"

He was alarmingly good-looking, in the kind of way that meant I never would have spoken to him normally, with bronzed skin and dark eyes and cheekbones sharp enough to slice hearts in half. He wore navy slacks and a white sweater. In one hand, he held a single flower with petals both yellow and purple.

"I'm—I'm, um . . ." Crimson embarrassment crept up my cheeks. I didn't dare name the catering company for fear of getting them in trouble. "I'm a cleaner. I'm cleaning."

"And all I wanted was some peace and quiet," he murmured, looking skyward before pinning me with his gaze again. "You're cleaning."

I winced. "Yes?"

"The study."

In for a penny. "Yes."

"In the middle of a party." His voice was low, almost melodic, as he coolly unraveled my story. "Without any cleaning supplies."

Right. Hm. "It's a—new. Kind. Of cleaning."

He lifted his brows in a mute response.

"I'm studying the room to see what I need in order to clean it."

"You're a terrible liar."

I know, right? I almost said. Instead, I sagged against the desk and spread my hands apologetically.

"Are you a thief?"

"No! God, no, I don't *steal* things."

"You just break into places."

I could see how one might be confused. "I didn't break in. I just—accidentally entered."

"What?" He stared at me like I'd spoken in tongues.

"It just happened. I was in the hall—and then I wasn't in the hall—"

"If you *are* a thief, you're the most incompetent one I've ever met."

All of a sudden, I had thief pride and he'd offended it. "Oh, and you've met so many thieves? What are *you* even doing here?"

He ignored me, gaze falling to the bottom shelves of the book-case. "You were looking at the photo albums?"

"No." I didn't even know why I denied it, unless, along with my thief pride, I had a heretofore unknown affinity for deception.

"Hm." He crossed to the fireplace, lifting a tiny vase from the mantel and placing the flower in it. "Why were you looking at them?"

"You're missing water."

"Thank you," he said, voice so dry that if any water *had* been present, it would have evaporated. "I hadn't noticed."

Eesh. What an honor, to meet the king of sarcasm. I looked at the strange multicolored petals again. "What kind of flower is it?"

"A poisonous one."

"Oh." I drew back. "Do you usually walk around fancy parties with poisonous flowers?"

"Only when I need to confront secretive thieves."

"I'm *not* a thief." I scowled, then held up my hands. "See? Nothing." I darted a glance at the door. He was several steps away. If I dashed for it—

I dashed.

He moved faster, throwing his body before the door. I skidded to a halt an inch away from him, and now we were too close, so close I could see each of his black lashes. My pulse ratcheted up and I hopped back, unable to catch my breath, unable to stop staring at him. His throat worked convulsively, his chest rising and falling like he, too, couldn't find enough oxygen.

But any momentary enchantment died when he opened his mouth. "Empty your pockets."

"These are girls' shorts," I shot back. "They don't *have* pockets. They're fake pockets."

He blinked. "That's ridiculous."

"I know."

"Your purse, then."

"Why should I listen to you? You're sneaking in here, too."

"Because I actually belong here."

I sighed and handed my bag over. I'd brought almost nothing—phone, keys, wallet. He flipped open the wallet. "Abigail Schoenberg," he read. His eyes flicked up. There were cues you looked for when you were trying to decide if someone else was also Jewish. Abigail could go either way, but my last name and my dark corkscrews were a strong signal. (And fine, my nose wasn't precisely subtle.) His gaze returned to my license. "Nice picture."

It was not a nice picture.

"If I was going to steal something," I said witheringly, "I wouldn't put it somewhere so obvious. I'd tuck it in my bra or something."

He looked up. The corners of his mouth twitched.

Shoot. "Which you're *not* checking. Obviously if I had, I wouldn't have planted the idea in your head."

"Unless you're really cocky."

"I'm not. Trust me."

"You do seem like a shitty thief." He held my bag high. "Tell me what you're doing here and I'll give it back."

"You can't take my stuff hostage."

He didn't say anything. Apparently he could.

"Fine. Whatever." I swept my hair out of my face. "I was snooping. What about you? What are you doing here?"

The knob behind him twisted. I inhaled sharply, and the boy jumped out of the way as the door swung open.

Uh-oh.

An older man entered, then stopped short, a frown etched on his brow. He looked me up and down, then focused on the boy. "Noah. I thought you might be here."

"I was getting a vase." He held up the flower. "Mrs. Greene picked this. It's endangered. Why don't people get that endangered means *you're not supposed to pick it?*"

"There are vases in the dining room."

"Giant vases. I wanted this one."

"Hm. Your parents are looking for you." His eyes slid back toward me. "Who is your . . . friend?"

"This is Abigail Schoenberg. Abigail, this is my great-uncle Bertie."

I gave a self-conscious wave. "Hi."

"Mm." He appraised my outfit. "Are you with Lindsey's?"

For a minute I stared blankly, before remembering Lindsey's was the name of the catering service. "Yes?"

"Then shouldn't you be out front?"

I glanced at Noah—ridiculous, since he had no reason to cover for me. But. Solidarity in youth. Old people clearly couldn't be trusted, not after they'd so casually ruined the planet.

For whatever reason, Noah stood up for me. "I wanted her help with something."

The man's brows rose perilously high.

Oh, great. Great-uncle Bertie definitely thought we'd been hooking up.

"But we're done now," I said hurriedly. "You're right, I should get back to my job. Those champagne flutes won't serve themselves."

Honestly, sometimes I said things so cheesy I made myself lactose intolerant.

"Someone else can handle it," Noah said.

"Noah." His great-uncle sounded impatient. "You should say goodbye."

Noah's lips pressed together, and I thought for sure he'd rat me out. Instead, he nodded. "Give us a sec, then I'll find Mom and Dad."

Looking mulish, the older man backed out of the room and closed the door.

Not entirely, though. Noah pushed it the rest of the way shut. Turning back, he hoisted my bag. "Well?"

But something had clicked in the back of my mind. "Your name's Noah."

He shot me an impatient look.

Why so interested? Jane had said when I asked about the Barbanel house, and Evan—wealthy, summer-people Evan, who ran in these circles—had said, *Noah?* "You're a Barbanel."

He nodded. "Be a little weird if someone outside the party ducked in here, wouldn't it."

A strange sensation swept through me—déjà vu, though of course we'd never seen each other before. "You're Edward Barbanel's grandson."

"So?"

I laughed, a little frantically. "It's just funny, is all. You. And me. Here."

He looked at me like I was insane. "What?"

I gestured. "The painting captures the light on the water."

"Is it *always* this difficult to talk with you?"

The doorknob rattled, and we both jumped. Noah glared at the door like he could will the outsider away. Instead, a girl's voice made its way in. "Noah! I know you're there. Your dad wants you, like, yesterday."

Noah sighed and opened the door. A girl a year or two younger than me squeezed in. "Uncle Bertie wouldn't say—" She stopped, and her tone shifted. "Oh."

Noah groaned. "Tell them I'll be there soon."

She ignored him and studied me. Against her, I definitely came up lacking. She wore a black dress with colorful flowers embroidered along the hem, and had curls the glossy brown of tempered chocolate. My own hair frizzed à la Anne Hathaway in the first half of *The Princess Diaries*, and even after I'd learned the First Hair Commandment (finger comb instead of brushing your hair post shower), my curls still dissolved as the day went on. She narrowed her eyes. "Who are you?"

"Abby. Hi."

She regarded me critically. "Are you . . . on the catering team?"

"Um." I tried to push my glasses up and poked my nose bridge. Right. I'd worn my contacts today. "Sort of."

"Okay." She turned an expressive gaze on Noah—*you're making out with the help?* "I'll tell Uncle Harry you'll be there in five. You owe me."

After she left, I spread my hands. "Seems like you really have to go."

"You're going to tell me more about this. Tomorrow." He pulled out his cell. "What's your number?"

I typed it into his phone. "I'm working tomorrow, though."

"I'll meet you after. Where and when?"

"Five. I'm at the Prose Garden."

He frowned. "You work at a bookstore as well as catering?"

"Oh. Um." I swallowed. "The catering is more of a—one-off thing."

He let out an exasperated breath. "You had better have a damn good excuse for being here, Abigail Schoenberg."

"I do. I swear I do."

Did intense curiosity count as an excuse?

I was so very, very screwed.

Four

March 30, 1958

You'll get over me. People say love is choosing to be together,
choosing the other person every single day. It's showing up for
each other. Well, we're not going to show up anymore, are we?
You'll stop loving me. Choose to love Helen. I mean it.
Be happy.

I wore my *Alice in Wonderland* dress for my first day at the Prose
Garden. The same shade of sky blue as Alice's dress, it matched my
mood of feeling lost in Wonderland; this wasn't *my* world, with its
too-big houses, strange characters, and enough wealth to have all the
roses on the island painted red—but I found it baffling and intriguing
and delightful.

Though early in the day, people already strolled through Nantucket's cobblestone streets, swinging their beach and designer bags.
A breeze ruffled the trees' leaves, carrying the ocean's tang, and the
morning sun made me feel warm without overheating. I still couldn't
get over the town's charm; I didn't think I'd ever be numb to the
quaint storefronts. Flowers spilled from window boxes and beauti-
fully lettered signs announced bakeshops and antique stores.

Jane had told me most of the buildings on Nantucket had gray
shingles not due to paint, but since natural cedar eventually weathered

into a calming gray. But the bookstore—tucked between two tall red-brick buildings on a side lane off Main Street—had white shingles. A rose-covered trellis led to the entrance. My nerves jangled as I walked beneath it. I'd worked at the public library long enough to have confidence in my bookish knowledge, but new jobs—new starts—were always scary.

I pushed open the door, and my tension sluiced away.

Light, air, and faint classical music filled the store. My shoulders relaxed. I breathed easier in rooms full of books, as if the paper retained the capacity of the trees they'd once been. So many books filled this room, more than in my own or my parents' or our living room, even though we had a wall of built-in shelves. The shop had alleys of books, towering cases of books. You could get lost here. You could be found.

A woman sat behind the front desk, reading a jacketless hardcover. I smiled with an excessive amount of brightness. "Hi. I'm Abigail Schoenberg. I'm here for the summer?"

"Oh, perf." She unfolded with unexpected grace to her feet. "Liz!" she hollered toward the back, then smiled. "I'm Maggie. Let's get you set up."

Maggie was the daughter of the family friend of the acquaintance of my hometown librarian's sister-in-law (all real connections). She wore a white-and-pink polka-dot dress and a headband, and her partner, Liz, had short purple hair and wore all black. A peanut-butter-and-jelly couple, Mom would call them. Perfectly paired opposites. They had three full-time staff, and hired more during the summer. The other seasonal employees were returning college students; I'd been lucky to get a spot.

It took only ten minutes to decide I adored Maggie and her noisy cheerfulness. She showed me how to run the register, how to check the shelves for what needed to be pulled and what restocked, how to read the maps for which books belonged on the display tables. One table featured World War II novels, their covers showcasing women with short bobs and long coats. *O'ma.* I'd spent half the night thinking about her photo. What had her life been like here and at Golden Doors?

Maggie trained me as people flowed through the store, effortlessly switching from instructive mode to helpful bookseller. Most of the time she seemed to know exactly what the customer wanted before they did. Once, someone said, "I heard about this book on NPR," and without any other details, Maggie plucked a book from behind her, and it was the *right one.*

"How—what—I'm speechless," I said.

Maggie laughed. "It's the book du jour right now. Also, this is as close as I'll ever get to magical powers, so I need to revel in it whenever I can."

She won over even the most difficult of customers. A twenty-something woman dismissed Maggie at first, then finally admitted she was a fantasy reader looking for a new author.

"N. K. Jemisin?"

"Read her."

"Sharon Shinn?"

"Read her."

"Kate Elliott?"

"Read her."

"Nnedi Okorafor?"

"Read her."

Yet with each rejection, Maggie became more and more excited. "Katherine Addison," she said. *"The Goblin Emperor."*

The woman paused. Tilted her head. "Hm. No. I don't think I have."

After the customer departed, novel in hand, Maggie collapsed in an overstuffed armchair by the fireplace and small café. She fanned herself with a magazine. I couldn't decide if it was an affectation or not. I perched on the arm of the chair across from her. "I'm impressed."

"I know." Maggie dropped the magazine to a side table and waved her other arm grandiosely. "As the keepers of knowledge, it is our sacred duty to unite texts and readers."

Liz looked up from the computer on the other side of the room. She took care of inventory and finances, and had built their website, where she maintained the blog and user outreach. Maggie handled more of the store's in-person interactions. "You're so weird."

"I'm brilliant. A wizard. She'll love the book. And remember the lady from last month who said her son didn't read, and I convinced her to buy *Pawn of Prophecy* and she came back three days later and bought the entire series? *And* the Malloreon?"

"She's been dining out on that story for weeks now," Liz told me.

"Because it's wonderful. Like me. So, Abby, this is your first time on Nantucket?"

I nodded.

"You're going to have so much fun. God, I would have loved to have been seventeen on Nantucket."

"No, you wouldn't have," Liz said. "You were an angry baby goth at seventeen."

"True," Maggie said amicably. "I've mellowed in my old age. I've become basic."

I loved Maggie and Liz's banter, yet the closer we came to the end of my shift, the more tension wound around my body, pulling me tight and stiff. By four thirty, I started every time the door chimes heralded a new customer.

And after half a dozen false starts, they heralded him.

It was almost a surprise, I'd gotten so used to it not being Noah. I froze in the middle of the Mystery aisle, the book in my hand half-shelved. Noah's determined gaze fastened on me almost immediately, and he stopped on the other side of my cart of books, his hair wind-mussed. "So you do work here."

"Yeah." I shoved the book firmly into place. "But I can't leave until five."

"Fine."

I shelved another book. And another. Then I looked at him again. "Are you just going to stand there?"

He shrugged. "Gotta kill these ten minutes somehow."

"Hm."

"You could help me find a book."

"Are you serious?"

"Sure."

"What kind of book?"

"You're the bookstore girl."

"Well, what do you normally read?" I looked him up and down. "James Joyce? David Foster Wallace?"

"Why are you smirking?"

"I'm not smirking."

"I like sci-fi," he said, which surprised me. "John Scalzi. And Le Guin."

"Huh." I reconsidered him. "Interesting."

He gave me a wary look. "Why?"

Because I'd been being judgmental and now I need to reevaluate. "Have you read the Ancillary books? By Leckie?"

"I don't think so."

"If you like Le Guin, you might like her. And maybe the Expanse books by Corey." Always good to recommend a book made into a TV show. I pulled the first books in both series and brought them to the register, taking his card when he handed it over. "Platinum. Cute."

He scowled.

Payback for mocking my license picture, bro. I studied his name. "Noah Ari Barbanel."

"You want to memorize the number, too?"

"I'll think about it." I handed the card and books back, receipt tucked beneath a cover.

"No bag?"

"We're in the middle of an environmental crisis."

"You're kidding."

"Nantucket's going to be buried beneath the waves in several centuries." I made a falsely apologetic moue as I delivered the tidbit, imparted to me by Jane alongside the cedar-shingle facts.

He looked annoyed. "You don't need to lecture *me* about Nantucket."

"Noah!" From the back room, Maggie emerged. "It's so good to see you."

"Hi, Ms. M." He smiled, and I looked away. Rather unsportsmanlike of him to be incredibly wealthy, well-read, *and* stunningly good-looking.

"How are you? Did you just arrive?"

"Last week, yeah. How are you?"

"We're great, ramping up for the season. Have you met Abigail? She'll be here all summer."

Now he turned the smile on me, but it sharpened. "We go way back. We're about to head out, actually, if she's done with her shift?"

"Oh, really?" Maggie looked at me curiously. "What are you two up to tonight?"

"Just some casual interrogation," he said lightly.

Why did I feel hot and embarrassed all over? "I'll go grab my bag."

Once we were outside, he slipped his books into my purse. "Since you denied me a bag."

"Hmph. You know Maggie?"

"It's a small island. Cross here."

We crossed Main and headed toward the harbor. "Where are we going?"

"We're walking."

"Anywhere in particular?"

"Nope. So what's your deal?"

I swallowed. "Straight to it, huh."

"You have me on pins and needles."

"Fine. What do you want to know?"

"Let's start with the basics." He fixed me with his gaze, and since he had at least a head on me, I had to crane my neck back to meet it. The sun cast a golden halo around his curls, as though the universe itself had decided to surround him with angelic light. "Why were you in my grandfather's study?"

We'd reached the wooden wharves, and I looked out at the harbor. Nantucket Sound lay flat as glass today. Small skiffs bobbed gently above their reflections. The ocean looked tamed, pinned down by boats, hemmed in by docks and land. A lie. The ocean could never be tamed. "He knew my grandmother."

"Okay . . ."

I shoved my hands in my dress's pockets and met his eyes. "He wrote her love letters. I found them a couple of months ago."

Surprise widened his eyes. "You think my grandfather's writing your grandmother love letters?"

"No, not now, decades ago."

"When?"

"From 1952 to 1958. She was eighteen at the beginning and he was twenty-two."

Noah shook his head decisively. "Couldn't have been him."

"Really? Because it was from an Edward at Golden Doors."

"Edward's a popular name. It might have been a gardener, a cook, a cleaner—"

Good lord, a regular *Downton Abbey* of staff. "*And* he wrote about painting light."

"What?"

"In one of the letters, he wrote about painting the light on the ocean. I saw one of your grandfather's paintings in his study."

Noah scowled. "Maybe they weren't love letters."

"Um." I thought about some of the more, ah, *romantic* passages. "They were love letters."

"Impossible."

"Why?" I took a stab. "Because Edward married your grandmother in 1958?"

"How do you know that?" he snapped.

I took a step back, surprised at his ferocity. "It's this newfangled device I call Google."

"Well." Noah pressed his lips into a fine line. "He did. So he wouldn't have been writing *love letters* to another girl the same year."

Oof. I stared at the soft-looking texture of his polo shirt. "I hate to break it to you . . ."

"Don't." He started walking

"What? I'm not passing judgment. But it's a possibility." I hurried a few steps to catch up with his long-legged strides. "Aren't you curious?"

"About if my grandpa was *cheating* on my grandma? No."

"Maybe your grandparents didn't meet until Edward and my grandmother ended. And, uh, married really fast."

"My grandparents dated for years before they got married."

I paused. Years? But Edward and O'ma had written love letters for *six* years. And some of the letters had been rather steamy. And he'd definitely never mentioned a Helen. "Maybe they were on and off? Or took a break? Which, totally reasonable. Who wants to stay with one person their entire life?" When he shot me a skeptical look, I expounded. "It's unrealistic to think your first love will be your final love. People change, you know? Maybe you're totally, madly in love one day, and then you're not."

He looked at me with a little more interest, as though seeing me as a person instead of a problem. "I take it you went through a breakup recently."

"Rude." I sighed. "My boyfriend dumped me four months ago. It's fine. He wasn't so impressive."

"Then why were you dating him?"

"Great question." Matt and I hadn't been friends first—I ran in a low-key artsy/nerdy crowd, whereas he'd focused on racking up achievements, be it soccer captain or president of National Honor Society or debate club. We'd been partnered together in Chem, and things had rolled from there. "He looked impressive on paper. Which I guess was his whole point. It turned out being in a relationship got in the way of building up his college resume."

"Rough."

"Not my fave life experience, yeah."

We walked a few more paces. "Okay," Noah said, "so you think since your relationship didn't work, no relationships work, and so my grandfather must have cheated on my grandmother?"

"Oh my god, are you for real? You're extrapolating way too much."
He laughed.

"Why are you laughing?"

He grinned at me. "Good use of extrapolation."

"Thanks. I think."

"And so you came to my house to—what?"

"Oh." I shoved my glasses higher on my nose. "I didn't mean to snoop, honest. But I've been trying to get in touch with your grandfather for months—"

"*What?*" He stared at me. "You want to talk to my grandfather?"

"Yeah. If he was writing my grandmother letters—"

"No." Noah shook his head firmly. "Don't drag him into this. What's your grandmother say?"

"She died. Last year."

"Oh." He cleared his throat. "I'm sorry."

"Thanks."

We stood in silence a few moments before another question burst out of him. "What do you want from my grandfather?"

"To know about my grandmother. We had no idea she'd ever been to Nantucket. We don't know much about her family; she barely said anything about them. Maybe this guy—your grandfather—knows more about her, more about them. Besides, it's wild to think she was in *love* with someone when she was my age, then never mentioned him again."

"Because you plan to tell future generations about Impressive on Paper?"

A reluctant laugh burst out of me. "No. Though I'm not sure I'd say we were in *love*. I mean, not the way these two were. Also—" I hesitated.

"What?"

I lifted my chin, aware this part could be contentious. "He had one of her belongings. A necklace. I want to know what happened to it."

He looked out across the flat, endless sea, then back. "No."

"Excuse me?"

"I get being curious about your family's past." He shoved his hands in his pocket and gazed down at me. "But prying into things from decades ago? This isn't worth talking to my grandfather about."

I bristled. "I didn't realize you got to decide which conversations have value and which don't."

"Look." He sighed. "I'm sure you're a nice girl. But you're not from here. You don't have the full picture. This isn't an adventure where you can play Nancy Drew. My grandparents are real people, and they don't need you stirring things up."

"I'm not trying to 'stir anything up'—"

"Aren't you? Because I'd say coming to an island for the *whole summer* says otherwise."

"I just want to talk to some people—"

He pinned me with an authoritarian stare. " 'People'?"

I hesitated, flustered. "Well, yeah. Your grandfather, and anyone else on the island who was alive then and might have known her—there's some names and places in the letters—"

"So you're *definitely* planning to stir things up." He looked furious. "This isn't your family. This isn't your island. Stay out of this."

Frustration gathered in my stomach, hot and tight. Usually I tried to reserve my attitude for my family and present everyone else with a softer, politer facade. Girls were supposed to be nice, after all.

I was so tired of being nice.

"You know what, Noah Barbanel? This isn't up to you." Our gazes tangled, angry and stubborn both. "You can't dictate what I do. I don't need your permission to talk to people."

He pressed his lips together. "I could pay you not to."

"Are you kidding?" Fury flashed through me, hot and sharp. Who did this guy think he was? "You can't buy me off."

"Why not?"

"Screw you." I didn't even know how to react; I'd been robbed of whatever small articulateness I'd ever possessed.

"I'm not trying to insult you. Think about it."

"I'm not going to think about it! You can't go through life paying people off to get what you want. That's not how the world works." At his skeptical look, I corrected myself: "It's not how the world *should* work. Not if you have any integrity."

His jaw hardened. "You do *not* have the high ground here, Abigail Schoenberg. You broke into *my* home. You went through *my* family's things."

"You're right. I messed up. But I have a right to try to find out about my grandmother's history."

"And I have a right to protect my family's privacy. I'm telling you, Abigail. Leave them alone."

"This isn't *about* your family! It's about *mine*."

"Really?" His eyes were flinty. "Because I don't see your family on Nantucket. They're not the ones who'll have to deal with any fallout."

"What *fallout*? I just want to ask questions!"

"Don't." His gaze bore into mine, hard as fossilized wood. "I can make your life difficult if you insist."

I stepped back. "Are you *threatening* me?"

"I'm just saying. I can help you or hinder you. Your choice."

"Screw you, Noah Barbanel." I pulled his books out of my bag and held them out. I couldn't even articulate my rage. "Seriously, *screw you.*"

His jaw worked, but he finally took the books. "You should think about this."

"You should think about not being an asshole." I gave him a tight-lipped, defiant smile. "Good luck with that."

Five

A list of things my grandmother wouldn't talk about:

—Traveling from Germany to the States, by herself, as a child
  of four
—Her first years in America
—Her parents, who were gassed on arrival at Auschwitz
—The war
—Nazis
—Being German
—Being Jewish

A list of things my mom wouldn't talk about:

—Her relationship with her mother

My fourth day on the island, Mom emailed me with a subject line
of ??? and no body, save a link to an *Atlantic* article about how teens
today spent less time with their friends in person than a decade ago
and reported feeling lonelier.

Thanks Mom!! I replied.

Mom couldn't always read inflection in my emails, but even she

would probably notice the sarcasm wrought by my double exclama-
tion points.

Gmail instantly alerted me to a new message, because Mom apparently thought email and texting were the same. Are you lonely??

In her case, the double punctuation signaled not sarcasm, but earnestness. She worried about me way too much. I called her.

"Hello?"

"I'm not lonely, Mom. I have a job—"

"Wait! I need to fix the ear thing—hold on . . ."

I rolled my eyes and clicked on a link in the article's sidebar about
climate policies to read while I waited.

"Okay. Hi. Did you like the article?"

"Do you think I'm lonely? I'm not lonely."

"I know." Her defensive tone made it clear she was lying. "But it
says . . ."

"Mom. Have you not noticed my million friends?"

"True." She switched to hopeful. "You have a very good group.
But what about on Nantucket? You don't know anyone!"

"My roommate is nice. I met her friends."

"Okay. Good. Because, you know, people are pack animals. You
need a pack."

"I'm fine, Mom."

"You haven't called me since you arrived."

Sometimes convincing Mom I was well-adjusted felt like my
raison d'être. She occasionally panicked about her parenting skills,
as though I was a soufflé in danger of collapsing. I suspected her
own parents hadn't been particularly nurturing, and so Mom felt
pretty in the dark about how to behave. (To be fair, O'ma and O'pa's
parenting had probably been influenced by their own childhoods.
They'd been a bit more like: Are the children alive, fed, and not in

imminent danger from Nazis? Cheers, everything's going great.)

"I've only been here three and a half days," I reminded Mom. "And I *literally* just called you. And texted you *every day*."

"I suppose." She still sounded woeful. "Should we Zoom?"

We video-chatted for forty-five minutes, my brother Dave wandering in and out, Dad quizzing me about the seashells on Nantucket (I had no satisfactory answers). Mom wanted to know about every person I'd come into contact with in enough detail to map out our relationships on a whiteboard. I was not, I must admit, reticent in complying with her demands.

My parents were cute. Painfully-in-love cute, write-mushy-Valentine's-Day-cards and forget-other-people-exist cute. They still flirted, about getting married and their first date. Dad joked about how he'd meant to marry rich, and Mom always retorted *she'd* meant to marry rich, and then the two of them wound up smirking and stealing kisses.

It did a number on you, growing up around people madly in love. It made you think their kind of love was not just attainable, but necessary. It made you think your partner should act like you made the tides move.

This was probably not healthy.

When we hung up, I flopped backward on my bed. Sunlight crossed the ceiling, and summer air drifted in from the open window. Sure, I'd been lonely once or twice in the past few days, but you don't say so to worry-prone moms. So what if sometimes I was lonely? Everyone was lonely. Re: this *Atlantic* article.

I wished journalists would go back to hating on millennials and leave my generation alone.

I picked up my phone, pulling up my roommate's number. Nothing ventured, nothing gained.

Me:

Hi! I remember you mentioning beach plans
this Saturday? If they're still on, I'd love to join

Jane:

Yeah, for sure! Also I'm at my aunt's tonight for
"quality family time" lol but I'll be home tomorrow

On Saturday, Jane and I headed to Jetties Beach, stopping first at
her family's bakery for picnic supplies. Pictures of the Azores hung
against one whitewashed wall, while shelves of dry goods lined another. Customers snaked up to the register, behind which lay pastries
and overflowing baskets of bread. We snuck me into the back, load-
ing up on containers of kale soup and linguica sausage and *suspiros*—
chewy meringues.

Next, we headed to Jane's aunt's house, which had a front yard
covered in hydrangeas and a handful of bikes in the back. Jane nodded at a baby blue one. "You can borrow Aria's. Sorry it's so twee.
Aria likes everything to be Instagram perfect."

The bike had a wicker basket attached to the front, with a pink
ribbon laced through the bands. "I love it."

We biked down narrow island roads lined with wildflowers, past
twisty trees and Cape Cod–style houses. The strips of sand between grass and pavement broadened until the road opened up at the
beach parking lot. We locked up the bikes and burrowed our feet in
the warm sand, grains sifting between our toes. Cotton-puff clouds
drifted across the bright blue sky, and people packed the beach. It
was a perfect summer day; the temperature hadn't risen high enough
to be painful, and a soft breeze tugged playfully at us.

The same group from last week sprawled across a haphazard map of blankets and towels, the corners of which were pinned down by shoes and purses. Jane's best friend, Lexi, sat shoulder to shoulder with a South Asian girl I hadn't met before—her girlfriend, Stella, I bet.

"We've arrived." Jane placed our baked goods in the center of the blankets. "You may thank us."

Evan, the preppy rich boy, grinned. "A little full of ourselves, are we?"

"Rightfully so."

Someone connected their phone to speakers, and music blasted out. Bags of chips and pretzels burst open and seltzers popped. Jane tugged off her crop top and wiggled out of her shorts, and I did the same, revealing the more conservative of the two bikinis I'd brought for the summer. Someday I'd wear the scandalous red one. But not today.

When half the group started a game of touch football, the remaining girls gossiped about relationships. I listened, pleasantly sunbaked, pinned by the heat to my towel. The warmth had the same relaxing properties as a massage, draining my tension down and away into the earth.

Stella turned to me. She wore a leopard-print wrap over her one-piece, and long earrings dangled against her neck. "So, what's your deal? Seeing anyone?"

"Nope." I remembered Niko's admonishment to have some chutzpah. "I wouldn't mind a summer fling. I, um—I dated a boy at home last year, but he dumped me to concentrate on college apps."

"Ugh, boys," Stella said. "Don't worry, though, this is a great place to get flung. Lexi says you met Noah Barbanel when you broke into Golden Doors." She waggled her brows.

Lexi tugged on Stella's hair. "It wasn't *technically* breaking in."

"It was. You're an accessory to a crime." Stella dropped a kiss on Lexi's lips. "It's why I love you. I've always had excellent taste in accessories." She returned her attention to me. "So?"

"He's a jerk," I said firmly.

Jane smirked. "Don't worry, you can always make out with randos at beach parties."

I refrained from admitting I'd never made out with a rando (though I had kissed Tessa Fogelson's second cousin at her bat mitzvah, but he turned shy and *ran away* from me, which, wow, what a confidence boost) because the rest of the group rejoined us then, flopping down on the blankets, animated and loud, a whirl of long limbs and sweat. Evan snagged Jane's water and chugged it. "What are you guys talking about?"

"Secrets." She grabbed her bottle back and used it to smack his shoulder.

Pranav folded himself down next to us, staring at his phone. "Sydney's coming."

"Sydney!" Jane chirped. "Great! How *is* she?"

"Good. She got in last night."

Sydney must have been Pranav's girlfriend—also from England, and also an architecture intern.

"You guys smell," Stella said. "Also, it's hot. Who wants to swim?"

"Gotta eat first," one of the boys said around a mouthful of sausage.

"I'll go," I told Stella.

We headed down to the water. The waves slipped over our feet, frothing at our ankles before pulling away in a web of white. Before us, the world was bright blue. "Count of three?" Stella said, and we plunged forward, shrieking. The ocean closed around me, silent and dark.

I popped my head out, shivering. Salt clung to my lips and my hair to my head like seaweed. Stella emerged, too, whipping her long black hair back. "Brr!"

We warmed up by swimming, fast and sleek like seals, arms scooping water along and feet kicking away. When we adjusted to the temperature, we floated happily. "Is this your first time on the island?" she asked.

"Yeah. You too?"

Stella nodded. "I came out a few times last year to visit Lexi, but never for more than a night or two. This is going to be even better. This year, we're going to have the perfect summer."

I floated on my back, watching the rays of sun streak through the clouds. The perfect summer. I was in.

"So, what's the deal with you and Pranav and his girlfriend?" I asked Jane later, as we stood over the twin sinks in our bathroom and readied for bed.

"What do you mean 'the deal'?"

"Well. You were *so* nice when she arrived. You embraced her like a long-lost sister."

"I don't know." She sounded miserable, or as miserable as one could be with a toothbrush obscuring half their consonants. "It's a weird defense mechanism. Like if I'm super friendly with her, no one will notice I'm madly in love with her boyfriend."

As expected. "Isn't that a stereotype, though? If you inquire a lot about someone's partner, it's because you're into the person?"

"Oh my god, what?" Jane sounded horrified. "No. That's not a thing. Oh my god, *is* it a thing?"

I started giggling and couldn't stop. "Pretty sure it's a thing."

We changed into our pajamas and turned off the lights. Moonlight spilled between our beds. I rolled over so I could see Jane's silhouette. "Thanks for letting me come today."

"For sure. It's hard not knowing anyone. And I could use another friend." She sighed. "I'm glad Stella came this summer—Lexi missed her so much last year. But—it used to be when Lexi and I had spare time, *we* hung out, and now she hangs out with Stella, which is normal and I'm happy for them, and I try not to be jealous. But I miss her."

I got it. I'd been thrilled for my friends: for Brooke, who landed a job as a camp counselor in Vermont; for Niko, off coding at Stanford; for Haley, seeing Spain during her immersion program. But each time I'd learned one of them would be gone, I'd chewed at my nails until my cuticles bled. And I'd run off to Nantucket.

I stared at the moonlight on the ceiling. In the late darkness, it seemed obvious I wasn't *just* running from loneliness, or searching for knowledge about O'ma's past, or fodder for a college essay. I wanted *more*. An adventure. A sense of purpose.

How hard could those be to find?

Six

On the Fourth, I woke to the scent of sugar and strawberries filling the house. "Good morning, girls," Mrs. Henderson said when Jane and I stumbled downstairs, lured by the scent, with no more will than Odysseus before the sirens.

"What are you making?" Jane asked.

Mrs. Henderson smiled with the serenity of a baker who knew her worth, and nodded to the cake sitting on the table. Dark ruby strawberries studded a yellow dough. "Strawberry cake for the bridge club's cookout. My grandmother's recipe."

Both Jane's and my shoulders slumped when we learned it wasn't for us. "Oh," I said mournfully. Ellie Mae twined her way between our legs, licked at our fingers, then abandoned us when it became clear we had no food.

Mrs. Henderson gestured behind her, and we realized a second cake sat cooling on the counter. "But I doubled the recipe, because why only have dessert after dinner when you can have it for breakfast, too?"

"And it's got strawberries, so it's healthy," Jane said happily. The three of us pulled up our chairs and tucked in.

After Mrs. Henderson left, Jane and I swapped our pajamas for real clothes and slipped on our sandals. Ellie Mae saw us heading for the door and howled pitifully. Jane grasped my arm. "Stay strong."

"We're abandoning her." I looked back, and Ellie Mae's barks fell to a tragic whine. Her soulful eyes pleaded with me. "We're evil incarnate."

Jane faltered. Ellie Mae wagged her tail, low and hopeful.

"Dammit," Jane said. "Fine, let's take her."

Leash in my hand, the three of us headed into town. Ellie Mae became more and more ecstatic with each new person she encountered, and there were many new people, an island full, shipped in from Boston and the Cape and who knew where else.

We found our group eating ice cream on a patch of grass. Lexi waved a tiny plastic flag printed with the stars and stripes as we approached. "Woo-hoo, America."

"Are we being ironic right now?" Jane asked. She sat down next to Pranav, whose girlfriend Sydney hadn't showed up yet, and gave him a bright smile.

This boded well.

After Sydney and a few more friends arrived, we joined the mobs of people downtown. Jane and I had our faces painted: an elaborate black-and-silver mask around her eyes; a red-and-gold phoenix curved over my cheek and temple. We watched a dunk tank and a watermelon-eating contest. A water fight erupted, long sprays arching above the cobblestones. We screamed and ran through, Ellie Mae happily tossing herself about before shaking the water on innocent bystanders.

When a parade wove down the street, Evan hoisted me onto his shoulders so I could see better. I grabbed hold of him for support, laughing gleefully, while Pranav raised Sydney similarly. Jane clutched Ellie Mae's leash and beamed up at Sydney like a star about to burn out. The crowd before us was a swirling mass of pale pink shirts and mint green dresses and lemon-yellow skirts. It moved, slow but constant, colorful and festive. More guys wore American-flag shorts than I'd ever seen before.

Then the people before us changed once again, revealing Noah Barbanel on the sidewalk, surrounded by half a dozen other teens who looked like they'd been airbrushed by wealth.

I saw Noah before he saw me, but only by a second. He froze when his gaze marked me. For a suspended moment, we both stared at each other, before I swallowed hard and tapped on Evan's shoulder. "Put me down?"

Evan bent his knees and I swung my legs onto the pavement, intimately aware of my sopping-wet hair and my T-shirt clinging to every curve. I looked like a drowned rat. Not exactly the way I wanted to present myself to my hot island nemesis. "Noah."

"Abigail." His attention shifted. "Hey, Evan."

"Hey."

Right. Evan and Noah were both rich summer boys. Of course they knew each other.

As Evan said hello to the others, Noah and I kept our cautious gazes on each other. Then the crowds swirled us apart, but my heart kept beating fast, like prey confronted with a predator. *I can help you or hinder you.*

Stella grabbed my arm. The red-white-and-blue sparkler headdress she'd secured on top of her braid crown bobbed. "Was that Noah? He's stunning."

"Too rich," Lexi said from her girlfriend's other side. "He'll give you a stomachache."

"He's not butter and sugar," Stella said.

"I was making a metaphor about how he's not healthy."

"I'm not sure metaphors work like you think they do."

My breathing slowly returned to tempo as my friends argued

about the merits of Lexi's metaphor. This was fine. I was fine. I bent over Ellie Mae, whose long pink tongue lolled as she panted. "We're doing great, right, girl? So great. We're so calm and great."

Ellie barked and sloppily licked my face.

Bleh.

"Hey." Noah's voice sounded behind me, and I whirled around, wiping dog slobber off my face, along with red and gold glitter. Oh, wow, I'd totally forgotten I had face paint on.

Noah, on the other hand, looked as beautiful and arrogant as always, though his curls spiraled more tightly and ungainly than usual, like he'd spent the morning on the beach. "We should talk."

"I don't want to talk." I glanced toward my friends, who'd meandered farther away while I'd consulted Ellie Mae. Noah and I were alone in the shifting crowds. Around us, the festivities and music continued, everyone so wrapped in their own lives we could have been in our own private room. A small child knocked into my leg, stared up at me with wide eyes, and kept going, towed away by his indifferent mother. "You threatened to blackmail me."

"Give me a chance."

"Why should I?"

"Because I'm asking nicely."

"This is your version of nice?"

His lips pressed together. Then he let out a deep breath. *"Please."*

I crossed my arms over my clinging top, feeling exposed and going on the offense to hide it. "What do you want to talk about? Are you going to tell me not to interfere again, and I'll tell you I'm not going to listen?"

"I want to call a truce."

"I wasn't aware we were at war."

"Weren't you?" He took a deep breath. "We should talk

somewhere—less distracting." His gaze dipped slightly, then flicked away.

Had Noah Barbanel just checked me out? He had. He definitely had. He thought this wet-shirt thing was *distracting*.

I felt a very non-nemesis-like flicker of delight.

Though maybe he merely found it unprofessional or whatever to talk to a sopping-wet girl. And in any case, talking to him was a bad idea. He'd just try to convince me not to do what I wanted to do. "I don't think so."

"Come on." He took a step closer and lowered his voice. "Please?"

This was unfair, a hot boy blasting his good looks in my face. "I should get back to my friends." I scanned the crowds, hoping to spot Evan's six-two frame or Stella's sparkler headdress.

He caught my forearm. Now we stood perilously close. Ellie Mae sat and panted up at us. "Seriously, what will it take for you to hear me out?"

Good lord. I could smell him, all beachy sunscreen and faint cologne. "Well, not threatening me, for one. And not grabbing my arm."

He let go and raised his hands. "Anything else?"

"Hm." I wrapped Ellie Mae's leash more securely around my hand, pulling her close to my side. A child walked by with a giant stuffed animal in her arms, holding it out for Ellie to sniff. My gaze transferred to the booth she must have come from, rafters full of stuffed animals. I smirked at Noah. "I'll talk to you if you win me a giant unicorn."

"What?' "

I shrugged. "I don't make the rules."

"You literally just did."

I raised my hands, palms skyward, and started to walk away.

He caught up with me, practically bleeding haughty dignity. "I don't do carnival games."

"Pity." I shot him a sickly-sweet smile. "I don't talk to threat-makers."

He narrowed his eyes at me and then, to my shock, stalked toward the vendor.

I blinked and trailed after him. "I didn't—I wasn't *serious*—"

"You had better damn well be." Noah exchanged his money for a giant water gun.

"No, I just said it because I knew—"

"I wouldn't do it?" Noah looked pained. He hefted the gun, took aim, and missed by a mile.

I couldn't help it. A laugh escaped me.

Noah sounded wounded. "It's harder than it looks."

"Is it?" I ruffled the fur behind Ellie's ears. "Who knew."

He took aim again.

Ten minutes and many shots later, Noah proudly presented me with a desolate-looking elephant. It sat on its haunches, staring out at the world with a tragic gaze. Its brows curved downward in an expression of despair.

I held the elephant at arm's length. At my feet, Ellie looked equally confused. "This is not a unicorn. This is the saddest elephant in the world."

"What are you talking about?" Noah sounded like a mighty hunter told his bounty was not worthwhile.

"He's so sad. Look at him. The last time an elephant was this sad, it was Dumbo and his mom had just been locked in a cage."

"He's going to be even sadder if you reject him."

Probably true. Sure, you couldn't anthropomorphize stuffed animals, but this elephant was one cruel comment away from sobbing beneath the bleachers. "What am I supposed to do with him? I don't want to look at a sad elephant all day."

"You could give him to a little kid."

"And what, make the kid cry?" I clutched the stuffed animal to my chest. "No."

"Can we talk now?"

I couldn't help it; I'd been charmed by his willingness to bend to my absurd demand, and won over by how earnest he'd been as he played the game. "Fine. We can talk. But later."

"Are you always this difficult?"

"At least eighty percent of the time."

He shook his head, but couldn't entirely suppress a smile. "Tomorrow, then."

I headed back to my group, who lounged on a side street with drinks and fried dough, getting powdered sugar and cinnamon all over themselves. Jane took Ellie's leash, struggling to keep the pup from eating her food. "How'd it go?"

"Where did *this* come from?" Stella snagged the sad elephant from my arms. "He looks tragic. Like he's been orphaned or had an enema."

"Thanks for the visual," Evan said.

Jane grinned. "It's from Noah, isn't it?"

"Don't make this a thing."

"It is *one hundred* percent a thing."

Our group spent the rest of the day indulging in too much food and silly games. At Jane's family's cookout, her uncle flipped burgers and charred corn on the grill, and her youngest cousins threw water balloons. After, we headed to the beach for the fireworks, crowding the sands with thousands of other tourists and locals. We danced to the music of a stranger's boom box. We were young and alive and filled with effervescent joy.

I snapped a picture of the scene and sent it to my best friends:

Happy fourth!! Love you all, wish you were here
♥🐱🐶🐾 Miss you all!!

The responses flooded in immediately:

Haley:
Happy fourth!!! Love you guys!!!

Niko:
I love you guys but would like my dislike of rampant patriotism to be noted

Brooke:
Noted
And omg fun!! Can't believe I'm missing the 4th.
Miss you guys!!

My cheeks hurt with the strength of my grin. Nothing could dim my love for these girls, no matter how far apart we were.

Slipping my phone back into my purse, I turned to Jane and the others. We ran into the surf as fireworks burst above us, golden sparks sizzling against the black night, giant red globes stretching out in long, arching strands. I breathed in salt and summer and threw back my head and laughed.

That night, when I went to bed, I slept deeply, and dreamed of floating.

Seven

The next day, I waited for Noah at Centre Street Bistro. The restaurant occupied the ground floor of a yellow Victorian. A privet hedge protected the patio diners from the hustle and bustle of the busy street, and umbrellas shaded them from the sun. I snagged an outside table at ten a.m. on the dot, looking around hopefully for Noah.

Twenty minutes later, the waitress swung once more by my table, where I'd almost finished a hot chocolate. "Can I get you anything else?"

"I'm sure he'll be here any second." After the waitress smiled sympathetically and left, I checked my phone again, all too aware no other single parties filled the tables surrounding me. No text, and I didn't want to text first. He'd asked *me* to meet. He'd picked the time and place. And now what, he was standing me up? Was this the Nantucket equivalent to asking a girl to prom and ghosting?

Whatever. People ran late and forgot to text. I'd wait ten more minutes.

I stilled my vibrating foot. Noah's surprisingly good-natured attitude regarding the sad elephant (now safely tucked in bed alongside my stuffed horse) made me hope he wasn't still on the help-or-hinder, I-rule-this-island kick. This conversation would be fine. Besides, he couldn't *actually* keep me from doing anything. He was a teenage boy; he didn't have any power.

Right?

He'd said he wanted to talk about a truce. What did a truce mean?

At 10:26, he breezed in. He wore a fitted oxford shirt, his curls carefully styled (at least, I hoped he'd styled them; if he woke up with them so perfectly done I'd be forced to shave his head out of sheer envy and possibly keep his locks. Note to self: that thought got bizarre fast, best never to share it with anyone).

He dropped into the chair across from me. "Hi."

"You made it."

"Ah, the passive-aggressive equivalent of 'You're late.'"

I crossed my arms. "All right. You're late."

"Had to help an old lady cross the street."

"Liar. What was this, some weird power play?"

He raised his brows. "Work went long."

"You work?" I sounded more surprised than I meant to.

"What, you think I lounge around all day?"

"Kind of. Also, it's very early for work to be finished. Unless you're a fisherman."

"I help out my dad. He wanted me to finish pulling a report for him."

"Oh." I liked the idea of helping out the family business. "That's sweet."

"Is it, though?" His voice had an edge.

The waitress appeared, beaming at Noah. She apparently shared my relief in not being stood up. "What'll you have?"

Noah ordered a breakfast burrito and a coffee, and I ordered buttermilk pancakes with berries. Once the waitress walked away, Noah took a swig of my hot chocolate and pulled a face. "Not coffee."

"I'd be sympathetic except you literally stole my drink."

He did not look repentant. "Okay, Abigail Schoenberg. What's your deal?"

"What do you mean?"

"I don't know anything about you."

"I don't know anything about you, either."

"Except you do, don't you? You showed up on Nantucket, in my house, prying into my grandparents' lives."

"That's your grandparents, not you. And this is very aggressive for a truce."

The edge came back to his smile. "Think of it as pre-truce. Who are you?"

I shifted in my seat, awkward and uneasy. I'd expected to talk about the letters and our grandparents, not me. "No one."

The chipper waitress appeared and set a steaming mug in front of Noah. "Here's your coffee!"

He thanked her, then turned to me as she departed. "Try again."

"I'm serious. There's not much to say."

"So you think it's *normal* for people to spend the summer on a re-mote island in order to find out more about their family's past? And to escape your ex."

"He doesn't have anything to do with it," I shot back, and, sur-prised, realized I hadn't thought about Matt at all in the last week. "Not that it's any of your business."

He tilted his chair to balance on two legs and slung his arm over the back, regarding me steadily. "I'm pretty sure we're each other's business now."

I could feel my cheeks turning red, with anger or something else. "What do you want me to say? I'm not getting anything else out of this except family history." I tried to sound glib, one of my favorite forms of defensiveness. "Unless, if I'm lucky, a really good college app essay."

His chair's front legs landed solidly on the ground and he stared at me, appalled. "You're prying into my family for a *college essay*?"

"No! God! I'm just saying I'm not going to get anything else out of this."

"Your essay doesn't even really matter. It's your grades and your well-roundedness."

That stung, mostly since I was afraid he was right. While my grades were fine, they were nothing to write home about, and did joining minimal-effort clubs count as being well-rounded? It seemed unlikely. I needed a perfect essay to convince colleges to give me a scholarship.

So I stung right back. "Oh? And here I thought it was how much money your family had donated."

He straightened. "I didn't get into college because of my family."

"I didn't say you did." I shrugged, overly nonchalant. "Though I *did* read an article about how several prominent schools often accept donors' children."

"My family donates to schools they *attended*. Alumni donations."

"Right." I widened my eyes innocently. "And I take it you're not going to any of those schools?"

"You're a real . . ." He pressed his lips together, then shook his head.

Bitch? Pill? Piece of work? Probably. I sighed. "Sorry. I didn't mean to jump down your throat. You stress me out."

"*I* stress *you* out?"

"Yes! I didn't think there'd be so much—*antagonism*—with me looking into O'ma's past. And I didn't mean to be rude about the college thing—I'm, I don't know, stressed about school, too, and getting

in, and having money. You're right. Maybe my essay won't even matter." I offered an awkward, apologetic smile.

He didn't look at me.

Welp. So much for our truce. I looked down.

"I'm going to Harvard," he said after a stretched pause. I peered
up from my drink to see him looking steadfastly away from me, two
dark swathes of color high on his cheeks. "My family does donate."

Ah. I'd pressed a hot button.

"But I had really good grades." He finally looked at me again. "I
was valedictorian."

Of course he was.

"You're starting in the fall?" I said, as an olive branch. "What are
you studying?"

"Econ."

"Cool. Do you want to go into . . . the economy?"

Wow, brilliant. I should get a Pulitzer in small talk.

His mouth twitched. "The plan is econ for undergrad, then business school."

Literally all I knew about business school came from my older
cousin Sarah, in the form of her disdain for the business school bros
she met via Tinder. "So you want to run a business?"

"It's kind of the deal."

It took a minute to click. "*Oh.* You mean—your family's company?"

He nodded shortly.

"Huh." I tried to process this. My life plan had no more details
than 1) get into college, 2) graduate from college, 3) get a job, 4)
support parents in their old age (and my brother, if necessary). "You
want to work at Barbanel?"

" 'Want' doesn't come into it. I have to."

"I mean, you don't *have to* have to."

He did not look amused.

I slowly put the pieces together. Edward Barbanel, chairman of the board, inherited Barbanel from his father, and grew it into the empire it was today. Harry Barbanel, Noah's father, was currently CEO. I blinked. "They don't expect you to . . ."

He raised his brows.

I laughed a little nervously. "I mean, you don't *have* to take over a giant firm if you don't want to."

"Someone does."

"Don't you have any cousins? Or siblings?"

"No siblings." He tossed back the rest of his coffee. "Shira's the closest in age to me, so she's kind of like a little sister. She wants to study sea turtles."

"Sea turtles."

"In Ecuador. They're endangered."

I digested the sea turtle news for a moment. Poor sea turtles. "Okay, well, what about your other cousins?"

"None seem interested."

"*You* don't seem interested. Why's it fall on you? Are you, like, the oldest son's oldest son or something?"

Embarrassment flickered across his face.

Oh my god. "That's ridiculous. And incredibly unfair. I mean, to you, yes, but also, what about everyone else?"

He looked away, then back, and spoke firmly. "So. What do you want to study?"

Fair, I'd been being pushy. "I want to be a historian, but . . ."

"But what?"

"Would it help anyone? Or are historians just modern-day Cassandras, doomed to cry warnings and be ignored?"

He looked surprised. "Do you think so?"

"Well, I think historians are important, but I also feel like they keep saying, 'Hey, this is how dictatorships start,' and everyone's like, 'Cool, got it, let's ignore you.' So does being a historian help? What helps?" I gestured at him. "I mean, besides being wealthy and directing your wealth in useful ways."

"Here you go." The waitress reappeared at our table, cheerful and sunny. "Breakfast burrito and pancakes."

"Thank you," we chorused.

She beamed at us. "Anything else?"

We shook our heads. I took a bite of my pancakes, finding it surprisingly deep in flavor, and deliciously soaked in butter. "Wow, these are *excellent*."

Noah cut his burrito methodically in half. "What counts as useful ways?"

"What? Oh, for money. You know, donating it toward useful causes and stuff."

"Like?"

I shrugged, swirling two square bites of pancake through the maple syrup on my plate. "Well, what are you passionate about?"

His gaze flicked up to mine. He smiled slightly. "I know what *I* consider useful causes. I wanted your take."

"Oh." Hot embarrassment flushed through me and I focused in on my food for a moment. Why had I assumed he wanted an explanation about how to make an impact?

He took pity. "I like the Nantucket Conservation Foundation."

"Oh?" If I kept asking questions, maybe my embarrassment would drain away. "Why?"

He shrugged. "My mom works in ecological conversation and my grandma gardens, so I guess I've always been tuned into the environment. And—well, my life has a huge carbon footprint, and my family uses up lots of resources, and I think it's important to offset it if you can."

I stared at him with surprise. "That's nice."

He looked embarrassed, turning to stare distractedly across the patio. When he turned back, his expression had shuttered. He leaned forward, a cryptographer faced with a code he couldn't quite crack. "What's it going to take to get you to leave this letter thing alone?"

I blinked. "Oh, I'm not going to leave it alone."

"Why not?"

"Why would I? How can you ask me to let my family history slip away?"

"I'm sure there's other ways you can find things out. Other people you can ask."

"You're so sure about that?" I tilted my head. "It's not like the Nazis left so many alive to tell their stories."

He paused, then blew out a breath. "You're kidding."

I smiled. Checkmate. "I'm really not."

"That's not playing fair."

"I know." You couldn't really turn away people trying to learn about their survivor grandparents. Sort of a faux pas. I took a bite of my pancakes.

He frowned at me. "Why don't you know anything about her?"

"Oh. She came here when she was super young, so she didn't remember much. We don't know where she's from originally—somewhere in Germany—or if there's any living family left over there. And even what she did remember, she didn't like to talk about. Mom says a lot of survivors don't like to talk."

"She's a Holocaust survivor?"

"Yeah. Well, to be honest, she didn't identify as a survivor, because she didn't live through the war in Europe. She came over here when she was four, right before the war started."

He dropped his fork to his plate. "She came over before the war. From Germany."

"Yeah."

"With her family?"

His intensity almost alarmed me. "No—they stayed, her parents. She was placed with a Jewish family in New York until she was eighteen."

He stared at me.

"What?"

There was a strange sort of silence when people hadn't quite finished saying what they wanted to, a silence where you had to gauge whether to urge or lie in wait. I lay down my fork and watched at Noah. Waiting.

"My family's from New York." His eyes stayed steady on mine. "They took in a German girl. During the war."

Pure satisfaction rocked through me, akin to the pleasure of trying one puzzle piece after another and finally having the right one snap in. *They took in a German girl during the war.* Of course they did. Of course O'ma had come to Nantucket because the family she'd lived with vacationed here, and she'd fallen in love with the son of the house. Why else would her picture be in a photo album? "That's it, then."

He shook his head. "It's too coincidental."

"It's not. It's why I'm here. She grew up with your family. It's why her photo was in one of your family's scrapbooks."

"*What?* Why didn't you mention that?"

"I forgot!"

He pinched his nose. "If she moved in with them when she was a little kid, they would have been like siblings."

"I hate to disappoint you, but they weren't."

He leaned forward, as though the sheer force of his personality could make me renege. "They grew up together. Siblings write letters."

"Not like these letters. Not outside of Westeros."

"Are you sure?"

"So very, very sure."

"You might have misread them."

"Dude. I didn't. Want to read them yourself?"

"Yes. No. Maybe."

He could sort out his feelings on his own time. "Let's ask your grandfather, then."

"Right. We could. But—" He shoved his fingers through his curls. "We can't."

"Really?"

He rubbed his forehead. "Look. My family worked hard to get where they are—"

"If this is a lecture about the American dream or pulling yourself up by your bootstraps—"

"It's about anti-Semitism."

"Oh."

"Yeah. People were happy to hire Barbanels, but they didn't want to socialize with us. We weren't Christian enough, we weren't white enough, we weren't *enough*. My family went through a lot to fit in on this island. If my grandpa had an affair when he was engaged to my grandmother? People don't need to know." He dropped his head in his hands. "And for it to be some weird pseudo-incestuous relationship . . ."

"Hey." I was bizarrely affronted on my O'ma's behalf. "It *wasn't* incestuous. And maybe they never felt like siblings! I mean, obviously they didn't if they fell in love, and maybe no one else thought of them sibling-like, either. And—I get struggling in the forties and fifties to be accepted, but I don't think anyone's going to care today."

"Yeah, well, you can leave the island afterwards, so it doesn't matter to you, does it? People like scandals here."

"But it's not even a very good scandal!"

"I think my grandma would disagree."

I digested his statement. "So this is the reason you don't want me talking to your grandparents? Because you think your grandmother would be mad? About—what, about Edward having an affair, or if other people found out about it?"

He ignored my question, which seemed to be his MO. "We can find things out without involving my grandparents. You're here all summer, aren't you? I'll help you. My help might be even better than talking to my grandparents. You said your grandmother clammed up about the past? Yeah. My grandparents aren't exactly oversharers, either."

Not a bad point. I'd been thinking of the boy who wrote *It has been too long since I last saw you*—but I should remember he'd also written *You're being ridiculous.*

"I can give you a tour of the house. I can get you access to the scrapbooks." He leaned closer, pinning me with his gaze. "You *want* my help, Abigail."

He wasn't wrong. What if his grandparents were like mine, and refused to talk about the past? At least this way I could look for more photos of my grandmother, and see the gardens at Golden Doors. *If you miss the rose garden so much, come back,* E had written. *They're blooming like crazy this year, and my mother planted a new kind, and you know she loves to show them to you. You know how much I love to see you in the garden, too . . .*

I cleared my throat. "But if I asked your grandfather . . ."

"Give me a month. One month. Then you can talk to him, if there's anything left to ask. And you get my help in the meantime. I can open doors for you."

"*Golden* doors?"

"Is that a yes?"

"I suppose."

"Good." He smiled, and it was like the sun. He speared a piece of my pancakes with his fork. "You're right. This is excellent."

Eight

❧

Over the next few days, an oppressive heat swept the island. Jane and I slept with our window wide open and a fan swiveling between us, damp towels pressed to our faces. We spent as much time as possible on the beach, where we could peel off the sticky fabric of our clothes and lie exposed to the elements, wholeheartedly putting our faith in sunscreen to ward off cancer and burns. When it became too unbearably hot, I'd fling myself into the water, stripping away the sweat and dirt and heat. I kicked and floated and splashed, and when I tired myself out I'd return to my towel, only to begin the cycle all over again.

During work hours, the bookstore's AC was a blessing: cool, breathable air I would down in gulps after coming in from the muggy outdoors. The walk from Mrs. Henderson's only took fifteen minutes, but by the time I arrived at work, sweat always pasted my clothes to my back. Customers came in to escape the humidity, saying over and over, "You must be so glad to be in air-conditioning!"

The Thursday after the Fourth, Jane and I had both gotten home from our respective shifts when her phone pinged. She turned it toward me so I could read the text from Lexi: We're going skinny-dipping—you in? We can pick you up whenever.

When I looked back up at Jane, she made an exaggerated face. "Are we doing this?"

I'd never been skinny-dipping. But you know what? Summer of chutzpah. "Hell yeah we are."

Lexi and Stella swung by to get us, and we drove out to a pond surrounded by trees and darkness. It was as though some cross-island memo had gone out to all the teens, telling everyone to meet here. Crowds gathered on the shores, laughing and drinking in the moonlight. We clamored down to the water's edge, where gentle waves lapped at the brief beach.

"Let's do shots first," Stella said.

"With what shot glasses?" Lexi said.

"Don't be so literal." Stella told her girlfriend, pulling a bottle of amber liquid from her brightly embroidered tote. Lexi groaned and Jane laughed.

"What is it?" I asked, wanting in on the joke.

"It's Fireball—it's cinnamon flavored," Jane said.

"Architect of many hot-mess nights," Lexi added.

"Don't be haters," Stella said. "I love it, it's delicious." She raised the bottle to her lips and took a swig, then handed it to me.

I took a more cautious sip, and still coughed as the liquor burned down my esophagus. It did taste like cinnamon, sweet and rather sickly. But I liked it significantly more than beer.

After a few more rounds, we looked at each other. "Ready?" Stella said. "We're doing this?"

We nodded, privates in an army, before bursting into giggles. "Go, go, go!" Lexi shouted, and we shucked off our clothes, shirts and bras everywhere, and ran screaming into the water. We windmilled our arms and laughed wildly as we fell into the cold, bracing lake.

"It's freezing!" Jane screamed.

I'd never been naked outside before, and I felt daring and exhilarated, sexy and childlike at once, utterly free. It was too dark to see anyone but my friends, and they were friends who only knew me as someone who would sneak into millionaires' homes and go skinny-dipping and drink shots (kind of). I loved it. I floated on my back, exposed to the wilderness. Above me, the waning moon shone, bright as a streetlamp.

"I feel like we should be casting spells," Stella said, her voice muffled by the water filling my ears.

"What kind of spells?" Lexi asked.

"Health, wealth, happiness."

"Acceptance to the colleges of our choice," Jane added.

"World dominance," Lexi said. "We can't be worse than the current leaders."

"Also, I look great in black." Stella again. "We'd make excellent witches."

"The moon is bright tonight," I murmured, and lowered my legs to the lake floor. "I'd cast a divining spell to find out where my grandmother's lost necklace is."

"Don't look now," Jane said. "But Noah Barbanel is here."

"What?" I whipped my head around and scanned the shore. Sure enough, he stood on the shore in a large group, which looked peak preppy in their pastels and polos.

"I *said* don't look!"

"I'm screwed."

"Honestly, he'd at least be worth making out with, don't you think?" Stella said.

No way was I climbing naked out of the lake in front of Noah Barbanel. Not in a million years. "I live in this lake now."

Jane smirked at me. "Do one thing every day that scares you."

"Thanks, Eleanor," I snipped.

I looked at Noah again, and almost screamed when he turned

right toward me. I could tell the instant he recognized me, because he stilled, then leaned forward, then stilled again—then raised his beer in a silent toast.

"Okay, here's the plan," I told the others. "I'm going to swim across the lake. You'll meet me on the other side with a change of clothes."

Jane glanced toward the far edge of the water, hazy in the darkness. "You're such a freak. No."

"You could go out and toss me a towel?"

"Also no. Don't show any weakness. You have to own it."

"Own what, precisely? Being cold and naked and wet in front of Noah Barbanel?"

Stella started giggling.

"I *hate* you," I said, splashing water in her face. Her makeup had miraculously stayed on. "This is weird, right? A bunch of boys standing clothed on the bank while we're naked in the water?"

"I mean, there's also a lot of naked boys in the lake and clothed girls on the beach," Jane said.

"Right. Fair. What do I do?"

I didn't get a chance to strategize, because I heard my name from the shore, carried in a low, amused tone. "Hey, Schoenberg," Noah called. "How's the water?"

Okay. We were doing this. I swiveled toward the shore, keeping my chin and everything below it safely submerged. "Great," I hollered back. "Coming in?"

"Nah." He shrugged, barely able to swallow a smirk. "I think I'll stay here. Enjoy the view."

My friends snickered and started dog-paddling away.

"You're on *my* side," I hissed after them, then raised my voice for Noah. "Coward."

"Really? What about you? Plan to stay there long?"

"Maybe."

He waded in, pulling his shirt off.

"What are you doing?" I squealed.

He balled it up. "Catch."

To my utter surprise, I did. Noah turned around and strolled back to his friends.

I watched him go, holding his shirt above the water. What was his deal? He could have left me to fend for myself. He could have made me more uncomfortable, or ignored me.

Was he trying to preserve my theoretical modesty? (Which, to be honest, I was glad for, because I was one hundred percent not up for owning it per Jane's suggestion.) I turned my back on the beach and shimmied into the shirt. When I'd made sure Noah had rejoined his friends and wasn't looking, I darted to shore and tugged on my bikini bottom, then did some careful maneuvering to get my bikini top on beneath his shirt.

I should have pulled off his shirt and pulled my own on then. I should have. But summer nights were not made for should-haves.

Instead, I looked up and found Noah again, and not a minute later, he glanced my way (did this mean he'd been periodically glancing as I awkwardly got dressed? Hopefully not!). A moment later, he strode over. "Didn't know you had it in you."

"What do you mean?"

"Nothing." I heard the smile in his voice. "I thought you'd be busy Nancy Drew–ing all summer. Isn't this a waste of time?"

"Rumor has it you're only young once." I tugged at the shirt and glanced over at the crowd of people he'd emerged from. "Those are your friends?"

"Yeah." I must have made some kind of face, because his eyes narrowed. "What?"

"Nothing. They look"—homogeneous and one-percent—"nice."

"You have a terrible poker face."

I knew I should keep my mouth shut, but I wanted to prod him, make him as uncomfortable as he made me. "The whole Nantucket vibe is a bit preppier than I usually go for."

"Because you didn't expect Nantucket to be WASPy," he said dryly, and I couldn't hold back a smile. "You're kind of judgy."

"Isn't everyone?"

"I try not to judge anyone until I know them," he said mildly.

Good lord. "Well, I guess you're just a better person than I am."

He grinned at me. "And I'll have you know preppiness is actually very Jewish."

"Sounds fake."

"Ralph Lauren went to a yeshiva."

"He did not."

"His parents wanted him to be a rabbi. His name was actually Lifshitz."

I laughed. "You're making this up."

"You can google it."

"I will." I looked over at his friends again, with their skins tanned and their hair lightened. "So you're saying you're preppy because you're Jewish, not because you're trying to fit in with the Nantucket elite?"

He gave a wry smile. "I mean, yeah, it's easier to be preppy on Nantucket."

"Easier? How?"

"You know. More comfortable."

I considered him, tilting my head. We were in our own little bubble, with the moon shining down on us, the lake water leaving me feeling silky and new. "Like you actively dress preppy so you'll fit in?"

He, too, looked over at his friends, then back at me. "Yeah, a little. Not in a bad way—it doesn't stress me out or anything. But—sure, in the past few years, I've noticed it's different here than at home, and it's easier to not stand out. Which sounds dumb out loud."

"I mean, it sounds real." I paused. "Stand out how?"

"Oh, you know," he said with a slight smile. "In New York, I don't have to think about being Jewish at all. No one blinks if you mention Solomon Schechter or Simchat Torah or the JCC. I don't have to represent Judaism, or even particularly *be* Jewish if I don't want to be, because other people are, and I can be nonreligious and have critical debates. Here—sometimes I feel like I have to think about it more, make sure I'm not doing anything that'll add to a negative stereotype." He looked at me. "Do you know what I mean?"

In my town, the Jewish community was so small I didn't feel like I had a match for either of Noah's experiences—I'd never felt surrounded by Jewish communities or references, but I'd also never really felt like I had to represent Judaism. Being Jewish was something my family did in private. But maybe that also made it easy, since I never felt like I had to represent anything? "A little. It sounds stifling."

"Maybe. I don't know. I never used to think about this as a kid—I was just so happy to be here, to escape the city and go swimming and sailing. But now—" He shrugged. "My family also cares so much about appearances. I don't want to do anything to stress them out."

Ah. "Which is why you care so much about if our grandparents had an affair?"

He opened his mouth to respond, but we were interrupted when a girl bounced up. "Noah!" She settled the full force of her smile on him. "What's up?"

Noah and I turned to her in surprise. "Uh," he said. "Just talking."

"About what?"

We exchanged glances, and I felt a familiar closing of the ranks, a keep-it-in-the-family emotion. "Nothing," Noah said, and we both smiled at the girl. "This is Abigail."

"Hey." She barely acknowledged me before returning her attention to Noah. "We need you to settle something."

"Oh." He glanced at me. "Sure."

I wrapped my arms around my waist, oddly bereft. "I'll see you later, then."

After Noah had followed the girl away, my friends came up to me. "What happened there?" Jane asked.

"To be perfectly honest, I have no idea." I watched as Noah's group enfolded him. "Just a little chat about preppiness and identity."

"That's super weird," Stella said, then waggled her brows. "Are you going to keep his shirt?"

I pushed her shoulder lightly. "*You're* weird."

I kept the shirt.

Nine

June 20, 1955

Sometimes I miss you like the sun must miss the moon, locked
in orbit but unable to move closer. It's a physical ache. There's a
tension in my shoulder blades and my back, a stiffness in my neck.
Being near you, touching you, relaxes me. But away from you I
carry the entire world locked in my muscles and I never breathe
as deeply as I do near you, as easily as on the island. Sometimes I
wrap my arms around my body and pretend it's you holding me,
your hands on my back.

   It never really works, though.

A few days later, I woke early. The island was hazy with heat, and the sun weighed heavily when I stepped outside. I splurged on a ride share, the only way to arrive at the Barbanel mansion without being a sweat-soaked mess. Birds warbled cheerfully when I climbed out of the car, and the ocean's tide wove in and out of their song. Before me, at the end of the circular drive of crushed shells, loomed Golden Doors, gray and elegant and calm. This house revealed no weaknesses, gave up no secrets. Golden Doors would go proudly into the sea itself should the shore give up in its eternal battle against the encroaching ocean, with nary a word of complaint. It made me feel like riffraff, small and unwanted.

I climbed the shallow steps to the veranda and rang the doorbell. I should probably stop assigning emotions to inanimate objects, especially active dislike. (At least Sad Elephant loved me, despite his own internal struggles.)

"Hey." Noah appeared in the doorway, dressed in sweatpants and a T-shirt, both branded with a high school crew team. Ah. Crew explained his perfectly sculpted arms.

Not that I paid attention to said arms. "Hi."

"Want to come in?"

I nodded, shy, as though I hadn't yelled at this boy multiple times. Different, I supposed, to be on his home turf after deciding to play nice.

"So what's the plan, Abigail Schoenberg?" he asked as we stepped into the airy foyer of the mansion. I hadn't been in the entryway before, and I paused to take in the high ceilings and massive staircase. "Where do you want to start your tour?"

I couldn't get over the unease this house wrought in me. "How about outside?"

We cut through the living room where I'd served champagne a few weeks ago, and out the French doors into the lawn. It was no less impressive sans white tents and sound systems than it had been with them; better, perhaps, with just the undulating roll of green, the thick gardens, and the ocean on the horizon. "Can we see the rose gardens? And the gazebo?" At his sharp glance, I added, "I read about them in the letters."

"Seriously?"

"You can read them, you know."

"Why, when you're already telling me the interesting parts?"

I let out a half laugh. "Not *all* the interesting parts."

"What do you mean?"

I pressed my lips together and shook my head, my cheeks warming.

His brows rose up. "What?"

"Nothing." One of the lines from the letters formed, unbidden, in my mind. *I wish I could see you surrounded by roses, naked and drenched in moonlight.*

Hard pass on sharing. "Come on. Let's go."

Flowers edged the lawn: romantic, soft-looking pinks against the dark green foliage; summer lilacs of all colors, vibrant magenta and pure white and gentle purple. A monarch butterfly landed on a plant with clustered pink-purple stars. "They like milkweed," Noah said. "The monarch population's declining like crazy, so if you want to help, plant milkweed."

I glanced at him, impressed but unwilling to let him know it. "Pro tips from Noah."

"Someone's got to save the butterflies."

"I take it your secret passion is entomology, not economics?"

He shot me a wry glance and led me through an arch in the dense privet hedge. We entered a winding maze of trees and bushes, covering the expanse from the lawn to the dunes. The trees here were spindly, salt-warped things, with peeling bark and thin, twisted trunks. Their needles looked hard and sharp, as likely to prick blood as Sleeping Beauty's spindle. "What are these?"

"Junipers. Their berries are used to make gin."

"And what about those?" I nodded at orange-red blooms at the base of the trees.

"Don't you know, bookstore girl?" He plucked one and tucked it in my hair, and I stilled, utterly shocked. I also felt bizarrely afraid of startling him away, because it turned out I *liked* Noah Barbanel touching my hair, even if he was teasing me, throwing me off my guard because he could. But maybe he wasn't. I'd never seen him so at ease. "They're poppies."

Poppies, a field of which lured Dorothy to sleep.

Once more I wondered if I'd wandered off the path, into Oz or Narnia or some strange world where the rules weren't mine and I didn't know when I broke them. I swallowed and lifted my chin, hoping to brazen through. "No roses, though."

Noah smiled and led me deeper into the gardens, down a path of hedges, the ocean peeking in and out of sight. Flagstones occasionally dotted the path, more a suggestion than a demarcation. His voice floated back toward me. "Botany."

I hurried after him. "What?"

He didn't answer.

It clicked. "You'd study botany instead of business? Why?"

He looked back. "I want to work on preserving biodiversity. If we can understand why species are going extinct, we can try to prevent it."

I nodded. "Thus, the monarchs."

"Thus, the monarchs." He smiled, a funny, almost sad smile.

"You don't think it's too late? I feel like everything I read about the environment is doom-and-gloom."

"I don't know." He touched the trunk of the tree beside him. "I think we need to try, no matter what. I think everyone has a responsibility to do whatever they can."

"We could just let the world burn."

"We can't." He pinned me with an intense, searing glance, which slowly lessened. "You're joking."

I bit back a smile. "Yeah. I think that's actually kind of a noble way to think about things."

He scoffed, the color in his cheeks heightening, and turned away from me. "Come on," he called over his shoulder, voice muffled as he ducked under a gap in the hedge.

I followed him into a wide, open space. Roses bloomed everywhere, a hundred kinds and colors, circling a gazebo in the very center of the clearing. I stopped. "It's beautiful."

"My grandmother's a gardener," he said, stroking the petal of a shoulder-high rose.

"Did she—make all of this?" But no—O'ma had been in this rose garden at seventeen years old, standing in the center of the gazebo. Unearned nostalgia filtered through me. How strange to walk through the same gardens she had.

"My great-grandmother—my grandpa's mom—designed it. But my grandmother added some of the newer rose varieties."

While Edward's current memories of O'ma in this garden had to be blurred by years with his wife, children, and grandchildren, I could only see this place through the lens of his letters. I wondered if O'ma's memories of being here had been crystallized, since she'd had nothing to overwrite them. Had they stayed with her throughout the decades, bright and clearly defined? *I wish I could see you surrounded by roses . . .*

It was too much—the setting, the inherent romantic nature of a rose garden and a gazebo. It made me strangely sad. I lifted my gaze, and it snagged on text carved into the inside of the gazebo's wooden cupola. *Quien no sabe de mar, no sabe de mal.*

Noah caught me looking. "'He who knows nothing of the sea, knows nothing of suffering.' It's an old Ladino proverb."

"Ladino?"

"A combination of Spanish and Hebrew."

"Very Jewish, a proverb about suffering."

"We like to stay on brand."

I smiled briefly, but it fell away. It was too bittersweet, the saying, this place, Ruth and Edward. "We should go back."

"Should we?" He looked at me, dark gaze intense, not a hint of teasing humor in his voice or expression.

My breath shuddered. I couldn't get a read on him today. Was he playing a game with me? But why? He had what he wanted; I'd promised not to talk to his grandparents for a month.

But maybe rich boys played games I didn't understand, games with roses and gazebos and summer girls. Part of me wanted to play, too, but I didn't know how, and I wasn't sure I'd be able to stop if I started. "Yes. We should."

And I turned away before I changed my mind.

Golden Doors rambled. Its interior reminded me of a Diana Wynne Jones book about a house whose many doors led to different places. We began in the modern addition, but quickly moved past it. It felt like we were winding back in time. The modern kitchen was connected to a semi-modern pantry, which led into a formal dining room from a much older era. A massive chandelier hung above a heavy oak table, and candlesticks decorated the sideboards.

"We almost never eat here," Noah said. "Most of the time we're in the modern section since there's more light and it has the sea view. But occasionally we have formal dinners here."

"Did your grandfather eat here? Growing up?" I tried to envision my grandmother sitting at one of the seats. Why *hadn't* the two of them felt like siblings? Surely she'd been treated like one of the family, hadn't she? "Or, wait, they were mostly in New York."

"Yeah. My great-grandparents moved there in the 1920s. Before then, though, the family lived here full-time."

For some reason, that surprised me. I'd imagined they'd started living on Nantucket, bought Golden Doors, in the 1950s or later— after accumulating their wealth in the modern era. "How long's your family been here?"

"They came from New Bedford in the 1800s."

"New Bedford? The . . . whaling town?"

"Yeah."

"Okay, I need help. How did Jews wind up in a nineteenth-century American whaling town?"

He laughed. "We're Sephardic. My family moved from Morocco to New Bedford in the early 1700s."

"You can trace your family back to the *1700s*?" I asked indignantly "And you're mad I'm trying to find out about my family history from sixty years ago?"

"I don't object to your goals, but your methods," he said loftily.

"How'd they end up here?"

"They were accountants—they'd been accountants in Fez, too— and New Bedford had strong Nantucket connections, because of the whaling trade. So when Nantucket boomed, my family opened a branch of the firm here. And built Golden Doors."

As he spoke, he led me into the next rooms—two parlors with no real purpose, and a music room. A baby grand showed signs of recent use, sheet music scattered around, the bench tilted out. "Do you play?" I asked.

"My dad does."

"Not you?"

"Tin ear," he said lightly.

I remembered mentions of piano in the letters. "Your grandfather plays, too?"

"Yeah."

"But you didn't want to learn?"

"Come on, you'll like this." He moved into a hall and pushed open another door, gesturing for me to enter first.

Okay. So this boy had zero desire to talk about his family.

"Oh." Books lined the walls. A fireplace stood on the far wall, a painting of the sea above it. Cozy couches and brocaded armchairs were scattered about the thick carpets. Foggy glass obscured the windows. A biography of Mark Twain sat on the round table beside one armchair, along with a box of Stoned Wheat Thins.

"It's wonderful. I always wanted a library."

A smile tugged at his lips. "I'm not surprised."

"What can I say, I enjoy being a stereotype."

Next, he led me upstairs, to a large, elegant room whose modern couches and entertainment system couldn't disguise its original grandiosity. Board games and books stacked shelves. "This is where the cousins hang out."

"How many of you are there? Where's everyone right now?"

"Anyone ever tell you you're nosy?"

"Literally my entire life." I crossed to the large windows overlooking the grounds and distant, crashing sea. I couldn't image my grandmother growing up here. "This view's stunning."

He came and stood behind me, shoulder only a few inches from my own. "There's twelve cousins on my dad's side."

"And you're the oldest."

He nodded.

"Must be a lot of pressure."

"You never give up, do you?"

"How would I learn anything if I did? *Is* it?"

He hesitated for long enough I thought he might stay silent. Instead, he gave a tiny nod. "It's not *not* pressure."

I waited, but he didn't say anything else. "I just don't get it," I said. "I mean, I understand how your family would want you to go into business if you wanted something they considered fluffy, but biodiversity? No one could stay that's not important."

"Sure," he said, an edge of bitterness in his tone, "but why should I be the one to do it? Other people will become scientists. Not everyone has a family business they're expected to join. Weren't we just talking about how rich people can raise awareness of causes? If I'd be better at making money than at being a botanist, shouldn't I make the money and donate it? Isn't it selfish to do what I'm interested in if I could do something else and have a bigger impact?"

I'd never had to think about my own future quite so intensely. "I don't know."

"Neither do I," he said, the bitterness stronger now, like it'd been brewing for a very long time. "Though my family has a definite opinion."

Then he took in a deep breath and exhaled it slowly, forcing his shoulders to relax, like he'd spent years teaching himself to calm down and dismiss his frustrations. He gave me a practiced smile and a firm nod. "Let's look for your grandma."

We wound back downstairs, into the wide hall between the old and new additions, where Edward Barbanel's study lay. I hovered on the brink of entering. "Will your family get mad if we go through this stuff?"

"Only if they find out." He shot me a lightning-fast grin. "My grandparents are at the club. They're not going to catch us."

We pushed open the heavy velvet curtains shielding the deep window alcove, letting light flood the room. Then we pulled the scrapbooks from the shelves and sat on the red carpet. "If she came when she was a kid, we probably want to start with the late 1930s."

"Let me find the one where I saw her picture—then I can show you what she looks like." I pulled out the 1947–1951 album. My fingers tingled as I opened the green cover. Had O'ma listened to Edward play piano in the music room? Had she ever been in this study with *his* parents, being disciplined, being disappointed?

Noah sat on the floor beside me, so close our knees brushed. In the silence, I could hear the sounds of our breaths, the turning of the pages. I scanned each black-and-white photo until I paused at the still I'd seen before. "Here."

She looked up at us, laughing with parted lips, frozen in time.

Noah bent forward, curls falling into his face. "You look a little similar."

"It's the eyes, isn't it? I hadn't realized we have the same eyes." I took a picture of the photo. "Do you think your family has any papers about her?"

"What do you mean?"

"Like how she came here? How she was placed with them? I want to find out where she was from, if she had any relatives who survived. I want to be able to trace our family back as far as you can." I turned the page, hoping for more photos. "We know her parents' names, and they're in the database of people killed at Auschwitz, but there's no other info. If you google my great-grandmother, *nothing* comes

up. Or, like, one German girl's Instagram account. Nothing else. The
records say they were deported from Luxembourg, so they must have
gone there from Germany after sending O'ma off, but there's no records of where they're originally from."

He nodded thoughtfully. "I'll see what I can find."

"Thanks. Oh, look." I paused on another photo of my grandmother, maybe fourteen, sitting on a sofa next to a grown woman.

Noah peered at her. "I think that's my great-grandmother."

Noah's great-grandmother. Edward's mother. I hadn't thought
about her before, but she'd raised O'ma, hadn't she? She'd taken her
in along with her own children. I studied the picture. Did they look
like mother and daughter? Had they *felt* like mother and daughter?

We kept turning pages, pausing every time we found one of O'ma
so I could record it on my phone. Most of the photos in the scrapbook
were family shots, meals or gatherings on the beach. Sometimes
I caught half a profile of O'ma, or her face in the background. She
didn't show up often, but she showed up consistently.

I wished I knew what the dynamic had been like. Had she felt like
one of the family, or not at all? Surely if she'd liked living with the
Barbanels, she would have talked about them. If she'd seen Noah's
great-grandmother as a mother figure, how could she *not* have mentioned her?

Here she was again, older this time, sitting on a porch chair with
her lips pursed flirtatiously. Maybe Edward had taken the photo. I
glanced at Noah, struck by parallel of us sitting here decades after our
grandparents. *History repeats itself,* the saying went, but why? Were
humans so predictable in our reactions and emotions? Were some
patterns easier to fall into than others? Why were we so bad at learning from the past?

I looked back at the picture, then sucked in a breath. "Look at this!"

Noah leaned ever closer to me. "What?"

"She's wearing the necklace." It rested high on her clavicle, the central pendant—a giant, clear sparkler—resting in the hollow of her neck. Smaller rectangle pendants connected with each other to form the band. It was vaguely art deco and gorgeous, glitzy and glittering.

"So?"

"I told you. My grandmother had a necklace, and your grandfather refused to give it back."

He removed his gaze from the photo to me. "What do you mean 'refused'?"

Oops. We'd been getting along so well, I'd forgotten we were on different sides. "Well—she asked for it back, and he wouldn't give it."

"Why did she think she should get it?"

"What?" I stared at him. "It was her necklace."

"How do you know?"

"What do you *mean* how do I know? Why else would she ask for it back?"

"Why wouldn't he give it to her if it was hers?"

"That's *my* question."

"And you haven't answered it. He probably had a good reason."

"Or maybe he was just being a jerk."

We glared at each other.

He finally sighed. "This whole thing is ridiculous. Are you *sure* they weren't basically siblings?"

"God, Noah. Read the freaking letters." I pulled out my phone and scrolled through my photos of the letters until I found the right one. I cleared my throat.

"'Sometimes I feel as though I'm grasping for something bigger than myself. Some people find it in religion and others in war, but for me it is you, it is this all-encompassing feeling you stir in me. You are bright and the world blurred, sharp and the world soft.' "

I looked back up to see Noah looking at me with wide, surprised eyes. " 'For me it is you,' " I repeated. "Not exactly sibling feels."

He swallowed. "No."

We sat there in silence.

"Actually, *maybe*—"

I sat up, glaring at him. " 'I wish I could see you surrounded by roses, naked and drenched in moonlight.' "

He stared at me. Then his gaze dipped to my lips.

Oh. I probably should have given the context. Red flags scored my cheeks. "It's from one of the letters."

"Mm." His gaze stayed on my mouth.

"I didn't—" My tongue darted out to lick my lips without permission, and when I realized I'd done so, I sat as straight as possible. It was very hard to breathe. "I didn't mean—I don't—"

"Don't worry, Schoenberg, I get it." He looked away, then back, wryly amused. "I can't decide if I'm turned on or grossed out."

I started giggling, relieved at the break in the tension. "Right?" I scrolled down to another. "They're our *grandparents*. It's *terrible*!"

"All right." He braced himself like a man going to war. "Send me the letters."

"So brave of you." I texted him a link to the album.

Stretching out on my stomach, I flipped through earlier scrapbooks as Noah looked through the letters. A little girl looked back at me, around four or five, with short hair, no smile, and a heavy coat. I wouldn't have recognized her as O'ma if I hadn't slowly gone back in time, seeing her at fourteen, then ten, then eight. But I recognized her now, the shape of her eyes, the curve of her chin. If I'd learned nothing else, I'd learned what she'd looked like.

Every so often Noah would read a portion of the letters aloud.

" 'Every time I touch a rose I'm reminded of your skin, soft as the flower, and I stroke the crimson petals between my fingers'—" He broke off, making a strangled noise in his throat. His cheeks turned red, his eyes bright. "My *grandfather* wrote this."

"Don't look at *me*!" I rolled onto my back and stared at the ceiling, hotly aware of Noah's gaze. "They were to my grandmother! Why are you reading them out loud?"

"I don't know!"

We lay there in silence a minute.

"Okay, we *have* to change the subject," I finally said. "I'm just thinking about rose petals now."

He started laughing, and I started laughing, and we curled up on the floor, laughing hysterically.

"Okay, but what happened?" he said, once we'd recovered. "If they were in love, why didn't they stay together?"

"What do you mean what happened? It didn't work out." I thought back to the letters. *Don't do anything crazy.* "I'm pretty sure she dumped him."

He looked stunned. "*She* dumped *him*?"

"Hey." His surprise struck me as slightly insulting. "Yeah, she turned him down. He begged her to come back."

He scowled. "I don't believe it."

I scowled back. "Read the last letters, then."

He did, his expression fading to a confused frown. "Why didn't she come back?"

"I don't know, she probably realized he'd also been seeing some other girl for several years and 1950s morality got to her."

"Why was he even dating my grandmother, though? If he was so in love with yours?"

"I mean." I shrugged. I'd done my research on Helen Barbanel (née Danziger, of Danziger Media). In the wedding photo I'd found online in the *New York Times* archive, she'd looked rich and beautiful, and the article had agreed, as had all the subsequent mentions of her I'd been able to dredge up. "My grandmother was an orphan girl from Germany. Yours was super wealthy and from high society. Checks out."

"No. It doesn't." He frowned again. "Doesn't this bother you? They were in love, and they didn't stay together."

Not really. At least, it didn't surprise me, not the way it seemed to surprise him. I tilted my head. "Why, Noah. Are you a romantic?"

His face closed. "You think I'm being stupid."

"No. I think it's . . . nice."

"Nice." He laughed scornfully and pushed his hand through his hair. "Cool."

I hadn't been using *nice* as a pejorative. I meant it. "Yeah. I *do* think it's nice. I don't think it's *realistic* to believe people stay together simply because they love each other, but I think—well, I wish I could believe it. I think it's really nice."

Our eyes held. *Be bold,* I could almost hear Niko saying. *Get flung,* Stella had said. A shiver went down my back. *History repeats itself.*

A voice sounded down the hall. "Hello? Is anyone home?"

Noah froze. "Oh, shit."

"Who is that?"

"My mom." He started shoving the scrapbooks back.

"I thought you said no one would care if we were here," I hissed.

"I exaggerated. Come on."

We slipped out of the study and down the hall. If this boy snuck me out the back like a servant, I was going to—

He led me into the kitchen. "Hi, Mom."

Oh no. I would have vastly preferred to be treated like a servant.

A woman in sleek, chic clothing looked up from where she un-packed grocery bags. Surprise crossed her face. "I didn't realize you were home, honey."

"Yeah." He cleared his throat. "This is, uh, Abigail."

"Oh, Abigail!" She said my name with too much recognition. "Nice to meet you."

"Nice to meet you too." Had the great-uncle mentioned me? As the girl locked away with Noah during the party? How awkward.

"What are you two up to?"

"We're just hanging out," Noah said. "I thought you had tea at the yacht club?"

"It was boring. I left as soon as I could." She smiled at me. "Are you staying for brunch? I'm making shakshuka."

Noah and I exchanged startled glances. Brunch! With a mom! She seemed lovely, but hard pass. Also, it was one o'clock—was it still appropriate to call the meal brunch? "Thanks so much, but I actually have work."

"Oh, where are you working?"

"The Prose Garden."

"I love it there. Are you here for the summer, then?"

"Yeah." Just here to dig into your family history, yup.

"Well, it's very nice to meet you. Maybe you can stay and eat an-other time."

"Okay, Mom." Noah said. "We should get going."

She gave a light laugh. "I'm always embarrassing him."

"Thanks, Mom."

"Nice to meet you, Mrs. Barbanel."

Noah steered us outside. A bird twittered somewhere above us. "Your mom seems nice."

"She is."

"Was it weird we met?"

"What do you mean?"

"I felt like I was lying to her. Since I'm trying to dig into her family past, et cetera. Or her in-laws' past, I guess."

"You don't feel bad making *me* help you."

"It's different with adults. And I felt like I was talking to her under false pretenses."

"Like what?"

"I don't know. She thinks we're friends."

"Right. False pretenses, got it." His voice was unexpectedly cold. "I'll call you an Uber."

Wait. Had I offended him? "I can call my own Uber. Are you mad?"

"About what?" He pulled out his phone and stared at it with the abject coolness of someone definitely not doing anything on their phone.

"I wouldn't think you'd *want* to be friends."

He stopped swiping but didn't look up. "Excuse me?"

"You know. You're—" Rich and hot. "We're only spending time together because you don't feel like you have a choice. I'm *forcing* you to talk to me."

"Abigail. Do you really think you could force me to spend time with you if I wasn't okay with it?"

"... Yes?"

"Your manipulation skills aren't as impressive as you think they are."

"Oh." I looked at my orange-pink toenails peeking out from beneath white sandal straps. "So you want to spend time with me?"

He just looked at me.

Okay. Right. Maybe we weren't friends after all. I flushed all over and tried to switch into professional mode. "Should we get together this weekend and look at the rest of the scrapbooks?" Oh no. Did I sound overly eager? "Or it's fine if you're busy. I'm busy. Saturday might not even be good. I might still be recovering from Friday."

"What's Friday?"

"I'm going to some beach party. With my roommate." Oh god, I was pathetic. Screaming subtext of *Look at me, I'm popular* never sounded convincing. "On Nobadeer Beach."

"Seriously?"

"Yeah. Why? What?"

"Nothing. Maybe I'll see you there."

Ten

"**M**om. Mom, you have to tilt the camera more, I can only see your forehead."

"What do you want to see me for?" The image rocked as Mom moved her computer. This was probably as close to seasick as I'd ever actually get.

"You should be able to see your face in the corner. Make sure you're centered, okay?"

She tilted the screen so the camera focused on her. I could tell she'd found her image when she finger-brushed her hair. Even though I could only see her face against the white square of the living room wall, I knew she was curled up under our blue fleece blanket, a cup of tea resting on one of our Klimt coasters.

I missed her. Zoom was almost as good as talking in person, but it wasn't the same as cuddling next to her on the couch.

"I found the family O'ma lived with," I said, after Dad and Dave had both come by, and we'd caught up on everything else.

"What?"

"Yeah. This family, the Barbanels, the one with the boy who wrote her letters, is actually the one she was placed with when she came here."

"No, she was with a New York family."

"I know, and they lived there, but they're originally from Nantucket and they spent their summers here."

Mom blinked. "She was placed with the *Barbanels*? Have you talked to them?"

"Um, yeah." I pushed my glasses higher on my nose. "There's a boy my age and we're sort of . . ." Acquaintances? ". . . friendly."

Mom's face transformed. God forbid I solve a huge gap in O'ma's history; the instant an eligible young man was mentioned, everything else vanished. Especially an eligible young *Jewish* man. "Is he cute?"

"Mom."

"Is he? How is that a bad question?"

"He's fine, I don't know." Stunningly gorgeous. "He's a person, he looks like a person."

"So he's *not* cute?"

"No, he *is* cute, okay?" I couldn't say a single thing without Mom mining it a hundred layers deep. "You're missing the whole point about O'ma."

She frowned. "Why are you always so reluctant to talk about boys?"

"Probably because you raised me in puritanical Massachusetts."

She sighed. If I ever wrote a memoir, it would be called *Sighs from My Mother* and would be a catalog of all the times I disappointed her. "I probably didn't make relationships seem natural enough growing up, and now I've given you these impediments."

"Oh my god, Mom, it's fine. You did fine. I'm fine. Okay?" Also astonishing: the speed with which I could go from missing Mom to being fully irritated. "He's very cute, he has dark curly hair, he's going to Harvard next year. Are you happy?" Sometimes I felt like a scientist feeding a mouse enough breadcrumbs to keep it alive but no more. "I should go."

"Are you mad? Don't hang up on me mad."

"I'm not mad." Just severely aggravated. "I'm going to a beach party and I need to get dressed."

"A beach party!" She practically wiggled in excitement before suddenly and expectedly transitioning into concerned-mom mode. "Don't go swimming. It'll be dark and there are sharks."

The amount I'd heard about sharks since deciding to come to Nantucket. "Mom, you've warned me about the sharks approximately fifty billion times, I'll be fine."

"And don't drink and drive!"

"No one drives. There are Ubers."

"Don't get in an Uber by yourself! Sharon told me—"

"I *know*, you've told me Sharon's story before. Don't worry. I'll stay with Jane."

"Good. I looove you."

I half sighed, half laughed. "I love you, too."

The day had been overwhelmingly hot: so hot your face broke into a sweat after thirty seconds in the sun, and breathing in the thick air hadn't felt substantially different from eating soup. But now, at eleven, the temperature had dropped to the high seventies, and a warm breeze stirred the humidity. The night was lazy and long; a fat moon hung in the dark sky. Occasionally, the low hoot of an owl trailed through the air as Jane and I headed to the beach.

Stella had lent me a faux-leather mini skirt which clung to my butt, and I'd paired it with a green top with a deep keyhole. My body and I were on pretty good terms, but I'd always downplayed my chest: when you developed cleavage at twelve and everyone in seventh grade

felt comfortable commenting on (and occasionally feeling) it, it dis-
couraged display. But the kids who'd made fun of me weren't here,
and no one knew I didn't dress like this all the time. *Be bold.*

I'd felt a little self-conscious about the tight skirt and the makeup
I'd put on, but it faded when we joined the other people on the beach.
For once, I felt like I fit in among the pretty people, and maybe it was
a shallow, stupid thought, but sometimes relaxing in the shallow end
was way more fun than treading water.

"Beer or something else?" Jane eyed the PBR floating around critically.

I still couldn't get into beer. "Something else."

"Same." We wound toward a firepit surrounded by kids I vaguely
recognized, casually saying hi before stopping at a blanket with two-
liter sodas and bottles half-filled with liquor. "Here we go!" Jane
handed me a red Solo cup and added soda, then topped it off with a
splash from a large jug. "Rum and coke. Easy to drink."

Rum. Drink of pirates. I could be a pirate, right?

I took a sip. It had a spiced kick and reminded me of the Fireball
shots we'd done before skinny-dipping. Definitely better than the
beer.

We squeezed back out of the center and Jane looped her arm
through mine. "Okay, back to this convo. Did Noah say 'Maybe I'll
see you there' like *maybe* I'll see you there or maybe I'll see *you* there?"

"Um. I don't know? What if there was no inflection? What does
no inflection mean?"

"There must have been some inflection. Is he a robot?"

"Honestly, who even knows."

"Friends!" Evan appeared out of the crowd, dressed in pink shorts
showing off his extremely attractive thighs. He flung his arms around
our shoulders. "What is *up*?"

"Seriously, Chubbies?" Jane looked at his very short shorts.

"Sexy, right?"

"Hm. Is Pranav here?"

Evan's easygoingness fell away and he dealt Jane a severe look. "Pranav is here *with his girlfriend*."

Jane looked flustered. "Wow, okay. I wasn't—look, there's Lexi and Stella." She grabbed my hand and towed me away. I sent Evan an apologetic look over my shoulder; he shook his head, and the crowd swallowed him.

It turned out I really liked rum and cokes.

An hour or two later, a boy slapped my shoulder and I spun around. "You're it!" he shouted, and spun away into the night.

I stared at my friends, appalled. "What just happened?"

"You're it!" Jane echoed, laughing. She waved her hands toward a half dozen teens running about by the water line. "Go get them!"

For a moment I didn't move. Then I grinned widely and handed Jane my cup. "Hold my drink."

By the time I came back to where our group spread around one of the firepits, I was exhausted from running and almost deliriously happy. I plopped down on a log beside Jane and watched flames lick the night. Above us, the stars spun, streaking and darting, like we could see their light traveling the void in real time. The world smelled like bonfire and ocean, tasted like salt and rum, and it felt like our world, like we owned the whole thing, like we were young and powerful and the kings and queens of existence.

I was so *happy*. Did this mean I was a happy drunk? Because I was happy. And drunk. And probably quite witty? Did everyone appreciate my wit?

I turned to Jane. "Do you appreciate my wit?"

"I do. You are the wittiest of wits. Your wit is like a wick, burning high and bright." She over-enunciated each word, which made them sound like poetry. I was impressed.

A nearby boy squinted at us. "You guys are weird."

I raised my Solo cup to him. "Weird is either the height of compliments or the most banal of insults. I shall accept it as the former."

"Me too." Jane knocked her cup against mine. "Chime chime. It's supposed to chime chime."

"Chime chime."

The guy shook his head and walked away.

Jane leaned her head against my shoulder. "Chime chime."

I stroked her hair and inhaled the woodsmoke, watching as sparks vanished from the fire into the night.

Suddenly, she sat upright. "Okay. Let's find some cute boys."

"Okay. Yours can't be Pranav."

She shook her head solemnly. "Not Pranav." Then she made a face. "Did you hear Evan? He scolded me!"

"Because he's your friend and wants you to be happy!"

"He's a jerk. I hate him. I hate rich boys."

"Me too," I said loyally. "Ugh."

She pointed at me. "You definitely need a fling. You said you were going to have one. You have to vanquish your stupid ex from your memory."

"Like an exorcism. Or like repelling a Dementor."

"Yes. Exactly. You need a ghostly animal."

"A Patronus. Yes. We must set a Patronus against my memory of Matt." Though Matt wasn't the person occupying my thoughts anymore.

"Yes. And your pat thing will be . . ." She gestured widely at the group before us. "One of these bros."

I inspected said bros and wrinkled my nose. "I'm not sure bros are my thing."

"Look at their arms. Their arms are works of art. They have been sculpted by Michelangelo."

Noah's arms were works of art.

Jane pointed. "I'm taking him."

"How?" I did not necessarily want to take a bro, but I did want to know, operationally, how this worked.

"I'm going to say hi, act like he's brilliant for five minutes, ask if he wants to go for a walk, and then make out with him."

I drooped. "You make it sound so easy."

"It is." She set her free hand on my shoulder. "I believe in you, Abby. Follow those steps and you, too, can have a bro of your own. Chime chime." She stood and walked away.

Chime *chime.*

I leaned back. I was at a beach party under a full moon, with the waves crashing and people laughing. If you could bottle this night, it would be eternal youth.

I did want a fling. I didn't want the last guy I'd made out with to be

Matt. I didn't want to think about . . . I didn't want to be focused on someone I couldn't have.

Okay. I was doing this.

I refilled my Solo cup. Rum and coke, easy peasy. No wonder they called alcohol liquid courage.

As I topped off my drink, a boy grabbing a beer nodded at me. "Hey."

"Hey."

Oh no. What came after hey? How did words work?

"What are you drinking?" He grinned, his teeth blazingly white. He wore a backward baseball hat, which was a choice.

"A rum and coke." I took a sip to give myself something to do, then repeated my thought from earlier. "Drink of pirates."

His laugh gave me a glow inside stronger than the alcohol's. "Are you a pirate?"

"Totally. I have a cutlass and a tricorn hat and everything." I wanted to make some weird joke about tricorn hats and pirates and Haman from the Esther story and American patriots, but decided it would inevitably fall flat. "I'm Abby."

"Sean. You here for the summer?"

It was surprisingly easy to talk to this boy, about our summer jobs and what we'd done on Nantucket so far, and our normal lives (he was a college freshman in Boston). Part of me knew the ease probably came from alcohol, but maybe part also came from my confidence in how good I looked, and from a cute boy's attention.

"Want another drink?" he said when we'd finished ours. "Or want to take a walk?"

I could do this. I could make out with him, like a normal, well-adjusted human being. Admittedly, I had limited experience making

THE SUMMER OF LOST LETTERS

out. But this was how you obtained experience, right? By mashing your lips against each other. Hopefully not *quite* as aggressively as Matt had done. (How could I have been *so into* someone who didn't even make out properly?)

Okay. I just had to say yes. Easy. So easy.

"Oh, I'm—" I made an awkward, truncated noise, and waved my hand vaguely. "I'm waiting for friends."

"Cool." He nodded, already scanning the area. "I've gotta find some of my friends, too. See you around."

I watched him go, my stomach sinking. What was wrong with me? So much for being bold and having fun. Why didn't I know how to relax?

Grimacing, I poured another drink, and downed it with more ease than I'd expected.

"Are you okay?"

I whipped my head up at the familiar voice. "Hi."

Noah Barbanel stood before me looking like he'd strolled off a magazine photo shoot in dark jeans and a gray shirt. Why were his clothes always so perfectly fitted? Was this what obscenely expensive clothes did for you?

He frowned. "You look pale."

Here I was, thinking about his gorgeousness, and he thought I looked sickly. "I'm fine."

"I saw you talking . . ." He hesitated. "Did that guy say anything?"

"What? No. Why?"

He studied me a long moment. "You look unhappy."

I pushed out a puff of air. "I'm not unhappy. I'm just—not sure I'm great at parties. It's fine, I'm just going to go home." I opened my ride share app. "You've *got* to be kidding."

"What?"

"These prices are ridiculous." I shook my head. "Whatever. I'll walk."

"*Walk*? You're on the other side of the island!"

"Right, which would be a bigger deal if it wasn't such a tiny island. It's only an hour."

"It's two in the morning."

"So?"

"Do you have a friend headed out with you?"

Oh. I got it. "Just so you know, I don't believe in chivalry. I'll be fine."

"I'm not trying to be chivalrous." He looked almost aggravated. "An hour walk. At two in the morning. After you've had a few drinks in a place you don't know."

"I don't need you to take care of me, Noah Barbanel."

"I'll walk you."

"You don't have to."

"I'll walk you," he said again, more determinedly.

My temper flared. "Maybe I don't want you to walk me! Maybe I'm sick of boys!"

"Fine." He pressed his lips together. "I'll call my cousin. She can drive you."

"No!" This boy. "Fine! Walk me! See if I care."

"Good."

It took me a few minutes to find Jane, who potentially had had a more successful hookup than me, given her shirt was inside out and she was smiling widely.

"Hey. I'm going to head out."

"You sure?" She looked reluctantly over her shoulder at a boy waiting several feet away. "Want me to come with?"

"Nah, Noah's going to walk me."

"What? Where?" Her eyes widened. "Did you hook up with *Noah Barbanel*?"

"No! Jane! Shh!" I looked frantically behind me. Noah was politely pretending he couldn't hear.

"Do you want me to like, come home at a certain time, or not come home, or what?" Jane asked. "I can crash with Lexi."

My stomach tightened. "Come home! There's nothing—we're not—he's just walking me home. Because it's late. I swear, he's just looking out for me."

"Abby." She leveled a look, half pity and half disbelief. "No. He's walking you home because he wants in your pants."

"Right, you'd think so, except I actually think he wants to, like, make sure I'm not murdered."

"Cute. No. Boys don't walk girls home because they're so goddamn nice."

I couldn't help myself; I burst into giggles. "Thank you for the warning. Are you okay if I leave?"

"Yeah, the boys and Sydney are still here. I lost Stella and Lexi, of course. God forbid my bestie wants to hang out with me." She closed her eyes and sucked in a deep breath. "That was mean and bitter. I am happy for them, I'm happy for them. I'm happy for them."

I hugged her. "See you later."

Noah and I left the beach, heading down the long, dark road. On either side of us, hedges loomed like dark shadows. Diamond-like stars scattered against the inky sky. Despite myself, I was glad to have Noah by my side. "Sorry you're missing the party."

"It's always the same party."

"How very existential of you." I slid him a look. "It's not like any party I've ever been to."

"No?"

"My friends and I aren't exactly drink-on-the-beach people. Also, we don't have a beach."

"What kind of people are you, then?"

"Standard-issue honors kids. Vaguely artsy and aspirationally alternative." My school was too small to have real cliques—the theater kids also played varsity sports, and the band geeks did Model UN. "What about you?"

"I don't know. Normal, I guess."

Suspicious. "People who think they're 'normal' are usually popular."

"Bold claim."

I raised my brows at him. "Are you saying you aren't popular? You're rich, confident, and classically good-looking."

"Classically good-looking?" He sounded amused. "Thanks?"

"I'm just stating facts."

"Sorry. I didn't mean to mistake it as a compliment."

"Apology accepted," I said airily. "Also you're tall, and everyone likes tall people. Tall people are more likely to be elected into public office. As are white men, obviously. Did you know, despite being less than one-third of the population, white men hold the majority of all elected positions?"

"Not Jews, though."

"Sure, though being part of a minority doesn't cancel out your other privileges."

"Are you always so political when you're drunk?"

"No idea. I've never been drunk before."

"You've *never*—"

"I heard me the first time, thanks."

We walked a few moments in silence. Then Noah leaned over

and almost absently ripped a plant out of the earth.

"Um." I glanced at the long stalks in his hand, tipped by bristly purple blooms. "Did those flowers do something to offend you?"

"Oh." He stared at them. "It's spotted knapweed."

"And what? They hurt someone in your family?"

He gave me his familiar wry grin. "They're an invasive species. It's one of the island initiatives, for volunteers to weed out the knapweed."

"So you just walk around pulling up bad seeds?"

"It's nice," he said. "I like weeding. You feel very productive. And relaxed."

"Do you spend a lot of time weeding?"

"With my grandma, yeah."

We walked a few more feet. "Thanks for walking me home. You didn't have to."

He shrugged. "Basic human decency."

"Even so. I'm impressed."

"Don't be." He half smiled. "Save your impressed-ness for more worthy things."

"Like what?"

He considered me. "I can tie a cherry's stem into a knot with my tongue."

"You cannot!" I let out a startled laugh. "People can't actually do that."

He locked his hands behind his back and looked up at the sky, feigning innocence. "Impressed?"

"Yeah, actually."

"Good."

Our eyes met, our gazes locking for a second too long. Warmth flushed through me. I looked away, overheated and strangely embarrassed. To distract from my discomfort, I stretched my arms high, fingers interlaced. "I guess I'll have to find a different summer fling."

"What?" Noah almost stumbled.

"Oh. You know." The words tripped out too freely—because of the late hour, or the alcohol, or the stars scattered high, or because we were alone on this lane lined with flowers and sand. "I can't spend all my time trying to uncover family secrets, can I?"

"I thought . . . You can't?"

"Of course not! It's summer! Look at this place! At what nights we have!" I flung an arm out to indicate our surroundings and spoke grandly, because if you're saying something over-the-top, you might as well be grandiose. "We're on a romantic, windswept isle. Perfect place for a whirlwind romance." I glanced over at him, my heart beating so loudly I imagined he could hear it. I was poking him, and I wasn't sure how he'd react.

"And you thought a drunk beach party was the place to find it."

"Why not?"

"Maybe not the best prospects hanging out there."

"*I* was there," I pointed out. I stepped in front of him, forcing him to stop walking. What was I doing? I should not be doing this. My skin tingled, and I felt cool and nervous and fluttery. "*You* were there."

He met my gaze. "I wasn't looking for a summer fling."

"Why not? Isn't this your last summer before college? You don't want a last hurrah?"

"Not really."

"No?" My stomach dropped, but I lifted my chin and prodded further. Why was I doing this? Why couldn't I stop myself? "If someone was flung your way, you wouldn't be interested?"

He didn't look away. "Depends on the person."

Oh my god.

What did he mean? In terms of me, where did I land in this "person" scenario? Where did I even *want* to land?

I didn't dare move. Didn't dare do anything for fear of ruining the moment.

He closed his eyes and stepped back. "You're drunk."

"I'm not."

"You are."

"Well, so what?" I said, because it turned out I did know what I wanted, and it wasn't a bro. "Just because I've had a few drinks doesn't mean my brain doesn't work."

"You said you've never been drunk before."

"I was drunk an *hour* ago! I'm not *still* drunk."

"We should get you home."

I wanted to stomp my foot, but I didn't want to respond to his condescendingly protective behavior by acting like a child. "You don't have to take care of me, Noah Barbanel."

"Well, you don't seem to be doing a great job taking care of yourself," he snapped, and we walked the next few minutes in tense silence. We entered town and walked over slate sidewalks buckled by tree roots, Main Street quiet and still. When we turned down Mrs. Henderson's lane, almost all the windows were dark.

"Thanks," I said stiffly when we reached her door. "I think I can manage from here. Unless you want to make sure I don't trip up the stairs? That I can untie my shoes?" I baited him one last time. "That I'm all tucked in?"

"Good night, Abigail," he finally said, firm and implacable. "Let me know what you want to do next about your grandmother."

Disappointment cut through me. Of course he only cared about our grandparents, our agreement. "Fine. Good night."

Eleven

Excruciating embarrassment came for me in the morning.

I opened my eyes to a dark room, the sky outside gray and low. Without the bright sun, I'd woken later than usual—and of course, I'd stayed up later than usual, too. Good lord. What had I done last night? I'd basically begged Noah Barbanel to kiss me. Noah. Rich, hot, popular Noah Barbanel.

Worse, he hadn't even been *interested*.

I squeezed my eyes shut as though I could block out last night. Why was I such a disaster?

Should I text Noah? Say something about my hot-mess state?

No. Better not.

I pulled up my covers and tried to read a few pages of *Moby-Dick,* which I'd picked up in an attempt to really get the historic vibe of Nantucket. I liked it well enough, save a casual dig about the ability "to detect a Jew in the company, by the nose," which, like, leave me alone, Herman Melville. But after a while I peeled myself out of bed and into a hot shower. More than books, I needed to debrief the night. And to eat a breakfast sandwich.

Fog lay across the town as I walked to Jane's family's bakery, pulling a hazy curtain over the cobblestone streets. I'd never been in a jungle, but I imagined this might give me a taste of the tropics. The humidity was so oppressive it was difficult to breathe, and I couldn't tell if sweat or condensation coated my skin. Beads of water gathered on clusters of hyacinth petals, and all the grass and leaves seemed overgrown and green and lush. Everything was heavy with moisture; even my limbs weighed down as though the water within them longed to return to the earth.

Jane's bakery, clean and cozy, was a welcome relief. She waved me behind the counter and handed me a tub of cookie dough. "Place those on sheets two inches apart from each other, stick 'em in the oven, let the previous batch cool for ten minutes before plating them."

"Can I eat one?"

"No. You can eat these broken scraps, though."

"Yum." I popped one in my mouth and it melted on my tongue. "Mm, delicious. I heard you wake up at, like, six. How much sleep did you get?"

"Three hours."

"Kill me."

"I'm gonna crash after this. What about you, how was the walk home with Barbanel?"

"Literally just a walk."

"Seriously? Not even a kiss goodnight?"

"He said I was drunk."

"Well, you were. Maybe he was afraid you'd be sloppy."

"Thanks. No, he's not interested. I mean, he'd be way too complicated. He was totally right not to do anything. One hundred percent."

"Wow, you've definitely convinced me."

"Ugh. What about you?"

"Well, I went back to make out with the guy you saw, and he was already hooking up with another girl."

I dropped my head into my hands. "I hate boys."

"Mood."

The cookies had just come out of the oven when a guy our age approached the counter. "Hey, Jane."

"Oh, hey, Mason." She pushed off from the counter she'd been leaning against. "The usual?"

I aspired to have someone, someday, ask if I wanted "the usual."

"Yes, please." As she rung up his order, he watched her with a nervously determined gaze. He cleared his throat. "Did you see Stoned Lake is playing at the Chicken Box on Friday?"

"Really?" Jane handed his card back. "Cool."

"Yeah. You should come."

"Sweet, thanks for the tip."

"No prob." He hovered for a second more, then smiled and left.

I waited until the door clicked closed behind him. "Explain."

"What?" Jane looked up from refilling the soup. "Oh, Mason. He's one of the locals."

"He's cute."

"Go for it."

"No, I mean for you!"

"For *me*?" Her whole body jerked. "What?"

"He obviously likes you. He asked you out."

"He did not."

"Pretty sure he gave you a time and a place to meet."

"He knows we both like the band. He was being nice."

"I don't think people smile so hard when they're being 'nice.' We should go."

Her eyes narrowed. Dangerously. Enough to make me suspicious. "What are you thinking?"

"Just . . . wondering if we should invite the group."

"No. Definitely not. You're not inviting Pranav and then flirting with Mason to make him jealous."

"What, who, me? God, Abby. So suspicious."

"Mason seems really nice, you should give him a chance."

"You literally don't know anything about him."

"Um. True. But he likes the same music as you! Clearly the mark of a brilliant mind."

"You're trying too hard."

"It's one of my many failings."

"Okay." She heaved a huge sigh, as though doing me a favor. "We'll go."

When the bakery got too busy, I headed out. The sky had splintered, letting out a loose, slow drizzle. I still had a few hours left before my shift at the Prose Garden, so I headed to Nantucket's town hall.

Twice in the letters, E had mentioned a woman named Nancy: *I ran into Nancy on Main Street today* and *when you and Nancy snuck into Tom's house.* So I got a hold of several phone books from throughout the years and started calling.

In general, I hated calling people, though it was, according to my mother, a Necessary Life Skill (Mom called our senators and representatives on a rolling basis to tell them how to do their job better. I'd only escaped having to do this myself because I couldn't vote yet, but I was fairly certain Mom planned to present me with a packet of phone numbers and scripts on my eighteenth birthday, like a political fairy tale).

So it was good practice, calling up Nancy after Nancy and asking if they'd known a woman named Ruth Goldman in the 1950s. I called them before work, during my work break, and after work, sitting on the sofa in Mrs. Henderson's living room with Ellie Mae curled beside me. Outside, the skies had opened completely and a downpour drenched the world. I hung up the phone and dialed again.

Each subsequent call became easier, especially since they all went the same way, with each Nancy politely letting me down.

Until one didn't.

"I did know Ruth," Nancy Howard told me. "When we were children."

I sat up straighter on the couch, my hand stilling on Ellie Mae's head. She swiveled her snout toward me, confused that the pets had stopped. "Really?"

"For years. You say you're her granddaughter?"

"Yeah. I'm trying to find out more about her life on Nantucket . . ."

When we hung up, I was practically shaking. My first real success. Well, other than the whole Barbanel situation.

And speaking of . . .

Noah had told me to keep him informed about what I planned to do next in my search for O'ma's history, but how much had he meant it? Did he want me texting him? But. What did I care what Noah Barbanel thought of me? "Get yourself together, Abigail," I muttered, and shot off a message.

> Found a woman who used to know my grandma—
> going to see her tomorrow if you're interested

I'm in, when?

> I told her I'd see her at 4 if that works?

Yeah sounds good

> Can we take your car? She's in Madaket

Using me for free rides, Schoenberg?

> Pretty much

I'll pick you up at 3:45

                                                    Thanks!

I'd expected Noah to text when he arrived, but instead, the doorbell rang at quarter of four the next day. I looked up from my seat at
the kitchen island as Ellie Mae darted to the door, tail wagging. Mrs.
Henderson opened it.

"Hi, Mrs. Henderson." Noah smiled at her, then bent to ruffle
Ellie Mae's ears. She barked, delighted. "How are you?"

"Noah, how lovely to see you. How are your parents?"

"They're great. Dad's managing to be here most weekends."

"How nice. I ran into your grandmother at Bartlett's a few weeks
ago, and she says you're going to Harvard."

"I am, yes."

"You must be excited."

He smiled politely and murmured something noncommittal, letting go of Ellie Mae, who promptly decided to run herself in circles
until she collapsed in a puddle of exhaustion.

We said goodbye to Mrs. Henderson and ducked out the door. I
slid him a look as we walked down the porch steps. "Everyone seems
to like you."

"I'm very likable."

"Really?"

"Don't *you* like me?"

I looked straight ahead, gathering my hair on the top of my head
and knotting it into a messy bun. Was he mocking me? Baiting me?
"You're all right."

We climbed into his car, one of the off-roaders popular on the island. The windows were already rolled down, and we cranked up the

music as we set off across the island. The rain last night had broken the relentless heat, and the temperature was a perfect midseventies, the sky blue and cloudless. I turned my face out the window to avoid revealing my deadly embarrassment. "Sorry if I was weird the other night. About the whole . . ." I waved a hand.

"The what?" I could hear a hint of a smile in his voice.

He was going to make me say it? "Never mind." I hung my arm out the window. "Is this how you expected to spend your summer? Carting a random girl around the island?"

He glanced at me briefly, before redirecting his attention to the road. "I don't hate it."

"But you must have had plans. You know. To uproot spotted knapweed, and all."

"Mostly I just wanted to be outside." He was silent for a moment. "Nantucket's my time to be free. To visit the marshes. To be out on the water. I like being the only person you can see in any direction."

I was silent a minute, too. "Not very like New York."

"It's why I like coming here so much."

"If you love nature so much, isn't it a bad idea to go to college in a city?"

"Boston's small. And you can go rowing early in the morning, or get out of the city pretty quick. But yeah." He paused. "Sometimes I feel like I need to soak up all the nature here, when I can. Like it's a recharge. I get three months, and then it's back to real life."

"It sounds relaxing," I agreed. "Except for the whole stressing yourself out to make sure your family doesn't get stressed."

"Someone has to do it."

I glanced over at him, at this boy who acted like he was some knight sworn to protect his liege lord. The old nursery rhyme ran through my head. *All the king's horses and all the king's men* . . . "And you think you can?"

His fingers tightened on the wheel, though he kept his voice light. "I guess we'll find out."

Madaket tipped the western edge of the island, past fields and bright yellow flowers and bushy trees. Nancy's cottage lay outside the village proper, tucked high up and covered in roses. Noah parked and we walked under an arbor to knock on the gray slate door.

A woman who looked to be in her sixties opened it. "You must be Abigail. I'm Laurie, come in. My mother's out back." She led us through the small and neat house. "It's so nice you came. Mom misses young people. She's been talking about this ever since you called."

"Oh." Great. Now I felt added pressure.

A woman in a wheelchair beamed up at us when we stepped onto the porch overlooking long, rolling fields. Despite the day's perfect warmth, she wore a sweater and long pants. "So you're Ruth's granddaughter."

"Yes. Thanks so much for seeing me. This is Noah."

"Of course." She smiled at him. "Noah Barbanel."

He jerked his head up. "Yes, ma'am."

"I know your grandparents."

Noah and I exchanged a quick look. But of course she did; Edward had written of her in the letters. And everyone on Nantucket seemed to know the Barbanels.

"Come, sit down. Would you like some lemonade?"

We took our seats in wicker chairs around a table with a pitcher and a plate of shortbread cookies. Mrs. Howard poured us tall glasses of lemonade, and the loose floating pulp made me think she'd made it herself. "I was so sorry to hear about Ruth's passing."

Another surprise. "Um. Thank you."

She nodded. "We hadn't seen each other in years, but we still wrote occasionally. Your grandmother wrote wonderful letters."

Apparently. "Had you known her a long time?"

"Since we were little girls." She smiled fondly. "My mother was the housekeeper at Golden Doors, and Ruth and I used to play together. We had quite the imaginations. Ruth said she knew the house was hers as soon as she heard its name."

Only it hadn't really been hers, had it? "What was she like as a kid?" I asked. "My mom and I don't know too much about her past. She never mentioned Nantucket."

Nancy smiled. "Most people would have called her quiet, but most people didn't know her, not like I did. She had a will of iron, Ruth. And there was a brightness about her, when we got older—when she talked, people listened. She didn't mince words. People wanted to hear what she had to say. And she was very pretty, of course, which helped."

"She was?"

"Oh, yes."

"Do you think . . ." I hesitated over the question, something I never would have dared asked O'ma directly. "She was happy?"

"Oh, well, what's happiness?" Nancy said, which wasn't the kind of response I'd expected. She smiled wryly. "It wasn't such a bad childhood. She and Eva were very close."

"Eva?" I echoed, confused.

"Mrs. Barbanel. Your great-grandmother," she added, with a nod to Noah.

Mrs. Barbanel. The woman who'd taken in my grandmother—who'd raised her. "How were they close?"

Nancy considered. "Mrs. Barbanel didn't have any daughters, so I think she bonded with Ruth differently than she had with her sons. They had a special connection. She didn't dote—she wasn't given to large displays of emotion—but I remember Ruth telling me they learned to bake together. Eva went out of her way to learn how to make German pastries, kuchens and gugelhopf, so she could teach Ruth. So Ruth would feel connected, and know something, about where she'd been born."

O'ma had taught *me* to make apple kuchen and gugelhopf. Crystalline memories of forming dough for the pie crusts flashed through my mind, of O'ma urging me to really *learn* how the dough should feel. Of O'ma showing me how to place dollops of chocolate batter on top of the vanilla batter in the gugelhopf pan, and using fork tines to swirl it in. I'd never questioned how she'd learned to make them. "That was good of her."

"Eva was a good woman. Tough, but good. I think she wanted to keep the memory of Ruth's parents alive—even if Ruth didn't have much of a memory of them."

Poor O'ma. Poor Eva. Poor everyone. "Did my grandmother tell you about her parents? I know their names, but nothing else, and I can't find anything online."

"Only once." Nancy met my gaze. Her eyes were a pale, filmy blue, gauzed over by time. "She wrote me, to say her parents had died. She'd suspected, I think. But she held out hope until some organization wrote to her, after the war."

I nodded, throat tight. "And she didn't mention other family, or people in Germany?"

"I'm sorry. None I remember."

I swallowed over an unexpected lump in my throat. "Can you tell me more about your childhoods? About growing up here?"

Her daughter let out a soft groan.

Nancy leaned forward. "Let me tell you about Nantucket, back in the day. The government almost took control of the island. The Navy planned to seize our ships and press them into war!"

From beside her, Laurie waved a hand parallel to the ground in silent negation. "It was a rumor, Mom," she said gently. "They weren't going to take anyone's ships."

Nancy scowled. "How do you know? Were you here?"

Laurie sighed.

Nancy ignored her. "The Germans sent one of their submarine packs here in '42. You've heard about them? The wolf packs?"

"U-boats?" Noah said.

"Exactly. They went up and down the entire eastern coast, torpedoing and sinking ships, tankers and merchant alike. American, British, Dutch, Norwegian. Over five thousand people died—did you learn that in history class? We had fuel shortages during the war because cargo ships couldn't get through. The Germans called it Operation Drumbeat, and our government pretended they didn't exist. The Navy didn't disclose anything, and the media agreed not to report on it. They pretended the U-boats weren't here at all, but they were."

Good lord. Where was this World War II blockbuster? "When did people find out?"

She nodded sagely. "A floundering ship ended up on our shoals, and some of our fishing vessels came across lifeboats filled with survivors from U-boat attacks. We knew what was going on." She leaned forward. "The government sent the navy here, and they built an auxiliary air facility where the airport is. They buried mines on our land in case the Germans took over. We thought the war was coming to our doorsteps."

"Wow."

"Wasn't good for tourism, either." Nancy stirred her lemonade. "The rich families decided to vacation elsewhere. Even the Barbanels, and they'd lived here before the war. But they were Jewish, and worried, I think."

I blinked. "Wait, so—were they not here during the war years? I thought my grandmother came here as a little girl."

"Maybe she came when they first took her in, in the late thirties, but then they went back to New York until the midforties. We met after; we must have been ten or twelve."

"Oh." I supposed if there were U-boats running around the island, you wouldn't want to chill here if you didn't have to. "So what was it like then?"

"Ah." She smiled, lost in thought. "It was wonderful. We used to run free all over the island. It was wilder then, only thirty-five hundred people during the winter months. A third of what we have today."

"And she kept coming here until she was eighteen?"

"Every summer. We wrote during the year, too."

"You don't have her letters left, do you?"

She patted my hand. "I'm sorry, dear, I got rid of all my old papers year ago."

"Did you know my grandfather, too, then?" Noah asked.

She looked at him consideringly. "Eventually. He was gone most of the time when we were growing up, off at his private school, then Harvard. But during the later summers, he was around more often."

Noah and I exchanged a quick glance. "So our grandparents didn't really . . . grow up together?"

"Oh, no." She laughed. "Not really. They were barely even in the same house except for holidays and several summers."

Very interesting. I considered asking about any romantic entanglements, but the force of Noah's presence warned me against it. Instead, I pulled out my phone, bringing up the photo of O'ma wearing the necklace and turning it so Nancy could see. "Did you ever see her wearing this necklace?"

She frowned. "It looks vaguely familiar . . ."

My heart jumped, and I looked at Noah.

He, on the other hand, frowned. "Did you know my grandmother, too?"

"Ah. Helen." Her smile bordered on a smirk. "Did we ever."

Noah kept his voice polite—a cool politeness I recognized as plastering over other feelings. "Oh?"

"We were teenagers the first time she showed up. What a time we had."

Something clicked, something that charmed me. Nancy had been my grandmother's best friend; she'd been on O'ma's side, the way I would always be on Niko's side, or on Jane's. Helen had probably been their nemesis.

Nancy switched from mischievousness to decorous, from past to the present. "Your grandmother is a real gift to the island, Noah."

Nice save. I took a sip of lemonade. "If Edward and my grandmother didn't really know each other until they were teenagers . . . did they not have . . . a typical sibling relationship?"

"Oh, no," Nancy said firmly, switching her pale eyes to me. "They were madly in love."

Noah started coughing.

"It was all very proper," she assured him. "Over and done with before he married your grandmother."

"You *knew*?" I said. "Did everyone know?"

She spat out a laugh. "Not likely! No. No, I think only we knew. I hope!"

"What happened?" I asked. "How did they fall in love?"

A smile teased her mouth and she looked away, into the rolling fields. "It was a long time ago."

I waited. Noah waited. Nancy's daughter waited, then finally broke the expectant silence. "Seriously, Mom?"

"A lady likes to keep some things private." She winked at me. "Though I'm not much of a lady."

"Why did they fall out of love?" Noah asked. "Can you tell us?"

"Oh, they never fell out of love."

Noah clasped his hands between his knees as he leaned forward, gaze intent. "They must have. If they loved each other, they would have gotten married."

"Sounds like a question for your grandfather."

"Something must have happened." Noah leaned back, frustration clear in every line of his body.

Nancy set her drink down, unsurprised and unfazed as she took in Noah. "He's a Barbanel," she said, clear and precise. "And Barbanels always do what's best for their family."

When we finished our lemonade, Noah turned us toward a path he said would lead to the sea. "If you don't mind," he said.

"Of course not."

We waited a respectable distance before talking. "This makes more sense, doesn't it?" I said. "If they mostly only saw each other as teenagers, it's not so weird they fell in love."

Noah took a moment to respond. "She didn't like my family very much."

"What are you talking about?"

"'Barbanels always do what's best for their family'?"

I was silent a few steps. "But you do, Noah. Not to beat a dead horse, but you're literally majoring in something you don't want to because it's best for you family."

A flash of surprise crossed his face. "That's different."

"Is it, though?"

"It's—" He made a frustrated noise. "I'm doing it because I *want* to. Because it's the *right* thing to do. Nobody's forcing me. While if Ruth and my grandfather were in love, the right thing to do—the thing they wanted—would have been staying together."

"You're splitting hairs," I told him. "Or you're holding yourself to a higher standard than you're holding other people. If you think Edward should have been able to choose someone he loved, *you* should also be allowed to choose something you love."

He shook his head, but his expression was troubled.

We reached the beach, one I hadn't been to before, with less people, more wilderness. The ocean melded with the sky. Our bare feet curved over smooth shells and rocks embedded in the wet, packed sand, our toes and heels leaving faint impressions. Today you could smell the seaweed strongly, pungent and alive and foreign.

At the water's edge, Noah stepped into the surf. He waded forward until the rush of water hit his calves, surging and curling around them before continuing on and breaking in a white froth. His chin floated up and his shoulders relaxed down. I followed, slower, the cold of the bracing water pebbling my skin with goosebumps.

"When I was a kid," he said when I drew up beside him, "coming to Nantucket was like escaping to some magic wonderland—like

Narnia . . . I feel like I can breathe easier here, by the water, than anywhere else."

"Like the ocean will drain away all your concerns?"

He shook his head, his profile unflinching. "No, like there aren't
any concerns. Like nothing else exists."

"Sounds a bit alarming."

"It's not. It's . . . freeing. Like everything is on hold."

I looked out at the water, and I could understand what he meant,
the meditative nature of the waves, the ceaseless push and pull of the
tide, the world of blue. My tension drained away, same as when I entered a bookstore. I glanced at Noah, and saw his face free of lines or
tension. "Why do you feel like it's your job to take care of your grandparents? Why isn't that your parents' job?"

He hesitated. "I guess it's all of ours. And I've always been close to
my grandma. I was the first grandkid—me, then my cousin Shira—
and our grandmother spent a lot of time with us. We all lived within
the same few blocks, and we'd go over to her place when our parents
and our grandfather worked. You know how Nancy said my grandfather's mom, Eva, wasn't very demonstrative? Well, neither is my
grandma. But she'd do things for us. Shira loves skating, so we'd
go to Rockefeller Center, even though Grandma despised touristy
things, and she took us to Disney on Ice and on day trips out of the
city so Shira could skate on ponds.

"And she'd take me to the botanical gardens, up in the Bronx, and
we'd spend whole afternoons with her teaching me to identify trees
by their leaves and bark, and watching videos about how dandelions
transformed into white puffs. So yeah. I feel like now it's my turn to
make *her* happy. And making her happy *does* make me happy." He
started moving again, feet slapping the hard sand as we walked parallel to the ocean.

"Is that why you're so fixed on whether our grandparents were in or out of love?" In the distance, closer to the dunes than the water, a strange collection of driftwood caught my eye. "Not because you hate the idea of your grandfather giving up on love, but because you're defensive of your grandmother? And you hate the idea of her marrying someone who didn't love her?"

"Neither makes sense," he said stubbornly. We left the hard, packed sand for the hills and valleys of soft grains. "If you love someone, you stay together."

We reached the driftwood. Pieces of wood were laid out in a circular maze, and in the center, a wooden enclosure had been built by boards stuck in the stand, forming a wall five or six feet high. Noah headed between the two charred wooden planks standing sentinel at the maze's beginning.

I followed. There were no junctures in the maze, just a winding path leading us close to the center, then away, then closer still. "I think it's time to talk to your grandfather. I don't think we're going to get answers any other way."

He turned back to me with a startled, almost betrayed expression. "You promised me a month."

"Well, I think we're at a pretty obvious block, don't you? What else can we find out without talking to him? We don't have to make a big deal out of it. Noah, please."

He gazed at me, wrangling with something internal, then turned away and continued walking. The path only allowed for single file, so his voice drifted back as we walked. "My grandparents' relationship is . . . strained."

Oh. "I'm sorry."

"I don't want to screw it up." He blew out a breath. "He's always doing things like missing anniversary dinners or birthdays for work.

Or last year, when Grandma's best friend died and she wanted to go over for shiva every day, Grandpa didn't. It was . . . rough. Shira and I went instead. I worry if my grandmother learns about *your* grandmother, it'll be the last straw."

"But she must know already, right? I can't imagine anyone has any secrets after so long."

"You'd never heard about Nantucket from your grandmother."

Fair point.

We turned inward again, and this time the path didn't zigzag or pull back—it led straight to the wooden enclosure in the center of the circle. One edge of the wall overlapped with the other, forming a narrow entrance, and we squeezed inside.

Soft sand filled the enclosure, and in the center, hundreds of pieces of sea glass filled a hollow—green and white and blue. Lucky stones, black with white bands, rimmed the pit, and other things: dried flowers and half-burned candles and seaweed.

I knelt down, sand pressing into my knees, and scooped my hand through the sea glass. "Who do you think did this?"

He sat down next to me. "Who knows."

"When I was little, my dad and I would search for lucky stones on the beach. We didn't stop looking until we found one, every time."

Noah also sat and trailed a hand through the stones and glass, picking up a teal piece and turning it over between his forefinger and thumb. "You get along with your parents?"

"Yeah. I mean, as much as anyone." Maybe more than most people: my parents were my prime example for how to be a good human. They were so staunch, so committed to each other and to me and Dave. Though thinking they were so ideal made the idea of ever disappointing them awful. "What about you?"

"My mom is good. My dad . . ." He shook his head and sighed.

"He'll be pissed if I singlehandedly ruin the entire family."

"Wait, what?" I twisted to focus on him. "Why do you think you could ruin the *entire family?*"

"If I bring all of this up . . . Even if my grandma knows Grandpa cheated, she'll be furious if anyone else finds out. She cares about their image. All of them do."

"But something decades old isn't going to affect the whole family! And *you're* not bringing anything up. I'm the one digging."

"I haven't stopped you, have I?"

I stared at him. "Your dad *can't* get mad at you for what I do."

He shrugged, a small, unhappy movement.

"That's crazy."

"Not really. I know what you're doing. I could keep you from talking to people. From stirring the pot."

"You know you're not responsible for my actions, right?"

He shoved his hand through his hair. "We don't need to get into my weird family dynamics. I just wanted you to know why I don't want you to talk to my grandpa. It could get messy."

"And your dad will"—unreasonably—"get mad at you."

He shrugged again.

"What if . . . we talked to your grandfather but made sure your grandmother didn't hear anything?" When he frowned, I hurried on. "No chance of scandal. A short talk with him about my grandma and if he knew where she was from or if his parents had records or anything. In and out. No one else needs to know."

Noah wrapped a hand around the back of his neck and looked up at the pale white disk of the moon in the blue sky. "He still might not tell us anything. He's not the easiest guy."

"Probably because the unbearable heartbreak of his youth turned him into a stone-cold man who existed only to make his millions."

He cracked a smile, which had been what I'd been after. "Probably."

"Please? We could meet in a coffee shop. The bookstore. Wherever." I held out the darkest stone I'd found, with two thin white lines. I was nervous and hopeful and barely able to believe Noah might actually introduce me to his grandfather. "I'll trade you a double-lucky stone for it."

He took the stone, his hand closing over mine, and the smile made its way to his eyes. "Deal."

Twelve

A few days later, the bookstore hosted a book club.

"We hold several book clubs," Maggie had told me early on. Today, she wore a puff-sleeved pink floral blouse and a pink skirt with buttons down the front, both amazing thrift store finds. "Mother-daughter, young adult, sci-fi/fantasy, mystery, classics, nonfiction. They're usually an hour, though sometimes the patrons stay longer, and we provide snacks and facilitate the conversation."

Despite never technically attending a book club, I felt like an expert. Exhibit A: School. Freshman year, we'd spent *three months* discussing *Great Expectations*. Pip was the worst, and Miss Havisham an icon. Ruined wedding dress, lace and cobwebs indistinguishable? Yes, please. I wrote my final English paper on *"Abandoned Wives: Why the Women in the Attic Matter"* in the form of a dinner party play between Mrs. Rochester, Ms. Havisham, and the unnamed narrator of *The Yellow Wallpaper*. *Very Imaginative!!* my teacher Ms. Lottie wrote. *But while this is charmingly written, it lacks grounding in facts.*

Thanks, Ms. Lottie!

Exhibit B: Mom had a "book club" who read articles, usually titled something like *"Emotional Labor in the Workplace"* or *"Statistical Analysis of Advocating,"* studies on power dynamics and salaries (everything sucked). Mom delivered the TL;DR version over dinner, thus contributing to my ability to be the girl always referencing *Atlantic* articles.

Exhibit C: Dad and I bought each other books for birthdays and Hanukkah, usually ones we both wanted to read (and sometimes read before gifting, oops). We'd gone through all of Scott Westerfeld's novels, and last year we'd traded *The Golem and the Jinni* and *The Song of Achilles.*

Exhibit D: My friends and I shared endless romance novels, plucked from the library sale rack for fifty cents each. We'd devoured Judith McNaught and Susan Elizabeth Phillips and old-school Harlequin Presents. Another paper I'd written, this time for Social Studies: *"How Romance Novels Empowered Women to Embrace Their Sexuality: 1940–1960."* (Mr. Brown had given me an A, though it might have been in order to avoid talking to me about the actual text.)

However. I'd never been to a *real* book club, with cheese plates and formal questions. Today, the readers would discuss *And Then There Were None.* I'd never read Agatha Christie before, and for some bizarre reason, I'd spent years thinking she was a fictional character, like an adult Nancy Drew. This was false, and I was an idiot. Good to know.

On the coffee tables in the back of the store, Liz arranged scones, cookies, and mille-feuilles on tiered stands. Flour covered her black T-shirt, and dusted the handkerchief tying back her purple hair. Next, she brought out a charcuterie plate with tiny wooden implements for each cheese. A honeycomb, the kind I'd only seen on a Cheerios box, lay atop a jar of local honey. We set out porcelain teacups, teal and pink flowers circling the rim and saucers. I hadn't known you could lust after teacups, but I lusted after these. I wanted a whole set of these teacups. I wanted a house whose decorating scheme could support these teacups.

Anyway.

The book club attendees arrived promptly, almost all women,

ranging from their twenties to nineties. I eavesdropped happily, organizing a new table display at the same time. Maggie facilitated the conversation, bright and bubbly and good at keeping things flowing, while Liz offered sharp insights and brought the discussion back on track when it wandered too far.

By the time the book club finished up, I'd finished my display and was surveying it with pleasure when I caught one of the attendees looking at me. She was white-haired and probably in her eighties, with a light blue jacket. "Can I help you find something?"

"What's your name, dear?"

"Oh, um, I'm Abby."

"And do you live here? Or are you visiting for the summer?"

"For the summer." I steadied my glasses on my nose, trying to get a hold of the situation. The woman's intensity had knocked me off-balance.

"You look so familiar. I thought maybe I knew your mother."

"I don't think my mom's ever been to Nantucket."

She studied me a little longer, then walked around the World War II table, her fingers trailing over the covers, a frown marring her perfect forehead. Every so often she'd pause, a diviner before her scrying pool. I stood there nervously, unsure of what she wanted. Did she need a rec? "Are you looking for anything in particular?"

"So many books about the war. So many brave men and women. So many people hiding Jewish children and protecting Jewish friends. But where are the ones where we save ourselves?" She looked up at me with familiar dark brown eyes. "What would your grandmother have thought?"

I watched her leave.

Shit.

I found Noah at the rowing club, and by *found*, I meant I texted him and showed up as boys poured out of the boathouse. He strolled toward me alongside half a dozen others, laughing and relaxed. He wasn't wearing a shirt, and his skin glowed with sun and exertion.

I swallowed and directed my attention to the horizon, squinting against the sun as it painted the sky a soft orange. Was it necessary for so much skin to be on display? Especially when I shouldn't be blatantly staring at it?

He waved his friends off and came over, tugging on a worn, soft blue T-shirt. "Abigail."

I focused on his ear to avoid anything more incendiary. "I met your grandmother in the bookstore. She knows who I am."

He froze. "What? Are you sure?"

"Pretty sure. She didn't seem thrilled." I shrugged. "So there's no reason to keep me a secret. Invite me to dinner. We can ask about my grandmother. I don't have to mention the romance or anything. We can just see if they know about my grandmother's family."

A tiny smile danced across his lips. "You want to come to dinner at my house."

"It seems easiest, doesn't it? Organic."

"Ripe for disaster."

"You're exaggerating."

"What's in it for me?"

Honestly, this boy. "What do you want?"

He grinned, sweaty and happy and too charming. "What's your best offer?"

"No one starts negotiations with their best offer."

He laughed. "I'm sure you can think of something."

No way was I flirting with him, when he'd be left smirking and unaffected while I'd be rendered a puddle of nerves. Best to act no-nonsense. "How's Saturday?"

He relented. "What do I tell them? I don't exactly invite tons of girls over for dinner."

"I'm sure you can think of something," I echoed back at him.

"Hm." He grinned down at me and my heart did a jump, skip, and hop.

What was wrong with me? Why couldn't I stomp these ridiculous flutters out of my body? Why did they need to show up every time I was in the same space as Noah? Obviously Noah was horrible fling material, given how 1) our families were weirdly intertwined and 2) he had, in fact, already flat-out rejected me.

"Noah! My man!"

And lo and behold, as though summoned by my desire for an appropriate summer fling, a blond boy approached.

Noah and the boy hug-slapped each other's backs. "Hey, man."

"How's your summer?"

"It's good. Got here last month. You?"

"Just flew in this morning." The boy was startlingly attractive, with hair like corn silk and the even, symmetrical features capable of landing a TV deal or a GOP endorsement. He flashed a blazingly white smile at me. "Hi. I'm Tyler."

"Hi, Tyler." I sounded dazed even to my own ears. "I'm Abby."

They exchanged updates for a few minutes, and when their conversation wound down, Tyler turned his grin on me. "Nice to meet you, Abby."

I watched him walk away, his long tan legs on display beneath his mint green Chubbies.

Noah took one look at me. "No."

"What?" I snapped my attention back to him. "No what?"

"You don't want to get involved with him."

I smiled a little too sharply. "Don't I?"

"Tyler wrecks girls."

"How so?"

"He's not serious about anyone, but people get serious about him. He breaks hearts."

"I want a fling, not a boyfriend," I shot back. "He can't break my heart if I don't let it get involved."

He snorted. "Because you're so good at not getting invested."

"What do you mean?" Could he tell how, the more time we spent together, the more my heart rate rose around him, and I couldn't stop looking at his arms, and sometimes at night—oh my god, of course he could, see: *me throwing myself at him*. Clearly, I had to act totally disinterested for the rest of forever to prove him wrong.

"You're obsessing over a failed romance from fifty years ago."

Oh. Right. "Because it's family history. Besides, like I said, I want no strings attached." So there.

"So you keep saying."

"Well, it's true."

"Seriously? That's what you want?" His brows rose and he looked exceedingly skeptical.

My heart started beating very quickly. Maybe he was about to offer himself up. To say *If you're looking for no strings attached, hook up with me.*

Maybe I read too many romance novels.

What would I even say in response? Anything with Noah would be an absolute disaster waiting to happen, since there absolutely would be strings attached. A Gordian knot's worth of them.

Instead, he leaned back. "Fine. Have fun."

My cheeks went hot with anger. *Have fun?* He seriously didn't care if I hooked up with Tyler? Then maybe I would, if it mattered so little. "Fine. I will."

I was irritable over the next few days, though I tried not to be, especially when I went with Jane to the Chicken Box to meet up with Mason from the bakery. It was a pretty good distraction, too, worrying about someone else's romantic dilemmas rather than my own. Like about how Noah's texts confirming dinner for Saturday night were terser than I liked. Which was ridiculous. He had no right to act haughty about my choice of potential summer hookups.

"What am I supposed to wear?" I asked Jane Saturday night, sitting on the bed in my underwear and holding up yet another shirt. Today had been a scorcher, the light white and hot, and I'd been thrilled to be in the Prose Garden's air-conditioning, helping customers with perspiration dripping from their brows. The necklines and armpits of their shirts had been damp, their skin tanned or burnt. After coming home, I'd showered and blown out my hair, and now I regarded my limited options with despair. "I've never met anyone's parents before. Other than Matt's, but I'd known them forever from school stuff."

Jane barely glanced up from her phone. "Understated money."

"Meaning . . . ?"

"You know. A hundred-dollar shirt. What do you think Mason means by 'thanks for coming by'?"

"Um. He's glad we met him at the show yesterday?"

"It's so *formal* though. Who *says* that? Isn't 'coming by' a little dismissive? We spent three hours there."

"Maybe he's being polite. Or making an excuse to talk to you. Do shirts really cost a hundred dollars?"

She yawned and stretched her phone above her head. She smelled like bread from the bakery, and a tiny dusting of flour still clung to her shirt. "Wear a sun dress. You have approximately five million."

True.

Wearing a lavender dress with a cinched waist, I arrived once more at Golden Doors. Though the evening retained the heat of the day, clouds had dialed back the worst of it, and now the warmth felt more like a decadent blanket. Still, I'd applied two layers of deodorant, and sweat gathered on the small of my back as I climbed the porch's steps. My stomach roiled as I listened to the echo of the doorbell. Should I have brought something? My parents always brought wine. Flowers? Dammit.

The door swung open. A woman my parents' age stood there, neatly dressed in white slacks and a blue linen shirt. How were all these people wearing pants in this heat? She looked at me curiously. "Hello."

"Um. Hi." If I'd had flowers, my hands would have had something to do besides floundering uselessly. "I'm Abigail Schoenberg. Noah invited me?"

"How nice. Come in." She stepped back.

Honestly, this entire summer had me feeling like a vampire awkwardly begging an invitation to other people's houses.

"Abby, right?" A girl stepped up next to the woman, wearing shorts and a halter top. The cousin. Shira. I immediately felt overdressed.

I forced a smile. "Hey."

"I'm Linda, Noah's aunt," the woman said. "He's probably in the living room."

"This way," Shira said, saving me from additional awkwardness. She glanced at me over her shoulder as we went down the hall. "You guys met during your catering gig here?"

"Uh. Yes."

She snorted.

We entered the living room. Dozens of people floated about: adults arranging food at the kitchen island, little kids running underfoot, an identical trio of prepubescent girls whispering to each other. Almost everyone had the distinctive Barbanel strong jaw and brows, dark eyes, and TV-worthy hair. "Full house?"

Shira shrugged. "Not really."

Cool.

Across the room, Noah chatted with a tall, broad-shouldered older man with graying hair. I crossed to his side as quickly as I could without running, and Noah turned to meet me. "Uncle Bertie. You remember Abigail."

I remembered *him*. He'd been the one who caught us in the study.

"Of course. Lovely to see you again, Abigail."

"Hi. Yes. You too."

After the conversation everyone had about where I was from and what I was doing on Nantucket, Noah excused us. I lowered my voice. "You didn't mention there would be *a gazillion people* here."

"You didn't ask."

"Why are there three tiny identical children?"

He laughed. "Aunt Joan's kids."

"Are you *all* on the island during the summer? Do you all stay here?"

He looked around the room, as though counting. "I think about twenty of us do. My dad has three younger siblings and everyone comes for at least part of the summer."

I took in all the other kids. "Are you the only one without siblings?"

"Me and Shira both, yeah. My parents had me pretty late in life. Sort of adds to the pressure of everything, being their one precious miracle baby."

"I'm sure they don't mean to add pressure." When he gave me a fiercely skeptical look, I changed the topic. "How was the house empty last time I came over?"

"Careful planning and expert manipulation."

"Why, Noah. I didn't know you had it in you."

A grin broke over his face. "I'll take that as a compliment." He nudged me. "There's my grandmother."

I whipped my head around. She stood across the room, dressed in slacks and a sweater advertising the Nantucket Atheneum—more casual clothes than at the book club. She looked older, too, in the way she moved, the way a woman my mom's age helped her lower onto the couch and a girl a few years younger than me curled up next to her.

It struck me, the three of them: three generations of Barbanel women. I'd spent so much time this summer thinking about my grandmother, my mom, and me. We'd been the center of my story, the pole everything rotated around. Maybe I needed to remember we weren't the only tale unfolding.

"Hi, Abby." A woman stepped up to us, a man at her side. Noah's parents. Mrs. Barbanel smiled. Though tight-lipped and tense, her eyes looked tentatively hopeful. "Good to see you again."

"You too. Thanks for having me." Was she having me? Or were the grandparents the hosts? Should I thank literally everyone over fifty? Ahhh, etiquette.

"This is my husband, Harry." She placed her hand on his arm. Harry Barbanel was tall and had a strong jaw and all his hair, and looked, I expected, as Noah would in forty years. I smiled hello and glanced at Noah, whose face displayed a cool politeness, like we were chatting with mere acquaintances. How unnerving. I might yell and roll my eyes at my parents, but I'd never treated them with this calm disaffection.

"Good to meet you." His dad pumped my hand. I couldn't remember the last time an adult treated me like anything other than an extra pair of hands to set the table or someone to grill about Gen Z's takes on political issues. It made me uncomfortable.

"I sent Shira to get your father," Mrs. Barbanel murmured to her husband. "Let's gather everyone." She raised her voice. "All right, dinner time! Let's go!"

"Do you guys do dinner together every night?" I asked Noah as we joined the crowd slowly meandering outside. Two tables had been set up in the lawn—nothing so fancy as when I'd first been here, but still nicely set.

"No, just on the weekends, when more people are here. My dad only comes Friday to Sunday, and so do some of the aunts and uncles—and cousins, too."

"What about your mom? She's here the whole summer?"

"Yeah, she works remotely. She's an engineer for a robotics company. Here, we're at the adults' table tonight."

We took our seats with the other dozen teens and adults, while the little kids sat at their own table several steps away. It was still light—the solstice hadn't yet arrived—but almost hazy, like we could see the heat surrounding us. A sea breeze lifted the humid air in little eddies.

Delicious foods weighed down the table: vegetable couscous with

chickpeas and plump raisins; tiny bowls of olives; peppers stuffed
with saffron rice; large clay pots of tagine. Cumin and turmeric per-
fumed the air. Everyone served themselves in a familiar, informal
manner, passing and stealing dishes.

Shira, Noah's younger cousin, walked arm in arm with an older
man as he made his way to the head of the table.

Edward Barbanel.

I hadn't come across lots of ninety-year-old men in my life: O'pa
had died when I was twelve, and my dad's dad hadn't hit eighty yet.
Edward Barbanel looked impossibly old, but he still had a full head of
hair and thick brows, both snow white. He didn't look thin and frail,
though his frame looked as though it had once carried more weight.
Still, I couldn't imagine him as young, couldn't make the mental
switch from this elderly gentleman to the man who'd written my
grandmother so many letters, who'd had said *for me it is you*. I could
only see an old man, with papery, spotted skin and sunken cheeks.

He'd written all those letters, and for the first time I felt guilty and
ashamed of reading them.

Shira pulled out his chair, and he squeezed his granddaughter's
hand in thanks. A chill went through me. I shouldn't be here. This
was a family night, a normal night. I should have picked a different
time, and a place where I wasn't intruding. I'd been in such a hurry
to get answers, so convinced we could be out in the open since Helen
Barbanel knew about O'ma, but I'd been wrong. I couldn't ask questions about my grandmother now, not when I'd read about how much
Edward had loved her, not in front of Helen, not with Noah's tense
parents and all these cousins. I'd come back some other time. Noah
and I would figure something else out.

I got through dinner quietly, smiling when everyone else did,
answering quickly when people addressed me, but all in all, flying

under the radar. Occasionally I caught Helen Barbanel watching me from her seat at one of the heads of the table. Who did she think I was—the granddaughter of the girl who'd been brought up in her mother-in-law's house, or the granddaughter of the woman who'd slept with her husband?

I met her gaze once, and it was as unwavering as Noah's. He'd said his grandmother taught him everything he knew about plants, had inspired him to want to study botany. What else had he learned from her? How to make his face an impenetrable barrier? How to handle not always being happy with your lot in life?

But I could be extrapolating. Maybe she was happy.

Noah's mom, on the other hand, looked at me frequently, but always darted her gaze away, like a nervous hummingbird. Yet when the meal had finished, and the adults had poured themselves tiny cups of coffee, and the sky had faded to a papery purplish-blue, she pitched her voice across the table. "So, Abby. Where are you from?"

Like a signal, the conversation around the table died and the focus turned to me. I resisted licking my suddenly dry lips. "I'm from South Hadley—it's a small town in western Mass."

Several of the adults laughed. Noah's mom smiled. "We're familiar with South Hadley."

Embarrassment slid through me, like I should have known they knew my town.

"And how are you liking Nantucket?"

"It's great. It's gorgeous." I glanced at Noah beside me, hoping for reassurance in the face of this gentle questioning. Beneath the table, he pressed his leg against mine.

"Abigail," Helen said, "is Ruth Goldman's granddaughter."

Edward Barbanel started choking.

He'd raised his drink to his lips, but now he set it down with a thunk, pressing a fist to his chest. The table's attention swung to him; even the kids' table fell silent.

"Are you okay, Dad?" Noah's father leaned forward.

Edward Barbanel waved him off, his attention on his wife. "Ruth's granddaughter?"

Helen took a measured sip of coffee. "Looks just like her, doesn't she?"

Now Edward's gaze swung to me. I sat very, very still. Beneath the table, my hand opened and closed in nervous fists. This was not the way I'd wanted this to come up.

After a long silence broken only by a toddler's babbling, Noah's mother spoke. "Who's Ruth?"

Edward took an excessively large swig of alcohol.

"Ruth lived with Edward's family as a child," Helen said. "Are you all right, dear?"

Edward Barbanel coughed into his napkin. Helen watched him, placid as a great lake and just as likely to be hiding an exceptionally dangerous current.

"Lived?" Noah's dad said, clearly confused. "What do you mean?"

"You remember. The little girl they took in during the war."

I glanced nervously at Noah.

Edward Barbanel looked at me again, but said nothing.

"She came over from Germany. Pretty little thing. She used to follow your father around everywhere." Helen's gaze switched to me, alarmingly piercing. "Didn't she mention?"

"I don't think so." I stared down at my plate. Beneath the table, Noah took my hand. I clutched his.

Helen's mouth curved in a very small smile. "Oh?"

"She never talked about—Nantucket."

"Never?"

"No." I felt very nervous. The beat of my pulse hammered through me. I wove my fingers through Noah's.

Edward thunked his beer down and finally spoke. "She doesn't?"

I shook my head.

Helen took a delicate sip of her wine. "How odd."

Now everyone was staring at me. I shrugged, but it didn't break the silence, so I finally managed to say, "I didn't actually know she'd lived here until recently."

"And is that why you're here?"

I glanced at Noah. He looked at his dad.

"Mom." Noah's father might not be sure what was going on, but his tone was clear: guests weren't to be bullied.

Yet his mother waved him off, her gaze on me. "Let her answer."

"I just—I realized she used to come here, and I was curious. So I came here."

"How sweet. Isn't that sweet, Edward?"

"She *never* talks about Nantucket?" Edward Barbanel repeated.

Talks. Present tense. My stomach clenched and I squeezed Noah's hand tighter, looking at him frantically before turning back to Edward. "I, um—no. I didn't know about—about anyone here. About the Barbanel family."

Edward looked gutted.

"Honestly, Edward." Helen's tone could scratch diamonds. "Did you think she was still carrying a torch?"

Well, she definitely knew Edward and my grandmother had a history.

Edward met my gaze. "How is she?"

Oh no.

Oh no oh no oh no.

I didn't want to do this. This wasn't how this was supposed to go.

I didn't want to tell the boy who had written *You are bright and the world blurred, sharp and the world soft* that Ruth had died.

I looked desperately at Noah. He stared back at me.

I cleared my throat and stared at a few chickpeas left on my plate. "She passed away last year."

Silence surrounded me, except for the hum of cicadas and the distant roar of the ocean.

I snuck a glance up, and saw Edward statue-like. Helen, too, looked horrified. She transferred her gaze to her husband, then back to me. "I'm so sorry to hear that."

Noah's parents and aunts and uncles looked baffled.

"I didn't know," Helen said.

"No—of course not . . ." I trailed off, helpless.

Edward Barbanel slowly pushed his chair back and rose. "You'll have to excuse me."

He walked away, each slow, faltering step taking an age. Helen smiled tightly at the table and went after him, offering her arm when she caught up to him. He didn't take it.

Everyone stared at me.

Noah, thank god, turned to his mom. "Can we be excused?"

"Sure, honey." She plucked a bottle of wine from the center of the table and topped off her glass. "I think it's probably a good idea."

Thirteen

A s soon as we were inside, I sagged against a wall. "What just happened?"

"Come on." Noah grabbed my hand and pulled me out of my collapsed state, leading me down the hall and toward the stairs.

"Where are we going?"

"Upstairs. Too many ears here."

Up we went, past hand-sized paintings of the sea, smudges of light set in wide frames. In the upstairs hall—one I hadn't been in, modern and high-ceilinged—we passed more of Edward Barbanel's paintings, large ones, unsettling: the moors of Nantucket under the silver moon, the snowy beaches in weak winter light.

Noah pushed open a door and I balked, tugging him to a stop— him over the threshold, me on the other side. "This is your room?"

"During the summer." He dropped my hand and moved farther in, and I didn't miss his touch, because who missed a hand only holding yours for directional input? I swallowed my impulse to say *You're allowed to have girls in your room?* because I didn't want to sound like a sitcom character from the nineties. Instead, I followed, pretending to be ever so calm. "Cool."

"Sorry it's not super clean." He blushed a bit as he pulled up the bed's rumbled covers—blue-and-white plaid. He grabbed a heap of clothes off the floor and threw them into his closet.

"Good solution." I nodded to the pile of clothing on the closet floor. "Into it."

His laugh cut the tension. "You can sit . . ." He turned toward an armchair, which was also covered in clothes. Then he looked at the bed, now made, but still decidedly a bed.

"Here's fine." I lowered myself onto the pale wooden floor. "So your grandma definitely knows about Ruth and Edward."

"Seems likely," he said, sitting down across from me.

"Seems one hundred percent."

He cupped his hands over his mouth and blew into them. "She was throwing you in his face, huh."

"Yeah. But why? She can't still be mad?"

"I think it's more how she's mad at him in general right now, and this is . . . more ammunition." His head sank. "Which I didn't want them to have."

The door burst open. Noah's cousin blazed through it, hair flying, eyes narrowed. "What's going on?"

Noah groaned. "Shira, go away."

She ignored him. "What's the deal with Ruth Goldman?"

"She was this girl Grandpa's family took in—"

"Yes, I know," she said impatiently. "The German girl."

"What?" Noah exchanged a stunned glance with me. "You know about her?"

"Of course I know about her."

"*I* barely know about her!"

She shot him a condescending look. "You're a *boy*. Boys don't pay attention to anything."

Man. I'd paired up with the wrong Barbanel. "What do you know?"

"Not much. She existed. Once I asked Grandpa if she'd come talk to my class on Yom HaShoah, but he said he didn't know how to get in touch with her." She turned to me. "What's the deal?"

"No deal." I glanced at Noah, who turned his palms face up. "She lived here. I'm trying to find out more about her past."

Her eyes narrowed. "While you just *happen* to be here on Nantucket, and you just *happened* to get a catering gig here?"

"Yes?"

"You're awful at lying," Noah murmured to me.

"Wow," Shira said. "Devious. And here I thought you were just another summer girl."

I raised my brows at Noah. "Just another summer girl?"

Shira looked at her cousin, too. "But what I want to know is, why is Grandma mad and Grandpa freaked?"

Apparently her question was less alarming, since Noah answered it. "Grandpa and Abigail's grandma had an affair."

"It wasn't an *affair*," I said. "He wasn't married to your grandmother yet."

"They were engaged."

"They were dating."

"Seriously?" Shira's head swiveled back and forth. "What, like sixty years ago?"

"Yeah," Noah and I said.

"Yet Grandma's still salty." Shira tilted her head. "I'm impressed by her tenacity."

"Probably because it surpasses even yours." Noah met my gaze, his own filled with determination. "If Grandma knows everything, there's no point trying to keep you hidden. So what the hell. Let's talk to my grandfather."

I stared at him, surprised and a little alarmed by the reckless glint in his eyes. This didn't seem like him, given how he spent so much time trying to keep his family patched together. "Are you sure now's the right time?"

"Why not?" He stood upright, decisive and driven, and strode out of the room.

Startled, Shira and I looked at each other. Then I ran after Noah, grabbing his arm before he reached the stairs. My heart pounded. "Noah. Maybe we should think this through. Slow down a bit."

"Why? I've *been* slowing things down—I've kept you from talking to my grandparents—and for what? I thought I was protecting the family, keeping any waves from being made—protecting my grandmother, keeping her from getting hurt. But she knows, so what's the point? And I'm sick of trying to keep anything even-keeled and smoothed over." He sounded furious. "I've been doing it long enough. So let's get answers."

"Right. Only—this seems a little confrontational?"

"Well, I'm feeling confrontational." He gave me his full attention, a muscle in his jaw pulsing. "My grandmother has dealt with my grandfather's shit for decades. He's been difficult and distant and put the company first every time. Why'd she put up with it? I thought they were in love. I thought it was because you commit to family. But what, he didn't even love her? He loved someone else he didn't bother to stay with? He cheated on my grandma for years, and wouldn't even have stopped if your grandmother didn't decide to. What the fuck."

I stared at him, heart in my throat. He was angry on his grandmother's behalf. I hadn't realized *how* angry beforehand. And now, since he knew *she* knew, he didn't have to be quiet. He could yell at his grandfather. Noah believed in promises and commitment, and his grandfather hadn't followed through on his vows. "Noah, I get it. I do. But let's wait until everyone's in a better mood—"

"I'm sick of waiting, sick of behaving. You want answers. So do I. Let's get them."

It was difficult to stop a boulder rolling down a hill. So we went. We went down the stairs, past the paintings, past the abandoned dining room. The house had eaten the adults.

Noah pushed open the door of his grandfather's study, the same study we'd met in, only now Edward Barbanel sat behind the desk. The velvet curtains around the window alcove had been opened, and warm moonlight spilled into the room. The elderly man leaned back in his leather chair, eyes closed, but they opened when we entered.

"Grandpa." Noah strode right up to the desk. "Did you date Ruth Goldman?"

Edward looked right at me, face blank. "She lived with us for a time."

"We have the letters."

Edward's brows rose. "Letters?"

"Letters you wrote her."

"Everyone corresponded by letter."

"*Love* letters."

"No, I don't think so." Edward's voice remained level, unmoved.

I couldn't believe it. Hedging, I'd expected, but a flat-out denial?

Noah's voice rose. "You did. While you were engaged to Grandma, you wrote Ruth letters. What's this bull you preach about supporting the family and the people you love when—"

"I have *always* supported this family," Edward cut in, a hard edge coming into his voice.

"Why didn't you marry Ruth? Why did you marry Grandma?"

Edward picked up a paper, peering over it at his grandson. "Enough, Noah."

"Would you have kept having an affair with Ruth after you got married if she hadn't ended things?"

"I said, enough." Edward's voice hardened. "You should take your friend home."

Grandfather and grandson stared at each other.

This was horrible. I wanted to leave—I hated confrontation with authority figures—but what was likelihood of seeing Edward Barbanel again? A second chance might not be on the table. I cleared my throat. "Do you know about her family?"

Both Barbanels turned my way with identical astounded expressions, like they'd forgotten I existed. Edward recovered first. "She didn't know much about her family."

"Did she mention anything? Where in Germany they were from? What her parents did? If they had any relatives who survived?"

His face softened. "She never talked about them. I don't know if she remembered much. But no, I didn't get the impression she had any relatives left—at least, none she knew about."

I swallowed, a crushing weight on my chest. I'd wanted a different answer. How terrible, to not remember your family. I pushed out my last question. "What about the necklace?"

All previous kindness evaporated, replaced with wintry dislike. "Excuse me?" Edward Barbanel said.

"She wrote about a necklace. She wanted it back. In your letters"—I couldn't believe I'd read his private letters—"I don't think she got it back?"

His face didn't move so much as solidify, muscles tightening beneath his composed expression, the change all the more unsettling for its minuteness. "I think we're done."

"Okay," I whispered, taking a step back. When Noah didn't move, I pulled at his arm, but he stayed stiff as a statue.

Fine. Heat laced up through my body. I couldn't handle any more confrontation today. Turning on my heel, I headed out the door and down the hallway, my vision tunneling. I brushed past Shira where she waited, and out the door and down the front steps of Golden Doors.

"Abigail, wait."

I kept going. Research I liked, but actual fights made me want to make like a turtle and never reemerge.

"Abigail." Noah caught my arm and pulled me to a halt in the middle of the sandy drive. The warm July night pulsed around us, moon bright, cicadas loud, hyacinths overwhelming. "Where are you going?"

"I don't know. Away." I shoved my hair behind my ears. "I'm sorry."

"What are you apologizing for?"

"Reading his letters. Making everything messy. I don't want your family to be mad at each other, or at you, Noah, swear to god. I just wanted to know about my grandmother's past."

"I know. Abby, calm down, I *know*." He took both my hands. "You were right, I should have waited. Blunt offenses never work in my family. But *I* was mad, so I went. I did this, not you. You didn't make anything happen."

"I hate fighting."

He smiled wryly. "You fight with me."

"You're a safe person to fight with." I drew in a deep breath. "He didn't want to talk about the necklace."

"He didn't want to talk about anything."

"Now what?" My hope crumbled. For the past few weeks, I'd been so convinced I could simply talk to Edward Barbanel and find out everything. I hadn't expected to be shut down. More fool me.

"We figure something else out. Hey. It's okay. This is a stumbling block, not the end."

I let out a strangled laugh. "Why are you being nice? You didn't want me looking into this."

He hesitated, staring down at our hands, then looking up at me with renewed resolution. "Abigail, you should know—"

"Noah."

We both jerked around, dropping our hands instinctively. Noah's father stood on the porch. He smiled stiffly, but his gaze was cold. "A word, please."

Noah closed his eyes briefly, then nodded at me. His expression had locked down, as stoic as his father's and as his grandfather's had been. "I'll see you later, okay?"

"Okay." I glanced at Noah's dad. "Um, nice to meet you, Mr. Barbanel."

Harry Barbanel's smile made it clear it was not nice at all. I'd never had a parent dislike me before, and I could have done without the experience. "Good night, Abigail."

"Good night. Bye, Noah."

And with a last look at the Barbanels as they were swallowed by Golden Doors, I fled down the driveway, feeling like I'd abandoned Noah to the wolves.

Fourteen

March 14, 1954

People have been asking me about my mother lately, in the unconcerned way strangers have. "What does your mother do? Where are your parents from?" I'm torn how to respond each time. Do I give them the scant details I remember, pretending they'd stretched on as they might have, had the actual timeline not occurred? (I almost never consider telling people the truth. The people who guess the truth know better than to ask.)

Often, I want to describe your mother, though I'm not an idiot; I know she wasn't mine. But at least I can remember her.

Sometimes I'm still so angry at her, though. Shouldn't she have done more? No more than two children to a room, the law said, and we had dozens of rooms in the New York house and at Golden Doors. Shouldn't she have taken in a dozen children?

Did you know we still haven't spoken? I thought she'd soften to us.

Sometimes I miss her so much it physically hurts.

Are you okay?

The reply came almost immediately:

I'm fine

A punch of humiliation sent my stomach swerving low. Well, then. So much for thinking he might want to talk. Fine.

Except.

I thought of how often I wanted someone to push when I'd said *I'm fine,* how rarely I meant the platitude. How when Mom and I fought, I'd go upstairs and tell her not to follow and wait, crying, until she did, always wishing she'd come faster. Noah wasn't me, of course. Still. Was anyone ever really fine?

Screw it. Why dash your pride against an impenetrable wall of someone else's pride once when you could do it twice?

Did you talk with your dad?

Yeah

How'd it go?

Could have gone better

He didn't think i should be airing
dirty laundry

You didn't air anything. Your grandparents did

I brought you to dinner and knew
what might happen

I basically insisted on coming

I'm still the one who invited you

I could have prevented this

This is why I didn't want you digging around
in the first place

I drew back and stared at his last text for a long time, my cheeks hot. What the hell? A few hours ago, he'd been saying I hadn't done anything wrong, yet now I deserved the blame? I tried typing a few things but they all sounded wrong and stupid.

                                                              Got it.

I put my phone down and crossed the tiny yard to bury my face in the lavender. Lavender had calming properties, right? Maybe I should sleep out here.

My phone buzzed again and I grabbed it.

I didn't mean it like that

Sure he hadn't. I'd said enough cutting things to Mom to know when someone had aimed words to hurt, and his words had been specifically designed to cut me down. I wished I knew how to convey cold indifference via text. Instead, I didn't answer.

My phone rang, shuddering into motion on the porch chair's arm. Good lord. What was he doing, calling? Phones only rang for death and library bills. Or perhaps he, too, knew not to let silence fester. "Wow. A phone call."

"I shouldn't have snapped at you."

"It's fine." This was better. Much easier to convey disdain via vocal tone than emojis.

"No, it's not. I'm mad at my dad and grandfather, and I took it out on you. But *they're* the ones who snap at people when they're mad. I don't want to snap, too."

I was silent a minute. "Learned behaviors, I guess."

"I'm going to learn other behaviors, then."

"What happened with your dad?"

"He was just pissed. You know."

"Not really. Why?

"Mostly what I was telling you about. My dad expects me to keep things together, you know? I *know* my grandparents are rocky right now, worked up about a hundred dumb little things, so I should know better than to introduce—variables."

"Me."

"Yeah." He sighed.

"I'm sorry. I shouldn't have pushed to come."

"*I'm* sorry. I shouldn't have blamed you. I was—striking out."

I hesitated, not sure how to frame what I wanted to ask. "Is your family always so . . . tightly wound? Your relationships with your dad and grandpa seem . . . strained."

He also paused before answering, navigating his words like travelers carefully crossing a rushing stream, stepping from slippery rock to slippery rock. "I think there's a lot of expectations. From my grandfather for my dad, and from my dad for me."

"Like you studying business instead of botany."

"I'm supposed to do what's right for the family. That's always been very clear. And I hate being a disappointment."

"You're not a disappointment."

"Yes, I am." He sounded flat. "It's fine. I'm used to it."

I had no idea how he could think such a negative thing about himself. "You were valedictorian. You got into Harvard."

He laughed without humor. "Yeah, and my family donated an obscene amount."

"Noah." I clutched my cell, hurt on his behalf. The smallest criticism from my mom made me want to cry, and she thought I was the best thing since sliced bread. How much more upsetting would critique be from a less-supportive parent? "Don't judge yourself so harshly, okay?"

He was silent a moment. "Sometimes I think I'm going to be just like him. Just like both of them."

"You don't have to be. We're not fated to repeat the mistakes of our family."

"Aren't we? Aren't we raised to be like them?"

"But you're not your dad or your grandfather. I'm not my mom or my grandmother. We have other parts of our family, and other things shape us. And—and maybe sometimes family traits do trickle down, yeah. But if we notice them, we can course correct."

He was so silent I asked if he was still there.

"Yeah. Just thinking. Maybe you're right."

"I am right. Noah—" I found it easier to say these words when I didn't have to look at him. "You're a good person."

He was silent a long time. "I'm sorry about how tonight went."

"It's okay."

"Okay." He paused. "Hey, do you want to go sailing on Tuesday?"

Something almost painful bloomed in my chest, I was so happy at the invitation. I had work, but I could trade shifts with one of the summer employees. "Yes!"

"Great. We're meeting at the yacht club at ten a.m."

Oh. Quick as my excitement had risen, it deflated. I'd thought he'd meant just us. "Okay. Awesome. See you there."

I'd never gone sailing before, and spent the morning debating proper attire. Did I wear my scandalous red bikini? It might stun Noah. And I hadn't worn it yet.

I tried it on and regarded myself in the mirror, only to be confronted by a rather excessive amount of cleavage, which, while sexy in the privacy of my home, seemed overboard for a daytime outing.

Never mind, then.

I pulled a gray tank and jean shorts over my more conservative bikini with the boy shorts. Into my beach bag went a towel, sunscreen, water, and a PB&J, along with a carton of strawberries in case this turned out to be a potluck kind of deal, and I headed out toward the yacht club (the *yacht club*!) for our ten a.m. meetup.

The day was so hot I found the idea of ever *not* sweating through my clothes painfully laughable; even in the short walk over, sweat accumulated under my breasts and at the base of my neck. I moved sluggishly, every step torture, every breath slow as my lungs tried to parse the oxygen from the water in the air.

Usually in this kind of heat, I couldn't understand how anyone could feel anything besides exhausted, or be anything other than a supplicant to the god of air-conditioning. Yet this morning, beneath the sweat and the heat, a terrible nervousness buzzed through me, a low-level anxiety I'd have excised with a knife if possible.

Why was I so worked up about hanging out with Noah's friends? It wasn't like Noah and I were dating. It wasn't like they'd even *have* opinions about me. I certainly never thought twice when a new kid appeared at one of the hangouts with Jane's group.

And yet.

I scanned the docks, one group after another, until I spotted a tangle of teenagers at the far end. Noah stood in the middle of the group, laughing and confident, surrounded by half a dozen other tan beachy kids. They all seemed to have received a memo about dressing in whites and stripes and Nantucket red. I clutched my beach bag tightly against my shoulder. What was I doing? I should have told Noah I had work and met up another day. So what if we got along in the closed bubble of the two of us? These were his actual friends.

My pace slowed as the distance waned, until I'd come to an awkward stop at the edge of the group. I was panicked and unable to glean enough air. Maybe I should bail. Slip away before anyone noticed me, and text Noah saying I felt sick. Why had Noah even invited me? We were hardly going to discuss family drama around others.

This was too much. Too stressful. I was bailing.

But then Noah looked up, his gaze unerringly finding mine.

Never mind, then. I managed a half wave and concentrated on breathing. At least if I passed out from anxiety I could blame the heat.

He came to meet me, smiling. "You made it."

I shrugged, suddenly shy. "Yeah."

"Come on, let's get you on the boat." He led me through the pack of teenagers, introducing me left and right, a social golden boy with a million friends and a smile for all of them—nothing like the angry, honest, guarded, romantic boy I knew. He helped me onto one of the boats, already filled with six others, then turned away to help a group of guys lifting coolers.

Cool cool. I didn't need a social crutch. No, sir.

The boats pushed off. A dozen people crowded on ours, with Noah somewhere near the front. Had I thought, for some crazy reason, this would be a reasonable time for the two of us to hang out and talk? Silly me.

Still, we were on a boat on the water, so how bad could this be? Sun soaked my skin, and I took a deep breath. Someone turned on music, blasting Top 40, and someone else distributed beer. Everyone peeled off their shirts, so I did, too, aware how even with a full-coverage bikini top, I had a lot on display. Whatever. Instead of being embarrassed, I had to own it, as Niko always told me.

A girl I hadn't met before dropped down beside me and offered a pink can. "Hi! I'm Alex. Rosé?"

"I'm Abby." I took the can but didn't open it. Was it kosher to drink before noon?

"Noah says you're family friends?"

"Uh. Yeah. I guess."

"Cool. Are you here for the weekend?"

"All summer, actually." We exchanged the routine introductions while two more girls folded themselves down by our sides.

"So, very important question," one of them said to Alex. "What are you going to be for Kaitlyn's party?"

"I'm thinking a jellyfish," she said. "You guys are pirates, right?"

"Ugh, we were debating. Maybe we could find a good trio costume?"

"Like what?"

"I don't know. Ursula and Flotsam and Jetsam? Katy Perry and left shark and right shark?"

"These costumes would solidly suck for two out of three of us," Alex said with a laugh. She turned to me. "The party's Blue Lagoon–themed."

"What's Blue Lagoon?"

"You know?" one of the other girls said—Chelsea, I thought. Chelsea and Jen. "The hot spring?"

"No." I took in everyone's shocked faces and decided to make a stab. "Is it . . . local?"

Chelsea and Jen exchanged the kind of look generally made when you thought no one could see you, not when you were directly in front of the person you were side-eyeing. Alex gave me a pitying smile. "It's in Iceland."

"Oh. I've never been to Iceland."

What a stupid, stupid thing to say. Did I have zero social skills?

"You definitely should go," Chelsea said. "You can get cheap deals through Reykjavík on your way wherever and extend your layover for a day or two."

"Iceland really is great," Jen said earnestly. "It's one of the best places to see the northern lights."

"Oh my god, don't remind me." Alex rolled her eyes. "I went for two weeks and didn't see them once. And Chelsea went for, like, twenty-four hours before heading to Croatia—"

"No, this was when we were going to Portugal."

"Oh, right. And she saw them! So unfair."

I smiled awkwardly. Though I didn't think the girls meant to make me uncomfortable, they lived in a world I couldn't relate to, and draped their sentences in wealth so expertly they'd practically made it an art form. When I mentioned how much I liked the *Hamilton* soundtrack, they launched into a discussion of which cast was superior—original or touring? When I mentioned my abiding love for pizza, they talked about how much better it was in Naples, the birthplace of my favorite food.

By the time we arrived at Coatue, the narrow strip of sand where we planned to spend the afternoon, an unwelcome stiffness had invaded my body, a sense of unbelonging. I looked for Noah as we pulled the boats onto the shore. I didn't want to be clingy, but he had invited me, after all.

I waited for him to jump off the boat. People surrounded him, tight-knit and chattering, but I stood there determinedly until he noticed me.

When he did, his eyes caught for the barest second on my chest, and he swallowed. Amusement and embarrassment and a *little* touch of satisfaction surged through me. Well, then.

He resolutely fastened his gaze on mine. "Having fun?"

"Yeah. It's—"

"Noah!" A girl bounded up to his side, tucking her arm in the crook of his. "Come on, I want to show you something."

He hesitated, still looking at me. "Uh—"

She squeezed his bicep. Literally. I didn't know people *did* that. "Please?"

"You okay?" he said to me.

I sent him a bright smile and kept my shoulders from slumping. "Of course."

Good lord, I was pathetic.

I watched Noah follow the girl away for half a second, then looked around for Alex and the other girls from the boat. Too late; they'd been absorbed by the crowd, which was made up of more than our one boat. People covered the beach, not a single one familiar. My shoulders inched toward my ears. Great. What a party. I should have kept the can of rosé.

I sat down and pulled out my phone, a sure safeguard against the world.

I didn't know why I was so upset. Or, sure, it objectively sucked to hang out with a group of people who all knew each other. But I knew most of my anger and unhappiness and the queasy, sick feeling in my stomach came from wishing Noah Barbanel wanted to hang out with me as much as I wanted to hang out with him. Which was *dumb*.

I shot off a selfie to Niko.

> Me:
> I'm alone on a beach and pretending to have fun

> Niko:
> Jesus you're still so pale
> Do you dip yourself in sunscreen every morning
> like Elizabeth Bathory

> Me:
> Yes I murder a hundred sun motes each day
> to collect their energy
> Do you think there'll be popular kids in college or
> will we finally be free of social hierarchy

> Niko:
> Hate to break it to you babe but civilization runs on
> othering ppl
> Go socialize!! I have to finish making a raspberry pi

> Me:
> Did you mistype pie or is the tech world trying to be cute

"Abby, right?"

I looked up. There, haloed by the sun, stood the beautiful boy from the rowing house. Blond and blue-eyed and glowing gold, he looked like he'd stepped out of a TV show.

"Hi!" I beamed up at him, pitifully grateful to have someone to talk to—and more than a little vindictively pleased it was a hot guy. Wow, my moral compass didn't point as true north as I'd expected. "Yes. You're Tyler?"

"Yeah." He lowered himself to the sand beside me, running his gaze over me with evident enjoyment, before flashing a grin. "How's it going?"

"Great." A beat of silence followed, and I babbled into it. "Trying to get used to this much sun."

He laughed. "This your first summer here?"

"Yup. I snagged a job at the Prose Garden."

Look at me go. Actual words exchanged with a hot boy.

A fling-worthy boy, in fact. Who maybe only wanted to talk to me because of my boobs, but whatever. I'd take what I could get.

I took out my sunscreen and started reapplying. Was I being too obvious? God, of course I was being too obvious, this was so clearly a hint for him to assist. No, it wasn't obvious, it was too *subtle*—boys never picked up on anything.

"You want help?"

"Oh!" My voice came out high, which hopefully sounded like surprise instead of suppressed maniacal giggles. "Sure."

I turned, gathering my hair on the top of my head with one hand. He smoothed lotion over my shoulders and I tried not to shiver at the touch. His hands were sure, and the sun warm, and the air filled with salt. A grin split my face. I felt like a girl in a teen movie. Could any scene be a more perfect summer stereotype? I'd achieved a level of basic-dom I hadn't known was possible, and I was riding it high.

I looked up and made eye contact with Noah.

A wave of red-hot heat crashed through me, followed by freezing ice, the whiplash like a slap. I felt like I'd been caught doing something terrible. Noah held my gaze for half a second, his own still and unfathomable. Then he looked away, expression unchanged, as though he hadn't even seen me.

I tried to regulate my breathing. Everything was fine. Why would anything not be fine? I wasn't on a *date* with Noah. He'd barely even spoken to me. I had nothing to feel bad about.

I wanted to throw up.

"There. Done."

Right. Another boy currently had his hands pressed against my skin. I let go of my hair and turned back to Tyler, forcing a smile of thanks. Yet the possibility Noah might be watching made me feel awkward and self-conscious, like an actor forced to perform before she'd memorized her lines.

Whatever. I tried to shake off my awareness of Noah. I needed to remember how very not into him I was. I focused on Tyler and upped the wattage of my smile. "Want me to do you?"

He smirked. "Definitely."

Why was it so easy to accidentally make innuendos?

He turned, and I poured a quarter-sized dollop of sunscreen into my palm, glad we were facing away from Noah. I could only see Tyler's back and the glittering ocean as I smoothed cold lotion over his shoulders. "You're super tan."

More points in the Abby-for-a-Pulitzer-in-small-talk bucket.

"I spend a lot of time swimming."

"Do you come to Nantucket every year?"

"Yeah, my parents have a house here."

"Lucky. And where do you live again?"

"I'm from LA. You?"

"Outside of Boston," I said, because everything in Massachusetts was outside of Boston. "How long have you been coming here?"

Tyler was easy to talk to. I wouldn't call our conversation scintillating, but hey, did I need a summer fling to have in-depth conversational skills? I had friends for those. Tyler was funny, and interested, and *here*. He made me laugh. He made everyone laugh. Soon we had

a whole group gathered, laughing and listening as Tyler told one out-
rageous story after another.

It felt good to have a guy pay attention to me. For his hand to occasionally touch mine. For his eyes to linger on me.

Noah didn't look over at us again.

I had fun anyway. The other kids weren't so bad once they weren't
talking about people they knew and gossip I didn't. A conversation
about blockbusters fueled us for half an hour; I brought up the
three-cheese debate from earlier this summer, which went over
equally well here.

Yet a slow anger simmered within me as the day wore on. Seriously, Noah wasn't going to talk to me *at all*? *He* had invited *me*. It was
rude to invite someone somewhere and ignore them.

By the time we headed back home, late in the afternoon, I was
thoroughly pissed off. I nursed a rosé as we sailed across the waters,
keeping my gaze fixed on Tyler as he spun story after story. (Rosé was
not as good as rum-and-coke, but better than beer.) As soon as we
docked, I hopped out of the boat, planning to storm home and sulk.

Except Noah managed to be right in my path. "Hey."

"Um, hi. Bye, I guess, I'm headed home." I navigated around him,
avoiding his gaze, because I didn't want him to see the anger in my
own.

"Want to get dinner?"

I looked up at him through narrowed eyes. "What?"

"I'm thinking sandwiches from Provisions."

Tyler climbed off the boat and strolled over. "I could use something to eat."

Noah transferred his gaze to Tyler, and his expression became
distinctly unfriendly. "We're going over some family stuff."

"You're related?" Tyler looked back and forth.

Noah blinked, looked at me, then back at Tyler. "Our grand-parents were friends."

"Ah."

"Come on," Noah said to me, picking up my beach bag. "Let's go."

For one recalcitrant moment, I considered digging in my heels and refusing. Instead, I sent Tyler a contrite smile. "See you later."

"Yeah, you too."

I caught up with Noah, and this time I didn't bother hiding my irritation. "I didn't say I'd get dinner with you."

"What?" He shot me a distracted frown.

"Dinner. I didn't agree. You just assumed I would."

He stopped. "Do you not want to get dinner with me?"

I glared at him. *No,* I almost said, but it turned out, irritated as I was, all I really wanted to do was spend time with Noah Barbanel. "Fine. Let's go."

We picked up food at Provisions, a sandwich shop on the wharf, be-fore hopping in Noah's car and heading to the lighthouse at Sankaty Head. "They moved it back from the cliffs years ago," Noah said as we parked and climbed out of the car. "Houses kept falling off the edge."

I regarded the fence edging the windswept cliff with newfound appreciation. "Are you serious?"

"Yeah. The island loses something like three feet a year from erosion."

"And houses have fallen *off*?"

"Not great, I know."

"You seem alarmingly unafraid."

He laughed, and I realized how much I liked his laughter, how much a single note of appreciation from him could warm my chest. I looked at the lighthouse to distract myself because I was still mad. "Can you climb it?"

"They open it to the public twice a year, I think. I went in a couple times as a kid."

Wind whipped at us as we crossed the grasses. Noah had brought a flannel picnic blanket from the back of his car, which we laid down at the top of the dune. Behind us, the land stretched in wide, empty plains. Before us, the cliff crumbled away.

When I'd first came to Nantucket, I'd thought it would be all boat shoes and curated wealth. And in town, I could forget how wild nature could be, since humans had shaped the land into something tame. But here, it was impossible not to remember. The wind seared the land, flaying the grass flat and driving whitecaps across the sea and filling my lungs with sharp, crisp air. Before us, a gull glided low on the horizon. You could feel removed from the rest of the world on Nantucket, lifted out of time and space and deposited in another life.

I wondered if my grandmother had ever stood by this lighthouse and gazed out at the waters. Had she thought of how the next land out from here was war-torn Europe? Had she wondered about her parents, the way sailors' wives wondered about their husbands? "It's funny," I said as we settled on the blanket, "how the sea can sometimes be so beautiful and sometimes so terribly, terribly sad. Or I guess it's always beautiful, whether it's happy or sad."

Noah unwrapped his sandwich. *"Quien no sabe de mar, no sabe de mal."*

He who knows nothing of the sea, knows nothing of suffering.

"Do you think you know something about suffering?"

"Not *real* suffering." He met my gaze. "But I think everyone knows what it's like to feel sad or alone."

I wrapped my arms around my knees. "The human condition and all that?"

"And I think when you're looking at something like the sea—at anything beautiful, really—you can feel your emotions more than usual. Like beauty is a magnifying glass."

I glanced over at him, surprised. "Noah Barbanel. You really are a romantic."

His cheeks heightened in color. "You're making fun of me."

"I'm not," I said hurriedly, and because it was important he knew I meant it, I touched his arm, though it made my heartbeat ramp up dangerously. "I'm really not."

He craned his head back. "I wanted to show you Coatue . . . but I think I messed up."

I kept my expression serene, afraid sharing any emotion would make him clam up. "Messed up?"

"Well . . . did you have fun today?"

I tilted my head. "Sure. I sort of thought we'd get a chance to hang out, though."

"Right." He nodded. "I did, too. I meant for us to. I sort of—so." He stopped and flushed. "There's a project on Coatue where you use ground-penetrating radar to look at what's under the surface, at low-growing trees and underground roots—I volunteered on it last summer, and I thought I'd show it to you, but . . ."

"But what?"

"I don't know." He shrugged, looking at the water, and a small, self-deprecating smile curved his mouth. "It seemed dumb once we were there."

"I don't think it's dumb." He gave me a skeptical look, and I shook my head vigorously. "I don't! I wish you had."

"Well." He shrugged, though he looked a little happier. "It didn't seem to fit the day's vibe. Besides—you seemed busy."

I stilled. "Excuse me?"

"You were talking with Tyler." His tone was utterly inoffensive, and yet my hackles rose. I recognized his blank, neutral voice. It wasn't one he used when he was pleased.

I concentrated on unwrapping my sandwich. "Yeah, because I didn't know anyone else."

"Really."

"And he was friendly."

"Hm."

I took a large bite of mozzarella and pesto and tomato and chewed aggressively. "Do you not like him?"

"I just don't think he's very smart."

Ouch. "Well, at least he was inclusive."

He looked at me sharply. "The others weren't?"

"They were fine. They just weren't . . . my people, I guess. And I also sort of thought—it might be just the two of us sailing."

"Ah."

I glanced over at him, but his expression was unreadable. He kept his gaze ahead. "So—you wanted it to just be the two of us?"

I shrugged. "I guess."

He looked at me, and I looked at him, and I was scared and nervous and uncertain. Maybe both of us were, hedging our languages in *maybes* and *guesses* and *buts*. So because I was an idiot incapable of letting moments happen, I asked, "Are you going to eat your pickle?"

"What?" He let out a burst of laughter. "No. It's yours."

"Thanks."

He leaned back on his elbows and considered me. "I thought we could go talk to the rabbi."

I almost choked on the pickle. "What?"

"As our next step. You want to know about your grandmother, right? I think talking to the rabbi is a good idea."

"I didn't even know Nantucket *had* a rabbi."

"Sort of. During the summer, she comes each Friday. What do you think?"

I thought Noah Barbanel making a plan to help me made me want to swoon. "I did look up if there was a Jewish community before I came, and the congregation was founded in the 1980s, so long after my grandma would have been here."

"True. But even so, the rabbi might know something we don't. She might have talked to someone, or know someone we should talk to, or have access to records we haven't even thought about. In any case, it can't hurt, right?"

"Good point." And it would give me more reasons to hang out with Noah. "I'm in."

Fifteen

I couldn't recall when the dementia arrived for certain. No distinct line existed in my memory, only moments before and after. Before, O'ma repeated the same stories every time we saw her, about working in New York, about buying lunch at a cafeteria for five cents and sitting on the steps of Trinity Church to eat it. She couldn't hear out of her right ear, and not well from her left, so if you wanted to talk, you had to lean close. Often, she refused to answer questions. "No, no," she'd say, waving a skeletal hand covered in paper-thin skin. "Don't ask me that."

After, she sat in her armchair in the nursing home. She had a hard time remembering us, but she remembered her routine: hair blown out once a week, nails professionally done, Chanel No. 5 applied. She could still do her lipstick in a car without a mirror. In the nursing home, she'd hung professional portraits of my mom and aunts from when they were little. Mom was maybe eight in hers and glowed with happiness. "Do you know who these are?" O'ma would grip my hand with her frail one. "These are my children."

Those were the sweet moments. The less sweet were when she didn't recognize us, when she asked where O'pa was over and over, when Mom shouted, "He's *dead*, Mom. He died fifteen years ago!" and O'ma stared at her with her pursed lips and said, "Who are you?"

My parents were terrified of early-onset Alzheimer's. Everything was a sign. If Dad forgot a word, he spent thirty minutes with a storm cloud embedded in his brow. If Mom put a pint of Ben & Jerry's in the fridge instead of the freezer, it was as good as a professional diagnosis.

Memory was a funny thing. Some people refused to disclose the past; some people recalled the same event differently; some people couldn't remember anything. Maybe this was why I wanted to study history: if only we could record everything, we wouldn't forget our pasts, and maybe we wouldn't be doomed to repeat them. We could turn over the stones of the past even if our own memories failed us, or if our family members shut their mouths.

But how did we record everything accurately? How did we make sure to pass the knowledge from one generation to the next?

How did we decide what deserved to be remembered, and what forgotten?

"Hey there, bookstore girl."

I froze on the step stool, my arms filled with sharp-edged children's books. I'd been arranging and rearranging these shelves for five minutes in order to fit a dozen copies of this title in a face-out. Now I carefully turned on the top of the stool. "Tyler! Hi."

He grinned up at me. "Need some help?"

"Actually, can you hold these for a second?" I spilled the books into his arms and jumped down. "I've been trying to shelve them for ages, but I think I'm going to have to reconfigure three other shelves before it works."

"Oh."

Right. Not everyone found the organization of bookshelves

enthralling. I took the books back, placing them on the cart where they could wait until I'd made room. "What's up?"

"Doing some gift shopping. It's my mom's birthday tomorrow. I'm getting her a book on her list."

"What a good son. What is it?"

"The new Karin Slaughter. Unless you have other suggestions?"

"You've asked my favorite question. What does she like?"

We chattered for a few minutes about books and his mom. Then I rang him up for the new Slaughter and a thriller by a debut author both Maggie and Liz had raved about. When I handed him his bag, his fingers brushed mine, and I was pretty sure it was on purpose.

"When are you done?" he asked. "Want to grab dinner?"

I blinked.

Oh my god. Tyler was asking me out. The hot rich kid was asking out the bookish girl. Even better, I looked *great* today. (Modesty has a place, but not in my head.) Noah and I planned to meet the rabbi later, so I'd picked out a particularly nice blue dress and added silver jewelry, because even if we weren't really going to temple, it sort of felt like we were. I'd tamed my flyaway hair with a dime of product and finagled a French twist to keep it off my neck. "Tonight I'm busy, but maybe next week?"

"Sure. What are you doing Monday?"

"Having dinner with you," I said, then stifled a wince because rom-com phrases sounded ridiculous in real life.

But it worked, because Tyler grinned. "Give me your phone. I'll put in my number."

I watched, rapt, as he followed through. As he handed my phone back, the door bells chimed. Tyler caught sight of the newcomer first. His grin froze for a moment, then widened. "Hey, man."

Oh no.

I turned to find Noah standing inside the shop's door. Apparently, the punishment for using a rom-com phrase was dealing with situational awkwardness. Noah stared at us, surprise clear on his face, and I stared back. He'd also dressed up, in a blue button-down, and his hair was slightly damp, as though he'd recently showered. He managed a curt nod. "Hey."

"Hi." I tried to push up my glasses, though of course today I wore contacts. "You're early."

He didn't deign to respond, which, fair.

"How's it going?" Tyler asked him.

Noah's gaze passed over him, cool and expressionless. "Good."

Cooool, I loved this. "I'll let Maggie know I'm leaving and we can go." I turned to Tyler. "See you later."

He held my eyes a bit too long. "See you Monday."

I tried for a smile, which might have come out more like a grimace, then darted away.

When I came back out, Tyler had left, and Noah lounged against one of the armchairs, paging through a Yotam Ottolenghi cookbook. Because, sure. Why not. I approached him with my bag slung over my shoulder, weirdly nervous after the scene with Tyler. "Ready?"

"Yeah." He put the book down and gave me his full attention. "You look nice."

A compliment. On my appearance. I was dead. "Thank you."

"I like your earrings."

I almost fell over, and I wasn't even moving. Good lord. Was it so easy to make me swoon, a boy complimenting my earrings?

Yes. Yes, it was.

We walked outside, into the glaringly bright day. In unison, we put on our sunglasses. It was hot, but not horrifically so, just blazingly bright, sun reflecting off every surface. "Want to get ice cream first?" Noah said. "We have some time before meeting the rabbi."

"Let's."

We made our way toward Jack and Charlie's on Straight Wharf, a gray-slated creamery with a white fence enclosing their redbrick patio. Seagulls hopped about, seducing crumbs from weak-willed tourists. Noah ordered watermelon sorbet, and I ordered a S'mores Brownie Batter sundae, because you only live once.

"That wasn't blandishment, was it?" I asked as we settled at the small wooden table we'd managed to snag from a family moving out. You had to be a like a vulture to get a seat sometimes. "You didn't have some secret motive for liking my earrings?"

God, what was wrong with me? Why couldn't I let a nice thing be a nice thing?

"*Blandishment?*"

"Oh." *Ergh.* Sometimes I swallowed uncommon words before they tripped off my tongue (*unnecessary*, adults had told me, *just be yourself*—but easy for them to say and less easy for me to believe). Still, I'd never felt the need to censor myself around Noah. "It means—"

"I know what it means. I was impressed. Great SAT word."

"Thanks." Now I beamed at him. "I got an 800 on the reading comp portion."

He snorted a laugh. "You worked your score in very subtly."

"You should feel lucky I'm comfortable enough with you not to pretend false modesty."

"False modesty would have been if your score came up and you pretended to be humble. This was straight-up bragging."

"True." I grinned and crafted a perfectly proportioned spoonful of ice cream, hot fudge, and whipped cream. "It *is* impressive though, isn't it?"

"Not as impressive as my ability to tie a cherry's stem into a knot."

I licked some stubborn fudge from my spoon. "That's still just hearsay."

"*Oh*. Shots fired." He got up and headed to the ice cream counter. When he returned, he dangled a bright red cherry from its stem. "Prepare to be blown away." He popped the whole thing in his mouth, and I watched in stunned fascination as his cheeks moved.

Oh my god. I was straight-up staring at his mouth. Just focusing on his lips. His very nice lips.

He popped the cherry back out, a knot threaded in the center.

I started laughing and couldn't stop. "Oh my god. Where did you even learn that?"

His lips tilted up the tiniest bit. "I'm very good with my tongue."

"Noah!"

"What?" His eyes danced. "Just stating facts."

"Sure."

"I can't help it if you have a dirty mind."

"I don't have a dirty mind."

He raised his brows. "No? What's in your mind right now, then?"

I buried my head in my hands, blushing furiously. *"Noah."*

He laughed.

"Ugh!" I scooped up some more ice cream to drown my woes in.

"You have some—uh—" He reached out and brushed at my nose. "Some whipped cream there."

Strange, you'd think my blazing-hot face would have melted any cream. "Oops."

"It's cute." He was looking at me again, but this time without the wicked humor of before. His gaze softened.

I *wanted* this boy.

No avoiding it. No pretending otherwise. Every nook and cranny, from my heart to my ribs to my fingertips, wanted him. Madly. Desperately. Unavoidably.

Of course I'd noticed a ridiculous crush growing. But I'd thought I'd had a hold on it. Crushes could be shunted aside and kept under wraps. This—this full-body desire—threatened to knock me over. I didn't have the time for complex, giant emotions: those were scary and difficult and blotted out reason. I didn't want to deal with them, not this summer, when I wanted to focus on finding out more about my grandmother. Sure, I'd been prepared to have a fling, but a fling was very different than obsessive longing.

So I couldn't handle Noah Barbanel looking at me the way he was right now. I couldn't handle opening up to emotions capable of consuming me.

I pushed my chair back and stood. "Time to head out."

He blinked. "We don't have—"

"I feel like walking a bit." I pitched my sundae cup into a nearby trash can. "Let's go."

Nantucket's Unitarian Universal meeting house didn't look too different from the UU church where my Girl Scout troop had met growing up. It had red pews and white walls and, every Friday night during the summer, held services for the island's small Jewish community.

I usually found temple boring in a familiar way, like eating oatmeal or unloading the dishwasher—occasionally tedious, rarely exciting, sometimes pleasant. At services, I'd see my friends from Hebrew school, and sometimes we'd sneak out to wander the halls and examine artwork by the little kids or the entry hall's Tree of Life mosaic. We had a massive congregation, made to accommodate five towns' worth of Reform Jews, at least on the High Holidays.

This congregation had to be tiny, which made me think texting wouldn't fly, nor would silently singing the songs in the back of the siddur, which was how I'd spent far too many hours entertaining myself instead of paying attention to sermons. ("My Country, 'Tis of Thee," verses 1–4, looking at you.)

Noah led me into the back halls, where Rabbi Leah Abrams had her office. He tapped lightly on her open door.

"Noah!" She rose from behind a desk piled high with books, and came forward to hug him. She was tall and on the skinny side, with a pretty purple scarf tied around her bald head. Placing her hands on the sides of his shoulders, she leaned back to see him better. "You look so grown-up!"

His cheeks pinkened and I bit the inside of my own so I didn't smile too hard.

"Your grandmother tells me you're going to Harvard next year."

"Yeah. I am."

"How exciting! Do you think you'll get to work at the Arboretum?"

"I'm actually studying econ, not botany."

"Oh." She sounded surprised. "Well! Very useful." She turned her smile on me and lowered her voice confidentially. "I studied theater. Not the most lucrative career."

"I'm thinking about history," I said, which surprised me, since I almost entirely tried to avoid talking to adults about college. "I'm Abigail."

"Yes, of course, come sit. It's your grandmother's past you're interested in?"

"Yeah." We sat in two matching chairs across from her. "She came over from Germany in 1939. She was only four, so she didn't remember much about her family . . ."

The rabbi nodded thoughtfully as we filled her in. When we finished, she pressed her finger tips together, hands splayed wide. "All right. Interesting. I do have a theory of where you should look next. Have you two learned about Kindertransport?"

The only kinder I knew was garten. I shook my head, as did Noah.

"Kristallnacht?"

This time we nodded. I'd learned about Kristallnacht in history class, taught about the event coolly and emotionlessly, like it was just one more bullet point to memorize—and perhaps to most people, it was. 1938, Kristallnacht, Night of Broken Glass: Jews were murdered and arrested throughout Germany and its territories; businesses were smashed; and almost three hundred synagogues were destroyed.

O'ma had never explicitly said she'd been sent away from Germany because of Kristallnacht, but the dates lined up.

"Kristallnacht made the international community sit up and take note. A lot of things can be brushed under the rug—but not rampant murder. Jewish, Quaker, and British leaders went to the prime minister, requesting England allow in Jewish minors. A bill was prepared the next day. It passed Parliament quickly, and three weeks after Kristallnacht, the first transport of children from Germany to Britain arrived. All in all, ten thousand children under seventeen came from Europe to live in the UK."

"So we also did this?" Noah asked. "Took in kids?"

She smiled wryly. "Not in quite the same way. Americans did try to pass a similar bill to England's, but it got shot down."

Welp. "Why?"

"A lot of people thought the refugees were someone else's problem—they were Jewish, and the States didn't want more Jews, and the Nazis were a European problem. However, some people refused to sit by quietly. These people started an unofficial American Kindertransport program, privately bringing kids to the States. They placed children with foster families until they were twenty-one. These private citizens saved over a thousand kids, who've become known as the One Thousand Children."

One thousand children. A huge amount, though not as many as ten thousand. Still, one thousand children, saved, without government intervention. One thousand lives saved though the acts of ordinary people.

"I thought I'd put you in touch with my friend, a postdoc in modern Jewish history," the rabbi said. "She'll know how to find out if your grandmother had any connection to the group."

"Yes, please," I said. "Thank you so much."

"Great." She glanced at the clock. "Time to start getting ready. Are you staying for services?" She read our expressions and laughed. "You don't have to."

I opened my mouth, and Noah kicked me under the table. "I think we're going to head out. Thanks so much for seeing us."

"Of course. Come by anytime. Very nice to meet you, Abby."

We left, and I glanced at Noah as we walked through the halls. "So what's the Arboretum?"

"It's a park in Boston."

"A . . . tree park?"

His lips quirked up. "I mean, you're not wrong."

"The 'etum' part gave it away," I teased. "What an overused synonym for park. People are always running around saying, 'Etum the cah in Hahvahd yahd.'"

"You're ridiculous," he said, laughing and pushing open the door to outside. He shook his head at me as I beamed up at him, thrilled with my terrible joke.

Noah stilled.

"What?" My head swiveled in the same direction—and I saw his parents walking directly toward us. I, too, froze, deerlike. "Oh no."

"Abigail!" Noah's mom paused as we reached each other. "How nice to see you again. And Noah. How unexpected. What are you doing here?"

"Abigail's concerned for my spiritual well-being."

His mom smiled nervously.

"He's joking," I said quickly. "We're . . ." *Oops.* I didn't actually want to bring up my grandmother. "Stopping by."

"Are you staying for services?"

Noah shook his head. "Nope."

His father spoke for the first time, tone rich with disapproval. "Why not?"

"We have plans already," Noah said. He took my hand, and I wasn't sure if it was for support or to pull me along if he started running.

"Hm." Harry Barbanel's focus landed on me. "And how is your . . . research . . . going, Abigail?"

I didn't like Harry Barbanel calling me by my full name. It felt like an attack, instead of sweet, as it did when Noah used it. And my *research*? Well. I didn't want to talk about it with him at all, not with the memory of how he'd beckoned Noah back into Golden Doors after the disastrous dinner, the way Noah had gone stiff and retreated into the Barbanel ranks. I gave Mr. Barbanel a closed-lipped smile. "Good."

Mrs. Barbanel tucked her hand around her husband's elbow. Possibly she, too, was prepared to pull her partner along. "Have a nice night, you two. We'll see you later."

We waited until they'd disappeared into the meeting house and we'd walked a minute before talking. Even then, I kept my words low-pitched. "Did your parents say anything about the dinner last week? What do they know about my, um, research?"

He shot me a side glance. "Pretty much everything now. We had a family discussion."

"Are you serious?" My voice rose several levels. "What does a 'family discussion' entail?"

"Not much. My dad pulled me into my grandfather's study with my mom and grandma. My grandfather told my parents about how Ruth grew up with him, but not much else. Afterwards, my dad asked me why Grandpa had been so upset and Grandma so—weird—and—" He shrugged.

"And what?"

"I told him about the letters. About Edward and Ruth. About how I'm trying to help you find out about your family history."

Emotions muddled together in my chest, baking soda and vinegar, the collision an explosion I didn't know how to deal with. Of course I wanted Noah to talk to his dad. But I didn't love Harry Barbanel knowing about my search—maybe because he so obviously disapproved of me, and I hated the squicky, dirty feeling being disapproved of gave me.

I guess Noah felt the same whenever he faced his dad.

"What does he think?" I asked. "About you helping me?"

Noah shrugged. "Want to get dinner?"

"Noah!"

He sighed. "He doesn't love it."

"I suppose he thinks you should stop me from digging any further."

He nodded briefly.

"So he probably wasn't thrilled to see us together here."

"Probably not." He grinned at me. "Though on the other hand, my last girlfriend was Catholic, and they were half convinced I'd marry her, so maybe they're thrilled."

Two bolts to the chest. One: being compared to a previous girlfriend, as though I might occupy a similar status (why did I overthink everything?). Two: Who was this previous girlfriend? When had they broken up? How could I subtly learn everything about her? "Oh?"

"There's a place on Main Street named after *Moby-Dick* I've been meaning to try," Noah said. "Let's go there."

So much for the girlfriend-prying. I went along with him into town, our hands still lightly held. "So you told your dad about the romance and the letters—did you also tell him about the necklace?"

Noah glanced at me and briefly paused. "No."

"No? You hesitated."

He half laughed. "No. I didn't think it would be helpful."

"Because he'd think I was prying even more?"

"It would have gone over really poorly, yeah." He paused in front of a restaurant's awning. "Here we are."

And we went inside, leaving lost necklaces and old girlfriends and disapproving families behind.

Later, sitting on Mrs. Henderson's porch as the cicadas sang and the moon shone down, I called Mom.

Mom already knew about Kindertransport, because moms knew about things like Kindertransport and taxes and the ins and outs of health care and whether or not the weird bump on your arm meant you were dying. But she'd never heard about American Kindertransport.

"What qualifies you as being one of these one thousand children?" she asked. "How's it an organization? It sounds like a loose collection of people with similar stories."

"I dunno, maybe it's a broad identifier."

I could hear her frowning. "But then it could be much more than a thousand, and what would they call it?"

"Maybe it's about a specific time period or they came over a particular way. I haven't looked it up yet, but the rabbi gave us the email of her friend who she said researches similar stuff. It *sounds* sort of like O'ma, right? O'ma's parents sent her away for safety, right?"

"True."

I listened to the cicadas for a moment. "Hey, Mom?"

"Mm?"

"Why don't you ever talk about O'ma?"

"I talk about her."

"No, but like—about what she was like as a mother."

Mom was silent a long moment. "I don't know. I guess it was sort of . . . difficult. It wasn't fun."

"Why do you think that was the case?"

"I think she had a lot more to think about than American parenting norms. I don't blame her. And she didn't really have a model."

Except for Edward's mother, I supposed. "Why do you think O'ma didn't try to learn more about her parents? I mean, I know she knew they died at Auschwitz, but why didn't she talk more about them, or try to find out if there were other relatives still alive?"

"I think it was too hard for her to think about it. It was too sad."

"Did you try to get her to talk about it?"

"I did," Mom sounded forlorn. "It never worked."

"I'm sorry."

"Me too."

"What about O'pa? Did he talk?"

"Sometimes. He wouldn't talk about it if you asked, but sometimes he'd mention a story in relation to something else—almost always unexpectedly." She almost laughed. "Once, I told O'pa I hated rutabaga turnips, and he said he hated them, too, because the Germans took all the potatoes for the last two years of the war and all they had left to eat were rutabagas."

"Wait, they took the potatoes and left the turnips? Why? Turnips are much better for you than potatoes."

She snorted. "I guess they tasted better."

"Hm. The Germans were making some real bad nutritional choices."

She laughed. "I miss you."

I gripped my phone tightly, overwhelmed by a sudden surge of love for her, and for Dad, and for how much they supported me and never, ever acted disappointed in or distant from me. "I miss you too. You're a great mom."

"I am?" She sounded surprised. "Thanks."

"Love you."

"I love you, too."

Who would you rather have, Mom liked to ask. *Niko's mom or me? Haley's mom or me?*

And though I would have picked Mom every time no matter my actual feelings, I didn't say *you* only out of filial piety: I said *you* because I meant it. Because I would always pick her. I'd pick her over any other person in the entire world.

Sixteen

July 25

Dear Dr. Weisz,

My name is Abigail Schoenberg, and Rabbi Leah Abrams gave me your email. I'm looking for information about my late grandmother, who came to the US in 1939. Her name was Ruth Goldman, and she was born in Germany in 1934. While we know her parents died at Auschwitz (here's their record in the US Holocaust Memorial Museum's Holocaust Survivors and Victims Database), their birthplaces/residences aren't listed.

 Rabbi Abrams suggested my grandmother might have been part of American Kindertransport, and thought you might have some ideas on research I could do to find out more about her history (I'm particularly interested in finding out what town she was from and if she had other relatives). If you have time to give me any pointers, I would really appreciate it!

Thanks so much,

Abigail Schoenberg

The next day, Jane and I and half a dozen others wound up touring the Hadwen House, a Greek Revival built by a whaling merchant in 1846.

We were doing this because Jane had showed an extreme amount of interest when Pranav started talking about the house, and now we were stuck here, me and Jane and Stella and Lexi and the rest (Sydney, Pranav's *actual* girlfriend, had passed). We drifted about the rooms, looking at paintings and ceramics and miniature ships. Occasionally I would get sucked in (I *loved* miniature ships! And learning about an all-Black whaling crew during Nantucket's whaling heyday was pretty cool).

Unfortunately, I kept thinking about other things.

Like O'ma.

And the necklace.

And what the hell I was going to do about this horrible, terrible, no-good crush on Noah Barbanel.

I knew the difference between casually liking someone versus diving into love. I had no interest in the latter. When I'd fallen for Matt, it'd been slow and easy: he'd asked me out and eventually we'd kissed and I'd thought, *Oh. I like this boy.* I'd never been madly passionate about him, never obsessed. Even so, breaking up had almost ruined me.

How much worse would it be to break up with someone you were crazy about? If your feelings for them eclipsed the whole world? Letting other people affect your feelings was *dangerous*. They could spin you around and around, and sometimes when you started spinning, you ended up places you shouldn't have gone.

Noah was going to college next year, not to mention our grandparents' complicated history. He didn't just have strings attached; he was wrapped up tighter than a kitten's ball of yarn. I wasn't a fool. I wasn't going to fall for him, because it wouldn't work, and I'd end up smashed to smithereens on the rocky bottom of a bad metaphor.

"This has to end," Jane said, staring longingly at Pranav's butt.

"Agreed," I said fiercely. "What about Mason? Text him back. Go on a date."

She made a face. "Our texting's so bland."

"Maybe he's better in person."

"Then why didn't he talk to me at the concert?"

"He might be shy! Give him a second chance. Suggest ice cream. Then at least if all else fails, you get to eat ice cream." Much easier to take risks on someone else's behalf.

Pranav drifted over. "What are you guys whispering about?"

"Abby's love life," Jane lied smoothly.

Traitor. "We are not!"

"Oh?" Pranav said. "What about it?'

"She's going on a date with Tyler Nelson on Monday."

I scowled at my roommate as the rest of the group wandered over just in time to hear Jane's remark. Evan cocked his head. "I thought you were into Barbanel."

"Do we have to talk about this?" I said plaintively.

"It's easier to go after guys you're not as into," Jane said. "Rejection doesn't hurt as much."

Maybe she had a point. Going out with Tyler seemed easy, while the idea of owning up to how much I liked Noah made me want to throw up. Only I wished Jane wouldn't use *my* story to illustrate her emotions, thank you very much. "Can we *please* talk about something else?"

"Did you know," Lexi said, leaning into Stella, "a whale's limbic systems—the part of the brain used to process emotions—is more advanced than a human's? So whales can feel more deeply than humans. Imagine if your best friends were being murdered and you were *even sadder* than humanly comprehendible. That's how whales probably felt when Nantucket whalers were hunting then."

We all stared at her.

"Jesus, Lexi," Evan said. "Couldn't you have shared a less depressing fun fact?"

Stella kissed her. "I would be sad as a whale if you were murdered."

Great. Now I had anxiety about the emotions of whales.

When the group dispersed again, Jane and I picked up our conversation. "Is that why you aren't going after Mason?" I murmured. "Because you're self-aware and realize you're using him? *Or* are you pushing away a viable candidate and staying hooked on someone you know you can't have?"

"Viable candidate?"

"Shut up. Come on, he'd be a healthy distraction!"

"Let's talk about Noah instead. I had a *great* thought about the two of you."

"Oh no."

"Pretty sure I sleuthed out the *real* reason the Barbanels don't want you poking around. What if"—she paused dramatically—"Edward Barbanel is actually your mom's father?"

"*What?* Oh my god, Jane, I can't."

"Stay with me. Maybe your grandma had an affair with Barbanel and got pregnant but pretended it wasn't him. But the Barbanels know. And now they're worried your mom has found out and she's going to try to claim *half the fortune*, as is her right. *Also*, you and Noah are cousins."

"Jaaaane!" My voice rose in an unhappy whine. "Why would you *say* that!"

"It's a good story though, isn't it?" She sounded pleased as punch.

"No."

"You're wondering now."

"Jane!" I dropped my head into my hands. "Gross."

"It's only gross if you guys hook up. Which you keep saying isn't on the agenda."

"It's *not*." Except I wanted to more than basically anything. "God, Jane!"

She waggled her brows at me. "You're lusting over your own cousin."

"He's not my cousin!"

Oh my god. What if he was my cousin?

No. Impossible. My mom was born years after the letters stopped. Both O'ma and Edward Barbanel were married to their respective partners by then.

"Okay, sure," Jane said, when I presented this infallible logic to her. "But they could have had a chance encounter, or an ongoing illicit affair."

"I hate you. They didn't."

They didn't, right?

"Why are you staring at me like that?"

"Like what?" I looked away from Noah quickly, focusing on my Triple Chocolate Mountain. We'd grabbed ice cream at the Juice Bar and taken it down to the wharves. It was seven thirty at night and still too hot, though a gentle breeze skirted over the water. We perched on the edge of the docks, our legs dangling. The sun was still high; the days were painfully long this time of year, the sun refusing to set until past eight o'clock.

"Like I'm an alien."

"No reason. You're not. We're not. Nothing."

I was not bringing this up. One: the theory was utterly insane. Two: Wouldn't admitting it bothered me be tantamount to admitting my interest in Noah? Otherwise, I should be thrilled to have a cousin. Yay, cousins!

Boo, kissing cousins.

Gross gross gross, moving on. I turned my phone around. "I got an email this morning from the rabbi's friend."

I watched him as he leaned over the screen, one of his curls flopping over his forehead. I didn't itch to push his hair back. Of course I didn't.

Dear Abigail,

Happy to help! It's definitely possible your grandmother was part of the American Kindertransport program, though many families made private arrangements to have children sent to the states instead of going through any organized effort. I'd recommend checking with museums/archives that might have records from the organizations involved in American Kindertransport (I've linked to a few below).

Do you know if she traveled through other countries on the way to the States? While England and Germany never officially released the names of the children involved in Kindertransport, there are several databases you could search. The late 1930s also saw a wave of German children coming through France, so the Mémorial de la Shoah might have helpful records.

I saw how incomplete your great-grandparents' Luxembourg deportation records were in the link you sent—the governments usually kept better records. Perhaps your great grandparents didn't have accurate papers on them if they were trying to escape through Luxembourg (or perhaps they were using fake ones). Still, might be worth contacting similar organizations in Luxembourg to see if they have more complete details about these deportations.

He looked up. "Wow. Are you going to follow through?"

"Please, I already have. I emailed the American nonprofits at the bottom of the email, but they don't have records you can search online, you actually have to go there in person and look through physically."

"Jesus." He licked a bead of ice cream off his cone. "Can you imagine doing this kind of research pre-internet?"

"Right?" I tried very hard not to think about his tongue. "They're not far—there's two in New York—but it's not super easy, either. I thought I'd email the French and Luxembourg organizations, too." I gave him my brightest smile. "You mentioned you studied French . . ."

He rolled his eyes. "All right, here goes."

We finished our ice cream while composing emails to international organizations. "What's the plan," Noah asked, "if they don't have anything helpful?"

"I'm not sure." I focused on the rippling blue-green sea. "I still wonder if your family has any records from my grandmother's arrival. I wish I could read her letters. Maybe she said something useful there."

"So what you're saying is you want to dig around in my family's papers some more."

"No. Yes." I let out a half laugh, kicking at the air above the water. "Yes, but I want permission. I want another try at talking to your grandparents. Unless you think it would go terribly?"

"Well, yeah," he said. "I'm for sneaking around in the study when they're elsewhere."

"Your family would have me catapulted off the island. And there have been sharks."

"We'll just need an alibi for why we're there."

"An alibi," I repeated. "For why we're . . . alone in your grandfather's study."

"You're smart. I'm sure you'll be able to come up with something."

I wrinkled my nose at him, feeling flushed. Was he suggesting what I thought he was? Had he noticed how much I'd been watching him? "I doubt I could come up with a single thing."

He laughed. "Sure."

Our gazes locked, and I could feel the heat traveling from my cheeks down my neck and spreading all through my chest. We stared at each other. I wanted to throw myself off the dock into the water. I wanted to kiss him.

Instead, I babbled into the silence. "So who was the girl your family thought you'd marry?"

A wide grin broke over his face. He looked delighted. "What?"

Shoot. Wrong question to ask. The dark waters below seemed more and more appealing. "Never mind."

"My ex. Erika. We broke up last year when she left for college."

Right. Very reasonable. "How come?"

He shrugged. "It didn't make sense for her to have a boyfriend in high school. She would have missed out on the whole college experience."

Would I have dumped a boyfriend in high school because I was going to college? Not one like Noah Barbanel. "How'd you take it?"

He glanced up at me, then smiled suddenly. "It was the right move."

"How long did you date for?"

"Two years. How long did you and what's-his-name?"

I bit back a smile. "Six months."

My phone buzzed, a reminder to head to the Prose Garden. I blew out a breath. "I should get going. I need to be at work in ten."

"I'll walk you."

We strolled casually, chatting about inconsequential things, though all I could think of was the look on Noah's face when we talked about alibis. I wanted to take his hand in mine, but even though they swung between us, even though we'd held hands before, it felt like an impossible step.

We dawdled as we approached the rose arbor leading to the Prose Garden's door. Noah looked at the arbor, then the sky, then me. "Are you really going on a date with Tyler?" he asked abruptly.

I blinked. "Where did you hear that? Did *Tyler* tell you?"

Noah shook his head.

"Then . . ." I ran through other options. "Evan?"

"Are you?"

"You're *so* bad at answering questions. And you're very obvious about avoiding them. So Evan did tell you?" He shrugged, which I took as a yes. *Oy.* "So what if I am?"

Noah's expression grew more and more austere. "I wouldn't have thought he was your type."

"Well, I guess my type is the kind of guy who asks me out," I retorted. "Is it so crazy for me to go on a date?"

"He's only interested in hookups."

"As you've mentioned before, thanks," I said through gritted teeth. "Maybe I'm also only interested in hookups."

"I'm trying to protect you."

"You don't need to protect me! It's not your job. You don't need to protect me, or your family, or anyone except yourself, okay?"

He didn't respond.

Screw it. "Do you not *want* me to go out with him?"

His face closed. "You should do what you want."

God, he was cold as ice. And I knew it was a bad idea, the two of us, I did. But I *wanted* Noah to be into me. I *wanted* him to say it. And if Noah asked—if Noah wanted—

Except . . .

"What *do* you want, Abigail?" Noah asked. "Do you want Tyler?"

What if we *were* cousins?

I stared at him, my mouth slightly parted, unable to speak.

He shook his head. "I'll see you later."

It's not my fault! I wanted to yell after him as he walked away. *I'm into you, just not into incest!*

Great.

Seventeen

July 26

From: The Jewish Children's History Foundation
To: Abigail Schoenberg

Dear Abigail,

We are sorry to report we do not have any records of a Ruth Goldman in our database. You are welcome to come look at our archives in person . . .

From: The Kanevsky Organization
To: Abigail Schoenberg

Dear Abigail,

Thank you for your inquiry. Unfortunately, we were unable to find anyone by your grandmother's name . . .

From: The New York Center for Holocaust Victims
To: Abigail Schoenberg

Dear Ms. Schoenberg,

We do not have any records of a Ruth Goldman in our databases. Good luck with your search.

I met Tyler the next night at a restaurant on the water.

He stood near the hostess station, all sunshine and summer, his corn-silk-yellow hair artfully arranged, a sky-blue shirt boosting the color of his eyes. His face was pink with sun, and he straightened when I walked into the cool air-conditioning. I gave him my best winsome smile. "Hi."

His gaze roamed over my pink dress and blown-out hair. "You look great."

"Thank you. So do you." My real takeaway from this summer was going to be learning to accept compliments. How did all these boys know compliments were the way to my heart? Was it simply because they'd dated enough to know this was standard practice?

"I put our names down, but if there's no room, there's a million other places we can go . . ."

The hostess looked up. "There's two of you, yes? We can seat you now."

"Really? Awesome." He beamed at me. "Great luck."

He put his hand on the small of my back and guided me toward our table, which was as new as getting complimented. The hostess left after handing us menus, and Tyler leaned forward. "This place is getting huge attention. My friend's mom is a food critic and she told us about it, and it's going to *blow up* as soon as her review goes live. We're lucky to get in while we can."

"Wow," I said, since some response seemed necessary. "Cool. I don't know anything about restaurants, I just look things up on Yelp."

He settled back in his seat. "People on Yelp are all haters, you can't trust them. You need somebody objective to know what's good."

The server came over with two glasses of water. Tyler looked up at him. "How long have you guys been open?"

"Three weeks," the server said.

"And how's it going?" Tyler looked around. "It's real busy in here."

"This is our busiest night so far," the server said, finally unbending enough to smile.

When he left, Tyler caught me smiling at him. "What?"

"You're a talker."

"Is that a bad thing?"

"No! I like it. You're friendly."

He grinned back at me. "I like people. I like knowing everyone's stories."

"Yeah? How come?"

"You never know who you're going to meet . . ."

We traded stories through dinner, of all the curious characters we'd met in our lives, pausing only to savor the food—a quinoa bowl with black lentils and avocado for me, and lemon-pepper salmon for him. I liked Tyler. He *was* friendly, and he was funny. Sure, Noah thought he was bad news, and maybe he was if he only wanted hookups and the people he dated wanted more. But if everything was on the table . . . then he might be the perfect guy for a summer fling.

If I wanted a summer fling.

If I didn't feel like, simply by being here, I was betraying someone.

Which was literally the stupidest thought in the world. So I buried it deep and tried to have a good time, which wasn't so hard, not with the way Tyler gave me all his attention and the way his knee touched mine under the table and the way his blue gaze pulled me in.

We split the check and headed outside, walking toward the docks. The setting sun slowly bleached the sky, spreading a line of orange at the horizon. The air was heavy, soup-like, and we moved languorously.

"How do you know Noah?" Tyler asked. His gregarious personality slipped slightly, a sharp, acute intelligence shining through.
"Family friends?"

A touch of wariness wound through me at his carefully casual
tone. "Our grandparents knew each other."

"Do yours also come to Nantucket?"

"Not really." I nodded at the sunset. "It's pretty, isn't it?"

"Not as pretty as you."

A laugh burst out of me, and I clapped a hand to my mouth. "Sorry."

Brief startlement crossed his face, but then he smiled wryly. "Too
cheesy?"

"Hey, good for you if it works."

"It usually does." He grinned, then cocked his head, studying me
as though I was an unusual specimen picked up on the beach. "I can't
tell what you want."

I blinked. "Um. You could ask me?"

"All right. What do you want?"

Oh no. Now I needed to answer. "Dinner was nice."

Great, now I was doing Noah's thing of very unsubtly changing
the topic.

"Are you and Barbanel a thing?"

"What?" I halted. "No."

"You seem like a thing."

Everything was awkward and I needed a hole to follow me around
so I could disappear into it when convenient. "If you thought so, why
did you ask me out?"

"I thought we could have fun. Why'd you say yes if you're into
Barbanel?"

"I never said I'm into him."

"Did you want to make him jealous?"

Did I?

"What's the deal between the two of you?" I asked. "Did you seduce his cousin or something?"

He smiled, a smaller, realer one than most of the others I'd seen so far. "Read a little too much Jane Austen?"

"I'm genuinely impressed you made a Wickham reference." I paused. "Or Willoughby, I guess."

"Don't be too impressed. I only read them to help me pick up girls." He flashed a smile, and I couldn't tell if he meant it or not.

"I see."

"And I didn't *seduce* Shira, but yeah, she had a crush on me. Which went nowhere, because she's a kid." He squinted upward. "I *might* have flirted with Barbanel's girlfriend last summer. But only when it was obvious they were on the outs."

Noah's girlfriend. "This is the one who broke up with him because she was going to college and didn't want a boyfriend?"

He smirked. "Is that what he told you?"

I blinked, confused. "What?"

"*He* broke up with *her*. She said there was some bull about her being free to date whoever she wanted to in college, but really he didn't want to do long-distance."

Huh. Okay. I nodded slowly, taking in this change of information. So Noah hadn't wanted to do long-distance. And maybe it hadn't been bull—maybe he really did think people should be single their freshman year of college. Maybe *Noah* wanted to be single next year.

"You wanna go down to the beach or something?"

I returned my attention to Tyler. "Is that a coded invite for making out?"

He barked a laugh. "Wow."

"I know. I'd be embarrassed, but turns out I'm really not."

"Cool. Well. Yeah, it was. I'm cool with you being hung up on Noah. Feel free to use me as a distraction."

I laughed, then threw back my head and laughed again. "I like you. You're refreshing."

He looked hopeful. "Refreshing enough to hook up with?"

"Nope. I'm going to head home, but thanks."

"Hey, you miss one hundred percent of the shots you don't take." He pointed a finger gun at me like he'd walked out of a bad nineties movie. "Good advice for you, too, Schoenberg."

"I'll keep it in mind."

During my Zoom call with my mom the next day, I said: "You don't think it's possible O'ma and Edward Barbanel were in contact later in their lives?"

"She never mentioned anything."

"No, I mean . . . Okay, you have to promise not to laugh."

She raised her brows. "I promise."

"It's not my fault," I warned. "Jane had this really weird theory. What. If." My words slowed down, then tumbled together in my embarrassed attempt to get them out quick as possible. "They hooked up later in life and it resulted in you, their *secret love child*?"

Mom burst into uncontrollable laughter.

"Mom! You promised not to laugh!"

"You said 'secret love child'!" she cried. "How could I avoid laughing?"

"Okay. Fine." My lips twitched, but I didn't back down. "Do you think it's possible?"

"Sweetie. No."

"You're sure?"

"Yes, I'm sure. If it makes you feel better, I'm a carrier for Gaucher because of O'pa."

I'd never been so glad for Ashkenazi genetic mutations in my life. I let out a huge sigh of relief. "Phew."

She leaned closer to the screen. "Does this mean you like Noah?"

"Mom!"

"Okay! Forget I asked." Her lips wobbled, and then her mouth broke into a smile and more laughter poured out. "I can't believe you thought I was a millionaire's secret love child."

I spent a moment in fake indignation, but then I joined her.

Phew.

The next night, two hours into watching Vikings try to take over England, my phone buzzed. A call, not a text. I glanced down, expecting it to be Niko or one of the other girls from home.

Instead, it was Noah.

I picked up immediately. "Hello?"

"Hi." He sounded tired. "What are you up to?"

"Nothing really. You?"

"Not much."

He didn't add anything. I stared at my reflection in the window, my face overlaid on the darkening night. Ellie Mae curled against my side on the bed, her golden fur shimmering in the lamplight as my fingers cleaved a path through her fur. "Are you okay?"

"Yeah." An odd note tinged his voice.

I waited him out.

Noah sighed into the phone. "My dad and I got into a fight."

"What happened?"

"It doesn't matter. He fought with Grandpa, it trickled down to me . . . Are you free? Do you want to . . . hang out?"

"Yes. Of course. Where should we meet?" I looked down at my pajama shorts, considering. I felt like I was on a precipice, daring and scared and about to force myself to jump. "Actually . . . Jane and Mrs. Henderson are out for the evening if you want to come over?"

I held my breath.

"Are you sure? Yeah, I'd like to."

Exultation rushed through me. "Of course."

It took twenty minutes for Noah to arrive, and I spent every last one of them cleaning. Why? Did I think Noah would turn around and leave if the drain stopper and faucet in my bathroom sink weren't polished? Would he deride me if my pillows weren't plumped? Why was I so nervous?

Because I was so, so nervous.

My phone buzzed. *Rapunzel, Rapunzel, let down your long hair.*

With one last look around my neat-ish room, I tripped down the stairs and opened the front door. Noah stood there, in jeans and a blue T-shirt, and at the sight of him, the tension I'd been carrying drained out of me. I grinned. "My hair's not *that* long."

He reached over and tugged one of my ringlets. "Long enough."

I flushed. "Want to come up?"

The nerves came back as I led him up the narrow stairs to my tiny room. Why had I invited him over? Why had he called me? Was it because we were the only ones who could understand each other's complicated, intertwined families? Or because of the more generic, baser, intoxicating reason a boy called a girl?

Also, was he looking at my butt as we climbed the stairs? I did have a nice butt.

We reached the third floor, and I swung the door open. "Welcome to my humble abode."

Why was I such a huge dork?

He grinned at me, and nodded at my bed. "This yours?"

"Yes."

He flopped down backward on it. Good lord. Noah Barbanel, on my bed. I sat at the foot, my back against the wall. Our legs were perpendicular, his pulled up with his knees pointed at the ceiling, mine laid straight.

He picked up Sad Elephant from my pillow and held the stuffed animal high. "You kept it."

"I told you. He's too sad to abandon, and I couldn't burden a small child with his tragicness."

"You should probably send him to therapy."

"But he doesn't have a mouth, see. Just a nose and sad eyes. So he wouldn't be able to talk about his feelings." Like, I suspected, Noah wouldn't. "What happened?"

"How was your date with Tyler?"

"No. You're not avoiding the conversation."

He raised a brow, looking cool and unruffled despite lying on his back. His T-shirt ruched up slightly, showing the flat, tanned skin of his lower stomach. "Was he the perfect summer fling?"

I tore my eyes away from the dark hair against Noah's abs, which were decidedly affecting my ability to breathe. I tried to match his disinterested tone. "It was nice. We went out to dinner at some new place on the Sound."

He scoffed, almost imperceptibly.

"What?"

He shook his head.

I wanted to pull my hair out. Why were boys like this? They

couldn't just make noises and expect me to pull the reasons out of them.

In fact, I wasn't going to play this game. If he wanted to tell me what his rude scoff meant, he could do it without prompting.

And he did, after settling Sad Elephant back on the bed, next to my stuffed horse. "Typical. Go to a brand-new restaurant. Probably finished with a walk along the water."

So apparently Noah knew Tyler's game plan. Fine. It wasn't like dinner and a walk were such an unusual or bad combo. "He said you broke up with your ex, not the other way around."

Noah's head jerked up, and a small smile curved his lips. "You talked about me?"

"Don't flatter yourself. It was small talk."

"Are you going on a second date?"

"Why do you care?"

"I don't like to see my friends date jerks."

Hm. Friends. Not the answer I'd wanted. "Well, we're not."

"Really? Why?"

I shrugged. "I decided he wasn't the right material for my fling."

"You're running out of time. Summer's half-over."

Our eyes caught. It felt very hard to breathe, the air thin, my heart working hard. I was minutely aware of how close my arm was to his legs, how if my hand moved slightly I could touch his calf. *Any suggestions?* I almost asked, but I wasn't brave enough. "Tell me what happened with your dad, Noah."

He looked away. "My grandparents got in a fight."

"Oh no. Why?"

He winced.

Guilt surged inside me. "My grandmother?"

"I don't think it's really about her. But. My grandparents'

relationship has already been on thin ice for a while. Everything with Ruth . . . it struck at their weakest part. And they just . . ."

"Cracked?"

"Cracked and geysered." He picked up Horse. "This guy seems a little tired."

"He isn't. He's stalwart. Why did your dad get mad at you because of a fight between your grandparents?"

Noah sighed. "My dad thinks I need to be better about my responsibilities. Be a better grandson. Protect the family's interests. It would ruin the family if my grandparents separated." He gave me a half smile. "And it would be my fault."

"First of all, it couldn't *possibly* be your fault, and second—what do you mean 'ruin the family'?"

Noah draped an arm over his eyes. "My grandmother's family brought in money when she married my grandfather. A *lot* of money."

I sat up. "What?"

"Enough to push Barbanel from a local firm to a national one. Enough to turn it into what it is today. My grandmother's brothers got stock in return. Not enough to control the company—unless my grandmother votes with them. She never does—she always votes with my grandpa."

"*Jesus*, Noah!"

He winced. "Yeah."

"So—what? If she votes with her brothers, what happens?"

"The Barbanels lose the controlling share and it goes to the Danzigers, and they could do whatever they want—oust my dad as CEO, give the control to his cousins, anything."

Wow. This was like a TV show. "So—it's about power? And money?"

"They do make the world go round."

"What do you want? Maybe if the Danzigers were in control, you wouldn't be forced to go into the business. Maybe some second cousins or whatever could take over."

"Yeah." He sounded unconvinced. "But my dad would be miserable. And he's my dad."

"And you don't want to disappoint him."

He nodded.

"Look." I hesitated. "I'm not saying you *shouldn't* go into business and become the CEO of a vast empire of men in expertly tailored suits. But. Your life goal shouldn't be making your dad happy. You're eighteen. You don't need to map your entire life out."

He made a face.

"I was watching this show where Vikings try to take over England, right? And people kept *dying*. Small child caught a cold? Dead. Dude looks at someone's wife the wrong way? Dead. Girl sleeps with the wrong person? Dead. Lots and lots of dead people. It's giving me an awful lot of life-is-short feels. Do what you want. Talk to your multitude of cousins and let them know running Barbanel is an option. Take *just one* freaking class on biological diversity."

He turned on his side so he could look at me directly. "So if you want something—even though you're not sure about it—you'll go after it? If you want something badly enough, you'll take the risk?"

I wanted Noah.

I wanted Noah and I didn't know how to say so, I didn't know how to lean forward and press my mouth to his. What was I more afraid of—rejection, or giving into this and then having it come to a halt at the end of summer when we inevitably dissolved?

"I'm not sure," I said. "What about you? Do you take risks?"

"It depends." He studied me. "It's easier when there's some indication the risk will pay off."

I wasn't sure I was ready to give that indication. I stared into my lap. "Talking to your grandpa about my grandmother, even if it made him mad, might pay off."

"That's the risk you want to take?" He sat up, sounding almost angry. "Fine. Let's do it."

"What?" I looked back, startled. "But you don't want to."

"But you do. And we *should* take risks, Abigail Schoenberg."

"So—we can talk to him?" I wanted, so badly, to have another chance to ask Edward Barbanel about O'ma and her family and her necklace. But Noah's energy right now was already making me re-think this. "You made it sound like he'd flip out."

"Then he flips. Didn't you just tell me I'm not responsible for his emotions? Come over for Shabbat."

"*Shabbat?* Are you serious? Besides, I thought your parents went to services."

"Not this week. A lot of the family is here, so everyone's staying home."

I hesitated. "Wouldn't it be better for me to come over when less people are around? Or have the conversation in a—neutral territory?"

"If we're having it, I don't think it matters where."

"Hm." I was still skeptical, but who was I to look a gift horse in the mouth? "All right, then. Friday it is."

"Good." He stretched, then grinned at me. "This Viking show. Think you can catch me up enough to watch your next episode?"

"Yeah." I smiled down at him. "I bet I can." Then I added, trying to sound casual. "Hey—I'm glad you called. And came over."

He didn't move or stay anything, but his stillness seemed not cold but watchful, like he needed more context.

I swallowed. "Because you can, anytime, you know."

"Okay," he said, which wasn't *thanks* or *yes this has been a meaningful experience,* but then he met my gaze and gave me a small, tremulous smile.

I smiled back and straightened. "Okay. So the Viking's name is Uthred, son of Uthred . . ."

Eighteen

Sometimes, late at night when I was reading in bed, I couldn't stand not knowing what would happen next in my book. I'd skip ahead a hundred pages and skim. I didn't want *spoilers*, per se, but I wanted to know the *feel* of the book so I could align with it: make sure I was rooting for the right love interest, find out if the plot skipped forward ten years, learn if the best friend lived or died. Then, after I'd come too close to a real spoiler—or stumbled across one—I'd close the book and go to sleep.

This caused confusion later on in my reading. I'd come across déjà vu–inducing passages and wonder—had the author written the same sentence earlier in the book, like a villanelle poem? Or had I dreamed these lines myself somehow?

No: I'd read them moments before bedtime, and only half remembered them later on. A practical answer. But it gave me the oddest feeling, like I'd been brushed by unnerving magic.

Golden Doors made me feel the same way.

How many times did you have to visit somewhere before it became commonplace? Before your neck stopped craning your head back so you could take in the sprawling mansion, with its gray paneling and dark windows? How long until something felt like an old shoe, until you didn't even notice the grandeur? Until you felt like you belonged?

A child opened the door when I rang it on Friday night—one of the ten-year-old triplets. She stared at me, speechless, then ran away.

Cool.

It'd been busy the last time, but dinner had still felt intimate. Now the size of the gathering had exploded. People spilled out the French doors and onto the lawn, where multiple tables had been set up. I made my way toward one with Noah and a cluster of other teens: some Barbanel cousins I'd met last week, some strangers with dark curly hair. Shabbat candles and challah sat in the centers of the tables. Everything was painfully familiar.

I almost felt like I belonged here, because I did belong to these traditions, which meant I almost belonged to these people—but I didn't belong to Golden Doors, and in any case, belonging wasn't my actual goal. My goal was to talk to Edward Barbanel. To see if he would share my grandmother's letters; to see if he knew about any records concerning her. To ask him about the necklace without making him shut down.

I stopped behind Noah's chair. "Does it ever bother you how the doors aren't actually golden?"

He swiveled in his chair and smiled up at me, a bright, beatific smile. "Hi."

"Hi."

"The poem doesn't even end with golden doors, actually. It's 'I lift my lamp beside the golden door!'"

"So everything's wrong."

"Pretty much."

"We tried painting the doors once," a boy across the table said. A cousin, maybe. "It didn't go over well."

"They used my nail polish," a girl said. "I told them it was a stupid idea."

"The nail polish was gold sparkles," Noah said. "They thought it would be subtle."

"It was not," the girl said.

Everyone smiled at me and I smiled back, then gestured to the seat next to Noah. "Okay if I sit here?"

"I saved it for you, so yes." He turned to the others. "This is Abby."

"Abby." The boy on Noah's other side leaned forward. He wore heavy eyeliner and had green hair and a few years on us. "The famous Abby."

"Famous?" I glanced warily at Noah as I sat. "Should I be alarmed?"

"Should *we*?" the green-haired boy said. "I hear you're a black-mailer."

I kicked Noah under the table.

"Ow," Noah said calmly. "This is Jeremiah. Our moms were roommates in grad school."

"Always a pleasure to meet a fellow delinquent." Jeremiah shook my hand, then turned to Noah. "The parental rumor mill says it's Harvard."

Noah nodded.

"Sorry you couldn't get into Yale."

"Screw you," Noah said with a laugh.

I'd never seen Noah so relaxed before, and it thrilled me to be allowed into his private circle. I couldn't stop smiling. I *liked* these people. They listened and laughed when they talked. They were smart and funny and attentive. I wanted to belong to them. I wanted this to be my place.

"All right, everyone!" Noah's mother called from the adults table. "Ready?"

Everyone quieted down. At our table, Noah's cousin Shira appeared and picked up the matches. As the sun started to set, we lit the candles and sang the prayers, and the sense of belonging settled deeper into my bones. *Baruch atah Adonai*, we said. *Eloheinu Melekh ha'olam, asher kid'shanu b'mitzvotav, v'tzivanu l'hadlik ner shel Shabbat.* This was belonging, to me, words I'd said since before I could understand them, candles lit, wine poured, challah ripped.

But no matter how familiar it was, no matter what sense of familiarity cloaked the evening, I was still an interloper at Golden Doors. I kept glancing at Noah's parents and grandparents, and more than once found their attention on me: wary, puzzled, cautious. Worse, though, was the way Edward and Helen *didn't* look at each other, but instead stiffly focused on anyone else. How could I talk to them if they were still so tense?

I tried to focus instead on the people in front of me, laughing and teasing and being teased in return. I ate couscous with tender carrots and zucchini and peppers and a dozen spices; stuffed artichokes in lemon sauce; baklava from Jane's bakery. When my leg brushed Noah's, I didn't move it, and he didn't move his, either. I spent the meal riding high on the light touch of skin against skin.

Like my own parents, Noah's adults were liberal about underage drinking on Shabbat. At home, I stuck to grape juice, but Nantucket had apparently done a number on me, so as the evening waned, I nursed a glass of wine. Only when the candles faded into smoke and the cousins cleared the tables and people milled about on the lawn did I lean in toward Noah. "Your grandparents haven't looked at each other all evening."

He grimaced in acknowledgment. "I know."

"They're still fighting?"

He nodded.

"Maybe tonight's not the right time to ask more questions." Much as I wanted to, we'd probably have the same results as if we threw ourselves against a brick wall.

He finished the rest of his wine, then turned to me with a familiar determined look on his face. "Okay, then."

"Okay?" I repeated warily. "Why does this *okay* make me nervous?"

"Come on." He wrapped his hand around mine and pulled me up.

God, I loved the feel of Noah's hand around mine.

I did not love being clueless as he dragged me across the lawn, through the milling people, and into the house. "What are we doing?"

We passed Shira, who caught my eyes and rolled her own.

We wound our way through the great room, then into the hall, and I started resisting as I realized where we were going. I dug in my heels when we reached the study. "Noah . . ."

"You want your grandmother's letters, don't you? You want her records. You want to find out where she came from."

I wavered. "I want to talk to your grandfather! Not go through his stuff."

"*Now* you have morals?"

"Won't your family be wicked pissed if they catch us?" And now, knowing more about Noah's relationship with his dad and grandfather, I didn't want them to be even more strained.

"They're busy hosting their friends. They won't notice." He pulled me inside and shut the door.

"I'd like the record to note I'm against this."

"Chicken. Come on." He peeled up the corner of the mouse pad on the desk, lifted a key, and unlocked the desk's top drawer.

"That's a terrible hiding place."

"Right? And look." He lifted a ring of keys from the drawer. "This is for everything else." He unlocked a floor-to-ceiling cabinet on the far wall from the bookshelves, revealing endless files.

I took in the determined energy shining through Noah as he moved about. He walked a tightrope, both constantly angry with his father and grandfather yet wanting to please them badly. If you didn't clean a wound before the scar tissue formed over it, it became harder to rout out the dirt. "You're closer to your grandma than your grandfather, right?"

He nodded, riffling through another drawer. "I used to follow her around when I was a kid. My mom always tried to fix things, you know? When I'd get in fights with my dad. Grandma didn't. She'd be out in the garden, and I'd join her, and she wouldn't talk—just clip here, plant here, this is a hybrid tea rose, this is a shrub rose, this is a climber."

"Are you still mad on her behalf?"

He let out a deep sigh. "Yeah. She's done so much for this family—not just bringing in money, but playing host for my grandfather, holding dinners and parties for his business associates, going to events, raising the family—and what, she was picked because she was rich? Not because she was the partner he wanted? He was writing *love letters* to someone else while he was dating her?" He shook his head. "It's shitty."

"Yeah."

"Would you do it?" He focused on me intently. "What your grandmother did?"

"It depends what you're asking," I said carefully. "Would I write letters to someone I loved? Sure."

"Even if you knew he had a girlfriend?"

I stiffened. "I'm pretty sure my grandmother was Edward's girlfriend before Helen was. Besides, why are we putting this on Ruth?

Why not Edward? *He* was the one making a choice—love or money."

"Ruth is the one who broke up with him."

"Maybe because she knew he was cheating on her! Maybe because he refused to choose between the two of them, so someone had to do something." I jutted out my chin. "So what would you do?"

"I'd choose the person I loved."

"So you say," I said skeptically. "But you can't really know."

"I do."

"Seriously? So—even if the first girl was a poor orphan, and the second a rich society girl who'd *also* bring the family company to another level, you'd pick love? Because I'd think the wealth of the second would go a long way to soothing any heartbreak."

"No," he said, and for whatever reason his decisiveness infuriated me. "I wouldn't be with someone I didn't love."

"You can't be certain."

"Yes, I can," he said, and maybe I'd infuriated him, too, because his voice rose. "Because I actually care about how other people feel. Though maybe I should stop, maybe I shouldn't care about my dad or my company or the family and I should only focus on me if that's just what everyone else does!"

I felt gutted. "Noah—"

He let out a deep *whoosh* of breath. "Never mind. It doesn't matter."

"I didn't mean to upset you."

"You didn't upset me. God, Abigail."

Now he sounded even *more* upset. "What?"

"Nothing."

"Um, it doesn't sound like nothing? You sound—worked up."

He tugged open another desk drawer. "If I am, it's for entirely different reasons."

"What did you mean?"

"Forget it."

"Then why'd you say it?"

"I don't know!" he shouted. "Because sometimes you drive me crazy!"

My stomach drew inward. My lips parted. Noah's and my gazes collided, his intense, mine surprised. And for one crazy, maddening instant, I thought—

I thought—

The door swung open.

Time slowed down as the door scraped against the floor. Noah grabbed my waist and thrust us both toward the window alcove, with the tall glass panes and the velvet curtains. We tumbled inside, landing on the window's ledge. Noah caught a fistful of the fabric and yanked the curtain closed. It whisked across the floor and shut us both in a tiny enclave of space, dark and private.

We huddled there, between the cool glass and heavy velvet, chests rising and falling. My hand clutched his arm. One of his had settled on my waist. His body radiated heat.

"We're in so much trouble," I whispered. A hysterical smile edged my mouth. "This is ridiculous."

"Shh," he said, but only barely. He was trying to muffle his own laughter.

Outside, we heard footsteps and the closing of drawers. We clutched each other, mirth more hysterical than entertained. Then, slowly, we stilled. The humor drained out of me. We were so close. I could see his individual lashes.

I drove him crazy, he'd said.

God, I wanted him so badly it felt like a physical ache. Only inches separated us. All I had to do . . .

The curtain yanked open. Edward Barbanel towered over us, expression inscrutable.

And hot, terrifying mortification swamped me. *Oh no.*

"What are you doing here?" Edward's voice was gravelly and low, and his gaze swung back and forth between the two of us.

"We're . . ." Noah's face displayed the same horror I felt. He pulled me to my feet and we stood side by side, frozen.

"Mr. Barbanel." I stumbled the words out. "I'm so sorry. We'll go."

"No." He nodded at the pair of Windsor chairs. "Sit." He lowered himself into the seat behind his massive desk.

Noah and I exchanged another nervous glance, then did as we were bid, pulling the chairs closer, schoolchildren before the principal. I placed my hands under my legs, then folded them in my lap, trying to look contrite but not cowardly.

"What are you doing here?"

Noah stayed statue-like, wearing the same unreadable expression as Edward, like they were two blank-faced rooks in a game of chess. Yet I could imagine what roiled behind Noah's mask. Should he offer silence, truth, or a lie? *I'm sure you'll be able to come up with something,* Noah had said to me. But now the alibi he'd alluded to felt impossible to voice, when it almost hadn't been a lie at all.

"I wanted to know more about my grandmother," I said. "I'm sorry. We shouldn't have come in here. I just—I just want, so much, to know about her life."

His eyes, so similar to his grandson's, held mine. "Then why didn't you ask her?"

Why hadn't I asked her?

I had asked her, hadn't I? Sometimes. But she hadn't wanted to talk about her past, about the years before New York City, before she met O'pa. She'd always redirected the conversation.

Wasn't it rude to push someone when they resisted?

Why was it so much easier to dig into someone's life when they weren't around to protest?

"Maybe I should have asked more," I finally said. "But for whatever reason, we didn't know about Nantucket. We didn't know about . . . you."

He didn't say anything.

My hands kneaded each other nervously. "We don't know where she's from, if she had any family, if they survived. I thought, since she had your letters—I thought maybe you would have hers, and she might have written things in them about her past."

"Those letters are private."

"I know. Right." Didn't I know? When did letters stop being private and enter the public sphere? Historians read old diaries and letters all the time. Was it when the people connected to them had died? Was it if you, the reader, had no connection? Or was it always an invasion of privacy? "I only wanted to find out more about her. Do you have any records from when she came to live with you?"

He frowned. "No."

I deflated. But then again, he had been a boy when O'ma arrived— his parents might have known, but why would he? "Okay."

His frown deepened, but whatever emotion it contained didn't seem directed at Noah and me. "You really didn't know about Nantucket?"

"She never mentioned it. Not once. I thought she'd grown up in New York. So when I realized I was wrong—when I learned she'd spent her summers here when she was my age—I was curious. It's a big secret to keep."

Edward studied me. I wondered what he saw: A girl with no respect for boundaries? A granddaughter who never bothered to ask questions? "Why do you think she kept it?"

I could have asked him the same thing. "I don't know. I always figured she was . . . sad. Too sad to talk about it."

Noah caught my hand and squeezed it.

Edward lowered his chin to his chest and kept it there for so long I thought he might have drifted off. But then he squared his shoulders and lifted his chin. "When she first arrived, yes. Sad like a cold you couldn't shake. Sad, sickly, frail, eyes too large. Like a persistent shadow, quick to scare away if anyone looked too long at her but always creeping back. She put me off, but Mother said it was tzedakah to take her in, and so we had, and we would be kind to her."

Tzedakah. Charity.

Hearing someone describe O'ma like a character out of a story was strange yet familiar, because I'd always seen her so myself. Except this was a different story than I was used to hearing; this was the lost second act, while I'd only heard the first and third.

Edward looked at Noah. "She was four, maybe five, when she arrived. I used to look at your father when he turned five, and try to imagine him going through what she'd gone through. Separated from her parents. Sent alone to different countries. Housed with a family who didn't speak her language. I can barely remember being younger than five, and she'd already lived an entire lifetime.

"But she grew up straight and sure and—and yes, maybe a little sad at times, but strong, too. She had a core of strength in her. Like polished diamond. I've—I've never seen anything like it."

Listening to this man as he grasped for words to describe a woman he'd known decades ago, at times sure and at times lost, I wanted to ask if he'd loved her. A question you could only ask certain people: friends, yes, but I'd never dare ask my parents, because what if the answer was no? And the answer *couldn't* be no, not the way they parented, as an indisputable team. The question was too much, too personal, the answers too dangerous.

And yet here, with this man who was practically a stranger, I could almost ask. He seemed almost like a character in a story himself, just like O'ma, and I wanted to drink in every word he was willing to spill.

Except he wasn't a character, and he looked so sad right now, and I hardly needed to ask, not when I'd read his letters. (*Don't do anything stupid. I love you.*) And O'ma wasn't a fairy-tale heroine, either. Her story didn't begin and end with the war. To act as though it did shortchanged everything else she'd experienced. Her story was complicated and messy, many stories wrapped in one, with no neat bows.

And right now, I wanted to know this story, with all its cuts and bruises. "How did the two of you . . ."

Edward looked at me again, but this time I didn't think he saw a granddaughter or a delinquent, but someone from the past. He smiled wistfully. "I came back one summer during college and she was here. I'd never paid any attention to her before, but—I don't know. She was pure emotion. She felt so much. I don't think we ever felt so much as when we were young." He blew out a long breath. "We were so young."

I waited for him to say more, but he didn't. "How did you feel?"

He leaned back in his chair and let out a half laugh. "It was so long ago. I don't remember the details so much." He pressed a hand to his heart. "I felt . . . like I'd been standing in a room with no light and she was an incandescent flame. I remember her smile. I remember . . ." He shook his head.

"What?"

He met my gaze. His looked, suddenly, tired. "I remember I cried when she left."

Regret pulsed through me. "I'm sorry."

Edward didn't respond.

Noah hadn't spoken in several minutes, but he'd tightly kept hold of my hand. I glanced at him now, worried he'd be upset about how emotionally his grandfather had spoken about a woman who wasn't his grandmother. Why was it so much easier to talk to strangers rather than family about intimate details? Because strangers judged less? Cared less?

Because we didn't have to worry about damaging carefully constructed family relationships?

I took a deep breath. "Why did she leave?"

"She wanted a job in the city. She wanted her independence. Her parents were gone—I think she felt like a charity case. She *wasn't*. But she felt like one."

"But why—why did you two stop seeing each other?"

"Ah, well." He let out a heavy sigh. "These things happen."

"How?"

He shrugged. "They just do."

All right, apparently it wasn't *always* easier to push with people you didn't know. "Why did she want the necklace back so badly?"

"The necklace." He waved a hand. "What a mess."

"Why?"

He shook his head. "It just was."

"What happened to it?"

Now he started to frown. "It was a difficult situation."

"How come?"

"It was," he said, his voice rising.

"Okay." I'd agitated him too much. "She wanted it back, right? Do you know why?"

His face crumpled, and he looked at his grandson. "Noah."

I put a hand on Noah's arm, as though to keep him from stepping between me and Edward Barbanel. "What happened to the necklace, Mr. Barbanel?"

He shifted in his seat, and his voice came out faster than usual. "It's gone."

"Gone where?" My stomach plummeted. "You sold it?"

"*Noah.*"

Noah hesitated, then nodded. He turned to me. "We should go."

"But *Noah*—"

"Look at him," he whispered harshly. "He's upset. We have to let it go."

I drew back. "Why can't I get a straight answer?"

"Come on." Noah placed his hand above my elbow and directed me out of my chair, steering me toward the door.

I twisted out of his grasp and faced Edward Barbanel. His face was still painfully contorted, visible even as he leaned it into one hand. The fight drained out of me. *We were so young,* he'd said, and yet I couldn't imagine it. I slipped out of the study.

My irritation at Noah didn't fade as easily. "Really, Noah?"

"Abigail, calm down." He followed me down the hall, and we paused, caught in between two walls of cream paint and surrounded by paintings of the sea.

"You tried to physically force me out of the room."

"It wasn't worth a fight."

"What *is* worth a fight, then? I don't get you. You act like you're on my side and ready to confront the family or whatever, but whenever they snap, you jump."

"He's my grandfather." Noah's calm cracked for a moment. "What am I supposed to do?"

"I don't know. I just don't understand why I can't get an answer."

"He's an old man. It was a long time ago. It doesn't matter."

"It mattered to my grandmother!"

"Did it? Because she had a lifetime to follow up and sounds like she never did."

"We have *no idea* what she did or didn't do."

"You're so convinced your grandmother was in the right, but how do you know? How do you know the details we're missing are in her favor?"

I glared at him. He glared right back.

I shook my head. "I should go home."

"Seriously?" If anything, he looked even angrier. "You can't storm away every time you get pissed off."

"Why not? It's a pretty good strategy for preventing blow-out fights."

"We don't have to fight, we could have a discussion—"

"And what are we going to discuss? How you're always going to be a shield for your family?"

"They're my *family*! What do you want me to do?"

"I don't know! Nothing! Protect them, I guess! But it just means we're on different sides, which is *fine*, but it doesn't mean I like it."

He stared at me, then let out a gust of air and pushed his fingers through his hair. "I don't like it, either."

I looked away. "I should call my Uber."

"I should go talk to my grandpa. Try to calm him down."

"Fine." I took a deep breath. "Even though it's not your job to manage your entire family."

He frowned at me, and I lifted my face toward him. Though still mad, I didn't want him to leave.

But he stepped back. "I'll see you later, okay?"

I shrank a little and nodded. "Okay."

I forced a smile and a stupid wave and went outside to call my ride. I sat on the porch steps and turned my face up toward the moon, sucking in deep breaths of the heady summer medley. What was I doing? Forcing confrontations and getting into fights. Maybe the necklace really didn't matter. Maybe I should be focused on what made *me* happy.

But O'ma had wanted her necklace back so badly.

The door sounded behind me and I jumped up, hope unspooling in my chest. It drained away when I saw Helen stepping onto the porch. "Hi, Mrs. Barbanel." I cleared my throat. "Um, thanks for having me."

She said nothing.

Jeez. Had all the Barbanels taken a class in intimidation through silence? I jerked my thumb over my shoulder, because apparently I turned into a cartoon from the fifties when nervous. "My car should be here in eight minutes."

In the fading light I couldn't make out her expression. "You asked my husband about a necklace."

Word traveled fast at Golden Doors. "I did, yeah."

"It's none of your business, but if you must know, he gave her that necklace." Her words were clipped. "He gave her everything, and she gave him nothing."

"What?" I blinked, trying to fit this new piece of information into the history of events. If Edward gave Ruth the necklace, why would she be demanding it back?

"He gave her the necklace, then took it back, and she was furious."

"What—why did he take it back?"

"They broke up. It didn't belong to her."

Could you simply take gifts back when you broke up with someone? Maybe. I hadn't even considered the idea of the necklace being a gift; I'd been so sure it belonged to O'ma. I'd thought it was a family heirloom, perhaps, brought with her from Germany. If it wasn't? If it was a necklace Edward had given her in the first place? Then maybe my digging into its history wasn't as appropriate as I'd thought. Maybe I didn't have a case at all.

Let it go.

I pictured the sparkling pendants dangling around O'ma's neck in the photo. It had been a romantic, beautiful dream, a lost necklace, a grandmother's legacy. In my head, my grandmother had always been the heroine of this story, but maybe Noah was right. Maybe there were other interpretations. What was Helen Barbanel's story? A young woman whose fiancé ignored her but married her anyway.

How much had I even really known O'ma, as a person instead of as my grandmother? Why was I so convinced she'd been in the right—simply because we shared blood? Was blood enough of a reason to back someone?

"Why—do you know why they broke up?" I asked.

"She met some other boy." Helen Barbanel looked me up and down. "Your grandfather, I suspect. He worked at a bagel shop."

I felt like I'd been kicked. Of course. What a convoluted web. And what a simple reason. She decided to marry someone else, and had to give back a gift, and didn't want to.

I looked up at the moon, feeling a little sick. "I'm sorry if this has all brought up a past you would have rather kept buried. I didn't mean to be trouble."

When she looked at me, her expression was unforgiving. "No one ever does."

Nineteen

November 19, 1953

I've accidentally landed a job! On Wednesday, I walked inside a bagel shop to order breakfast and entered a madhouse instead. People were shouting and covered in flour and someone kept yelling for the cornmeal and I saw it on a shelf behind him, but no one would give it to the poor man, and finally I couldn't help it, I walked right behind the counter and handed it over.

Afterwards he kept giving me tasks to do, cutting and wash-ing things and pummeling the dough and flipping bagels as they boiled, and eventually someone asked who I was and he said to her, very aren't-you-an-idiot, "This is Saul's daughter, she's come to help us for a while." I should have said something, but it was nice to be called someone's daughter. And then someone asked me my name and I said Michal, which I thought witty, but everyone nodded, and there's nothing worse than making a joke and having it fall flat.

Except later, after everything settled down, one young man said, "And is your husband's name David?" and I laughed and we started talking and I admitted I'd actually wandered off the street. He laughed but I could tell he was embarrassed by the way his ears went red (he has very large ears). So he introduced me, properly this time, to the man who thought I was Saul's daughter, who wasn't embarrassed at all and offered me a job on the spot.

felt horrible the next day, horrible for pushing Noah, for how my conversations with Helen and Edward Barbanel went, for deciding to come to this island in the first place. I composed half a dozen texts to Noah during my shift at the Prose Garden, but didn't send a single one. At lunchtime, I went down to the docks with a sandwich and ate it woefully as I regarded the boats.

Surprise replaced woe when I opened my email and saw a response from one of the many emails I'd sent earlier in the week. By now, I knew better than to get my hopes up, but knowledge doesn't necessarily correlate with emotions, and my heart beat a little bit faster as I clicked on the message from the French organization Mémorial de la Shoah.

July 26

Dear Mlle Schoenberg,

Thank you for your email. It looks as though your grandmother came through Paris and left, bound for New York, on the *SS Babette*. We have included the records of her passage below.

My breath caught. I stared at my phone; then my gaze slowly drifted higher, toward a boat coming into the harbor, then higher still to a triangle of gulls flying in formation. Just like that, here it was. They'd pulled her names from the records, found her ship, had the data my mom and I hadn't had for our entire lives.

The *SS Babette*.

I opened the attached PDF. There: *Ruth Goldman, née 7 avril 1934.* It listed the ship's date and berth of both departure and arrival.

I wasn't even sure what I'd do with this information yet, but I could do *something*. If O'ma had been on this ship, maybe other

Kindertransport kids had been, too. Maybe people who were still alive, who'd known O'ma.

SS Babette, I googled. The first option linked to a wiki article on the ship itself; I amended the search to "*SS Babette* passenger list" and still landed four million results. Luckily, three out of the first four led to searchable archives, and one of the three let me download the ship's passenger list for free.

I impatiently skimmed through the list for the Gs. There her name was, smack in between *Frederick Godfrey* and *Jean Guerrant.*

I scrolled back up to the first name on the list. *Gemma Allenson.*

And I started googling, name after name after name.

I looked up the passengers on the *SS Babette* during every second of downtime I had on my shift, then for hours after, curled up on Mrs. Henderson's sofa with Ellie Mae by my side. I read LinkedIn pages and Wikipedia articles and obituaries and wedding announcements. Many of the passengers weren't easy to find, or had little or no information. But some had information.

And some were Jewish.

When I pulled my list, I emailed Dr. Weisz, on the off chance she'd have other ideas. Then I let out a huge breath and closed my laptop. It was past eleven; Jane and Mrs. Henderson had both come home and gone to bed. With one hand curled in Ellie Mae's fur, I pulled over my phone, hoping to see a text I'd somehow missed from Noah.

Nothing.

All right. Cool. Now what? Maybe I *should* take more risks. Be bold. Show some chutzpah.

Not, like, *huge* risks, but a teensy little risk wouldn't hurt. An olive branch. An indication of interest.

A corgi dressed like a sailor.

Me:

Here's a picture of a corgi dressed like a sailor

Noah:

How is the hat staying on

Where did you find said corgi

Me:

On the docks

He faced off against a seagull and emerged victorious.

Noah:

He's half the size of a seagull

Me:

Right??

Also I'm sorry about getting stressed last night

Also I talked to your grandmother after I went outside

Noah:

Er

Why?

Me:

She came out

And told me Edward actually gave Ruth the necklace originally

So that's a thing

Noah:

Wow

Really?

Me:

Yeah

Also, Ruth broke up with Edward to marry my grandfather

Noah:

Whoa

On the other hand

Maybe they were madly in love

If it makes you feel better

Me:

Lol I hope so

Or at least had better power dynamics

Noah:

?

Me:

The disparity in wealth thing

So

I feel bad about all of this? Can I make it up to you
by buying you ice cream tomorrow

Noah:

You realize you already owe me two ice creams

Me:

I had no cash!!

Noah:

I will accept three ice creams

But tomorrow's supposed to be nice, actually,
so I'm thinking of sailing

Me:

Monday then? I'll tell you the latest developments
in the Girl from Germany story

Noah:

Abigail.

I meant let's go sailing *instead* of getting ice cream

I wore the tiny red bikini.

"Is it too much?" I asked Jane the next morning, standing in front of our mirror. "Like, am I going to fall out of this?"

"Don't make any sudden movements. Or dive. No diving or you'll lose the bottoms."

"I'll stay very still."

"And you're *sure* you're not cousins?"

"I hate you."

I checked my email on the way to the yacht club, anxious for a response from Dr. Weisz—or maybe I was just anxious all over. I hadn't had time to process everything that had happened at Golden Doors. When Noah had said I drove him crazy. The conversation with his grandfather.

The moment in the window alcove.

I wasn't sure if Noah would want to talk about the alcove, or about our arguments, or not talk at all. I couldn't tell if this meant something, inviting me to be alone on the water with him, when aloneness and nature were two things he prized so highly. What was in my head and what actually existed? Was he waiting for me to make a gesture of interest, or was I reading things unwritten?

Luckily, Dr. Weisz *had* written, and her words were plenty distracting:

Hi Abigail,

Good digging! I had an additional thought—while the other passengers might have already passed away, it might be worth cross-checking their names against this collection of oral histories from survivors. If any of them left a testimonial, they might mention your grandmother or where they went afterward—and if they're also part of the American Kindertransport, they might share a similar path as your grandmother.

If any of the passengers did leave testimonies, you do unfortunately have to visit, in person, one of the institutions with access to the records (you can find the list of institutions, mostly colleges, here). The closest to Nantucket are Boston University, Harvard, and Brandeis—if you do come to Boston, I'd be happy to meet up (and some of these universities might actually require you to be an affiliate in order to gain access, and I could definitely bring you in as a guest).

I was so excited I almost ran over a tourist. Then I spent the rest of my walk plugging in the names of the Jewish passengers

I'd discovered—and all the other passengers as well, for good measure.

And lo and behold, two passengers *had* left oral records: Else Friedhoff and Michael Saltzman.

When I reached the yacht club, I ran right up to Noah. "Guess what I got!"

He raised his brows. "Gold? A winning lottery ticket?"

"Passenger records!"

"What? For your grandmother?"

And we easily fell back into our rhythm, as though we hadn't fought at all, as though I hadn't told him we were on opposite sides.

Noah directed the sailboat with long-practiced ease. It would be August in two days, and I felt like I existed in a snow globe of summer, the glitter of sun scattered everywhere, and heat baking into my bones. Noah stood against the sky, listening, strikingly handsome. We were alone in the world, the two of us. As I finished talking, I could feel my heart pounding in my throat. I felt so light and tight with nerves my mind might break away from my body and float into the blue, blue sky.

And Noah was smiling. "So you're basically Sherlock Holmes."

"Exactly, my dear Watson." I licked my lips, then felt embarrassed. "Unfortunately, it's yet another archive where you have to go in person. Why have digital recordings you can't transfer digitally?"

"Would Dr. Weisz be willing to listen to them?"

I made a face. "I thought about asking, but they're upwards of five hours."

"You could go to Boston."

I shot him a quick glance. Boston, where he'd be in a month for school. "I could."

A silence fell. I looked around us, at the water and sky. We were a speck of humanity, just two people, and yet we carried so many emotions with us.

"I brought lunch." Noah lifted a cooler and canvas bag out of the storage. Then, in a move I should have expected due to the heat, he stripped off his T-shirt and tossed it aside before sitting across from me.

"You did?" Oh god. Where did I look? Why was I having so much trouble breathing? I was like a Victorian heroine, ready to faint. Was it kosher to stare at his chest? I swallowed hard and looked down at the canvas bag.

He lifted out a baguette, Brie, grapes, and chocolate. "I hope it's okay."

"It's perfect." Like him. Okay. I needed to get a hold of myself. "Friday was intense."

Noah tore off a hunk of bread, and handed it to me. "Yeah."

"Was your grandpa okay when you went back in to talk to him?"

"He—" Noah hesitated. "You know how you said your grandma didn't like to talk about her childhood? He's the same. He shut down. My grandmother was there when I went back, but she left—you said she came and talked to you?"

His hand brushed mine as he passed me the Brie knife. I suppressed a shiver. "Yeah. I've been trying to figure it out—I don't know why anyone would give someone a gift, then ask for it back, but it's not such a big deal, I guess. Not as big a deal as if it was a family heirloom."

Noah was quiet a moment, opening the fig jam, spreading it methodically over his bread and cheese. "Maybe it was a family heirloom. Just not yours."

"What?"

"Maybe it was *my* family's heirloom. And Edward gave it to Ruth, but then when they broke up, took it back."

I was already shaking my head. "Why would she demand it back, then?"

"I don't know. But why else would he take back a gift?"

"Wouldn't he have mentioned if it was a family heirloom? And then he'd still have it, instead of it being gone."

"True. Maybe he wanted to avoid talking about it, because it brought back too many memories."

We paused, stumped, under the hot sun, smearing more Brie and fig jam across the white interior of our baguettes.

"I should ask my grandma," Noah said, almost more to himself than to me. "She should know."

"She certainly seemed more willing to talk about it than your grandfather was."

"And maybe it wasn't an heirloom," Noah said. "But maybe, if he bought it for Ruth, if it was expensive, he still thought he could take it back if they weren't going to be together."

"Maybe," I said. I wanted to follow up and say, *And maybe they were lying,* because part of me *knew* the necklace had belonged to O'ma, how could it not have, how could I have come to Nantucket searching for a necklace of no importance?

But I tried to calm myself down. To remember O'ma didn't have to be perfect. And besides, I wanted more than a fancy necklace. I wanted her past. And I was getting closer. Maybe I *would* go to Boston. "Are you excited? About being in Boston next year?"

"Cambridge, technically."

I rolled my eyes. "*I* know. I'm the one who's actually *from* Massachusetts."

He laughed. "True. Does western Massachusetts count, though?"

I sat up straighter. "Excuse me? What does *that* mean?"

He raised his hands. "Not in a bad way! I was thinking about sports. Doesn't western Mass cheer for New York teams?" He grinned. "A good thing, since we have better teams."

Okay. Wow. I drew my spine up as straight as it could go, the top of my head reaching toward the cloudless sky. "Excuse *you*."

"Am I wrong?"

"About literally everything in those statements."

He sounded amused. "I didn't think you were a sports person."

"I am a *Massachusetts* person."

His lips twitched. "Okay, but you can't deny the Patriots suck."

"One, I *can*, and two, I'm not having this conversation with you."

"Why?" He openly grinned now. "Because you don't actually have a defense?"

"Because people from New York will be mean about us no matter what, so it's not worth engaging."

"I didn't realize you had the Boston chip on your shoulder."

"I don't have a chip."

"Inferiority complex, then."

I picked up the remaining half of the baguette and struck him in the shoulder.

"Ow!" Laughter spilled out of him, bright as the sunlight on the water. "Violence!"

"You *maligned* my home!"

He fell backward on the boat, all mirth. "You're ridiculous."

"You take back your vicious insults."

He grinned. "Make me."

I launched myself at him. We tussled. I landed half on top of him, and he grabbed my wrists, trapping them between our chests.

I became very, very aware of all his exposed skin and how close our faces were to each other.

God, he was beautiful. Beautiful and interesting and way too complicated and intense and I could not keep up with him, nope, not at all.

His eyes focused on mine, liquid pools of dark brown, rich and warm as chestnuts in color, as bright and deep as emeralds or rubies. The black of his pupils exercised as much gravity as a black hole.

I didn't have the energy—or the desire—to fight this anymore. Maybe it would be a mess. But I didn't care. God, I didn't care.

He swallowed, then sat up so quickly I half fell off him. "Do you want to go for a swim?"

A swim. When I'd been about to throw myself at him. Well, my entire body blazed like I'd been scalded by fire, so I could probably use a cooldown. Did we depict Cupid with a bow and arrow because infatuation felt as painful as being shot?

Good lord, liking Noah had turned me into the kind of person with worse analogies than eleven-year-old Ginny Weasley.

"Swimming. Yes." Maybe he'd attribute the red of my cheeks to the sun. "It's pretty hot."

Now all I had to do was remove my clothes and bare the tiny bikini.

Avoiding Noah's gaze, I peeled my shirt over my head and dropped it lightly on the bench. Then I unbuttoned my shorts and slowly stepped out of them.

Raising my gaze to his took all my willpower. My cheeks felt like miniature suns had embedded themselves. Good lord, I was practically naked. Thank god the bikini top had enough lining I didn't need to worry about other troublesome situations.

Noah's eyes were dark, his body still. The breeze ruffled his curls, but the space between us felt thick and weighty. I could feel my heart slowing down and thumping hard against my rib cage. I could feel the very flow of my blood in my chest.

We were surrounded by all the air in the world and I couldn't breathe.

He swallowed. "Do you need any sunscreen?"

If he touched me, I would spontaneously combust. "I put some on already."

"Cool." He turned away and dived off the side of the boat.

I gaped after him. Wait! What if I changed my mind? What if I *did* want his help with sunscreen? What if I decided to be brave? To take the risk?

Oh god, I couldn't.

But didn't he even want to *look*? Wasn't he interested in this teeny-tiny bikini?

Or maybe he was *too* interested.

Okay, no, I was getting ahead of myself. I didn't need to read every little detail as Noah secretly being wild with lust/love for me.

(Though maybe he *was*??)

He surfaced, water sluicing over him, dragging his curls flat against his head. "Come in. It's great."

I stepped up onto the boat's edge, raised my arms into a bow, bent my knees, and launched myself skyward. My body curved through the air, then dove beneath the surface. Cold water submerged my body in one clean, satisfying sweep.

And the ocean peeled my bikini bottoms down and away.

Shit.

Shit shit shit shit.

My eyelids flung open, then immediately shut at the sting of the ocean. I'd never been able to open my eyes underwater. Kicking upward, I broke the surface, sputtering and coughing, salt everywhere. "I lost my bottoms!"

"What?" Noah treaded water, eyes wide.

"My bikini bottoms! They came off. They—they weren't very secure."

He started, honest to god, *cackling*.

"Don't laugh!" I would have shoved him if we were closer, but you couldn't pay me to go within ten feet of him, despite the opacity of the water. "This is terrible!"

"Okay. Okay." He caught his breath. "Don't panic, we can find them."

"I can literally never leave the ocean. I'm doomed. I live here now."

He laughed again, this time so hard he had to paddle over to the boat and grab the side of it so he could expel his amusement without drowning.

"I hate you," I told him, with no little sincerity.

"I know. I'm so sorry."

"I can't open my eyes underwater."

"Okay. Don't worry. I'm going under."

"Don't look!"

He shot me a wry expression—obviously he'd *have* to—before gulping in air and diving. I scurried backward, much as one could scurry in the water.

He reemerged, dashing water from his eyes and hair. "Sorry. Nothing. Let me try again."

"Noah—"

But he'd already vanished.

He dove a third time, but we both knew it was hopeless. I sighed mournfully. "This is the first time I ever even wore that bikini."

"Really?" He grinned. "What inspired you to wear it?"

I splashed water at him from a good fifteen feet away. "Get over yourself."

He laughed. "Okay. Well, you have your shorts, right?"

"And I have underwear." Embarrassingly, I went red *again*. Apparently I couldn't even mention something utterly mundane without blushing.

"I'll turn my back when you get on the boat and you can put them on."

"Swear to god you won't look, Noah Barbanel."

"I swear. I swear so hard." He was laughing again as he held up three fingers. "Scout's honor."

I climbed up the boat's ladder, face blazing hot, and wrapped my towel around my waist. I dug the underwear I'd brought with me for post-beach wear out of my bag, and quickly pulled them and my shorts back on.

"Besides," he shouted as I changed. "It's not like I haven't seen you naked before."

"Noah!" I yelped. "You did not!"

"No—you're right—" He could barely speak for laughing. "I didn't."

It was amazing, though, how different this was than the night weeks ago when I'd gone skinny-dipping, when I was mortified about the idea of him catching me naked because I didn't want to feel vulnerable. I would have done *anything* then to keep him from seeing me, even swum to the opposite side of the pond, as I'd half joked to Jane.

But now—

Now keeping my clothes *on* felt way more difficult.

"You're good," I called to him, and two broad strokes brought Noah to the boat. He closed his hands around the ladder and half hoisted himself out of the water. He draped his forearms casually over the top of the rails. Droplets streamed down his body, causing him to glitter like a diamond. He grinned at me, eyes bright and hair straightened by the weight of water. "Now what?"

"Now what, what?"

He swung himself into the boat. "I'd thought we'd swim a bit, get some exercise . . . now what are we going to do?"

Would my cheeks ever not be red again? "Well, I have no idea."

"No?" He picked up a towel, rubbing it through his hair and down his body. Good *lord*. "None?"

I swallowed. I didn't need exercise, because I wasn't going to have a body after I spontaneously combusted from sheer lust. "None."

"Okay, then." He slung the towel around his shoulders and sat down cross-legged. "This is my favorite thing to do."

"Go out on the water?"

He nodded, leaning back on his hands. "I'm not really religious, but I think—this is what I find the most moving. What I want to save. When I was a kid and I came to Nantucket, I loved it so much, because it was just me and the stars and the sea and I didn't have to be hemmed in by buildings and I could be totally, completely alone. Even in Central Park, you're never really alone. It's different now, there's the weight of the family and what I'm supposed to do and I'm not oblivious anymore, there's the whole history of Nantucket and the British taking it from the Wampanoag, and I can't pretend it's all nice, but the *nature* . . ." He shook his head, as though robbed for words.

"You do seem more relaxed."

He shot me a half smile. "Weirdly, I find you relaxing."

I grinned back at him. "Why is that weird? I'm *very* relaxing."

"No." He shook his head with, perhaps, an insulting amount of certainty. "You shouldn't be. You're hyper and nosy and aggravating. But. You're real. I never have to pretend anything with you."

"I wouldn't want you to," I said, not sure whether to be insulted or complimented. "I *might* want something a little nicer than 'aggravating' though."

"Do you?" His gaze caught mine. When I flushed, he smiled to himself, and looked up at the sky. "When should we go to Boston?"

"*What?*"

"To listen to the recordings."

"We?"

He shrugged. "You're seventeen, right? I'm eighteen. You need to be eighteen for most hotels or Airbnbs."

Boston.

An overnight.

Noah.

"You can't be serious." Traveling with a boy—alone with a boy—seemed incredibly intimate. And adult. I hadn't even traveled alone with my friends anywhere. Traveling with *Noah* . . .

"Why not?"

"Wouldn't your parents be fazed? By us traveling together?"

"It's not the kind of thing they usually have a say in."

"How can they not have a say?"

"You've noticed their lack of parenting skills, right?"

"I sort of thought your mom might have opinions . . ."

"Mom's busy keeping Shira in check. Besides, they decided a few years ago I'm old enough to make my own decisions." He cocked his head. "Unless you don't want me to come with you?"

I swallowed a hysterical laugh. "I want you to come with me."

I couldn't believe I'd *said* that. I couldn't believe any of this. An army of butterflies had taken up residence in my stomach.

"Okay, then, it's settled. When?"

"I can ask for two days off next week. Maggie and Liz are pretty flexible."

"Nice. And it's not a long flight."

"I'm not going to *fly*."

"Why not? It's quick."

"It's expensive. It's just as easy to take the ferry and the train from Hyannis to Boston."

"Cool, so we'll take the ferry."

Traveling together. A night at an apartment. Maybe I was reading this wrong, because until people said things out loud, nothing could be sure. But I was pretty certain we were thinking the same thing here. I was pretty sure a trip together to Boston might have more consequences than listening to several recordings.

And I was pretty sure I wanted it to.

Summer of chutzpah.

Twenty

The sun blazed across the water, bleaching the world of color. I'd paired contacts with my sepia-toned sunglasses, which made the world look like I'd used a nostalgia-inducing filter on it. The sunglasses' oversized shape made me feel like Audrey Hepburn.

Noah and I claimed two seats on the ferry's top deck. I scrunched my hair up on the top of my head and pulled it up in a messy bun so the constant wind wouldn't whip strands into my eyes and mouth. "Want to know a really terrifying theory my roomie had?"

"Yes." He angled himself toward me.

"Okay. So." I took a deep breath. "She thought maybe Edward and Ruth met up later in life and had an affair. Resulting in my mom."

"What?" His brows arched and a tiny smile pulled at his mouth.

"Yup."

"So—" He started laughing. "Wait, so . . ."

"Yep."

"Wow. Well." His smirk broadened. "I'm sure you'd be welcomed into the family."

"Unless I tried to take over the business."

"True." He tilted his head. "You didn't actually *believe* . . ."

I turned bright red. "I considered it."

"That we were cousins?" He let out a whoop of laughter.

Then I did, too. "I know! I didn't really believe it, but it lurked in the back of my mind. It seemed like a totally valid possibility."

"Jesus, I'd hope not."

"Right?"

"Right."

We stared at each other. My breath caught.

"So," Noah said slowly. "Since you know we're not . . ."

"Noah? Noah Barbanel? Look at you!" A middle-aged women crossed the deck, beaming. "What a nice surprise."

Noah closed his eyes briefly, then turned toward the newcomer with a polite smile. "Hi, Ms. Green."

Honestly, was there a conspiracy to keep me and Noah from concluding a romantic moment?

We spent the rest of the ferry ride talking to Ms. Green, a Barbanel family friend. From Hyannis, we caught the Cape Flyer to Boston's South Station, and then the Red Line whisked us to Harvard Square, that bastion of red brick and ivy.

We'd booked an apartment behind the Cambridge public library, a fifteen-minute walk from the train station in Harvard Square. We emerged from the subterranean metro into a bustling area filled with bookshops and restaurants, crowded with busloads of tourists and students who traveled in packs. We strolled along brick sidewalks until we'd left the heart of the square and traveled up quieter streets, past stately Victorians and small parks. Lush gardens fronted the homes, some carefully tended, others chaotic riots of color and lush green.

"I think this is it." I looked up at a narrow town house, pale yellow with white fringe. We'd made it to the apartment. The apartment for just me and Noah.

Ahhh.

Mom had originally been appalled I planned to spend a night

alone with a boy. I'd thought about not telling her about the Boston trip—thought *really hard* about not telling her—but keeping a secret from her would be worse than dealing with her shock. After a quick round of her telling me about safe sex and me yelling, *Mom, we haven't even kissed,* we calmed down, and she moved into a "please don't drink/do drugs/get abducted" spiel, which I vastly preferred.

I'd told Niko and Haley and Jane about the trip, too, and their suggestions had been diametrically opposed to my mother's. And Jane had told me if we didn't at least make out, I was canceled.

We punched in the code and opened the front door, also painted yellow with a frosted glass window. A narrow staircase brought us to the top of the house and into a third-floor apartment filled with light and plants. Two bedrooms lay on either side of the central living room, and a tiny kitchen and bathroom were off it.

"Do you have a preference?" Noah asked.

A preference. Did I have a preference about the room I slept in, in the apartment which also had a boy in it. No, I did not, because my brain was too busy with other things like *the boy in the apartment.*

"This one's fine." I tossed my bag in one room, with a wall of books and a painting of the Boston skyline, with the Prudential and Hancock towers and Citgo sign. "Should we head over?"

"Let's."

Back we went down the red brick sidewalks, until the houses turned into stores and people replaced the gardens. A bakery piped out the scent of freshly baked bread in the center of the square, and we turned into it exactly on time for our meeting.

"There." I nodded across the café at a woman who matched the photo we'd found. Dr. Genevieve Weisz wore jeans and a T-shirt and looked like she needed a nap, despite clutching a thermos to her chest with the desperation of a toddler clinging to her blankie. We headed toward her, and I was surprised to find I was nervous. I cleared my throat. "Dr. Weisz?"

She looked up and smiled. "Abby?"

"Hi." I did an awkward wave, then realized she was an adult, so I stuck out my hand.

She shook it firmly, then Noah's. "Let's go order."

We wound up with a spread of pastries, while I got a hot chocolate and Noah an iced coffee. Dr. Weisz added an espresso to the order, clearly afraid her cup might runneth dry.

It was lucky Dr. Weisz had already claimed a table, because people packed the place. Most of them looked a few years older than me— college students, which made sense, with the school right across the street. There was a scattering of adults with laptops, even though it was three o'clock on a Thursday. Dr. Weisz slid her own computer into a backpack, then shoveled in several papers as well. "How was your trip in?"

"Great. Thanks for meeting us." I nudged Noah, unable to stop picturing him walking these streets, studying in this café. "Noah's going to be here next year, actually."

"Really? What are you studying?"

"Um." He glanced at me, and the words he said next came out fumbling and awkward, which I wasn't used to from him. "Econ, but I think—I might take a few biodiversity classes."

I blinked rapidly and smiled at him.

I tried a chocolate croissant as they talked about the college, closing my eyes as the layers of buttery dough and thick bar of dark chocolate melted on my tongue. *Mm. Delicious.* When they'd covered enough ground to be polite, I leaned forward. "What about you? How did you end up studying Kindertransport?"

"My grandmother was part of the British Kindertransport effort," she said. "Which I thought I'd do my thesis on, but when I looked into it, I became curious about whether America had a similar situation."

"It didn't, right?" I glanced at Noah. "Rabbi Abrams gave us the general explanation about Kindertransport, and it sounded like it was less organized here."

"Right." She inhaled a gulp of coffee from her thermos. "In the UK and Europe, Kindertransport got around ten thousand Jewish children out of Nazi-occupied countries, but the States shot down a similar bill. Kids need to be housed and fed and schooled, and the government didn't want to pay. In British Kindertransport, private organizations had to agree to sponsor the kids so they wouldn't be a financial burden."

"Wait," I said, slightly confused. "So if British Kindertransport wasn't about supporting the kids, what even was it?"

"Basically expediting visas and legally allowing more kids to enter the country, all at once. Applying for immigration was messy and expensive. You needed documents, the documents cost money, they expired, you had to get them again—you needed a sponsor so you wouldn't be a financial burden—you needed ship tickets and interviews with the US State Department." She shrugged. "The UK expedited the process so the Kindertransport children could enter, but the US didn't. So people simply didn't have the money to come here."

"But they did, somehow, right?" I said. "Because there *was* some sort of American Kindertransport?"

"Right. Individuals pooled their resources. The German Jewish Children's Aid association brought over two hundred and fifty young German Jews in 1934. Then they brought over children fleeing the Blitz, a wave of kids from Central Europe helped by the French *Oeuvre de Secours aux Enfants*, and kids from Spain and Portugal."

"And they were all placed with families?" *Like O'ma.*

"Pretty much. Though American law, unlike European, stated foster kids had to be placed with families of their own religion. At first, there weren't really enough Jewish families to go around, and people were nervous to advertise publicly because of anti-Semitism. Orthodox families did try to volunteer, but the Children's Bureau often wouldn't qualify them because their homes were too crowded."

"I'd think it would be better to live in a crowded house than no house," I said.

"Bureaucracy is filled with red tape. Luckily, families heard about the program through word of mouth and opened up their homes." She nodded at Noah. "And look at what a difference what a single person, what a single family can make. His grandfather's family took in your grandmother, right? And here you are."

Here I was.

Harvard's Widener Library presided over part of Harvard Yard. Dozens of steps led up to the Corinthian columns fronting the red brick structure. Dr. Weisz walked us inside. "There's over three and a half million books here," she said. "And five miles of aisles."

Clearly I wasn't the only one with a library/book obsession.

She got us set up at the listening stations, and helped us find the two recordings by the people who'd been on the same ship as my grandmother. "Let me know if you find anything out," she said. "I hope you do."

After she left, Noah and I plugged in our headphones and looked at each other. Noah nodded. "Let's do this."

We pressed play.

At some point during the recordings, Noah took my hand. I

glanced at him, and found him staring at the ceiling, while he idly ran his thumb across my palm.

I supposed that was the thing about Noah. I didn't have to explain anything to him. I didn't have to tell him I would like a hand to hold right now. I didn't have to explain how I was feeling, because he had the same emotions tied up inside of him, too.

Two hours into Michael Saltzman's recitation of his life, he described the ship from Paris to New York. I perked up, but the description was over in a moment, and he didn't mention anything about my grandmother. Instead, I listened to him talk about being separated from his older brother and sent off to distant relatives in California, none of whom spoke German, while he didn't speak English. He liked the palm trees, though.

Twenty minutes later, Noah's head jerked up. "I think I have something."

"Really?" I paused Michael's recording. "What?"

"Here." He set the recording back a minute and we both put an earbud in. "Ready?"

I nodded, and a warm, scratchy voice filled my ear, coated in a thick German accent. "—a girl named Ruth attached to me early on at the église in Paris. She was four years old and from a town close to mine. She was a quiet thing, and used to watch me closely. I think she missed her parents very much, and half expected everyone else to leave her, too. That was the first time I realized I had to be strong for other people. I had to take care of this little girl because no one else would, and I was older than her and a stand in for an adult. We were together on the SS Babette, which took us from Paris to New York in one week. Some of the actual adults were terribly seasick, but we never were. It was wonderful. I'd never been on a boat before. It felt like a vacation.

"The German Jewish Children's Aid society placed Ruth and me and

a few of the other kids in the Holtzman House in New York until families
could be found to take us. We were there together for a few weeks, but I
don't remember what happened to her. I suppose a family took her in,
but I just remember her following me around, ghostlike, and then her
being gone. I remember thinking—you don't learn how much you'll miss
people until it's too late.

"Anyway, the Holtzman House wasn't a bad place to be, even if it was
packed. I was fifteen, not so appealing to families, and I wanted to get a
job and live my own life . . ."

We listened for a few more minutes, but she didn't mention O'ma
again. I paused the recording and looked at Noah. I could feel how
wide my eyes were, feel the adrenaline coursing through my body. "I
didn't really think we'd find anything."

"But it's her. It has to be, right?"

"It has to be. Ruth. The *SS Babette*. Four years old." I shook my
head. "I can't imagine having to take care of *myself*, not to mention a
little kid. And thinking it was like a vacation."

"Kids are resilient. And it probably was, compared to what they'd
been through already."

"True." I blew out a breath. "Okay. So. What do we think 'a town
close to mine' means?"

"She said where she was from in the beginning—let's find it."

The woman, Else Friedhoff, came from Hamburg. We looked it up
and studied the map on my phone. Hamburg lay northwest of Berlin,
not far from Denmark, a port city on the confluence of three rivers.
Dozens of names of smaller towns doted the map around it, many of
them coastal: Bremen, Lüneburg, Schwerin, Lübeck, Cuxhaven. "So
she's from northern Germany."

"It's a start."

"Definitely a start."

We emerged from the library into the early evening, with the sun still high and the sky still blue. In the yard, tourists took pictures on the library steps while students lay beneath tall trees. We passed through an arch in one of the walls surrounding the school and reentered the bustling square. Our arms swung gently between us, our hands occasionally grazing as we crossed one final street onto the embankment with a boathouse and paths in either direction. We walked to the right, past long reeds edging the banks and geese waddling about.

A small pedestrian bridge arched over the Charles, and we climbed to the middle, looking out. Long banks edged the water, lush with greenery, and colorful domes rose against the skyline. Noah leaned against the wide stone rail. "My dad used to take us here to see the regatta each fall. He rowed for Harvard."

"So you're a legacy?"

His mouth turned up humorlessly. "Yeah."

"I don't suppose he expects you to row, too?"

This time some wryness permeated his expression. "Nailed it."

"Do you want to?"

He glanced back at the water, at the next bridge painted against the sky. "I want him to be proud of me. And he loved rowing. He loves the regatta. He's always so happy when we come here."

We were silent. I didn't know how to comfort someone about their difficult paternal relationship. But maybe the point wasn't for me to comfort him; maybe the point was simply for me to listen.

"I think he tried really hard to fit in," Noah said. "Maybe I do, too. And I think he does want me to be happy, theoretically. But he thinks this will make me happy in the long run—the college, the company, everything."

"And do you?"

He shook his head. "I don't know."

For several minutes, we leaned against the railing in silence, watching the sailboats and rowboats moving along the river. "I had an idea," I finally said. "I looked up the Arboretum after the rabbi mentioned it. Why don't we check it out?"

He looked wary. "Abigail . . ."

"What? You like plants. There are plants there. I like plants, too! It'll be great."

He shook his head but couldn't contain a smile. "You're ridiculous."

"But also convincing? It's supposed to be *really* pretty."

"But also convincing."

We caught a Lyft across the river and down through Boston, passing large, stately houses and circling a giant pond before pulling up to the Arboretum. In the most basic of terms, it was a park—but unlike any city park I'd visited before. It covered hundreds of acres, and was filled with meandering paths and endless, giant trees and shrubbery.

We meandered first to terraced gardens, where vines climbed up trellises, then followed signs pointing along to a bonsai garden. "Pretty sure these aren't bonsai," I said as we passed yet another sign leading us to a row of evergreens.

"It's supposed to be one of the best collections in the US," Noah said. "We'll probably notice it."

"Are you an expert on bonsai, too?"

He laughed. His enthusiasm was endearing, the way he admired the plants the way I did Ellie Mae. "No, but it's impossible not to think they're cool. Here!"

We'd reached a hexagonal shade house. The walls opened to the elements, and a walkway ran around the interior. We walked, counterclockwise, peering close to read the signs and admire the miniature trees. "This one is a Hinoki cypress," I said. "Over two hundred years old."

Noah leaned a little closer to see it, and a soft voice piped out "*Please KEEP BACK* from the trees."

He jumped back and looked at me guiltily, as though he'd hoped I hadn't seen him leap. I started giggling. "So much for a bonsai heist."

Next, we walked through the rest of the park, wandering up hills and past massive trees. At the farthest end from where we'd entered lay the highest point of the park, a gentle hill with a view of the Boston skyline. Noah and I dropped down on a plank of stone. To our left, a man took pictures of a woman as she posed; to our right, two men played with a dog.

"You could work here," I said. "Harvard runs it. You could take classes here."

He nodded. Obviously this wasn't news to him, but I thought maybe he'd actually begun to consider it as an option.

The park closed with the setting sun, and by then, we'd worked up an appetite. We ate at a Cuban place recommended earlier by our driver. It was ten by the time we arrived back at our Airbnb. Late enough to be a reasonable hour for bed.

Instead, we sat on the couch. Nervous energy ricocheted throughout me. Now what? Surely we weren't *actually* going to go to bed.

Here was the thing. I totally, absolutely, one hundred percent wanted to hook up with Noah Barbanel. I wanted to so badly it hurt. My longing for him twisted up my insides and shortened my breaths and made my very lungs ache.

And yet. The transitional period, going from not making out *to* making out, seemed so utterly terrifying, so fraught with potential rejection, I thought I might rather jump off a bridge than face it.

Niko said this state of not-kissing got better with practice. She said eventually, you became such an expert you could sense the way kisses fell like commas in sentences; the silence before them, the expectation in the air.

I hadn't reached that point.

Noah shifted on the couch. "Do you want to watch something?"

No. I did not want to watch something. I wanted to make out with him.

"Sure," I said, because god forbid I communicate like an adult.

He switched on the TV and we found the first episode of a show we'd both been talking about trying, and turned it on.

Okay. Fine. I would sit here, watching TV like there was any *possible* way I could concentrate on it, when all I wanted to do was jump his bones. We sat shoulder to shoulder, but without actually touching, and not touching made me want to throw up. I was as aware of the spare inch between us as I'd ever been of *anything* in my life.

The show ended.

"Do you want to watch another one?"

Obviously I didn't want to watch another, which I communicated by shrugging. Great. I needed to say something. To make a move. But I couldn't manage to part my lips, to make anything come out of them.

Say something say something say something.

"No," I blurted.

"No?" He raised his brows.

"I don't want to watch another show."

He shifted again, but this time toward me on the couch so we faced each other. "Really," he said. "Any other suggestions, then?"

My head felt so light I thought I might pass out. My breaths came quick and shallow, and the nerves in my stomach hadn't disappeared. All I could manage was the smallest nod.

"Like what?" He lifted a hand and toyed with a strand of my hair.

"Um." I swallowed. Could he hear my heart? I couldn't hear anything over the roar of blood in my ears.

He wound my hair tight around one finger, then released it, brushing the strand back in a long, lingering motion, palm sweeping against the side of my head. I shivered. His hand slid over my neck and jaw to cup the back of them. His eyes never left mine. "No suggestions?"

My heart was about to burst from my chest. My words came out as the barest whisper. "Kiss me."

A slow, radiant smile covered his face. "Kiss what?" He brushed his lips, light as a feather, across my cheekbone. "Kiss this?"

I managed a tiny, wordless nod.

He pressed his mouth to a soft spot beneath my ear. "Kiss this?"

Heat rocked through me. I hadn't known that spot *existed*. My head fell back. "Oh, god, Noah."

I could hear the smile in his voice. "Kiss this?" He pulled the lower lobe of my ear into his mouth and I gasped, hands reaching for him as sensation washed through me. Ears. Why had no one ever told me how great ears were?

My hands found his head and I pulled him toward me, twisting so our lips finally met. My whole body seized. It was like I had both expected it and had no idea at all the kiss was coming, like I'd been preparing my whole life and was stunned senseless.

His mouth was firm and warm and I couldn't get enough of it, I couldn't get close enough to him. We pressed against each other, hot and insistent and together. His tongue slid into my mouth, twining around mine until I gasped. All my bones seemed to loosen, my muscles coming undone. Fire rolled over me, hot and slick and dangerous, and I would have been quivering if I hadn't been pressed against Noah so closely.

His hand reached for my leg and pulled it over his own so I straddled him, and he let out a small groan as I settled on top. His hand clasped the back of my neck and pulled my mouth down to his for several long, burning minutes. Then he pushed me back slightly, both of us breathing hard, my hair dangling down, a curtain between us and the world. "Is this okay?"

"Yes." I pressed a kiss to his brow, which was weird but seemed right. "Yes, it's great." Then realization clicked and I pulled back, bracing my hands on his shoulders. My cheeks turned bright red. "Oh! Um. I'm not going to sleep with you."

He grinned up at me, eyes sparkling. "Okay."

"Okay? Okay. Good. Just making sure—we're okay."

"This isn't, like, an express train or anything. We can stop whenever we want."

I couldn't keep a grin from breaking. I already knew I liked Noah Barbanel, but I liked him even more when he was being considerate and making nerdy analogies. "I like you, Noah Barbanel," I announced. "You're a good person."

"Thanks?"

"You're welcome," I said, and kissed him again.

Twenty-One

February 3, 1953

Remember how when I was little, I used to pace the widow's walk? I told people I was pretending to wait for my whale captain husband to return from sea. Your mother had told me about past women of Nantucket who'd done so, and it sounded terribly romantic. I used to stand on the widow's walk for hours. "She has such a rich imagination," guests used to say.

I lied.

I wasn't looking for some imaginary husband. I was looking for my parents. Even though I'd come by boat to New York, even though I knew most people arrived there, I had the idea my parents would come to Nantucket. They'd have learned, somehow, I was there. And I would see their ship sailing close, see it curving over the horizon, and it would draw closer and closer and they would be at the rail, waving.

I can't believe I got the letter. I feel like I've been waiting for it a hundred years. And I know I told you it would be better to know, I know I said this state of suspense hurt too much, but now I'd give anything to go back to last week when I thought, Maybe. I'm not an idiot; I knew it was a pipe dream. I knew. But I didn't really, did I?

1943. Gassed on arrival.

I hate this world, Ned.

I wish you were here.

woke before Noah. We'd fallen asleep in his room, because the idea of separating from him, even to sleep, had seemed untenable. He faced me, his chest rising and falling peacefully, his lashes a sweep of black against his cheekbones. I gently dislodged his arm and slipped out of bed, padding toward the bathroom.

I'd never slept in a bed with a boy before.

Well, to be honest, I hadn't done much sleeping. Turned out it was *hard* to sleep with another body right next to you. But in a good way? I kept waking up, but instead of being irritated, I glowed with happiness and snuggled up to Noah.

Noah. Noah, Noah, Noah.

After showering and pulling on a lilac sundress, I sat in the unused bedroom and called Mom to give her the rundown. "One of the records mentioned O'ma!" I told her. "She said O'ma was from a town close to hers, and she was from Hamburg, in northern Germany."

"Really? What else did she say?"

Suspecting Mom might ask this, I'd copied down Else Friedhoff's words, and now I read them to Mom. "I was thinking, since we've narrowed it down to a region, I could double-check O'ma's parents' names against the 1930s censuses from the area, and see if we could find them?"

Mom let out a startled laugh. "Not a bad idea."

"Except I have no idea how to get a hold of censuses."

"There must be genealogy websites which can help. How are things going with Noah?"

I glanced at the other bedroom. "Good."

"Is he there right now?"

"Yes."

"What did you guys do last night?"

Nothing! "We went to the Arnold Arboretum and out to dinner." Thank god I'd called her instead of Skyping, so she couldn't see my red face.

By the time Mom and I hung up, Noah had jumped in the shower. I googled German census records, and found more information than I'd expected, but no concise search engine—mostly places I could pay for in order to download census results from different towns. I bookmarked the pages for later.

Next, I looked up the Holtzman House, which Else Friedhoff had said she and O'ma had been placed in by the German Jewish Children's Aid society, the principal organization for getting children over from Europe. Like the GJCA, the Holtzman House was a privately funded refugee organization. It provided temporary housing for Jewish children.

Perhaps they'd been the ones who'd informed O'ma her parents had passed away, which meant they might have more information about them—or perhaps they'd have more information about O'ma's arrival itself, including family facts.

The Holtzman House no longer existed, but another Jewish nonprofit had inherited their records. Like many of the other organizations I'd come across, it didn't have digitized records and suggested coming to New York to search their archives, but nothing ventured, nothing gained. I shot them an email, grateful to have actual information to impart: My grandmother, Ruth Goldman, came over on the SS *Babette* in 1939. She stayed at the Holtzman House for several weeks. Do you know if there's any mention of her in your records?

Noah came out of the shower, rumpled and half-awake. He wore a towel slung low over his hips. "Morning."

"Good morning." I felt unexpectedly shy, as though we hadn't spent half the night with our bodies pressed against each other.

He filled a glass with water from the tap. "Were you on the phone?"

"With my mom, yeah."

He drained half his drink, then looked at me. "You're okay?"

"About my phone call?" I said, slightly confused.

"No, I meant—" For the first time, he fumbled. "I wanted to check about last night. Make sure we didn't go too fast or anything."

I couldn't stop a smile from springing to my lips. "No. We didn't."

"Good." He came over and kissed me full on the mouth, then grinned his heart-melting grin. "Because I thought it was great."

This boy was going to kill me.

"Should we get breakfast?" he asked. "I'm starving."

We went to a café down the road with sandwiches named after streets and schools. We ordered breakfast burritos and Noah got a coffee while I added on a cookie (to each their own). Then we took the T downtown and spent the afternoon walking around the Common and Public Garden, which (as Noah told me) was the oldest in the country. Then we took the T to the train, the train to the ferry, and the ferry all the way back to Nantucket.

Returning to the island after a night away felt odd. You weren't supposed to *return* to your vacation land once it had ended, and the vibe of Boston had been far different than of Nantucket. Not to mention what had happened between Noah and me. I felt nervous as we walked down the dark, familiar streets to Mrs. Henderson's house. Now what? Had Boston been a fairy tale, and Nantucket, however odd it sounded, our ordinary lives? In the city we'd existed in a bubble of our own making. What would happen here?

Noah walked me to my door, and we lingered on the steps. He hitched his duffel bag strap higher on his shoulder. "I'll see you soon."

Right. Because now we were parting. "I'll let you know if the archive has any info."

"Good."

"Good."

We stayed locked in place. Then Noah's hand came up to cup my cheek and he lowered his lips to mine, soft and light as a whisper. The worried tension inside me unwound. "See you later, then."

"See you." I slipped inside, then leaned against the closed door. I grinned at the ceiling, unable to suppress the thrill of the weekend. I'd *kissed* Noah Barbanel! And, you know, extensively made out. I gave a hop of sheer joy.

The house was dark but moonlight streamed through it. I danced upstairs, silently entering my room where Jane already lay sleeping. I floated down atop my bed like a maple seed helicoptering down to earth, blissful and dream-filled.

I fell asleep thinking about Noah.

I woke up thinking about Noah.

Okay, wow, this could get real time-consuming real fast.

Did people usually feel so *destroyed* by hookups? Utterly all-consumed? Was it normal, craving another person like a drug? It couldn't be.

Of course it could. My body chemistry had probably changed, addicting me to Noah's hormones. The biological imperative was laughing its little brain off, encouraging me to procreate even though Earth had too many people, and it would be nice if humanity had an off switch for a while, or at least until we'd terraformed Mars.

God, I wanted him so badly.

"You're back!" Jane bounded down the stairs and joined me at the kitchen table. "How did it go?"

"It was great. We found this one recording—"

"Tell me about Noah." She dashed milk into a bowl of Cheerios. "You spent the night together! And don't tell me only technically. Your texts were very coy."

I put my spoon down, a smile worthy of the Cheshire Cat crossing my face. "Well . . ."

"Oh my god, what happened?"

Jane made all the right noises and exclamations as I told her. When I finished, she let out a whoosh of air. "Finally!"

"What do I do now, though?"

"You could text him."

Right. I could. I did, theoretically, have command over my phone and the English language. Except. What did you text someone after you hooked up? Why wasn't this covered in school? Why did we learn pre-calc and bio, and yet I didn't know how to respond to a human who'd stuck his tongue in my mouth? How the hell *did* we manage to propagate the species? I scooped up my last three Cheerios. "No. Definitely not."

Jane smirked. "The bravest girl in Nantucket."

I made a face.

For the rest of the day, I was a nervous wreck. At work, Maggie paused in the middle of a conversation and asked if I was all right. I pulled myself together for the rest of my shift, but honestly, I wasn't sure.

Most of the time in the books I read, hooking up served as the culmination of the romance, and after, everyone was happy. Or, perhaps, the couple made out because they were in a fake relationship or a marriage of convenience (I read a lot of historical romances) or because of a fit of angry passion, and were in situations where they kept running into each other.

But what if you hooked up and weren't in a relationship or forced to keep interacting? What if you just made out once, and were really into someone, but had no guarantees? How did you figure out how to communicate afterward?

I'd resolved to text him when my phone finally buzzed in my pocket. I froze in the middle of shelving a book. I couldn't bring myself to pull out my phone: At the moment, I existed in the Schrödinger's cat–land of text messages. The moment I looked at my phone, I'd either be deliriously happy or wildly upset.

I waited as long as I could, like a child holding her breath underwater, until the uncertainty became worse than potential disappointment. Then I whipped up my cell.

Mom:
did you know teens spend an avg of 17 HOURS A DAY LOOKING AT SCREENS

WHAT R U LOOKING AT

GO PLAY OUTSIDE

Mom. Disappointment poured through me in a gale, followed by a wry laugh.

Me:

I'm literally spending 6 hours today looking at books,
not screens

Also I bet you read this in an article ON A SCREEN

My phone buzzed again. I glanced down and let out an audible *eek*, throwing my gaze away from the screen, panic and hope now battling for supremacy. Breath coming fast, I forced my eyes back down.

Noah:
What are you up to tomorrow?

Oh my god. Noah. A text. Why had he rendered me verbally incompetent? Would I ever recover? Was this my life now?

How did I answer?

Oh. By answering the question, yes, good, quite.

Me:

Jane and I were planning to go to a party at
Kaitlyn Phan's house. You?

I watched intently as the three dots danced on my screen, willing them to resolve into words, desperate as a seer trying to interpret signals before a mercurial king.

Noah:
Same

What kind of response was *same*?

Meet you there?

Meet you there was not the same as *Let's go together*, as *Be my girlfriend, let's go steady, wear my letterman jacket* (why did all my examples of dating and romance come from 1950s musicals?). But it did imply we'd see each other. Tomorrow.

And for now, that would be enough.

Twenty-Two

Kaitlyn Phan's house stood on the brink of a cliff. (Maybe if you have a lot of houses you don't mind if one falls into the sea?) Jane had sworn it would be okay if we showed up, even though neither of us knew Kaitlyn—apparently she threw amazing theme parties, and as long as you tangentially knew her crowd, you could get in. We arrived at 10:15, trailing glitter and nerves. We'd followed YouTube makeup tutorials with the precision of neurosurgeons, applying dramatic eyeshadow with white liquid liner on top, contouring with teal and pink, and painting our lips blue. We pulled fishnet stockings across our cheeks and temples, pressing cream eye shadow through them to create scales, and carefully applied sequins to our skin.

For costumes, we'd scrounged up metallic scaled leggings and crop tops from friends; Maggie had lent me a pink-and-green-and-blue wig she usually wore for Pride, and Jane twined green strips of fabric through her hair like seaweed.

"I feel like I'm in a teen movie," I told Jane as we walked up the path. Thumping music radiated out from the house, while lights flashed through high-up windows. Luckily, there were no neighbors within earshot to complain. "No one has parties like this at home."

I wished, suddenly and strongly, we'd arrived with Noah, so we'd feel like we belonged. He'd offered to swing by our place, but I'd told him not to bother—it would have been out of his way, and I'd had no intention of showing up at Golden Doors dressed like a mermaid.

Obviously, a stupid mistake on my part.

We opened Kaitlyn's front door and stopped short. A curtain of flowers and seashells hung from the ceiling. Jane and I glanced at each other, then pushed through, into the foyer. Teal and aqua lights undulated throughout the two-story entrance, giving it an underwater effect. People were dressed like pirates and mermaids and sharks. Girls wore flowers crowns and boys wore spikey chokers I recognized from looking up the *Blue Lagoon* movie. In the middle of the space, where one might expect a table with flowers, or a tree at Christmas, stood a giant ship.

"Oh my god." I had to yell slightly to be heard. "This is crazy."

"I've never seen anything so extra," Jane said. We approached the ship, tilting our heads to consider it, an island of bemused silence in the midst of chaotic noise. Tiny sailor figurines were falling to their deaths. "I'm in love."

"How do you think she got it through the door?"

"Maybe she had it built in here?"

Gelt-like gold coins lay scattered around the base of the ship, interspersed with plastic gems. "What a world. Where do you think her parents are?"

"Maybe they're back in Boston for the work week?"

"And left Kaitlyn here? I don't understand rich people."

From the entryway, we let the—ahem—current carry us to the kitchen, where beer and wine covered the counter. I snagged a rosé can and popped the tab.

Who knew rosé could grow on you so much in one summer?

Jane knocked her Cisco IPA against my drink. "Chime chime."

"Chime chime."

We wandered through the house, oohing to each other as the

decorations shifted, from a grotto sure to be the scene of many hook-ups, to a desert island replete with real sand. (Who would be cleaning up later?)

In the massive living room, which had embraced a general beach theme, Jane grabbed my arm. "There's Sydney." Her eyes narrowed. "Who's she talking to?"

Pranav's girlfriend stood by a cute boy in board shorts and a collared shirt. "Jane. No. Just because she's talking to another boy doesn't mean she's about to break up with Pranav and you'll get him all to yourself."

"But are you *sure*."

"Talk to someone else." I flung an arm out and accidentally smacked a boy in the chest. He gave me a dirty look as he walked by. *Oops.* "This party is full of boys!"

She surveyed the multitude of Sperrys and Chubbies. "They're all tools."

"Jane! You're the one who wanted to come here."

Her gaze wandered back to Sydney. "Maybe I should investigate. Make sure nothing weird is going on."

"You one hundred percent should not." My gaze latched on a familiar face across the room. "Look, there's Evan! Let's talk to him!"

I dragged her over to where Evan stood with someone I didn't know. Jane glared at our friend. "What the hell. What are you doing here?"

"Uh." Evan looked confused. He hadn't dressed up, but as a nod to the occasion, he'd worn a T-shirt with a lobster on it. "Hanging out?"

"You didn't say a word about coming to this party! I wouldn't have felt so much like we were crashing if I knew you were here!"

"So glad to know my sole purpose is to invite you to parties."

She narrowed her eyes. "What else are you hiding from me?"

"I'm going to do a loop and see if I can find Noah," I said, deeming Jane out of imminent danger. "Have fun fighting!"

I looked for Noah by way of the snack table, methodically eating chips and salsa before I realized it would probably ruin my lipstick. *Oops.* Also, only sheer luck had saved me from dropping a hunk of tomato on my shimmery gold top. Forcing myself away from the food, I found myself trailing, enthralled, in the wake of a boy who'd dressed as Ursula. I sipped my rosé and examined the construction of his tendrils. Perhaps he planned to grow several sizes and sink the ship in the entryway?

Which was where we'd wound up, the foyer with its teal lights and seashells suspended from the ceiling. Intent on taking a good picture for Niko and company, I lifted my phone, tilting my head to find the best shot—and I caught sight of Noah.

He stood on the second-floor balcony, wearing a captain's hat and a blue blazer that fit him very, *very* well. I'd never thought captains were hot before—if I'd been asked to describe one, I would have said scraggly beard and oversized sweater, or all crisp whites.

Noah was undeniably hot.

For a moment I gazed up at him, reveling in the chance to look at him uninterrupted, to absorb how attractive he was, to let my sheer amount of liking for this boy wash over me, warm and sweet and strong enough to make my heart beat extra hard.

Then I slowly took in all the people surrounding him, the people I'd have to make my way through to reach his side. It seemed daunting to approach him, while he was laughing and confident, bracketed by people who belonged to this strange world of underwater parties just as he did.

I needed fresh air.

I slipped out through the living room, out the French doors, past groups of people. At the edge of the property, the land fell away into the dunes, the dunes to the sand, the sand to the sea. I stood on the cliff's edge. Despite being high summer, the breeze tonight carried a chill. I lifted my gaze to the endless dark and inhaled the night and the ocean.

Did everyone feel this way when facing Nantucket's sheer nature, like the wind and moon and water stripped them bare? Did everyone, no matter how poised, feel as alone and vulnerable and insignificant as I did when facing the ocean? Perhaps anyone wrapped in wind and salt would be overawed; perhaps this connection to the ocean that felt so personal to me was universal.

I had to talk to Noah about what we were doing. Not talking was tangling me up inside.

"Hello there, Ariel."

Delight thrilled through me, so strong and instant it burned away every last shadow and doubt. I turned to beam up at him. He'd sought me out. His very presence, even without words or touch, made me glow with happiness. "My hair isn't red. And your eyes aren't blue, Prince Eric."

"Fair. And I don't remember Ariel being quite so . . ." His gaze ran over me, lingering on my hips, hugged tightly by my metallic leggings, and on the skin exposed by my crop top. ". . . scaly."

A laugh bubbled out of me. I tapped my chin, studying his achingly familiar face. "Good point. And you're a captain, not the prince. Maybe I'm one of the sisters, then, not Ariel. Maybe we're in a different story."

"Oh?" He took a step closer to me, sliding one hand around my hip. His thumb stroked the bare skin above my waistline. "And how's our story go?"

A shiver shot through me at his touch, and I fought to keep my body from trembling. "Less murder and self-sacrifice than the original *Little Mermaid*, I hope."

His brows rose. "I missed those parts."

"In the original fairy tale, it felt like a thousand knives stabbed the little mermaid's feet every time she took a step." I gave him my most beatific smile. "Her sisters tell her to murder the prince to save herself. She can't bear to, so she winds up dying."

He swayed nearer. "Unfortunate."

"Wait until I tell you what happened to Cinderella's stepsisters and Snow White's stepmother." I tapped his chest. "Disney churns out the sanitized versions. There's always undercurrents of violence and tragedy."

"Always?"

"Always." Our faces were a whisper apart and I wanted him to kiss me. I wanted *him*. We weren't the little mermaid and her prince. We were a new story, and maybe there didn't need to be any tragedy here at all. We weren't our grandparents. We could work.

What are we doing?

Four simple words. Why couldn't I make them trip off my tongue? Why did I find it so difficult to talk to Noah about us? Was it my damnable pride, my fear of rejection? Because if he said we were just hooking up, I wouldn't be able to handle it. I'd have to break this off immediately, because it would hurt my heart too much otherwise.

And he would say we were only hooking up, because he was off to school next month, and who wanted to go to college with a girlfriend in high school? He'd broken up with an *actual* girlfriend when she went to college because he thought having a long-distance partner was such a bad idea.

Maybe it didn't matter what we were doing, if we were happy

while doing it. Maybe we didn't need to talk about expectations. Ariel hadn't talked, after all, and—well. It'd worked out for her in the Disney version.

Just not the original one.

What are we doing? I said in my head, the words held in my mouth. I should force them out, propel them into the world with my breath and my tongue and my vocal cords. Because I did need to know what the expectations here were, on both of our sides. I needed us to be on the same page.

"I like your captain's hat," I said instead.

"Do you?" His other hand rose past my waist and my throat went dry. "I like your . . ." His forefinger brushed my cheekbone. "Everything."

What was I supposed to say to that?

Nothing. I couldn't say anything, because anything I said would ruin things, and this was too precious to ruin. I was incapable of anything other than throwing my arms around him and kissing him, so that's exactly what I did.

Twenty-Three

The next morning, I woke to find Jane staring at me from her bed. I yawned and scrubbed the sleep from my eyes. "Morning. Why are you being so creepy?"

"I'm not looking at you, I'm staring into the middle distance. But. Since you're up—" She turned her phone to face me, as though I had good enough sight to read it without my glasses on or contacts in. "Evan asked me out."

That woke me up more than a splash of cold water. I gaped at her. "*Evan?* Our Evan?"

"What do I do?" She pulled at the braids on either side of her head.

"Oh my god. What happened?" I propped myself up on my elbow, all sleepiness burned away. When I'd checked in last night, she'd told me to go off with Noah, and she'd be fine getting home on her own. She'd been in bed and asleep when I got back. "Walk me through this."

"We hung out at the party yesterday, and . . ."

"Did something happen?"

"No! Nothing. Except I guess we flirted. Or—I mentioned Pranav, and he got mad, so I told him about Mason to prove I wasn't hung up on Pranav, and he was—I don't know, he was sort of snarky, *very* unlike him, but also he was giving me vibes? But obviously he's *Evan.* Now he's texting and he wants to hang out."

"Like a date?"

"No. He literally said, 'Want to hang out?'" She handed her phone over.

I put on my glasses, Sherlock on the case. "These texts *do* sound a little flirty. And it's barely ten, which is an aggressively early time to text if you're not into someone."

"Right? Unless you're *so* not into someone you aren't worried about the timing of your texts."

"Hm. Well. Do you *want* it to be a thing? Do you like him?"

"Of course I *like* him, he's Evan," she said scornfully, then bent when I gave her a look. "I don't know! He's so—so—I don't know, I'm basically a townie, and he's super rich, and it's very complicated."

"It's not so complicated. Also, you're not a townie."

"Obviously, objectively, he's very hot."

"True." I nodded. "Can confirm."

"But I've never considered *liking* him. He hardly seems attainable, and then there's Pranav."

"Except there isn't *really* Pranav."

"Evan and I have never even hung out alone together. What if we have nothing to say? What if we hate each other?"

"You don't hate each other. Hang out! Find out! Shonda Rhimes believes in the power of saying yes."

"Oprah says it's fine to say no."

"Well, Oprah's not here right now."

"Neither is—"

"Go! Talk!"

She scoffed. "Like you've been so good on the talking front."

"Do what I say, not what I do."

"I'll hang out with Evan if you talk to Noah about whether you're actually dating, because hooking up does not a relationship make."

"Rude." I blew out a breath, then straightened my shoulders. "I did tell Noah I'd meet him for lunch today. Maybe I'll put my money where my mouth is."

"Hopefully not literally."

"No, money touches too many hands, gross."

I arrived at Golden Doors at noon. When I got off my bike and pulled out my phone, I saw a text from Noah: Sorry, my dad's grabbing me for a quick talk—you can hang out in the living room if you want, I'll be done soon.

A nice offer, but I didn't plan to wander through Golden Doors by myself. I shot him a quick text—I'll be in the gardens!—and headed around back, preferring nature to the imposing gray beauty.

The lawn, like always, was stunning, full of lush summer plants. Emerald green blades carpeted the lawn, their fresh-cut scent mingling with the perfume of flowers. The sky formed a translucent dome, and the sun shot through tree leaves, turning them a transparent, glowing green. Small birds warbled from branches and I caught sight of a rabbit hopping away from me. It was like stepping into a painting.

"There you are, Abigail. I'd been hoping we'd see each other soon."

Helen stood in the middle of the lawn, at a long table draped in white cloth. She wore pink linen pants and a long-sleeved white sweater. Roses, lilies, dahlias, stalks of greenery, and white baby's breath lay on the table.

"Come here."

I trailed over, soft and nervous, my attention caught by her hands.

They trembled even when still, and her skin was both crinkled and drawn tight around the bones. But her movements remained decisive as she arranged the plants, the Queen Anne's lace, the small white roses and larger yellow ones. She cut stems and held the lengths against each other like a painter comparing color swathes. I paused across the table from her. "It looks beautiful."

"I'm teaching a flower arrangement class later. It's very popular." She picked up a green plant with a brown stem and oval leaves. "Do you know what this is?"

I shook my head.

"It's myrtle. A beautiful scent, but a horrible taste."

I shifted uneasily. Had her comment been pointed? Surely not. Hoping to contribute something, I said, "Queen Esther's original name came from the word for *myrtle*."

"Hm." Helen picked up a dahlia, hot pink at the center and edged in white, studied it, then set it back down. She did not look at me. "And what does *Abigail* mean?"

"Father's joy. Or source of joy."

"She was King David's wife, wasn't she? Beautiful, like Esther. The Talmud called them two of the four women of surpassing beauty in the world."

Okay. Was this another weird insult? Or a compliment? Or a statement of fact? Was my Talmudic knowledge being tested? Should I be able to offer up the other two women? (I couldn't.) "Helen was beautiful, too. Launched a thousand ships."

She looked up, startled, like I'd said something off script. "So she was."

I clasped my hands behind my back, nervous, and tried to think of something utterly inoffensive to say.

"Your grandmother," she said, then sighed and started again. "We met for the first time here, when I was eighteen and she was sixteen. I won't deny she'd had a hard life, but she acted very put-upon, playing up the poor orphan, the unwanted relation. Still, everyone liked her. *I* liked her."

I resisted pointing out how O'ma *had* been orphaned, and hadn't even been a relation but a charity case, so it might not have been an act.

Helen held up a piece of baby's breath against the flowers, studied it, then sliced away a quarter inch of the stem. "There are some people who everyone wants to be around. People with a special energy. Your grandmother was so, despite her mood swings and silences. She drew everyone to her."

I knew the energy she spoke about, the spear of light striking through a person, magnetic as an iron rod. I saw it in Stella, where it manifested as exuberant extraversion, and in my best friend, Niko, whose sharp wit gathered people close. These were the moving centers of a party, the people who exuded energy instead of drinking it.

"Then there are the rest of us, the moths. The moths get too close to those people, and are burned to a crisp."

I opened my mouth, but she cut me off. "My husband didn't choose me. *Ruth* chose to *not* be with him. I've made my peace with this. But we don't need history repeating itself. Be careful with my grandson."

"We're not—it's nothing like—"

"You're not a couple?"

Oof. Great question. "I meant—it's a different situation."

"I see."

All right. If everything I said was going to be difficult and strained, I might as well ask what I really wanted to know. "You knew my grandmother fairly well?"

She nodded slowly. "When we were young. Or at least, we saw each other fairly often."

I wanted to know about their relationship. Had she been aware of anything between Ruth and Edward? Had she viewed Ruth as competition? But those questions paled compared to the one I'd been carrying all over this island. "Did you know anything about her family?"

"This *was* her family," she said without hesitation. "The Barbanels raised her. They raised her from when she arrived on their doorstep."

I hadn't thought about it like so before. "They didn't keep in touch with her, though."

She pinned me with her gaze. "My mother-in-law called Ruth every week for her entire life."

"What?" I stared at Helen. My throat closed up. "Really?"

She smiled, the corners of her mouth held up by a myriad of emotions. "Every Sunday."

"I had no idea." Impossible. Surely I would have known? Or Mom would have known. Daughters knew these sort of things about their mothers' lives.

Didn't we?

It felt almost inappropriate to ask more questions, but when would I get another chance? "What was their relationship like? My grandmother and—Edward's mother?"

"Better than my own." Her expression turned stark. "The Barbanels were Ruth's family more than they were ever mine."

I couldn't imagine what it must have been like, having a mother-in-law more invested in your husband's previous partner than you. Only it hadn't been like that, had it? It was more having a mother-in-law invested in her own daughter.

How could O'ma have never have mentioned a surrogate mother? I talked about Mom all the time. She was so much a part of who I was.

And *why* would O'ma have kept her a secret, if they talked every week?

"I'm sorry," I said. "It doesn't sound easy."

Helen Barbanel picked up a rose and snipped it.

It felt like a dismissal. Maybe I'd overstepped; maybe it wasn't my place to have sympathy. I should go find Noah, but I hesitated. I wanted to make one thing clear. "I'm a moth, too, you know."

"Not to Noah. He thinks you're the sun. If you're going to disappoint him, do it now. Don't let his heart get so invested you shatter it." She smiled, but humorlessly. "We don't need another Goldman girl breaking another Barbanel boy."

I walked around to the front of the house and sat on the porch steps, hugging my knees to my chest, desperately trying to calm my buzzing mind. The thought of ever seeing Helen again made me want to hide beneath a blanket.

I hated this. I hated being disliked by an *adult*, someone who was supposed to have their shit together. How did anyone stand up against the disapproval of their families? No wonder Noah felt pressure to do whatever his family wanted, whether it was studying business or protecting the family's name and company. I'd known I was lucky to have a low-key, flexible family, but this really rammed it home.

Yet on some things, I knew Helen Barbanel was wrong. Noah didn't see me as a blazing sun; he probably didn't even consider me a light bulb. Helen Barbanel thought I would hurt him? Ha! *He* was going to hurt *me*.

Still—did she have a point? If we weren't going anywhere, if either of us would end up hurt, should Noah and I end things now? Maybe this wasn't worth it.

I pulled out my phone to see if Noah had texted. No dice. Maybe I should go home. I didn't want to be here. My stomach hurt and I felt small and sick and pathetic.

And yet, even with Helen casting doubt, even with my own confusion about what we were doing, one overriding emotion made me stay: the undeniable desire to be in Noah's company. I wanted him to look at me with his steady gaze and take my hand and laugh.

I took a deep breath. Okay. Noah would probably be free soon, and maybe I could walk my nerves off in the meantime. I got to my feet and set off along the front façade of the house, in the opposite direction from the way leading around back. Piano music floated from one room—Noah's dad? No; Noah was talking to his dad right now. Edward, maybe. Or Shira.

I passed another open window, and voices blasted out.

"She's a bad influence."

"She's not a bad influence!"

I froze, a horrible certainty hooking through me and tugging me toward the window. Through it, I could see Noah facing off against his father, two versions of the same mold separated by decades. Noah's rage boiled high, his fists clenched and eyes bright, while his father's simmered low, shown only in his tense shoulders and implacable voice.

"Three months ago, you weren't talking about *plants*—"

"I'm going to see her whether you like her or not."

I felt like I'd been sucker punched.

I turned back toward the porch, walking slowly, each step through a haze. I aimed for my bike, which still looked cheerful and merry, all twined with ribbons. Pulling it upright, I got ready to throw my leg over the seat and escape.

"Abigail." My name in Noah's voice stilled me once more. I turned, letting my bike lie back against the porch's side. He strode out of Golden Doors and down the steps, tension draining from his face. "There you are. Thank god."

I stared at him.

"Are you leaving?" He frowned and raked a hand through his hair. "God, I'm sorry I'm so late. I'm so glad to see you." He stepped forward and wrapped his arms around me, kissing me firmly. Then he drew back, frowning harder. "What's wrong?"

I pushed out of his embrace. "Is this a good idea?"

"What?"

"This." I gestured between us. "Us."

He looked baffled. "I happen to think it's a *very* good idea."

My heart pounded so fast I felt like it would burst out of my chest and fall onto the lawn, red and bloody and flat. "Your family doesn't think so."

"What are you talking about? Are you serious?"

"I don't know! I've never had adults dislike me. I hate it. Your grandmother thinks I'm awful."

"Abigail, my grandma disapproves of *everything*. It doesn't mean she doesn't like you. So she thinks you stress out my grandfather. So what?"

"What?"

He hesitated. "You—what were you were talking about?"

"She thinks I stress out your grandfather?"

His eyes closed. "Damn."

"How? What did she say?"

"Nothing. It doesn't matter. What were you talking about?"

"She thinks I'm bad for you. I think she called me a myrtle. But in a bad way?"

"A *myrtle*?"

"Noah. Tell me why she thinks I stress out your grandpa."

He sighed. "She said it's not healthy for him to be reminded of the past so often."

I leaned back. "Do you think she has a point? About me stressing out your grandfather?"

"Honestly, Abigail, I don't care."

"What about your dad?"

"What about him?"

"Why doesn't he want you seeing me? Why *are* you seeing me? What are we doing?"

"What do you think?"

"I don't know!" I yelled, finally at my breaking point, unable to handle my anxiety and bouncing nerves anymore. "I don't know what we're doing! Are you just hooking up with me to piss off your dad?"

"Why would you *say* that?"

"Because it makes as much sense as anything else I can come up with! I don't even know what we're doing. I mean, we're not *serious*, are we?"

He rocked back on his heels. His voice went flat. "You said you didn't want anything serious."

"What?" I felt thrown, like I'd suddenly gone from the attack to the defense.

"You're looking for a summer fling, right?" His expression didn't change. "Something casual."

My throat went dry, though my eyes did not. I blinked rapidly. Really shot myself in the foot there, hadn't I, spending all summer talking about flings. Of course he thought I'd be fine with one. "I don't want a fling."

He looked at me sharply. "What?"

My throat was too clogged to speak, so I shook my head instead.

"You said you wanted a summer fling."

"I meant in the abstract." Blinking hard, I looked down at my feet, my pink nail polish glinting in the light. "Not with you."

"Be a little more clear, Abigail."

"How much clearer can I be?" I cried. "I don't want a *fling* with you, or to be your revenge hookup to get back at your dad. I *like* you! I want to spend all my time with you and I wish we were serious and it's tearing me apart not knowing what we're doing!"

He looked stunned.

Hot shame rolled over me. I was an idiot. *Stand your ground*, I told myself, even though I wanted to cry. No one could be mad someone liked them. It was flattering, even if they didn't return the sentiment—wasn't it? "Don't worry," I said stiffly. "I won't be a bother about it."

"A *bother*?" He closed the space between us. "God, Abigail. It's not a *bother*."

"It's not?" I looked at him warily.

He let out a disbelieving laugh. "Why would it be a bother?"

My whole body trembled from trying to hold myself together. "I don't have any interest in being with someone who isn't into me, or who thinks I'm being clingy. If you thought I'd be a chill hookup because I said I wanted a fling, I'm sorry. But I'm not feeling very chill. Honestly, I think hooking up isn't going to work for me because I want more."

"Abigail. So do I."

"You—what?"

"I *like* you." He swept the hair out of my face, hand lingering on my cheek. "You did notice we've been going on dates, right?"

"Um." I starred up into his warm brown eyes, feeling utterly confused and uncertain and a tiny bit wonderfully hopeful. "Maybe?"

"We went out to lunch and we went to the party and we're picnicking today?"

"But—it's August. You leave for school in two weeks."

"Cambridge isn't so far away from South Hadley."

"You shouldn't go to college with a partner. Everyone knows that."

"Who's this everyone?"

"You know. Everyone." I lifted a shoulder. "College is for making new friends and experimentation and reinventing yourself. You don't want to be tied down. Didn't you break up with your ex because you didn't think a college student should date a high school kid?"

He studied me. Then he picked up my hand and started tracing the lines. "I broke up with Erika because we'd outgrown each other, not because of some arbitrary college/high school thing. And besides. Here's something I've learned from a very smart girl." He smiled at me, steady, serious. "Sometimes you should do what *you* want to do, not what everyone else thinks is correct."

I let out a strangled laugh. "Practical advice for majors and life goals. It wasn't about—I don't know, feelings."

"I'd argue feelings are practical. Emotional well-being matters, doesn't it?" He cupped the back of my neck. "I want to date you, Abigail Schoenberg. Do you want to date me?"

I swallowed. There were so many reasons this didn't make sense and would fall apart, but right now, none of them mattered. "Yes."

"All right, then. We're dating. Why are you fighting this so hard?"

"I don't know," I said despairingly. "I mean, I do. Honestly, your family freaks me out a little. And I'm nervous you might mean it now but you won't mean it in a few weeks when you go to school."

"Then we check in and if we want something else, we want something else. We don't stop ourselves because of what we *might* want, in the future." He smiled at me. "We live in the present, Abigail Schoenberg. We commit."

"Okay. Okay." I breathed out. "I want that. I want you."

"Yeah?" A small smile curved his lips and grew, and grew.

"But what about your family?"

"My family isn't dating you."

"Your grandmother thinks I'm going to break your heart. She thinks we're going to repeat the mistakes your grandfather and my grandmother made."

"I have a solution, then," he said lightly. "Don't break my heart."

A sudden, horrible premonition rose in me. You couldn't promise not to break someone's heart. I knew that. And I also knew Noah believed, absolutely, if you loved someone, you did anything to make your relationship work.

"We're not going to make the same mistakes as our grandparents," I said. We *weren't*. We were going to get a happy ending.

He pressed his lips against mine, soft at first, then hot and undeniable. "All right, then. Let's make our own."

When I got home, I sat cross-legged on my bed and called Mom.

"Noah's grandma says the woman who raised O'ma called her once a week for *the rest of her life*," I told her without preamble. "Is that true? Have you ever heard of her?"

"I don't think so." Mom sounded startled.

"Seriously? How can you not have known?"

"Don't yell at me!"

"I'm not yelling at you! I'm just surprised."

Mom was silent a minute. "I remember she used to get these phone calls when I was a little kid from some woman named Eva, who I'd never met, and whenever she called, your aunts and I knew to get O'ma. But we didn't think about it too deeply."

"You didn't ask?"

Mom made a *tsk*ing noise. "And what do you ever ask me?"

"I don't know! Do you have any secrets about surrogate mothers you haven't told me?"

Mom laughed. "I don't think so. Do *you* have any secrets?"

I hesitated, then decided to throw her a bone. "Don't freak out. But Noah and I are dating. It's not a big deal."

Mom freaked out.

And I didn't hate it.

Twenty-Four

From: The New York Jewish Archives
To: Abigail Schoenberg

Hi Abby,

Thanks for your interest in our archives! While our records aren't searchable, we do have an intern currently working on a digitalization project, and she'll be scanning and digitizing the 1938–39 records from the Holtzman House soon—we can have her send you a link when it's all online.

Noah and I spent the next week all over Nantucket.

We walked across the moors as storms threatened, the heavy air carrying the particular fresh scent preceding summer rain. Dramatic lighting scored the sky: dark, striking clouds, and white light on the horizon. We walked through Nantucket's protected forests, where golden rays filtered through tall trees and swept across the oceans of ferns blanketing the forest floors. We went out in his boat and, out of sight of everyone, he pulled me into his lap, and we kissed and kissed until we fell flat on the boat's floor, laughing.

I could say things to Noah I couldn't say to anyone else, inane, incomplete things. I plucked unfinished thoughts straight from my head and gave them to him. We stood at the edge of the water and talked about the vastness of sky and sea, of feeling infinite and small. We played keep-away with the waves, dashing as close to the water as possible, then back before the inward tide could touch our feet.

It felt like the island belonged to us.

On rainy evenings, we curled up in Mrs. Henderson's living room with Ellie Mae at our feet. Noah browsed through Harvard's biological-diversity-related classes and looked up their professors. I combed through German censuses, searching for my great-grandparents' names. I checked my email intermittently, in case the records had arrived from the Holtzman House.

Interns! Who knew!

"Have you talked to your dad again?" I asked one day. Humidity hung in the air and painted a sheen of sweat across our faces, even though today wasn't intolerably hot. I was scrolling idly through yet another census, and had found I could hold a conversation while scanning for O'ma's parents.

"I mentioned one of the classes I'm thinking of taking. He grunted instead of saying anything, which I'm taking as a win. I figure if I plant the seed and keep mentioning it as a possibility, at least it won't come as a surprise."

"Do you feel better having mentioned it?" I opened another town's census: Lübeck, Germany, from 1912. Germany had done minority censuses in 1938 and 1939 to help them locate Jews; I'd looked at the 1938 census before, but to no avail, which had made me think my great-grandparents might have headed for Luxembourg by then (perhaps immediately after putting O'ma on the train to Paris). 1912 seemed a little *too* early, but it was accessible, so here we were. Like most of the other documents, it was a PDF and not searchable, so I scrolled endlessly with an eye out for Goldmans.

"Yeah, a little."

Herman Goldman.

Sara Goldman.

I gasped.

"What? What is it?"

"I found them." My great-grandparents. My mother's grand-parents. I swiveled my laptop so Noah could see. "Look!"

"Wow! Excellent sleuthing."

I took Noah's face in my hands and smacked a loud, triumphant kiss on his mouth.

In painstaking German, crafted mostly through Google Translate, I wrote to the organization through which I'd downloaded the censuses to see if they had any related paperwork. And I looked up Lübeck, the town where my grandmother had apparently been born. It was a German port, with inhabitants since Neolithic times. Jews weren't allowed inside, so in the early 1700s they set up in a nearby town of Moisling; when Lübeck annexed Moisling in 1806, they came along. By the early 1900s, over seven hundred Jews lived in Lübeck.

How hard could it be to find a handful of Goldmans among a mere seven hundred Jews? I wrote to the Lübeck city hall to see if they had my grandmother's birth record, or my great-grandparents'—then shot off a similar request to the Lübeck synagogue, which had been around since 1880, and was apparently the only still-functioning pre-war temple. It looked like it, too. Quite a lot of red brick.

Three days later, the synagogue sent me birth certificates for O'ma and her parents, as well as a marriage certificate for the latter.

"I'm shocked," I told Noah next night, when he picked me up as I finished closing the Prose Garden. "I felt like I was looking for a needle in a haystack."

"But you said they didn't tell you about any relatives?"

I sighed. "No. And I tried googling, but nothing came up. Still, it's proof they existed. Proof they had a life." I looked out the car's window at the moon. It was ten thirty, and usually I'd go home and to sleep, but Noah had been insistent I come out. "Where are we going?"

"It's a surprise."

"I hate surprises."

He leaned over and kissed me. "Tough luck."

We drove up North Beach Street, but instead of turning toward Jetties, we took a slight right, then turned up Cobblestone Hill. We drove along a road I'd never been on, passing land with massive dark houses, and parked along an empty lawn in the center of a cul-de-sac.

"This way," he murmured after we parked. Even this late, the air was hot and humid, a lackadaisical breeze barely stirring the heavy air. Noah took my hand and led me to the end of the pavement. A sandy path took over, squeezing its way between two sets of tall hedges marking different properties. This no-man's-land ended at the top of wooden steps built into a dune and leading down to the beach. Standing at the brink, we had a sweeping view of the water.

I froze. Turned out I didn't *always* hate surprises. "Oh my god."

Noah wrapped his arm around my shoulders and pulled me into his side. "I know."

The water glowed with neon blue sparks, washing to shore and back, eerie and beautiful and unearthly. Awe cascaded through me. I hadn't known the world could be like this. "What *is* it?"

"Bioluminescent jellyfish. They're called comb jelly."

We walked down the steps to the sand, kicking off our shoes and approaching the water. The waves crashed against the shore, beautiful and glowing and strange, pulling at something deep within my gut. Sometimes, when I saw nature like this, stunning and bizarre, I felt like I'd been presented with an aching secret I didn't understand, something tremendously ancient and important.

Only this time, I didn't ache as much as I often did. Noah's presence filled the hole in my chest. With him, I could appreciate the beauty. And it didn't make me long for something I would never have.

Noah pulled off his shirt, and my thoughts narrowed back on him. "What are you doing?"

"Going in." Happiness lit his face as he grinned at me.

"Are you serious?" I gaped at him, then at the glowing water. "Is it safe?"

He walked backward toward the water. "Guess we'll find out. Unless you're scared?"

"Fighting words, Noah Barbanel."

His grin was as bright as the moon. "Guess you'll have to fight me, then." And before I could protest, he dove forward and picked me up, throwing me over his shoulder and running into the water, the spray splashing up at me. I struggled valiantly, laughing and hollering. "Don't you dare!"

"Can't stop me."

I smacked his butt. "I will *bite* you—"

He dumped me in the water.

It closed over my head, suspending me in a silent, isolated world. My limbs stretched out and my hair drifted slowly away.

Then I burst up and jumped on him.

"You're wet!" he yelped. "And cold!"

"You deserve it." I tried to off-balance him and knock him into the water by kicking at his legs. He caught one of mine and pinned it to his side. Then, for some reason, hoisting my other leg around his waist seemed like a good idea, and then I had both legs wrapped around him, his arms holding me in place, and we were grinning wildly and staring into each other's eyes.

Then we were kissing and laughing and back in the water, swimming and playing, until we tired ourselves out. Slowly, the glowing green-and-blue jellyfish we'd scared off surrounded us once more. We floated on our backs, suspended by water and salt, drifting in between water and sky.

Here was the thing.

His family didn't like me, or the idea of the two of us together. But I did. I liked Noah so much I thought my entire body might break if I went more than a day without seeing him. I liked him so much I pictured him every time I closed my eyes. I craved his touch, his laughter, his gaze. Maybe other people didn't think we were a good idea, and I'd given their opinion due consideration. But we *were* a good idea, the two of us.

We might be the best idea in the world.

Twenty-Five

"How do you feel," Noah asked a few days later, as we lay on the beach after I'd finished work and he'd finished crew practice, "about garden parties thrown by obscenely wealthy people?"

I propped myself up on my elbows so I could gaze down at him. He was so beautiful, this boy, with his curly hair and his dark eyes and his smile, which came so easily and often when we were together. "Like, say, the one I served drinks at?"

"Swap out summer-beginning for summer-ending. My grand-parents throw one every year."

"I am *slightly* skeptical of going to a party with your family."

"They'll get over themselves the more they see you. Exposure therapy."

"Hm."

"My mom likes you. My dad's just salty because of botany, but he'll chill out. Especially if he realizes we're serious."

Serious. There was something tantalizing about how he said it, so matter-of-factly. He had no doubt about us. He wanted his family to know me. He was serious.

Still. "And your grandparents?"

"We'll avoid them." He tugged me closer, his tone imploring. "Please. I have to go. And it's my last night on the island before I leave for Boston. I want to spend it with you."

A pang shot through me at the idea of him leaving so soon. I'd leave a scant week after, and then we wouldn't see each other for who knew how long. I forced my lips up. "How very full circle."

"Please. We can even break in to the study again if you like."

This time my smile was more genuine. "If you're lucky."

He grinned up at me. "You can serve me champagne, too."

I smacked his chest lightly. "I'll pour it *on* you."

"Oh, I think I'd like that, too," he murmured. When my mouth fell open he laughed and pulled me down for a kiss.

"You're bad."

He rolled us over and pressed his lips to the underside of my jaw. "Only if *you're* lucky."

So we went to the party.

This time, I wore a gauzy pink dress and heeled sandals. Instead of sneaking through the house, I arrived early and hung out with Noah and cousins during setup. And instead of early summer flowers, we were deep in August, everything lush and green, soaked with color like the world couldn't hold itself back.

Yet I couldn't forget how fall would soon arrive. In the morning, Noah would leave for Cambridge, and soon I'd return to South Hadley. I tried to picture the world cold again. It seemed impossible winter would ever come here, where the sun seeped so thoroughly through to my bones. Perspiration beaded on my skin, and the heady perfume of flowers soaked the air. Yet I could feel the seasons readying to turn, the world shifting. *My* world shifting.

"Stay close," Noah said as the guests started arriving, scanning the incoming adults from our safety within the pack of cousins.

"What happens if I don't?"

"I won't be able to protect you from conversations about whether or not snakeskin print is in or out."

I blinked. "Which is it?"

"Okay, maybe I should leave you to those conversations."

But none of the conversations were so mundane—or maybe they were, but I hardly noticed, because each time we merged into a new group of people, Noah said, "This is my girlfriend, Abigail," and by the time I'd come down from the high—his *girlfriend*—we'd moved on to the next group.

I did stick to his side, and closely, because I didn't want to lose a moment of this night, even if we had to share it with other people. But at one point I found myself across a circle from him—and the next thing I knew, Noah's mom stood before me.

"Abby. I'm so glad you came."

Mrs. Barbanel was probably the only member of the Barbanel clan who might be happy to see me, so I returned her tentative smile. "Hi, Mrs. Barbanel. Everything is so nice."

"Oh, no thanks to me. Noah's grandmother does all of it." She tilted her head, rather birdlike. "Noah tells me he's going to take a biological diversity class next year."

I tensed, afraid of being politely reamed out.

"It sounds nice," she added, to my surprise. "He was telling me about the program and he's very excited about it. He's always been fascinated by nature. His grandmother taught him all about gardening, every summer we came here."

"Oh?" I squeaked.

She smiled. "She tried to teach me, when I first married Harry, but the outdoors isn't really my thing. She was thrilled when Noah showed interest. It's a bit of a family tradition—my husband's grandmother taught Helen." Mrs. Barbanel's clear, steady gaze made me wonder how much she knew about this summer. "It was one of the few things the two shared."

"I'm glad," I said, and I meant it. Because even though most of my support belonged to O'ma, part of me hurt for Helen, for anyone made to feel like a second choice. Because of course she'd wanted to fit in; of course she wanted her mother-in-law's approval. And my heart hurt for Eva Barbanel, too, who used to show my grandmother the flowers she planted. Had Eva felt like she'd lost a daughter when O'ma left Edward?

The sun sank into the sea, and the moon intensified, a perfect pearl in the sky. The night whirled on in laughter and conversation. At a little past ten, I stopped by the hedges on my way back from the bathroom and breathed in the night air, taking in the scene. People filled the lawn, adults, teenagers, the occasional child. A palpable joy and delight in summer traveled like a current between guests. Even the windows glowed with a cozy, warm light. For the first time, Golden Doors looked like a home to me.

I pulled out my phone to capture the moment, framing Noah where he stood with a group against the house. An email alert flashed across the top of my screen: a new message in my exchange about the Holtzman House. I sucked in a breath, and surprise and anticipation jolted through me as I tapped the email open.

> Dear Abigail,
> Hi, my name's Megan Wolfe and I'm the collections intern at the New York Jewish Archives. I was forwarded your request for photos from 1939 from the Holtzman House. I've digitized the collection of images from those years and attached the file. I hope this contains what you're looking for! Please let me know if there's anything else we can help you with.

I was going to send this intern a gift basket.

Noah was still talking with people halfway across the lawn, laughing with two men in seersucker. He wouldn't miss me for a few more minutes. I opened the PDF.

The pictures loaded slowly, so I scrolled the same way, taking in each one. Children and teenagers, girls my age holding toddler boys, solemn expressions, heavy coats, old-fashioned hats, the rare smile—

And there she was. O'ma. I wouldn't have recognized her if I hadn't already seen a picture of her in the Barbanel scrapbooks, which had showed me what she looked like at only four years old. She wore a heavy jacket and a cloche hat.

And—

My breath caught in my chest, like my heart had snagged on a rib bone. I enlarged the photo, bringing my phone closer. A furrow dug deep between my brows.

There, resting across her collarbone, hung the necklace.

But. She was four years old. Why would a four-year-old be wearing a necklace? And—she didn't *have* the necklace yet. She hadn't met Edward yet. Edward gave her the necklace.

Unless he hadn't.

Unless it really was O'ma's necklace. And it had to be—how else could she be wearing it in this photo? That was the only option.

And it made sense, didn't it? Because why else would she have wanted it back so much? She'd wanted it back because it had always been hers. It had belonged to her all along.

Why had Edward lied? How dare he? For what possible reason could he have had to lie to us?

Except—

Actually, *Helen* had told me Edward gave O'ma the necklace. She, technically, had been the one to lie. Had she done it to keep Edward from looking like a thief? To protect the family reputation, which Noah said she valued so much? But for god's sake. They shouldn't have lied. Maybe they'd had a reason, but they should have owned up to it, especially now, years later. Was it really easier to try to sweep the truth under the rug and hope I would go away?

I had to tell Noah.

Quick and light-footed, I crossed the lawn, and took a small step up to his side. I placed my hand on the back of his arm. "Hi."

He beamed at me and took my hand. "This is my girlfriend, Abigail Schoenberg."

Girlfriend.

I nodded politely during the introductions—*ah yes, Representative, nice to meet you, and you, too, news anchor who looks shorter in person, best not to mention*—quivering with suppressed tension. When the others returned to their conversation, I stood on my tip-toes and whispered in Noah's ear. "I have to tell you something."

He looked at me, took in my expression, and nodded. "Nice talking to you," he said to the others, and let me drag him away to the edge of the lawn, where the privet hedge rose. We stood in an archway leading to the gardens and roses and gazebo and ocean, a spot of privacy with the rest of the guests drifting before us.

"What?" he asked, half laughing.

"Look at this." I showed him the photo on my phone, practically bouncing on my toes. "That's my grandmother's necklace."

His eyes focused on mine, confused, intent. He transferred his attention to the screen. "What?"

"The nonprofit I emailed, with the records from the Holtzman House, where my grandmother went. They emailed me their pictures from the year she arrived."

He took the phone from my hand and enlarged the photo, just as I'd done. "This is her?"

"Yeah. From when she first arrived in the States." Unable to resist, I gave a little jump. "Noah, she's wearing the necklace. It was *hers*."

His mouth worked, a frown swallowed. "But my grandfather gave her the necklace."

"He didn't. He clearly didn't, because they hadn't even met at this point. He must have—" The word *lied* died on my lips.

His gaze clouded with confusion. "I don't understand."

He did. But I couldn't force him to admit his conclusion. He had to decide to take it in himself. "Noah."

He nodded, pressing his lips into a thin line. "I don't suppose we suspect it's a bizarrely identical necklace."

"We don't. I'm sorry." To be honest, I cared less about the deception than finding out it *had* been Oma's. She'd been right to want it back; I'd been right to try to find out what happened. "Maybe they got confused, who knows, I don't care."

"Why would he have said he'd given it to her, then? Why wouldn't he have returned it when she asked?"

"I have no idea. But we have to talk to him, again. This is proof, Noah. If we show him this photo—if he knows we *know* the necklace belonged to Ruth—he'll have to tell us the truth."

He nodded. "Abigail . . ."

"Yes?"

He blew out a breath and shook his head. "I don't know. I don't understand. I just . . . I didn't think they would lie. I thought—I thought they must have reasons for keeping things to themselves."

"Maybe they did have reasons." *But probably not good ones.* "We'll find out what we can."

He rubbed his temple. "I need a drink." He grabbed two glasses of champagne off a passing waiter's tray, taking an alarmingly large swig. He didn't meet my eyes, and finished off one flute in a matter of seconds.

"Noah, what is it?" I'd spent too much time with this boy not to know something was off. "What's wrong?"

"It's nothing."

"I'm not sure I believe you." I studied him. I'd never seen his face like this, or his body so stiff. Ice began to spread through my veins. "What aren't you telling me?"

"I don't believe in—I don't know, airing family business." His gaze flicked over my shoulder and his face went even more expressionless. "Let's go over here." He took my hand and tugged me one way, but I dug in my heels and turned in the direction he'd been facing.

And went cold.

I hadn't seen his grandmother yet tonight, but now she glided out of the crowd toward us, immaculate in a blue gown, her white hair blown out. Around her neck, a necklace glittered, cold and clear as ice. "Hello, dears."

I felt like I'd been punched in the stomach.

Slowly, slowly, I pivoted to Noah. He stood utterly still.

"Tell me," I said, remote and precise, "you didn't know she had it."

He closed his eyes. He was impossibly handsome, this statue of a boy, with his artful curls and crisp white shirt. When he opened his eyes, he didn't need to speak.

He knew. He had known this whole time. We'd found the photo of my grandmother wearing the necklace as a teen, and he'd thought, *I know this necklace* and *Better not tell this girl,* and he'd never changed his mind. He'd known his grandmother had the necklace, and he'd concealed it, despite knowing how badly I wanted to find it.

I had to escape and there was nowhere to go, no way to get through the mass of guests to the exit. So I did the next best thing. I turned and walked through the arch in the hedge into the deep, flourishing garden.

"Abigail—"

I picked up my skirts and ran.

Flowers and trees whipped past me. Juniper trees, with their sharp needles. Late summer blooms, orange and yellow, reminders of the autumn to come. I turned into the rose garden. Now what? I'd pinned myself in. There was nowhere to go, just the gazebo, the high ground in the storm. I bolted up the steps, as though it could protect me, this structure with no walls, no entrance or exit.

"Abigail!"

I whirled around, the sheer fabric of my dress swirling around my legs. Each detail of the evening intensified, like I'd put on glasses after walking through the world without. Ivy choked the gazebo's posts; golden light gilded the deep green leaves. Rose perfume saturated the air. Tawny sunlight stretched in long lines across the gazebo's floor. "You lied to me."

Beneath Noah's golden tan, his face was pale and set. "I didn't lie."

"You knew your grandmother had the necklace, and you didn't say anything."

He shook his head, putting his foot on the first of the gazebo's three steps. I moved backward into a pool of light let in from the roof's cupola. "I thought you were wrong. I thought you were digging into my family's history, into our possessions. I thought it was my grandmother's necklace."

"But it wasn't *your* grandmother's, it was *mine*."

"I didn't know!"

"Well, then, why didn't we talk about it? Why didn't you say, 'Oh yeah, that necklace. I know it,' instead of letting me flounder blindly?"

"Because we barely even knew each other."

I drew back as though struck. "I see."

He moved forward. "Don't. Don't withdraw."

"Why shouldn't I? God, Noah! What about later, when we *did* know each other? We had dinner with your family, and *Shabbat*— we went sailing together, we talked to the rabbi, we ate hundreds of ice cream cones—you made me think we were friends and you were *helping* me and you knew where it was the entire time. Were you just trying to throw me off course?

"No!" He raked his fingers through his hair. "I mean, yes, when we started this, I was trying to keep you from getting too close. And then—I was trying to decide what the right thing to do was. I was trying to protect them."

"Well, good," I said. "You succeeded. You protected your family and kept your secrets, good job. You could have kept my grand-mother's necklace, too, if yours hadn't insisted on wearing it."

"God, Abigail, obviously I would have told you now. After learn-ing the necklace belonged to your grandmother."

"Sure," I said scornfully. I was so hot, so terribly, terribly hot. The only way to protect myself was to ice over, a shell of unyielding cold. "Which is why you said something right away instead of taking a shot of champagne."

"I was processing."

"How long does it take you to process? Dammit, Noah." I gripped my skirt, fingers crushing the pale tulle. My voice went high and tight. "You didn't even tell me after *Boston*."

His face softened and he reached for me. "Abigail—"

I stumbled back. My face was hot and my heart fast as a hum-mingbird. "You don't keep secrets like this."

"By Boston—I thought it was a moot point. It didn't matter. We'd

figured out—we thought the necklace belonged to my grandfather.
Why add fuel to the fire?"

"It's about trust, Noah. And being honest."

"It would have upset you."

"Then upset me! I'd rather be upset than oblivious! God!" I raked
my hands through my hair. "You should have told me. You shouldn't
have pretended to help me when you weren't."

"I was trying to balance—"

"But you didn't, Noah. You didn't balance me and your family.
You chose them." I shook my head. "You know what? You're right.
We barely knew each other. We still barely know each other." I summoned the ice again, stiffening my spine and lifting my chin. "I want
it back."

"What?" He almost looked confused.

"I want the necklace back."

"You're being impulsive—"

"Don't tell me what I'm doing or being. It's my grandma's, isn't it?
She asked for it back. She told him to send it to her, and he refused."

"That was *ages* ago."

"And so was Elgin stealing the Parthenon's marbles, and so
was the Rosetta Stone, and it's still a terrible excuse." Maybe those
weren't the strongest examples, given how the British Museum still
hadn't returned the items to Greece or Egypt. "I want it."

"It's been my grandmother's for fifty years!"

"And who knows how many years it was in my family for? Either
you can talk to your family, or I will."

"Abigail—" He grabbed my arm.

I shook him off. "I mean it, Noah." I pushed past him, back through
the rose garden, barely keeping it together as I reemerged onto the
lawn. The guests smiling faces blended in a chaotic, maddening

mess, a swirl of too-bright eyes and high-pitched laughter. I stumbled through them, heading toward the front.

I hadn't meant to confront Helen Barbanel. I really hadn't.

But when then she was in front of me, in her blue gown like an ice queen. The jewels glittered at her neck. The words burst out of me. "Why did you say your husband gave my grandmother the necklace?"

"Excuse me?" She turned her cool, impenetrable gaze on me.

"I know it's not true. I found an old photo of my grandmother wearing the necklace."

Her expression didn't even flicker. "What do you mean, dear?"

"A photo from when she was a child. It was Ruth's necklace. It was always her necklace."

Helen tilted her head, a pitying smile on her face. "It belonged to Edward's mother. Ruth probably borrowed it to try on."

"No." I stood my ground. "This photo is from before she ever came to Golden Doors." I turned my phone toward her. "See?"

She took my phone. Blinked. "What is this?"

"It's from the Holtzman House in New York City. From when my grandmother arrived there as a kid."

Her mouth parted. "How did she get that necklace?"

"Probably from her family before she came over." Why would she lie to me? I'd known she didn't like me, but you couldn't just *lie*.

"No." Helen shook her head. Her voice was oddly hollow, surprise echoing through her words. "It was from Edward."

"Oh." A terrible inkling slipped up the back of my spine.

"He gave it to me. It was his mother's."

I stared at her.

Helen's lips pressed together, so like her grandson's. Then she handed my phone back, and her motions became precise and sharp. "Come along. I believe we both need some questions answered."

Twenty-Six

Helen swept across the crowded lawn and I followed in her wake. No one seemed to notice the fury in every line of her body. She paused in front of her husband, who sat in a chair facing two older men. "If you'll excuse us," she said to the pair, her bearing regal. "I need a moment with my husband."

They practically bowed as they left.

Helen Barbanel did not sit. Instead, she towered over her husband, righteous fury in a sky-blue gown. Her voice didn't tremble when she spoke, but I could see the quiver in her fingers as she unclasped the necklace. She held it up. "This young lady says the necklace never belonged to you."

Edward Barbanel closed his eyes.

"Is this true?" his wife pressed. "This necklace doesn't belong to your family? It came from Ruth Goldman?"

Still he said nothing.

"Answer me," Helen hissed, so low none of the nearby guests could overhear. "Or at least tell me it's not true."

He groaned, deep in his throat.

She sucked in a deep breath, then turned to me. Pulling my hand from my side, she pressed the necklace into it. "Take it."

I stood stock-still.

She turned back on her husband. "I am not a thief, Edward

Barbanel. You've embarrassed me." She strode away, flinging herself back into her guests with a wide smile and a laugh as bright and cold as diamonds.

Leaving me facing Edward Barbanel. I blinked at the elderly man, then looked down at the sparkling pendants in my grasp. "Do you . . . what . . ." I held it out to him uncertainly.

He turned his head away. "Go," he said.

So I did. I stuffed the necklace in my pocket, and walked right out of the party. With shaking fingers, I summoned a car, then tried to calm myself by taking giant, gulping breaths and staring up at the moon.

"Abigail."

I turned. Noah stood behind me. His hair was tousled, by his fingers or the wind, his expression bleak. "You're not leaving?"

I was so mad at him. I didn't know if my anger was rational or ridiculous, but it was *there*, a deep-seated, unyielding fury. A sense of betrayal and humiliation. He'd known what I wanted and treated it as unimportant. Fine. I didn't need that in my life.

"Can we talk about this?"

"No."

"*Abigail.*" He strode closer. "I'm *leaving* tomorrow."

"So leave." I turned away from him.

He stepped in front of me. "We can't end things like this—"

"Actually, we can. Pretty sure this is what we call a deal breaker."

"You think I should have picked you over my grandparents? My family? The company?"

"I don't know. Maybe you made the right choice for you. But you didn't make the right choice for us. Lies and distrust are no foundation for a relationship."

"Neither is breaking into someone's house! But people change."

"But you didn't change enough, clearly. You didn't trust me, or you would have told me."

"You are so goddamn proud."

I shrugged.

"What will it take to get over this?"

I quenched my molten anger in ice, turning it hard as tempered steel. "We're not going to get over this. Look, we had a good run. But we're done."

He stared at me. "You're breaking up with me because of this?"

I shrugged again and wrapped my arms around my stomach. If my shell cracked, I would dissolve into a puddle, which I couldn't handle right now. I couldn't put myself back together if I let myself break. Instead, I started to uproot my emotions, pulling back each tendril I'd wrapped tightly around Noah. "We should have known this wouldn't work. We're too different."

He frowned furiously. "You're scared, Abigail Schoenberg. Scared to really put yourself out there."

"And you're confused. You think this is all about you? It's not." I pulled the necklace out and gestured with it wildly. "Maybe the happy ending to this summer isn't a cute little love story but a family heirloom reclaimed."

We both flinched, gazes locked. Neither of us had used the word *love* before.

He stepped closer. "You think you'd be happier without me?"

And because I knew how to aim words like arrows, I said, "Yes. I do."

"You're wrong." His jaw worked. "You're wrong and you're too proud to admit it."

"Well, it doesn't really matter, does it?" I said, making my tone cold enough to freeze the ocean. "It's not your call to make."

"You'll make yourself miserable, Abigail." He was cold now, too, chilly as the longest night.

"That's my choice."

He cursed low and hard. "We're not going to be able to see each other again and work this out, you know. My flight's at ten a.m. tomorrow."

I shrugged. "Fine."

"It's not fine. None of this is fine." He stared at me. "You're *fine*?"

If I spoke, I would break, so I only nodded.

He closed off, iced over. "Fine." He nodded at the necklace. "I hope you're happy."

I wanted to hit him with it.

"Goodbye, Abigail." He turned on his heel and walked back into the house.

I wanted to scream after him. I wanted to hurl the necklace at his head. I wanted to fall into a puddle on the ground and cry and wait until he came back. Because already, I wanted him to come back.

Instead I gathered myself together and looked at my phone. Two more minutes until my car got here. I looked at the moon and tried to breathe.

At home, I curled up in my bed and hugged Sad Elephant to my chest.

Moments of the summer flashed through my mind. Standing in the garden at Golden Doors for the first time, looking at butterflies, the sad look on Noah's face when he'd said, *Thus, the monarchs.* Walking through the driftwood maze; handing him a lucky stone. *Quien no sabe de mar, no sabe de mal.* Meandering through the Arboretum in Boston; leaning against the bridge's railing over the

Charles. The whisper of velvet curtains. The glowing ocean.

Usually, I wasn't moved to tears by real-life events. I remained stoic and suppressed (thanks, New England reserve!). Then, when I was deep in the safety of a book and came across an emotional scene, I would cry deep, wrenching tears, out of proportion with the text. The tears would dissolve the calcified lump of emotion I'd been carrying around, leaving me hollow and shaky. Then I'd continue reading, and the book would fill me back up, restoring my levels like an aquifer pouring into low rivers. They were aquifers of emotions, books. They were miracles.

Now I tried to pick up my novel, but I couldn't make the words move. I couldn't replace my mind with the words on the page. Instead, my e-reader fell to my side, and tears leaked onto the pillow in a great, damp spread. No words could regulate my emotions, could tell me when to cry and when to hope. Instead, nothing stopped the tears, and they came jagged and constant all through the long night, and even my books couldn't comfort me.

I didn't want to tell my parents what had happened.

Telling them would be embarrassing—Noah and I had barely been together, and now we were over. Worse, it would make the breakup feel real. And worst, they'd be sympathetic, and sympathy might make me crack open.

But better to tell them than risk a question about how Noah was doing. I did it at the end of our next Zoom call, attempting to keep my voice light and detached. "One other thing—Noah and I broke up."

Mom straightened on the couch, shock on her face. "Oh, honey, I'm so sorry. What happened?"

I shrugged. No way I could keep from crying if I got into it. "It doesn't matter. He's going to college in the fall, anyway. It wouldn't have made sense."

"Oh, sweetie, I wish I could hug you." Mom's face and voice were a canvas of tragedy. Beside her, Dad rubbed her shoulder, looking distressed.

"It's okay," I said quickly. "My friends are being great. And we really only dated for a few weeks."

"But you really liked him."

I shrugged again, wrapping my arms around my chest. "Yeah. But I'm fine."

"You don't have to be fine, Abigail." Mom looked worried.

"I guess. I will be, though."

"I know you will. You're so strong, honey."

"Yeah. Okay. I just figured I should tell you. I'm going to go to bed now."

"Are you sure?"

I couldn't take any more of her sympathy or I'd start bawling. "Yeah. I'll see you soon."

"We love you, honey," Dad said, his quiet, measured voice the straw that made the camel weep.

"Love you, too," I managed to get out, and hung up right before the tears came once more.

I wasn't actually sure I'd be fine.

I hadn't wondered if I'd been in love with Noah until now, because falling in love was terrifying and immense and best left to adults, not seventeen-year-olds with overactive imaginations. But when I broke down while walking on the beach, when snot ran down my face as I howled like a wounded wolf, I didn't have to wonder. When I waited for Jane's breath to fall into the rhythmic cadence of sleep so I could sob with Sad Elephant in my arms, I didn't wonder. "I loved him," I whispered, ragged and broken. "I *love* him."

And because I wasn't unaware of my melodramatic nature, I told myself other things, too: "You're being stupid and pathetic. Get a grip. You're seventeen, this is so normal as to be unnoteworthy."

"But I *loved* him."

"'Tis better to have loved and lost. This is a good life experience. A growth opportunity."

"But he was supposed to love me *back*. He wasn't supposed to let me walk away."

"You literally told him to. You were mean. Why would he stay with you?"

Honestly, I felt a bit like Gollum.

Stella took me out for ice cream. "You have to be as nice to yourself as you'd be to a friend," she told me, serious as I'd ever seen her. "That's what my therapist says."

"I guess."

"Not 'I guess.' I mean it. Moping doesn't make you stupid. You got hurt. You're allowed to feel feelings."

"What if I don't want to?"

"Ah." She crunched on her cone. "There you're out of luck."

I had my last shift at the Prose Garden the next day. Liz baked me a miniature cake, and Maggie gave me earrings of dangling stacked books. "Come back next summer," Maggie invited. "We'll let you choose one of the book-club books."

I launched myself at her, and after a surprised moment, she hugged me back. "Thank you," I told her, then hugged Liz, too. "You guys have been amazing."

I expected that to be the most memorable part of the day, but an hour later, Edward Barbanel showed up in the bookstore's doorway, dressed in jeans, a sweater, and a windbreaker, as though it wasn't eighty degrees outside. Seeing him outside his home jarred me; he looked much frailer than when seated behind his massive desk or at the head of the table, surrounded by the home and family he'd built over decades.

Great. What was I supposed to do? I couldn't exactly be rude to a ninety-year-old man when I wasn't fueled by rage. "Hello, Mr. Barbanel."

"Abigail." He smiled at me, the expression unexpected on his weathered face. "Do you have a moment to talk?"

Did I have a moment to talk with my ex-boyfriend's grandfather who'd stolen my grandmother's necklace? "I'm working right now . . ."

"It'll only take a minute. Where can we sit?"

Oy. "In the armchairs. Let me tell my boss I'm taking a break." I hesitated, hostess instincts kicking in. "Would you like anything from the café?"

"An Earl Grey would be perfect, my dear."

Blargh, old men calling me *my dear.* I gave him a pained smile.

When I returned, I placed his tea on the table beside him and settled into the opposing armchair, a green juice in hand.

He opened his eyes. "I wanted to tell you about the necklace."

Did he, now. After avoiding the topic for months. I sipped my juice. "Okay."

It took him a moment to start. "The necklace was Ruth's, it's true."

I did not say *No shit, Sherlock,* for which I should have been commended.

"It was one of the few things she arrived with—the clothes on her back, a small case, and the necklace. She hid the necklace itself in the hem of her dress before she came to New York. She planned to sell it after the war, to bring her parents to America."

I swallowed over a sudden lump.

His eyes were kind. "Yes. After the news, she wore it everywhere. She bought her whole wardrobe to set off the necklace—she only dressed in reds and blacks for a year." He paused. "We decided to get married."

My eyes widened. I wanted, instinctively, for Noah to be here—Noah, who I was so mad at. Yet he'd been part of uncovering this story from the beginning. "What happened?"

"My mother." He sighed. "And before her, the collapse of the family fortune. Ruth knew, of course. She said we should sell the necklace and use the money to help the company survive. To help us survive. It wouldn't be enough, but it would be something."

He drew something from his pocket and passed it over to me. "Then she sent me this."

I am going to try to explain, the letter started, and for the first time, I read one of O'ma's letters, as she tried to set Edward Barbanel up for disagreement. She loved him, she said. She loved him, but romantic love was only one kind of love, and she prized other types equally as high.

> *Yesterday, your mother showed up at my apartment. I haven't seen her in ages, and I threw myself into her arms right away and started crying. And she hugged me back, and Ned, it was—I don't even know how to explain it. I feel stupid, since she's your mother,*

and obviously you've always had her. But I barely see her now
that I've moved, and I've missed her, and here she was.

We went inside and I wanted to die from embarrassment
because the room I rent from Mrs. Schwartz was so cramped and
small and messy, and I'd left clothes everywhere and didn't even
have tea to offer her.

But it didn't matter and we talked for hours, and I felt like a
sunflower reaching toward her, soaking in her rays. And then she
said, "You know you can't marry Edward."

And I said we were in love.

And she said, "I know. But the company will go under if we
don't get help, and then where will the two of you be? We'll have
to sell Golden Doors and maybe even the New York house. And
you'll be poor and he'll resent you and all our employees will be
out of a job and the Barbanels will be done. So I'm asking you not
to marry him."

And the thing is, Ned—she's the closest thing I have to a
mother.

The page ended. I looked up at Edward. "That's it?"

"Another page or two, but this is the important part. My mother
asked her not to marry me. So Ruth decided not to."

"She must have loved your mom a lot," I said slowly.

He nodded. "I never understood. Or maybe I did, intellectually,
but I never would have chosen my parents' wishes over my own. I
wouldn't have put the family first the way she did."

What would I do? If my mom asked me not to marry someone I
loved? I wanted to say I would stick to my gut, but—my *mom*. If she
asked me, she would have a reason. And my mom had put her everything into raising me. I owed her everything.

I cleared my throat. "So my grandmother gave you the necklace—but why didn't you give it back?"

He stirred his tea. "Because I was foolish, and stubborn, and hopeful. I didn't believe she'd leave the necklace behind. I thought if I had it, she'd *have* to come talk to me. I'd be able to make her change her mind."

"But she didn't?"

"No."

Oh. "Then—then what? You decided to go along with her plan and marry Helen?"

He nodded, not looking at me.

Poor Helen. "Why didn't you send the necklace back to my grand-mother, then?"

"I don't know," he said softly. "I like to think I might have, if she'd ever asked again. But she didn't. I guess . . . I thought if I still had the necklace, she might someday be forced to talk to me."

But she never had. Why not? Had she just decided to cut her losses? Had she been too angry? Had she already been swept away by my grandpa?

Too late to find out the answer.

"And you gave it to your wife," I said. "Why?"

He met my eyes, his own sad and calm. "I don't know."

What an unsatisfactory answer. But then again, maybe I could an-swer my question myself—anger, revenge, nothing pretty to own up to. I'd thought people grew up once they became adults, but maybe no one ever really grew up. Maybe people were always capable of be-ing petty and cruel, even people with all the power in the world.

But maybe they were also capable of changing.

"I'm sorry," Edward Barbanel said. "I came by to tell you, to apol-ogize. I was wrong to keep the necklace; wrong to give it to Helen. It was unkind to both women. I'm glad you have it back now, even if I didn't make it easy." He hesitated. "I hope you won't take it out too hard on Noah. He tries to do the right thing. More than I ever did. But he's young, and young people make mistakes. What matters is how they handle them afterwards."

After Edward Barbanel left, I stared up at the slowly moving ceiling fan. O'ma had chosen her mother over Edward. He hadn't chosen money over love; she had chosen being a daughter over being a lover.

Why were there so many choices in life? Why couldn't things be easy, one simple current carrying us along to our destination? But there were so many branches, so many opportunities to mess up or upset people.

Noah had chosen his family over me, and even though his choice had made me feel like he didn't trust me, I understood why he'd done it, why he hadn't known what to protect, his family or our trust.

Should I apologize for pushing him away? Should he apologize for keeping a secret? Should we both apologize for everything? If we both stood by our stances—mine being a relationship needed honesty, his being he'd been right to protect his family's privacy—did it make us incompatible?

I had no idea. All I knew was I missed him like a phantom limb. I wanted to text him desperately.

But what good would getting back in touch do? He had lied to me. He'd said I was overreacting, though it had been my grandmother's necklace and he'd known and this would never work, so why bother trying? How could I trust him again? How did you let go of something so painful? Even if you wanted to, how did you actually do it?

And he was gone to college, and of course a relationship between us wouldn't work in the long run. Wasn't this better, this clean break? So what if we *did* work out our differences—what if we gave us a second go? Then what? Then we were in a long-distance relationship and time and space would break our hearts all over again.

No. There were too many arguments against trying to get back together. It was smarter not to. Maybe this was why O'ma had avoided seeing Edward again: Because she knew if she saw him, it would be too hard not to be drawn back together. And then it would be even harder to separate, which she knew would happen in the end.

Twenty-Seven

July 12, 1952

Did I ever tell you about the first time I saw the house?

Some people will say I wasn't old enough to remember arriving. But I do. I remember other scenes, too, scenes too sad to relate, and this was the first good memory in a long time.

The social worker held my hand. She must have been well-intentioned to have taken her job, but mostly I remember her as having a brash accent, square jaw, and little patience. She'd scolded me nonstop since we'd left the city, and had for some unknown reason become convinced I meant to foil her care by diving off the ferry.

"Usually, the family is at the New York house," she'd told me. But not during the summer. They'd offered to have the nanny and chauffeur pick me up at the wharf, but the social worker wasn't giving up her chance to see Golden Doors, so we loaded ourselves into a car and wound our way up the island. Past those trees wizened by salt and sea, past the Portuguese hydrangeas. I'd already been in so many worlds—New York City and Paris and home— and here was another one.

The house came into view. You know how it does, unveiled like the brass sounding their horns in Holst's "Jupiter." I'd never seen something so stately yet so undeniably American. These were the people who planned to take me in? What could I possibly have in common with them?

A woman opened the door. She crouched down, eyes at my level. "Hello," she said, speaking in German, though her accent was poor and I could have understood hello, at least, in English. But she'd learned these phrases for me, to make me feel more comfortable. "You must be Ruth. I'm Eva. Welcome home."

Mom showed up on the next ferry.

"You didn't have to come," I said as she descended onto the docks, but then I hugged her tightly and didn't let go. She smelled like Pert shampoo and Tom's soap, like home and safety.

"Of course I did." She cupped my cheek in one hand while trying to smooth out a line in my brow with the other.

"But you don't take boats." She'd *never* taken boats, not once in my entire memory. She *hated* boats.

"I'm an adult, you know. I can take boats."

"But you *don't*." My voice wobbled embarrassingly.

"Oh, sweetie." She pulled me close again, and the tears shook out of me as I clung to her. "You poor thing."

"I really liked him," I whispered into her chest.

"I know you did."

Mom's presence salved the deep, constant hurt pulsing through me. She was better than chocolate, better than books. We went to the inn where she was staying and ordered pizza and watched *13 Going on 30* on TV.

She'd be staying for three nights, before we both went home. I wanted to show her Nantucket—show *off* Nantucket. In the morning, I led her from shop to café to beach. "I can't believe you spent all summer here," she said as we walked barefoot along Jetties Beach, the water lapping at our feet. She walked higher on the wet sand than

I did, only occasionally getting licked by the tides, while I sloshed through the water.

"Isn't it gorgeous?" It was a stunning late August day, with enough of a hint of chill in the air to be reminded fall would soon arrive. "Wasn't it a good idea for me to come here?"

She scoffed and bumped me gently.

"It *was*," I pressed. "But you were so against me coming. How come?"

"Oh, honey." She stopped walking and stroked my hair. "You were so upset earlier this summer. I didn't want you to be upset far away from me, where I couldn't hug you when you got sad. You're leaving so soon, anyway, for college—I don't want you to leave me. I don't want you to get hurt. I don't want to not be able to protect you."

"Oh." I felt small and ashamed. "You don't have to worry about me."

"Of course I do. I'm your mother. I'm always going to worry about you."

I hugged her, quick and impulsive. "I love you."

"I love you, too."

In the afternoon, I took her to the Prose Garden, and introduced her to Maggie and Liz. Then Jane met us for ice cream, and we told Mom a curated list of the best summer moments. Sans Noah, of course.

Mom let my boy-exclusions pass until dinner. The two of us ate at one of the bougie restaurants I'd eyed all summer, with tables on a deck overlooking the ocean. Umbrellas provided shade and flowers twined up against the railing.

"Why did you two break up?" she asked. "You seemed so happy."

I buttered a yeasty white roll. "It's complicated."

"Do you want to talk about it?"

Her hopeful, sad eyes made me feel obligated to tell her. "He knew his grandmother had O'ma's necklace the entire time. And he didn't tell me—what?"

Mom looked appalled. "You broke up with him over a *necklace*?"

"No! Not *over* the necklace. It was more—he didn't *tell* me. He lied."

"Did he lie, or did he not bring it up?"

"Mom, it's the same thing!"

She cut into her salmon. "Well, honey, I think it's a shame if you end something so important because of a necklace."

"Mom!"

"Did he want to break up, too?"

I stared at her, furious. "You're supposed to be on *my* side."

"I am! Of course I am. But you liked him so much."

"It doesn't even matter. I'm being practical. He's going to college."

"Don't be practical! When did I ever teach you to be practical?"

"Um, I'm literally only allowed to go to a state school or somewhere I get a full ride because you refuse to let me graduate with student loans."

"Okay, yes, but—"

"Practical!" My voice rose a little too high.

She stared at me, then held up her hands. "Okay."

"Okay, we can move on?"

"Of course."

Of course, we couldn't really. Several hours later, when we'd retreated to her hotel room and were watching TV, she brought it up again. "We should talk about why this necklace matters so much to you."

"What do you mean?"

"I don't understand how you became so obsessed with an object.

Why do you care so much about material things? Did I make you? How? It's not one of my values."

"God, Mom, it's not about *material things*. This necklace—it was O'ma's."

"But it's just an object."

"It was an important one! She cared about it! Why can't I care?"

"Of course you can care. But you care so much, I worry you'll hurt yourself. You throw yourself so hard into something like this, and it ends up upsetting you. Why can't you let it wash over you instead of fixating on it? Why would you let a necklace ruin a relationship?"

"It was the principle of the thing. It was because he *lied*. It was because—"

Because I was too damn proud?

Because he hadn't fought for me, while he'd always made it clear he'd fight for what mattered to him?

I shook my head, trying to clear it of Noah. "I *wanted* to do this, Mom. I wanted to find out about O'ma's past. So I got a little hurt— it's worth it. I wish you could *get* that." I could feel the tears welling up. "I wish you could be proud of me for finding out everything I did, instead of thinking it was messed up. I found out where O'ma was from! I found out who her parents were, and got their records. I found out about O'ma's *entire childhood*. I found a family heirloom from Germany."

"I am proud of you!"

"Are you? Because all summer all you cared about was about whether or not I was interested in Noah."

"Well, Abby, that feels a lot more real. That's the *future*. O'ma's history is the past."

Her words rang in my ears.

I swallowed. "Well, I care about the past. I wanted to know about it. Besides," I said, setting my jaw. "Now this is the past, too. So can we move on? I don't want to talk about Noah."

She studied me. "Okay, honey."

The worry in her voice effectively deflated my anger.

She forced a smile. "Do you want to show me this necklace, then?"

I did. I hadn't looked at it since I'd come home from Golden Doors, when I'd stashed it in a sunglasses pouch, but I'd put the pouch in my purse this morning. I'd always intended to show it to Mom today. Now I pulled the pouch out and handed it over.

Mom loosened the drawstring and poured the necklace into her palm. It landed in a pile of glittering rectangle stones. She held it up, her brows raising. "It's very pretty."

"Right?" The sunlight glinted off the cut pendants.

"What are these? Glass?"

"Probably. Or what's it—cubic something?"

"Cubic zirconia? That's synthesized—I'm not sure they'd even figured it out in the thirties." Her eyes twinkled. "What if they're *diamonds*?"

I laughed, relieved our tension had dispersed. It was always like this with Mom; highs and lows, anger, then calm. We were cyclical tides, the two of us—or maybe the ocean and the moon, tided together, eternally inseparable even when out of sight of each other. "They're not diamonds."

Except.

I cleared my throat. "I mean—Edward Barbanel, Noah's grandfather, did say they considered selling the necklace for money."

"He did?" Mom turned the necklace over, peering at the main pendant—twice the size of the others, and oval in shape. "How do we even tell what it's made of?"

I shrugged. "I don't know, try scratching something?"

We looked around. There was nothing to scratch, except the glass tabletop of a coffee table. I didn't think the hotel would appreciate such a choice.

"I'll google it." A moment later, I read from my phone: "'Breathe on it—a real diamond will fog only briefly, then disperse the heat instead of remaining misted like glass would.'"

We looked at each other and shrugged.

"Here goes." I took the necklace back from her, raised it to my mouth, and exhaled.

The pendant misted over. The mist immediately vanished.

A shiver went down my back.

I swallowed and looked at Mom. She turned her hands, palms out, eyes wide. "Maybe you didn't breathe hard enough?"

I breathed again. Hard. Still the fog barely lasted.

Mom coughed. "Well, I can certainly tell you had those garlic knots."

"You're hilarious."

"Give it here."

But when Mom breathed, it still barely fogged over.

"Maybe fog usually only lasts a second," Mom said.

"Maybe," I said skeptically. I consulted my phone. "One of the other tests says to rub sandpaper over it."

"We don't have sandpaper," Mom said (irrefutable Mom logic). She squinted. "It's probably some other similar jewel. There's a few other clear gems, I think."

I wilted. "Yeah."

Mom smiled. "Still, no harm asking. Didn't you say Nantucket is big on antiques? We can get it appraised."

I agreed, and we divvied up some ice cream and hot fudge we'd bought earlier, and climbed into bed and pulled up the covers. We watched *Stargate* and I haltingly told her a little more about Noah, and she told me about her first boyfriend, from when she was nineteen.

It was very late when I dared voice the thought. "Mom," I said. "What if it *is* a diamond?"

Mom looked at me. And then, to my surprise, she started laughing. A grin split her face with childish delight, and her eyes closed in the familiar squint signaling utter amusement. "Hell if I know."

I laughed and closed my own eyes, a smile still on my face.

But it slowly faded as another thought surfaced.

What if Mom had been right, as she usually was? What if I *had* picked the past over the future?

Was it too late to change my mind?

Nantucket had a long history of antiques: they had antiques shops and an annual antique show and this year, they'd decided to host an *Antiques Roadshow*–style event. It took place on the lawn outside the Boys & Girls Club, in peaked white tents filled with long tables and clumps of people.

Mom and I waited in line for forty-five minutes to speak to a jewelry appraiser. Mom hummed and pointed out funny characters while we waited, her arm looped through mine. Every time my thoughts drifted to Noah, her words pulled me back, making us laugh until our sides hurt. A deep, effusive love filled me. She drove me mad, of course. But she was the best mom in the whole world.

When we finally sat down in front of the appraiser, he greeted us with a weary politeness enunciated by his British accent. He was a bit of a stereotype, and I loved him for it.

"What have we here?" he asked politely as I pulled the necklace from my purse. I'd put it back in the glasses pouch, and now felt silly, like I should have worked harder on presentation. I felt weirdly embarrassed, too, like a child taking up an adult's time with something unimportant. "It's my grandmother's necklace. It might be worth nothing. I don't know. I thought it'd be fun to find out."

I unspooled the necklace and laid it carefully on the table

"Oh." He sounded slightly surprised. For a moment he didn't move. Then he picked up the necklace, carefully, sifting it through his fingers, the pendant coming to rest in his hands. He lifted his jeweler's loupe.

Even though I knew the necklace probably only had sentimental value, I couldn't help hoping it would be worth real money. Mom and I had spent the morning watching *Antiques Roadshow* clips, and they kept valuing old jewelry at three to five thousand. I knew we only saw the highlights reel, but still. It could be worth something! Edward Barbanel had implied as much, hadn't he?

When the appraiser looked up, his face was professionally blank. "Can you trace the providence?"

I looked at him, confused. "What's providence mean?"

"Where it comes from. Can you establish the path of ownership? You might have received a certificate when you bought it."

"It belonged to my mother," Mom said.

"Where did she get it?"

"I'm not sure."

"Hmm."

Mom and I exchanged a glance. She leaned forward. "Why does it matter?"

He laid the necklace down, turning it over and pointing out a stamp on the back of one of the metal settings. "Do you see the mark here?"

We nodded.

"That's the maker's mark. It tells us who created this. This was made by the Goldman family, but without knowing the history of the purchase, it loses some of its value—especially since it might have been traded illegally at some point. The Goldmans were a German Jewish family who had most of their possessions seized by the Nazis."

A tiny shiver went down my back, tracing the line of my spine from crown to neck to spine, a dance of disbelief and anticipation. I glanced at Mom, whose wide eyes must have mirrored my own. She carefully crossed her hands in her lap. "The Goldman family," she repeated. "Are you sure?"

"Of course."

"They're our family."

The appraiser went very still, like a hunter wary of startling his prey. He spoke with the soft, calm tone of the emotionally suppressed. "Excuse me?"

"It's my mother's family," Mom said. "We've never heard of them being jewelers, though—but my mother was very young when she moved here from Germany."

"Where was she from?"

Mom looked at me. "She was from a little town called Lübeck," I said. "Her parents were Herman and Sara Goldman. They were both born in Lübeck."

He pressed his lips together, looking back and forth between us. "You're sure?"

Mom bristled. "Of course we're sure."

"We have birth records and death records and everything," I said, because I'd done a lot of hard work to find said records.

He nodded several times. Then he cleared his throat. "To be perfectly honest, I wasn't expecting this sort of situation today. I have some due diligence to do, and then if you're—interested—I might have a few more facts to share with you."

Mom and I exchanged a glance. "Of course," she said. When he asked, she scribbled her number and email down on a piece of paper for him.

"Thank you," he said. He had the air my brother had when our parents interrupted him from gaming—polite but itching to dive back into his own world. Clearly we'd been dismissed.

Yet as we stood and I put the necklace back in its bag and my purse, my curiosity was too strong to be denied. "What about the necklace? Did you have an estimate?"

He looked up. "A necklace from the Goldmans of Lübeck, of yellow cut diamond?" He smiled, brief and wry. "I'd like to look into it a bit more, but I'd tentatively appraise it at eighty thousand dollars."

Mom and I wound up at the Juice Bar.

"The Triple Chocolate Mountain flavor is very good," I said.

"Is it. Well."

We both ordered the flavor, took our cones, and sat down at one of the wooden tables. We stared at each other. Then we started laughing, small giggles at first, then loud, reckless, near-hysterical laughter.

"I tried googling them," I said when we recovered. "O'ma's parents. But nothing came up. Shouldn't it have, if they're well-known?"

"Maybe they're only well-known in the antiquing sphere," Mom said. "And maybe it's like with all those archives—the actual records about them haven't been digitized."

I placed the necklace between us on the wooden planks of the table. The stones (the diamonds, real diamonds) glistened in the sun. "What are we going to do?"

"What do you want to do?"

I shook my head, still too blown away to have any actual response. What do you do with eighty thousand dollars? I wouldn't even know what to do with eight hundred extra dollars. Put it in my savings account?

"Well," Mom said. "We could sell it and put it toward your college fund."

Yet another exceedingly practical Mom answer. "I guess."

"Did you want to spend it?" she asked with a smile. "I think it'd be better spent on education or your IRA, but a discretionary amount for something fun makes sense."

Education made sense. Fun made a *ton* of sense. Even if Mom only let me have a thousand dollars, I could do so many things—take a trip abroad, buy a million books. Maybe some new dresses.

What else?

What did anyone want? A vacation home, a house on the shore, Golden Doors. But I didn't *need* anything.

O'ma had needed Golden Doors, because O'ma had needed a home. "We could sell it and donate the money. To a refugee fund."

Mom took a bite of her ice cream. "It's a very sweet thought, Abby."

It wasn't just a thought. It had clicked. It was right. "Let's do it."

"You should think about it a little bit first . . ."

Sometimes I did need to think about things, to sit on them, to sleep on them. But this time, I didn't. "Do we need the money? I thought we were fine if I went to state school." I frowned. "Do you and Dad need the money?"

"No. No, you don't worry about us. But, sweetie, you could go to a private college with this. You could go anywhere you got in, even without a scholarship."

"For one year."

"There are loans and financial aid."

I licked my ice cream. "We never even expected to have this. So it's not much of a loss."

Mom set down her tiny spoon. "Okay."

I hadn't been expecting her to fold so quickly. "You're not going to fight me? It's your necklace."

"You found it. And it's a good idea."

"Maybe we can do an auction," I said, more excited by the moment. "Get it on BuzzFeed and HuffPo and everything."

Mom smiled, tremulously. "I'm *very* proud of you," she burst out. "Remember that."

When I got home, I found Jane lying in bed, holding her phone above her.

"Guess what." I tossed the necklace toward her.

She caught it. "We're going to go reenact *Titanic?* Because, for real, we could."

"It's worth eighty thousand dollars."

"*What?*" She shucked the necklace away and onto the blankets. "Are you kidding me?"

"Nope. Crazy, right?"

"Jesus."

"I'm going to sell it to raise money for refugee relief."

"You're mad," Jane said. "Sell it? Eighty thousand dollars? Are these, what, *diamonds*?"

"Yellow cut, whatever that means."

"Don't *sell* it!" she cried. "Keep it! Wear it to the Met Gala."

"Jane. I'm never going to be invited to the Met Gala. You've seen *Ocean's Eight* too many times."

"No defeatist thinking. You won't be invited if you don't have something to wear. Wait, you could sell it to the Met and part of the price could be an invitation. Oh my god, I'm a genius. Yes. Two invitations, I'm your date, screw Noah."

"I'm done with Noah."

"Right. Sorry. I forgot." She cautiously picked up the necklace and held it close to her face. *"Shiny."*

I didn't feel done. I desperately wanted Noah to text me. It felt like more than a want; like a *need*, like I might pass out if I didn't hear from him. Every day, I looked at my phone over and over, in case I'd missed the buzz of an incoming message. I opened our last exchange, in case a new text had slipped in unnoticed. I even restarted my phone.

But I'd told him we were done, and he must have believed me.

My last night on Nantucket, my friends went to the beach one last time. The air hung heavy with moisture, almost chilly. We wore sweatshirts and huddled close to each other. Everyone was going home soon, back to school and regular life. Pranav and Sydney had already left; Evan would be gone tomorrow morning; Stella and Lexi were leaving in three days.

Jane and I sat side by side on a towel, watching the bonfire spark orange into the night. "Come back next summer," she said. "You can avoid Noah. I need you to be my roommate."

"You could use a wing-woman, for sure."

She made a face, her gaze trailing after Evan. "You want who you want, right? Even when it doesn't make sense."

I rubbed her back and we watched the dancing flames. "Go talk to him. What do you have to lose? Even if it goes poorly, you'll have a whole year to recover."

"True." She stood up. "Here goes nothing."

Not nothing, I thought as I watched Evan's face light up when Jane approached him. I let out a sigh, pushing to my feet and walking down to the water.

I hadn't realized how different breakups could be. With Matt, I'd been so angry. So furious and hurt and determined to move on and get over it. I hadn't wanted to see him again. I hadn't wanted to be anywhere near him.

With Noah—I was still angry, but mostly, I was hurt. Mostly, I ached for him to come back from Cambridge and to knock on my door and to say *I'm sorry. Let's fix this.*

Mom had asked why it mattered, the necklace, an object, the past over the future. Why *did* it matter? *You're too goddamn proud*, Noah had said. Was that it? *You'll make yourself miserable.*

But I didn't think pride alone would keep me from someone who brought me intense joy. What else had Noah said?

You're scared, Abigail Schoenberg. Scared to really put yourself out there.

I wrapped my arms around my belly, shivering in the night wind. So easy to say *Be brave, take risks, show some chutzpah.* Harder to do it, to risk getting destroyed, to put yourself and your emotional well-being in someone else's hands.

The waves beat the shore, over and over. The moon glided across the water, a bright path you could follow forever without reaching the end. I watched the ripples of white on black until the wind off the ocean became so cold I couldn't stop shivering, and then I turned away and walked back to my friends.

The next morning, before we left, Mom and I found Mr. Barnes—the appraiser—in a well-appointed sitting room on the first floor of his hotel. The walls and curtains were done in muted off-whites, the floor and furniture dark brown. Paintings of ships hung in elegant frames.

Mom and I settled on a sofa, kitty-corner to Mr. Barnes's armchair. He stood when we arrived, then sank back into his seat, taking off his glasses and rubbing his brow.

"I got in touch with some industry folk last night," he said. "After I looked through the paperwork. I should have told you this yesterday, but I was surprised, and a little . . . skeptical, maybe. It's not often people appear saying they're the descendants of a notable jeweler family."

He folded his hands and leaned forward, addressing Mom. "As you're aware, the Goldman family lived in Lübeck during the years leading up to the war. Your mother was sent away. Soon afterwards, the family's work was seized by the Nazis."

He cleared his throat, while Mom and I nodded. So far he wasn't telling us anything we hadn't heard before.

"Much of the jewelry ended up in private collections. However, some wound up in museums after the war. Goldman jewelry can be found in the British Museum, the Hofburg, the Louvre. I pulled a file of the pieces I know about." He slid a glossy printout across the coffee table.

Mom picked the file up, but instead of flipping through the papers, regarded them with an almost bewildered expression. I leaned my head against her shoulder.

"You might be familiar with some cases where families recovered their family's work. The most famous is the *Woman in Gold*"—Mr. Barnes cracked a smile—"popularized by the Helen Mirren movie. There are other similar cases. It's possible for the families to get restitution or the return of their property." He paused. "The Goldman collection is—lucrative."

Mom stared down at the file. "You're saying there's more? More jewelry?"

"I'm saying there's *much* more." His rather bemused smile grew larger. "I'm saying, Ms. Cohen, that if you claim your inheritance, you will be a very, very wealthy woman."

When we walked outside, the sun broke over us, so bright we squinted and reached for our sunglasses. Mom raised her face to the sun and smiled, bright and all-encompassing as a star. She would burn forever, my mom. Then she looked at me. "How do you feel about raising money for refugee relief *and* going to whichever college you want?"

"I feel great."

"Good." She pulled out her cell, dialing a number, and I could hear Dad pick up on the other end.

"Hello, darling." Mom met my gaze, and her eyes crinkled up with pure delight. "I'm happy to report you did, in fact, marry rich."

Twenty-Eight

Let me tell you a story:

Once upon a time, a girl was born to a family of jewelers in a forested town by the sea. She was loved and cossetted and happy, but when she was four years old, her family had to send her away for her own safety. They sewed an exquisite necklace made of diamonds into the hem of her dress. She traveled across an ocean to a country where she didn't speak the language, and went to live with strangers on a windswept island, in an exquisite house called Golden Doors. She fell in love with a boy she was too poor to marry. A boy who betrayed her in the end because he thought it would bring her back to him.

Let me tell another story:

Once upon a time, a girl was born to a family in Upstate New York. She helped her parents at their deli, and she studied, and she helped her little sisters with their homework. She was very smart and she put herself through college and married a kind man and had two children and landed a job that paid for a mortgage and vacations and college funds.

The second story wasn't as exciting as the first. No one would gasp or widen their eyes or cry while listening to it. It wasn't mournful or melancholy or romantic.

But it was an *active* story. It was a story where the girl took charge, where she owned her agency, where she went out and forged her own path. It was a real story. It was a powerful, heroic story. We didn't tell it enough. We didn't always acknowledge this story was a story at all, a story with a heroine, and the heroine was my mother.

I left Nantucket amid a whirl of tearful goodbyes and hugs and promises to text. I hugged Mrs. Henderson and Ellie Mae and Jane, and waved goodbye, and bumped my suitcase down the steps of the porch, just as I'd bumped it up months ago. Mom and I rolled our luggage through the colorful downtown, still picturesque, still all-American. I mentally said goodbye to everything we passed, trying to print it on my memory. The heavy tree branches, the uneven sidewalks, the sign posts, the flower pots.

Then it was time to climb aboard the ferry, to say goodbye for the final time. Mom and I stood by the rail of the Hy-Line catamaran, watching Nantucket shrink into the distance, until it disappeared into the brilliant blue sea.

Within a short hour, we reached Hyannis, where Dad waited with the family car and a hug. We swung our luggage into the trunk and set off across the Cape. We waded through the traffic at the bridge, and merged onto 495. The ocean was replaced by trees, the salt by the scent of the forest. It took less than three hours to get home, to turn off the highway onto the winding roads of South Hadley, to drive down streets I'd memorized a decade ago, to pull into the driveway of home.

And Mom set everything in motion.

She hired a lawyer. She contacted the museums. She talked to specialists in restitution. The museums and private collectors might have more lawyers than us and more money, but they didn't have our story, and Mom made sure *everyone* had our story. After our local paper published the story, Twitter ran with it. BuzzFeed, HuffPo, the *Boston Globe*, and the *New York Times* covered it. A story containing diamonds, Nazis, and lost history? People ate it up.

Goldman jewelry might be worth a fair amount of cash, but most museums decided good PR was worth more.

"What are we going to do with all of these?" Mom asked in bewilderment after we heard a pair of sapphire earrings valued at twenty thousand dollars would be sent to us.

"Are you kidding?" Dad asked from behind his laptop. He pushed his glasses higher. "I'm going to wear them to work."

Mom's question wasn't too serious: we'd keep a few pieces and sell most back to museums, to pay for my college education and Dave's college education and the college education of all our cousins, since, of course, the money didn't belong to Mom alone, but to her two younger sisters and their families as well. We reached out to the Museum of Fine Arts in Boston to see if they'd be interested in hosting an auction for many of the pieces, and they said yes.

"We don't have to do this," Mom said, before we sent the confirmation email. We were in the living room, windows and tabs spread across our computer screens. I'd inherited my messiness from her; Dad kept his email at inbox zero (Mom's currently numbered close to ten thousand unread messages, which caused Dad visceral pain). "For O'ma's necklace, in particular. You could keep it."

I looked at the necklace, which I'd draped across my knee for no better reason than I liked to look at it. My great-grandparents had been *jewelers*. *Good* jewelers.

Part of me did want to keep it. O'ma had wanted this necklace so badly, and no wonder—it was the only thing she had left of her parents, and a huge piece of financial stability. And I'd spent all summer trying to find out what happened to it.

But.

It was so tangled up in Noah, this necklace. I wanted to look at it forever and I never wanted to look at it again.

"No," I told Mom. "It's the most valuable piece in the collection. It'll bring in the most money. And I think it's important to donate the money."

So Mom sent the email, which—stupidly, bizarrely—felt like I'd cut ties with Noah all over again.

Focusing on the Goldman jewelry scattered throughout Europe served as a solid distraction from him. Most of the time, he didn't infiltrate my thoughts. Most of the time, I could pack him up into a little box in the back of my head.

But at night the box opened and all the demons came out and there was no Pandora at the bottom, no hope, no anything.

I missed him.

But missing someone didn't mean I'd made the wrong decision. Better to have a clean break. Better to move on.

Wasn't it?

Was I just afraid? Was I more scared of actually being in a relationship than of my pride getting hurt? Maybe. After all, being in a relationship meant letting someone else in completely. It felt like flinging myself into a void with utter abandon. And that was *terrifying*.

Because what if I did, what if I flung myself at Noah and told him I wanted him, I adored him, I loved him, I was one hundred percent committed, and he wasn't? What if he broke my heart?

Again.

Or what if he said yes, he did want to be with me, and three months passed, six months passed, a year passed, and then he said no, he was done, we were done? We would fall apart and I would fall apart and it would be worse than this time. It would be worse than anything.

And he didn't care about me as much as I cared about him, if I was thinking about it logically. You had to believe what people told you, and he had told me he would never give up on the person he loved; he would be with them, no matter what. Noah believed if you made promises, you kept them. He believed if you loved someone, you fought for them.

But he hadn't fought to stay with me. He hadn't texted. He'd let me go after one fight. Yes, I'd told him to go. Yes, a relationship was a two-way street. But if Noah actually wanted to be with me, he wouldn't have let me walk away so easily.

And he had.

So I would let him walk away, too. It would be better for us both, in the end. People recovered from heartbreak. We'd be fine. I couldn't regret what had happened, because while my heart had broken, if I thought about it, really thought it through—it'd been worth it.

A week after I came home from Nantucket, school arrived, as inevitable as the changing seasons. Niko picked me up in her old beat-up Toyota, with the top peeling off the ceiling and a side door no longer capable of opening. ("Barack took Michelle out on a date in a car with a hole in the floor," she liked to remind us. "I'm destined for great things.")

Brooke already sat in the passenger seat, and she handed me a hot chocolate from Dunkin as I climbed in. "Woo! Senior year!"

"Go Turtles," Niko said. (Turtles were not our mascot, but Niko had spent the past three years insisting they were.) She craned her head to give my outfit a once-over: a red skirt and a black top, with earrings to match. "Solid choice. Should have worn the necklace though."

"I didn't get my matching evening gown dry-cleaned in time. And look at you! Really breaking out of your mold!"

Niko, as per usual, wore all black.

My brother scooted in after me. "Hey, Davy." Brooke beamed at him from the front seat. "Ready for high school?"

Dave, whose sole contribution to the Goldman jewelry discovery had been to ask if it meant he could get a tattoo (I worried about his disjointed logic), said, "I hear it's a barrel of monkeys."

We opened the windows and blasted music as we drove down the winding road. Canopies of golden leaves arched above us. I could smell fall in the air, fast approaching, crisp and cool with the promise of leaves crunching under our feet and pumpkins and apple pie and cozy sweaters.

This could be the beginning of my story. There were always new beginnings, new school years and college and the world after. My story didn't have to be of a girl on Nantucket, looking for a necklace and breaking her heart. Or I could reframe my thinking entirely: each person was a continuous story. We didn't begin or end, rise and fall. We weren't so contained. We were endless. We were infinite.

What would your grandmother have thought? Helen Barbanel had asked, looking at the table of World War II books. O'ma's story had not been limited to the space of ten years, to her childhood and her teens. It had spanned more than being ripped from Nazi Germany and sent to America and raised by strangers. It had kept on going, through the fifties and the hippies and the now. It didn't end bittersweet or optimistic; it didn't end for decades.

And neither would my story.

The auction for the necklace happened the second week of September, a week so warm it could have still been summer, if not for the way the light had changed—a slight softening, a golden glow. I left my sweater at home when I headed over to Niko's house. I didn't want anything to do with the auction; I didn't want to think about never seeing the necklace again. One day, Mom had placed it in a box, placed the box in a canvas bag, and carried it away. I tried not to let it distress me too much.

"Aren't you desperate to know?" Niko asked. We sat on the swings in her backyard, idly pushing off the ground and drifting through the air. We faced the forest of oaks and maples behind her house, watching as the occasional bunny dashed purposefully by. "I'd kill to be there."

"I'll find out soon. I didn't want to have to see someone buy O'ma's necklace. It's what I want to do, but it still sort of sucks."

"Do you still miss him?"

I dug my toe into the grass, sending myself on a more forceful swing. "When you spend so much time with someone, it's impossible not to."

"But do you *miss* him?"

I could feel how much I missed him in my stomach, in my throat, in my eyes. I shrugged.

Her eyes were sharp. "Do you still want to be with him?"

"I don't even know what that would look like."

"You don't have to *know*," Niko said. "You're allowed to try to figure it out."

A few days later, we learned the amount of money the necklace had raised: six figures—over *one hundred thousand* dollars. And the pang at giving up O'ma's necklace was soothed over by the knowledge of the good this money would do.

When my grandmother came to the States, she was lucky. She had people willing to take her in. She had had a woman who called her *once a week* for her entire life. When your people lived in a diaspora, that was what you did, whether in 1940s Europe and America, or sixteenth-century Spain and Morocco. You looked after your own.

But not everyone had the resources and community and luck O'ma had had.

We donated the money, and we did several interviews, and then we carried on. I wrote a killer college application essay and didn't even feel too guilty about exploiting my family history to get it. Rosh Hashanah came and went. We ate sweet apples dipped in honey and tart pomegranates and dense kugel. Dad and I braided and baked round challah like O'ma had taught us. In services, we were reminded to ask for forgiveness from anyone we had wronged in the past year, before Yom Kippur arrived in ten days.

I sat outside on the back porch and stared at the light filtering through the trees and thought about how I was still madly in love with Noah Barbanel.

"Are you okay, honey?"

I looked up. Mom leaned against the frame of the French doors. When she met my gaze, she stepped outside, closing the screen behind her and sitting next to me on the bench.

I stared straight ahead at the trees. "I'm fine."

She put her arm around me and pulled me toward her, my head resting on her shoulder. "You sure? You were quiet today."

I could feel tears welling in the back of my eyes, but I tried to keep my voice steady. Despite myself, it cracked. "I'm just a little sad still. I feel like I should be over this. Over him."

"Are you sure . . ." Mom started, then hesitated. "He didn't break up with you, right? You broke up with him?"

"Technically, I guess. I felt like I had to, though." He'd hurt me so much. He'd lied to me.

Her hand was soothing against my head, her warmth familiar and calming. "Sometimes people mess up. You have to decide if it's worth forgiving them. And, honey, I don't know if it's worth holding a grudge if it makes you so unhappy. What if by forgiving him, you'd both get to be happy?"

After Mom went back inside, I stayed outside, drained of tears. Was Mom right? Should I just wave a hand and forgive him?

The stark truth stared back at me. I didn't need to forgive him; I already had, because I understood why he'd lied to me. He'd lied because he loved his family. I'd used my anger at being lied to in order to push him away, because I was scared. Because I didn't believe he cared about me as much as I did about him.

It was the stubborn fear of getting hurt that held me back, keeping me from reaching out to him. Because what if I got my heart broken again?

I stared out at the trees, taking deep, steadying breaths. Maybe I *would* get my heart broken again. But so what? At least I would have tried. I'd have no regrets. I'd never wonder—*what if?* Maybe, like Mom had said, I'd get to be happy.

So I decided to lay my cards on the table.

The sun lowered into the woods, stretching long shadows against the lawn. The wind tugged at my maxi skirt. The days were shorter now; it was only around five, but soon it would be full dark. I pulled out my phone and opened my messages with Noah.

Looking at the blinking cursor made my heart speed up. Too much, too quickly. I put my phone down and had to catch my breath.

I leaned my head back and stared at the sky. My backyard was thick with trees, their branches reaching out across the expanse of dark blue. When I was away from the forest, I craved it, craved deep greenery and endless trees. I could breathe in the woods like I could breathe in a bookstore: fully and easily. Now I took one deep breath after another.

Hadn't this all started because of a handful of letters? Maybe we could work it out through letters, too.

I pulled my computer to me, and began to type.

Dear Noah,

I don't really know how to start this letter. So I guess I'll just start.

I was angry and hurt you lied to me, yes, but the anger should have led to a fight, not a breakup. I think you're right; I *am* proud, I'm proud and I'm scared, and I should have responded to all those feelings in a better way, but instead I responded by slamming my walls up. It's easier for me to shut people out than let them in. It's easier to walk away than wait for someone else to leave.

I don't want to walk away from you. I've never liked someone as much as I like you. I'm terrified of putting myself out here, but here I am. I miss you, and I want to be with you.

And I'm sorry, because I hurt you, too. I wanted to make you hurt as much as I did, which is horrible and unkind. And I want you to know that being without you *does* make me miserable. I want to be with you. So badly. You're all I want.

And if you don't want to be with me, I get it. We broke up. And I yelled at you, and you're in college. But god, I want to be with you so much, it's like a physical ache thrumming through my entire body.

You don't have to answer this letter. But I wanted you to get it. To tell you I'm sorry. To tell you how much I care about you. To tell you I never should have responded the way I did, by pushing you away. To tell you I understand that choosing between me and your family was not a choice you should have had to make, that you should be able to pick both of us, that I should have been more understanding.

I love you.

Abigail

Twenty-Nine

A week later, the doorbell rang. I put down my book and went to the door in my Friday post-school outfit: leggings and an oversized T-shirt. Hopping through the mudroom, I opened the door, but no one was there.

So I looked down. And found a package sitting on my parents' doorstep.

The paper was brown.

The string was twine.

But this time, the package was addressed to me: *Abigail Schoenberg, 85 Oak Road, South Hadley, Massachusetts.*

Déjà vu washed over me. The lightest, strangest feeling fluttered in my head, glitter and cotton candy and the sea. I looked down the driveway, half expecting to see the same delivery truck from months ago pulling away down the road.

I carried the box inside. Dad was at work, Dave at soccer practice, Mom upstairs in her study. I settled on the living room sofa, late afternoon light spilling over me. My hands trembled as I unwrapped the brown paper, then used a key to open the taped box inside. I lifted the box's flaps and revealed a white creamy envelope. *For Abigail.*

Hands trembling, I lifted the envelope and stared at my name for a long, careful moment. Then I set it aside and turned back to the box. A black velvet case fit snugly within. I placed it in my lap and ran a finger across the top, watching as the threads of fabric reversed directions.

Throat dry, I pulled the lid up. It opened with a concentrated snap. O'ma's necklace glinted against the black velvet backdrop.

I looked away, out the French doors at the trees heavy with leaves, blinking back tears. My pulse pounded in my throat and air raced through my lungs. I'd known as soon as I'd seen this package what it would be. What it was. It felt inevitable.

I closed the box and opened the envelope.

Dear Abigail,

I'm sorry I didn't tell you about my grandmother having the necklace earlier. I should have; should have told you the first time we talked to my grandfather. I tried, and I chickened out. I should have told you the second time we talked to him and I knew he wasn't telling you everything. I was trying to protect my family, but I don't need to protect them by keeping their secrets from you.

I'm even more sorry I left Nantucket when we were mad at each other. I mean, yes, I had orientation. But I should have called you and worked this out.

The thing is, you're not the only proud, scared, stubborn one. I don't want my words to be tossed in my face or to be rejected. Here's the other thing, Abigail Schoenberg: I love you. I love you and I want to be together.

I know you're nervous about a long-distance relationship. And yeah—maybe our relationship will end in property theft and we'll marry other people and bury our feelings for the rest of our lives (but we should probably not, because it seems unhealthy and unfair to other people). But maybe we won't follow in our grandparents' footsteps. This could work. I want it to work. I think we're worth it.

P.S. Please, please don't be mad at how much money the neck-lace cost. My mom says to think about it in terms of percentage of income, and the money is being donated to charity, and also we get a tax write-off.

I was still sitting there, stunned, a few minutes later when the doorbell rang again.

Oh god. I swiped at my eyes. My whole body felt light and jittery and like it hardly belonged to me.

"Abby, can you get the door?" Mom called from upstairs.

It took me a few seconds to regain control of my vocal cords. "Yes!"

Each step felt like I was moving in slow-motion, pushing through molasses as I stepped into the chilly mudroom, then, ever so slowly, unlocked the front door and pulled it open. I thought my entire body might stop working. I thought my legs might turn to jelly.

Noah stood there, framed against the fall colors, wearing a crimson sweatshirt. His hair was mussed like he'd driven his hands through it moments ago. We stared at each other.

I gripped the door's frame and waited for the world to stop spinning.

"Hi," he finally said.

"Hi."

It was September 20, his third week of classes (I'd checked) and seven days after Rosh Hashanah.

"You're here," I said stupidly, because I couldn't think of anything else to say. "You—you bought the necklace."

He nodded.

A small laugh wobbled out of me. "It was a *very* expensive necklace."

He winced. "I know. Did you read the letter?"

I nodded.

"I mean it, Abigail." His eyes were steady and focused on mine. "You said we shouldn't make our grandparents' mistakes. So let's not."

"Okay."

"I shouldn't have kept the necklace a secret; I'm sorry. I shouldn't have tried to keep you from researching your family's past. I . . ." He paused, a look of confusion on his face as my words caught up with him. "Wait, okay?"

I started grinning. "Yes. Okay. I overreacted. I get it, they're your family."

"So—you—we're—"

I grinned harder, my chest so warm and full I felt like I'd swallowed the sun. "Yes."

He let out a blazing laugh and shook his head and very deliberately held my gaze. "I should have fought for you."

"You did. I did. Did you get my letter?"

He looked confused. "Your letter?"

A surprised laugh jolted out of me. "You'll get it soon."

"What did it say?"

I took a step closer and hesitantly raised my hand to tame one of his flyaway curls. "It sort of said what your letter said. Brilliant minds and all that. And I'm sorry I told you I'd rather be miserable than be with you."

A smile started spreading over his face. "Yeah, you were pretty cold."

"I'm sorry." I wanted to launch myself into his arms, to hug him so tightly every line of our body fit together, but even now I was being slightly cautious. In his letter, he'd said . . . but I needed to hear it out loud. I needed to hear it two times, three times. "I don't want to be miserable. I—I have been miserable."

"You have?"

I made a strangled noise. "Of course I have."

"Really?"

"How can you be surprised?"

"I wasn't sure! You're *so* good at walking away. You sounded so rational."

"I wasn't being rational! I was trying to protect myself. It's *hard* to let someone in. It gives them the power to hurt you."

"True." He swallowed and stepped forward. "I want to let you in, Abigail Schoenberg. I love you."

I pulled in a breath. He was so vulnerable, standing there, all his walls down, the layers peeled back, soul bared and helpless. Noah Barbanel was proud and determined and protective to a fault, and he didn't like to show weakness—and he'd done so anyway. He'd decided to do this, to come after me, to say we were worth it. To fight for us. To choose us.

I chose us, too.

I chose to be with Noah Barbanel, who I was in love with, who made me happy. I chose delight and butterflies and incandescent joy, and I could have this, this good, wonderful thing. I could fling myself off the cliff with utter abandon. I wanted Noah Barbanel. I wanted *us* and so did he. "I love you, too, Noah Barbanel."

His head jerked up, his eyes wide. "You don't have to say that."

"I know. But I do. Love you. And," I said, my own smile breaking as his broke over his face, "you make me want to be better, too. And

I will be. I won't run away. Or—I'll come back, if I run. I think I'm always going to want to come back to you."

His grin widened even more, and he stepped up onto the stoop with me, sharing the space toe to toe. He wrapped one of his arms around my waist. "Now what?"

"Now . . . Now you're in *my* home."

"True. You can send me away if you want. But it is Friday. And I don't have to be back in Cambridge at all this weekend."

"No?" I tilted my face up.

He tilted his face down. "No."

And then we were kissing, so easily, like we'd been born to kiss each other. Heat uncurled deep in my belly and I pushed onto my tiptoes so I could press closer against him.

When we separated to breathe, I realized we were standing there on the doorstep, in full view of anyone passing by. "Do you want to come in?"

"Sure. Is anyone else home?"

"My mom."

"Do I get to meet her?"

"If you're lucky." I led him inside, and he looked about curiously. I took him to the living room, where the necklace lay gleaming up at us. "It seems like cheating." I said. "To be willing to give the necklace up, and to get it back."

"You could give it to a museum. Or sell it again."

"I could." I smiled up at him. "But I guess I'll keep it."

The corners of his mouth curved ever so slightly. "You guess?"

"It does have some sentimental value. For my family."

"For your mom, maybe."

"Exactly. Actually—one second."

"What?"

"Stay right here." I kissed him quickly, then planted my hands on his chest and studied his eyes. I'd never told a boy I'd loved him before today, and it felt good. Right. "I love you," I said again, firmly.

He kissed me again, this time slow and thorough, so thorough I almost forgot what I'd meant to do. When he finally let me go, he said, "I love you, too."

"Good," I said, grinning. Grabbing the necklace box, I snapped it shut, blew Noah a last kiss, and ran upstairs to my mom's office. With my free hand, I swung around the doorframe. "Hi."

She looked up. "Hi, sweetie. What's up?"

"Got you a present."

"And it's not even my birthday." She looked wary, which, understandable. Had I ever gotten her a present spontaneously? Probably not. Maybe something I should start doing. Also, now did not count as starting.

I handed her the box, beaming. "Open it."

Still wary, she drew up the lid. For a moment, she stared inside the case with an expression of bewilderment, before transferring her gaze to me. "How . . . ?"

"It's from Noah."

"Noah—" Comprehension dawned, and she looked queasy. "He *bought* it? It sold for six figures."

"Don't think about the money right now," I said quickly. "It's here. It's ours. It's yours, from O'ma."

"I'm still thinking about the money."

"His mom said to think of it as a tax-deductible charitable donation."

Mom snorted. "Well, then."

"Also they're super rich and so it's not such a big deal for them."

"I don't know if that makes me feel better or worse."

"It's really just like Noah donated to refugees and happened to get a necklace at the same time—"

Mom held up her hand. "It's okay. You don't have to convince me." She tried to hand it back.

I stepped backward. "No, it's for you."

"Oh, honey, no. I'm sure Noah bought it back for you."

"I want you to have it." Emotion surged through me, stronger than reason. "It should be yours."

"I don't even wear jewelry—"

"It's from *O'ma*," I said. "She would have given it to you. She would have wanted you to have it."

Mom blinked rapidly, then nodded. "All right."

I went over and kissed her cheek. "I love you."

She looked surprised. "I love you, too." She looked back at the necklace. "You know . . . I can't stop feeling like we stole this from Helen Barbanel."

"What?" Startlement filled me. I hadn't felt anything of the sort.

She nodded. "It was hers for so many years. It meant something to her. It doesn't mean anything to me."

"It was O'ma's."

"It was," Mom agreed. "And it shouldn't have been taken from her. But . . . I just feel like we shouldn't take it from Helen. I mean, really, honey, we can do whatever you want, but I would give it back to her."

I stared at Mom. Give back the necklace? Helen could have bought it back instead of Noah if she'd wanted it. Noah giving it to me had felt *right*. Me giving it to Mom had felt right.

But maybe giving it to Helen felt right to Mom. And I wouldn't gainsay her, even if I didn't understand. "Okay."

She pulled me into a hug, then leaned back, a smile forming. "*Noah* sent this to you? What do you think about that?"

"I think we're both working on being less dramatic about things. Though, admittedly, this was pretty dramatic." I grinned and twisted back and forth in a little dance. "As was showing up on the doorstep."

"*What?*" She started laughing. "He's here?"

"Come down and meet him," I said, taking Mom's hand and pulling her out of her chair. "I think you'll really like him."

"So you like him again? You're happy? You *look* happy."

I smiled, embarrassed and thrilled all at once. "I'm happy."

"Good." She hooked her arm through mine, and arm in arm, we walked out of her office and went toward Noah.

Author's Note

My maternal grandmother arrived in the States from Paris when she was seventeen years old, right after World War II. She went to live with relatives in New York, while her eleven-year-old sister was sent to St. Louis. My O'ma loved talking about New York City, but avoided stories about the war; but since she was a teenager during those years, teenage me was obsessed with learning more.

I drew on that curiosity for this book. Like Abby, I love history, and I'm interested in how each generation is independent and yet interconnected, and how certain issues appear time and time again, even if they wear different faces: like immigration and refugee rights, something top of my mind while I wrote this book in 2019. These are topics that will always be in our lives, and I can only hope we'll learn to handle them with more kindness and empathy.

In this book, I wanted to capture the magic of my childhood summers. I grew up going to the Cape every year, a land of endless seashore, rambling roses, and sandy dunes. I was later enchanted by Nantucket, an isolated island both like and unlike the towns I knew. While writing this book, I was helped by several amazing visits, talks, and books, including *The Other Islanders: People Who Pulled Nantucket's Oars* by Frances Ruley Karttunen; *Away Off Shore: Nantucket Island and Its People, 1602–1890* by Nathaniel Philbrick; and a whole lot of Elin Hilderbrand and Nancy Thayer.

I also delved into the fascinating history of Sephardic Jews in America. The first group arrived in New Amsterdam (New York) from Brazil in the 1650s, fleeing the Portuguese Inquisition. By 1763, a synagogue had been built in Newport, Rhode Island—now the oldest surviving synagogue in the US. Several Jewish Newport merchants had dealings with the town of New Bedford, MA, which was connected to Nantucket through the booming whaling trade. My invented family, the Barbanels, is based on the idea of Sephardic Jews landing in New Bedford, and then expanding to Nantucket—a bit of alternate history I truly enjoyed creating!

Acknowledgments

This book sold in March of 2020, a time when the whole world was shutting down, and working on it has brought a golden lining to this year. It's been nice to have something to do between staring at my screens and staring at my ceiling. (Kidding! This book also meant staring at a screen). Jokes aside, this book has been a lifesaver, and I am deeply, deeply grateful to all the people who made it real. I am especially grateful to you, my readers. Thank you for taking a chance on me. I hope this story made you smile.

The first step in turning my smattering of thoughts into a novel was talking it through from its very inception with my agent, Tamar Rydzinski. Thank you for always being my sounding board: for listening to all my nervous worries and endless questions. Thanks for editorial insight that is nothing short of brilliant and for always being a staunch champion of my work; I feel so incredibly lucky to work with you. Thank you, also, to my wonderful film agent, Mary Pender, for believing in this book and for championing it in Hollywood.

A huge thanks to my editor, Jess Harriton, whose kindness, notes, and vision shaped this book into what it is today. Your warmth and excitement over this story has meant the world to me. Thanks as well to the entire team at Razorbill: I am so thrilled this book found a home with people who have cared about it so much. Thanks to Gretchen Durning, who kept me on the ball; to my publisher, Casey McIntyre, for answering all manner of questions; to Jayne Ziemba and Vanessa DeJesús and Susie Albert, for your hard work and enthusiasm. Thank you to Marinda Valenti, Abigail Powers, Maddy Newquist, and Briana Wagner for catching my millions and millions of mistakes, because it turns out that while I can write I can't always spell. Thanks to interior designer Rebecca Aidlin and cover designer Maggie Edkins for creating such a beautiful cover and manuscript—I couldn't be happier with it!

My friends are my rocks. Thanks to friends-my-friends; to Annie Stone, who introduced me to Tamar and who told me you can't actually study business at Harvard undergrad (whoops!). To Diana and Mary, who've listened to me freak out about literally everything under the sun. To Carlyn and Sonja for much needed Bachelor/ette and nail painting sessions. To Kayti, Nadia, Zan, Bridget, Madeleine, Sara, Danielle, Meredith; everyone's support and excitement made this year, especially as we took it virtual. Here's to you and here's to happy lamps and just, like, insane amounts of snark and emojis and all caps and book recs.

Thanks to Rachael, Madeline, Heather, Mary, Allie, and Sam, for keeping my spirits up this year with our necessary virtual chats—even though we're scattered across the country I still feel so close to all of you. Thanks to Emma, Laura, and Ann, for unconditional love and making me laugh as hard today as we did at sixteen. Thanks to Reiko—can't wait to be lying in a park or strolling through a bookstore someday soon.

Also, without doubt, I wouldn't have come as far as I have without all my writer friends. They've kept me sane (or perhaps shared in my insanity). Thanks to Diana Urban, who in the beforetime had endless teatimes with me where we hashed out our books, and afterwards suffered in the cold outside a Tatte. Thanks to Akshaya Raman, for always reminding me to stand up for myself. Thanks to Julie Dao, for much-needed jaunts to the country. Thanks to Janella Angeles, for hot goss in Davis. Thanks to Jo Farrow for emails and enthusiasm and excitement. Thanks to Emily Cataneo: I wish we were doing yoga or drinking fancy cocktails right now.

And as with every book I've written, thank you to Monica Jimenez, who has heard every idea and every problem with this novel (and my life) in real time, and who has sat across a hundred different tables with me as we wrote. One day we'll be able to sit in one of the cafés of Camberville again without freezing our hands and feet off.

Lastly, thanks to my parents, for endless love and support. I swear these characters aren't based on you (except, of course, when they are; I can't help that you guys have really good one-liners). Sorry there aren't any dragons, Dad. Mom—she gave the necklace back! Love you both loads.

Return to Golden Doors in
EIGHT NIGHTS OF FLIRTING!

This Hanukkah, sparks will fly.

CHAPTER ONE

When I saw Tyler Nelson at Nantucket's tiny airport, I ignored him, because Tyler Nelson was the absolute worst. I watched him from the corner of my eye, feigning indifference as I brushed away the snow clinging to my coat from crossing the tarmac. He took the prime position at the start of the baggage carousel, so I moved to the far side and stood with my back to him. Outside, white flakes swirled madly. The wind—which had spurred nerve-racking turbulence—howled like a lone wolf given wild, maniacal form by motes of snow.

My phone buzzed, and I pulled it out. "Hi, Mom."

"Shira?" In just two syllables, Mom's tone conveyed worry and bad news. "Where are you? Did you land?"

"I'm at the airport. Are you at the house?"

"We're still in Boston. Our flight was canceled."

"What?" I'd expected her to be at Golden Doors by now, along with the rest of the family, lighting up my grandparents' house with laughter. Their plane had been due to arrive an hour before mine. "Did you get another?"

"They're all canceled—the winds are too strong. We're going to take the Hy-Line tomorrow, if the ferries are running. Will you be okay alone tonight?"

I'd been looking forward to seeing my family, to burrowing into their warmth. The idea of being alone for an extra day made my stomach feel hollow. But it wasn't worth telling Mom and stressing her out. "I'll survive."

"Make sure you pick up something to eat, okay?"

I glanced outside again. I'd be lucky to get home in this storm, let alone get takeout or delivery. But surely Golden Doors had food in the pantry. "Will do. How was Noah's ceremony?"

"Good, lots of speeches. Noah looked very grown-up. How did you do on your final?"

"Aced it," I said, because if your daughter had expensive tutors, she damn well better ace her exams. "Are Grandma and Grandpa okay?"

"Oh, well," Mom sighed, "Grandpa's complaining about how we should have predicted the weather, and Grandma thinks he's being foolish. She's worried about the decorations, though. She thought she'd be back today and have them up before the littles arrive tomorrow, but now everyone will show up at once . . ."

Mom lacked even the smallest drop of subtlety. "You want me to decorate."

"Not if you don't have time . . . But you *will* be there . . ."

So would you, I wanted to say, *if you'd stayed home and flown out of JFK instead of going to Noah's thing in Boston*. But I'd told them it was fine, so it was fine. "Sure."

"Okay, great, darling. We should be there around three tomorrow. You're sure you'll be okay?"

"I'll be fine," I said. "See you tomorrow!"

When we hung up, my fake smile fell away, and I stared blankly at the swirling snow. Alone for the first night of the holidays. I could do this.

Only I was so lonely.

Nope. Nope, I was fine. Besides, I didn't have time to be lonely. I could work on my plans for this break. Because I had big plans. Plans involving Isaac Lehrer.

If my life were a movie trailer, the voice-over would say, *This holiday season, Shira Barbanel is determined to win over Isaac Lehrer no matter what*. A series of slapstick shots would follow of us running into each other in Central Park, flicking latke batter at each other in my kitchen, and ice-skating at Rockefeller Center (where he'd witness me landing a triple axel).

The narrator might add something along the lines of *Shira Barbanel is a lost cause at love*, the appropriate-for-all-audiences version of *Shira Barbanel is a hot-AF mess who can't get a boyfriend*, a situation I planned to change over winter break.

I'd met Isaac—my great-uncle's nineteen-year-old intern—sporadically over the last year, at family and company events. He was six-three, lanky, and as dreamy as Morpheus. His grandfather and my great-uncle had gone to college together, so when Isaac's parents decided to spend six months traveling through Europe and Asia, my great-uncle offered to bring Isaac to Golden Doors for the holidays. And now (*this holiday season*), I would turn our occasional small talk into a genuine connection.

And maybe I didn't have a *great* record getting boys to like me, but that could change. Besides, not everything could go as badly as it had with Tyler.

Who, in a cruel twist of fate, was now the only other person left at baggage claim. Also, while I was blatantly ignoring him, I found it insulting that he so easily ignored me. To add insult to injury, our belated bags came out nestled together. I looked pointedly away while Tyler pulled his duffel bag free, and instead of walking over, waited for my slow-voyaging suitcase to reach me.

When it did, I heaved the bag off the conveyor belt and lugged it across the nearly empty room. Nantucket's small airport was almost more like a train station—the whole of ACK could fit inside Grand Central. Still, a broken wheel on my suitcase left me panting and awkward as I reached the doors, where I accidentally made eye contact with Tyler.

He smirked.

While the plane ride had turned my normally impeccable curls both frizzy *and* greasy, and I could feel a zit poking out of my chin, Tyler looked like he'd stepped out of central casting. His soft golden hair gave him the aura of a Disney prince, and even the amusement in his blue eyes didn't detract from his angelic looks. "Hey, Shira."

"Tyler." I dragged my suitcase another few feet.

"Need any help?"

"No."

"Suit yourself." He turned away, buttoning up his woolen coat and tossing one end of a scarf over his shoulder. It was sixteen degrees outside. He should have been wearing a puffer jacket and Bean Boots, like me. But god forbid he look like anything other than an ad for expensive cologne.

Whatever. I didn't care if he froze to death or ruined his fancy leather shoes. Tyler Nelson came in at No. 1 on the list of Shira Barbanel's Disastrous Attempts at Romance, and I wanted nothing to do with him.

The list, in no particular order:

1. Jake Alvarez. Asked him to homecoming last year only to have him blink, stumble backward, and stutteringly tell me he already had a date.
2. Dominic Hoffman from Camp Belman. Mocked him

relentlessly in an attempt at flirting. Made him cry
and leave for home early.

3. Siddharth Patel from driver's ed. Lusted after
him silently throughout the entire course. Finally
exchanged numbers on the last day. No response to
my one, brave text (**Hey**).

4. Tyler Nelson. Spent four summers madly in love
with him, only to finally make a move and be utterly,
devastatingly rebuffed.

Isaac—handsome, smart, sophisticated Isaac—would not be
another example of me failing at boys. He was way more grown-up
than any of my other crushes, sure to be better at conversation,
and easier to hang out with. And this time, I'd master the art of
flirting. Or I'd at least follow the steps laid out by Google, for
as much as they were worth. (*Step three: start talking.* Possibly,
Google needed as much help at flirting as I did).

In any case, I knew better than to expend energy on Tyler
Nelson. I tore my attention away from him to check Uber and
groaned at the surge pricing. And—

No car available.

Impossible. I tried Lyft with the same result.

With a sense of looming dread, I looked out the windows
again. The snow obscured the world. Hard to believe leaves had
still clung to trees a month ago, yellow-green and orange-brown.

The chill in the air had only been enough to make boots acceptable. But today, a nor'easter had swept the Eastern Seaboard with the reckless speed of Elsa icing Arendelle, painting the world white—even Nantucket, where the sea usually whipped the island wet and bleak.

Outside, a car pulled into the taxi lane, careful on the snow-dusted asphalt. By the terminal doors, Tyler gathered his duffel bag, tightened a hand around his suitcase handle, and walked into the blizzard.

Pride warred with desperation, and the latter won. I dashed after him, heaving my suitcase off its broken wheel. It banged against my legs, the pain and embarrassment warming me against the hideous cold. Snowflakes smacked into my skin, dissolving in icy pinpricks. "Tyler!"

He stood by the back of the taxi, placing his bag in the trunk. "Shira."

"Can I share your car?"

"Let me guess." A close-lipped smile curved his perfectly shaped mouth. "You can't get one. Tough break."

"Tyler, come on. You live next door to me."

The driver pushed his head out the window. "That you, Shira Barbanel?"

"Phil!" I beamed at the driver, who I'd known for years. "How are you?"

"Doing well, doing well. Where's the rest of your family?"

"Snowed in in Boston. Their flight was canceled."

"Really?" Tyler said. "Same with my family. What were they doing in Boston?"

"Noah had a thing. I had to stay home for a final."

"Toss your stuff in the back," Phil said. "I'll give you kids a ride."

Throwing a triumphant look at Tyler, I maneuvered my bag into the trunk, then slid into the back after he beat me to the front.

Phil pulled away from the curb. "You two have a good flight?"

"Some turbulence, but not bad," Tyler said. I made a noise of agreement. I couldn't believe I hadn't noticed him on the plane. Maybe I'd boarded after him, and he'd been in the back. Maybe he'd boarded at the last minute, when I'd already been absorbed in my book. Maybe, I thought with a shot of hope, I was no longer so tuned in to Tyler's presence that I noticed every move he made.

We drove down Old South Road. Though the storm might have been a transportation nightmare, I adored how the snow powdered the pavement white, like we'd been transported to a time when horse-drawn carriages traveled on dirt paths, where people hurried down the streets in velvet capes and fur muffs, and sleigh bells mixed with the sound of laughter. The island already had a quaint, old-timey atmosphere, and winter just heightened it. This was my favorite season on Nantucket: I loved the stark, cold beauty, the snowy beaches and brilliant stars.

The drive only took fifteen minutes, winding past the cedar-shingled island houses outfitted for the season, decked in sparkling lights, yards populated by light-up reindeer. Windows displayed Christmas trees and candelabras whose branches I always counted. There were wreaths twined with pine cones and holly, and red and gold everywhere.

But Tyler's house, when we reached it, was dark. The lawn was a sheet of white, the bushes snowy heaps, and the house—usually an elegant beauty—a blank monolith under the darkening sky.

"Thanks," Tyler said to Phil. When he climbed out, icy air swept in, and goose bumps rose on my neck. Tyler tossed a look my way. "See you around, Shir."

"Shir*a*," I muttered. Being called Shir always made me think of sheep or transparent tops. But he'd already shut the door and gone to unload his bag.

"We'll wait to make sure he gets in all right," Phil said as Tyler trundled to the front door, then stepped inside. Relief broke over me as Phil put the car in reverse. With Tyler out of the way, I could focus on Isaac—on the future, not the past.

"How's Aimee doing?" Phil's nineteen-year-old daughter was a lifeguard during the summers and had just started college in Boston. "Is she home for Christmas?"

"She got back two days ago. Brought a suitcase of dirty laundry." Phil laughed, hearty and familiar. "She's loving college. Next semester she'll have to declare her major, and she's teetering between computer science and physics. Her mom and I tell her—" Phil paused, and I saw his frown in the rearview mirror. "Huh."

I twisted. Tyler was running toward us, waving his arms for attention.

Phil rolled down the window. "You okay?"

Tyler reached the car, his breath coming out in white puffs. Snowflakes glittered in his golden hair. "The electricity's out. The heat, too; the panel didn't work."

Oh no. Surely he wouldn't *deign* to suggest . . .

He met my gaze and smiled, more ironic than charming. "So, Shira. Can I bunk with you tonight?"

"You want to stay with me. At Golden Doors." *Why don't you stay at a hotel?* I wanted to ask, but I didn't want to bicker in front of an adult. And while Tyler could afford it, why would he shell out money for a last-minute room when he could stay at my grandparents' place for free? Besides, then Phil would have to take Tyler to a hotel, spending even more time driving in these conditions.

Still . . .

But no. I couldn't turn him down. Our families ran in the same social circles; we'd be attending their Christmas Eve party later this week, and they'd be attending our Hanukkah celebration a few days after. "Fine."

"Great." With a flash of his white, even teeth, he retrieved his bag and returned to the car, his long legs once more cramped in the front seat. "We'll have a good time."

I didn't dignify his lie with an answer.

Tyler's moms' summer home abutted my family's ancestral property, the sprawling estate of Golden Doors, so the ride took a scant minute. The house loomed as we pulled up the circular drive, not gold, but gray: gray shingles covered the original nineteenth-century building as well as the modern expansions. Endless windows reflected the gray-white sky. Someone had plowed and shoveled the porch steps, but even so, a blanket of snow had gently returned.

"Thanks so much," I said to Phil, and Tyler echoed me. Then we were pushing through the drifts, our legs struggling against the snow. On the porch, where a lighter layer carpeted the wooden boards, we brushed ourselves off as best we could.

I let us in to the dark foyer and flicked the light switch, my chest tight—what if the power had died here, too? But the chandelier lit up and the HVAC panel summoned the telltale whir of heat. I stepped back on the porch, directing two thumbs up at Phil. He gave a friendly honk and sped away.

Leaving me and Tyler Nelson alone.

We stared at each other. I had never met anyone else with such perfectly sculpted features, with eyes so blue and hair so gold. This boy could get away with murder or fraud or heartbreak, and people would chuckle and pat him on the cheek and say, "What a rascal!"

"Well, Shira," he drawled, and even his voice was beautiful, damn him. "This should be fun."